THINGS ARE LOOKING UP

MAXINE MORREY

Boldwood

First published in Great Britain in 2021 by Boldwood Books Ltd.

Copyright © Maxine Morrey, 2021

Cover Design by Debbie Clement Design

Cover Photography: Shutterstock

A CIP catalogue record for this book is available from the British Library.

Paperback ISBN 978-1-83889-047-6

Large Print ISBN 978-1-80162-817-4

Hardback ISBN 978-1-80162-816-7

Ebook ISBN 978-1-83889-048-3

Kindle ISBN 978-1-83889-044-5

Audio CD ISBN 978-1-80162-722-1

MP3 CD ISBN 978-1-83889-045-2

Digital audio download ISBN 978-1-80162-720-7

Boldwood Books Ltd
23 Bowerdean Street
London SW6 3TN
www.boldwoodbooks.com

For Shirley Ann Hill

1

The London traffic rumbled past me as I tapped the toe of my suede Louboutin ankle boot on the pavement impatiently, glancing up at the traffic light. Checking the phone clutched in my hand, I saw there was still plenty of time. I was pretty punctual in general but today was the one day there was no room for error. This was it. This was the chance I'd been working towards for... well, since I could remember. The reason I'd grown up reading about the greats of fashion, done a degree in fashion journalism, and a Master's in fashion history. The motivation for all the late nights, early mornings and complete lack of social life. I'd worked so hard for this, to the detriment of pretty much everything else. There was a twist in my stomach as my mind fluttered back to that day four years ago. The emptiness of the flat. The silence. The overwhelming sweep of loneliness that had washed over me when I realised he'd gone.

A car horn blasted, bringing me swiftly back to the present. Good. The last thing I needed now was memories like that encroaching. Today just proved I'd done the right thing. This was the future. This was my future. And it was going to be bright and beautiful!

I finished my mental pep talk and rolled my shoulders, trying to release some of the tension, then gave Instagram a quick scroll to see if I'd missed anything vital that might come up in the interview. *Just relax*, I said to myself as I scanned the line of traffic. Were these lights ever going to change? I brushed a tiny speck of dust from the slim black Chanel trousers and pulled the long camel-coloured Marc Jacobs coat around me a little more as I adjusted a large tote bag by the same designer on my shoulder. I'd probably brought too much with me, but better to be over-prepared than under. Running a hand quickly back over my hair, I was pleased that it still felt smooth and shiny. It had taken long enough to style but I'd got there, and although I wasn't one to toot my own trumpet, I'd done a good job. The long, dark auburn layers had almost shimmered as I'd turned to check my work, the natural gold highlights catching the light from the slightly small, definitely grimy window of the bedroom in my shared flat. With a bit of luck, I'd finally be able to change that circumstance as well soon. My phone beeped a message.

Something's come up. Need to bring the meeting forward half an hour. Trust that is OK with you?

Shit. I checked the time again. OK. I could still do this. Assuming this bloody crossing light ever changed! Was it broken? A few others waiting had clearly begun wondering the same thing and a couple had already rushed forward to weave between the traffic. I'd have preferred to keep to the original appointment time but the question mark on the message was, of course, ironic. When you had a meeting with the editors of *Vogue*, you adjusted things for them, not the other way around. But that was fine. I was used to that. I'd been freelancing for long enough to know that the client is always the one in charge, even if it wasn't convenient for me. Having no money to pay the rent would be even more inconvenient so I made it work. I was just glad that I'd given myself plenty of time to get to the offices today so that I could tap out a jaunty reply.

Absolutely. No problem at all.

'Oh, for God's sake,' I muttered as the light resolutely remained green. Ooh! A gap. I dashed out, ignoring the beep from a taxi that was miles away anyway. My phone dinged again. I opened the message as I hurried across the road.

Great. See you then.

I felt a smile spread over my face. This was it. What I'd worked for. My ultimate aim was within sight. Just getting the interview was a large part of the battle and I knew these people wouldn't be spending any of their precious time on me if they weren't already pretty sure of the outcome. An hour's time and life was going to change!

Actually, it took far less than an hour. Just a few seconds, in fact. With my eyes still on my phone, I hadn't seen the bus round the corner and the next thing I remember was a squeal of brakes and the horrified look of the driver as I suddenly looked up from my phone to lock eyes with him a split second before the vehicle hit me.

2

So, it turns out that being hit by a bus really, really hurts. My one piece of luck that day was that an ambulance heading back to its base was close to the junction I'd just helped block when the call came in and so was on the scene pretty quickly. The screaming had now stopped – it turned out it wasn't me as I'd initially thought, but an onlooker. Fair enough. I don't think I'd like to see someone knocked down by a bus either. I was even less en-thusiastic about being the one under it. OK, under it is a bit dramatic. I definitely wasn't under it as I could see the big, red, square front of it looming a few inches from my face. Admittedly it was a bit of a fuzzy image, not helped by the cracking headache I now had but I would deal with all that later. Right now, I just had to get to my interview.

One of the paramedics was talking to me.

'Can you tell me your name, love?'

'Milly,' I replied, my voice sounding faint and croaky and odd.

'Hi, Milly. I'm George.'

I raised my hand to wave but it didn't work.

'Try not to move too much, Milly,' George said. 'Just while we get you comfortable.'

I was beginning to think that might be an impossible task with the pain that was now starting to radiate out from various parts of my body. But again I pushed it away. I'd felt like I was breaking once before. It hadn't been physical damage but the pain had been just as intense – I'd got through that and I'd get through this too. I'd obviously managed to collect quite a few bumps and bruises as I bounced off the front of the vehicle but, right now, nothing was more important than getting to the *Vogue* offices. Oh, God, what was the time? Where was my phone?

'Can you move your fingers for me?' I didn't

have time for this but did as he asked, just to get it over and done with. I was fine. A few bumps. Getting me up off the road – oh, my poor coat – would be the most helpful thing.

'Good,' he continued. 'And your toes?' How the hell he was going to be able to see my toes wiggling in my boots I had no idea, but I obeyed anyway. 'That's great.' He turned away from me and had a short conversation with his colleague, who was busy doing something with my right arm. My phone had been in my right hand. Perhaps George's colleague had it.

'What's that, Milly?' George asked as I croaked out the question. He'd been busy putting a collar thing around my neck, which stopped me being able to see exactly what his colleague was up to. That would obviously have to come off before I went in! Accessorising was key and I didn't think the editor of *Vogue* would buy that it was a choker by a new, *avant garde* designer.

'Where's my phone?'

'I'm afraid you're going to need a new one of those, love.'

Great. I knew I should have taken out the insurance the guy had tried to flog me.

'What's the time?'

George was coordinating something with his partner and the next moment a board thing slid under me and they started strapping me to it.

'What's the time?' I asked again, the words sounding even fainter now as the pain in my head began to almost blind me.

'It's ten to two, Milly,' George replied, his kind face smiling at me, the words measured and calm.

'I have to get to an interview. It's really important.' I was struggling to keep my eyes open now.

George had leaned in to hear me, his face was close, and I felt him touch my fingers, a gesture of reassurance. 'I'm sure they'll be able to reschedule it for you,' he said gently, the voice drifting into the darkness.

I tried to shake my head – *No, they won't* – but it didn't move.

'Milly?' The voice was so faint now, I could barely hear it. Everything that had been so loud before now disappeared and drifted away into nothing. 'Milly, can you hear me?'

* * *

It was dark when I woke up. At least, that's what I thought at first. As my eyes, feeling heavy and still tired, began to adjust I realised that there was a little light filtering through the partly closed blinds. I shifted slightly in the bed.

'Milly?' My brother's voice was quiet. I turned to see him pushing himself hurriedly from an upright armchair, rushing towards the bed. 'Oh my God, Milly.'

Henry bent over me and placed a gentle kiss on my forehead. Even in the low light of the room, when he pulled back, I could see tears shining in his eyes. Henry and I were close and I spent as much time as work would allow with him and his family, but he wasn't the gushy type. He was sensible, reliable, dependable Henry and the expression on his face was one I'd never seen before. Apart from looking like he hadn't slept in over a week, his eyes were filled with – what? Frankly, my brain felt a bit on the foggy side, but if I had to try and rootle out a name for it, I'd say it looked like relief. He reached out and pressed a button before focusing his attention fully back on my face.

Trying to make sense of it, I supposed it must have been a bit of a shock to receive a call saying your sister's just been knocked down by a bus. Oh, goodness, poor Henry! It wouldn't surprise me if he asked to step down from the position of emergency contact after this, but with Mum and Dad off finally pursuing their dream of travelling the world in a camper van, and not always contactable, Henry had drawn the short straw. But it was all a bit dramatic – they must have really put the wind up him to make him react like this. Going by the faint traces of daylight, I could only have been out for a short while. An hour at the most. Unless... oh, God, had something happened to Mum and Dad? Was that what he was actually upset about and now he had to tell me!

'Are they OK?' I scrabbled about in my brain for the right words.

Henry frowned and sat down on another chair that he'd pulled up to the bedside. He took my hand and I noticed there was a thing sticking out of the back of my hand, which in turn was attached to a drip. A cannula? Was that what it was called? Most of my medical knowledge had been gained from watching *Grey's Anatomy* years ago and, as most of the time I'd been more interested in Patrick Dempsey's anatomy, there was every chance I might have got some terminology wrong.

I moved my head, an action that felt stiff and slightly unnatural. My right arm was in a cast from the wrist to just below the elbow and the hand itself was also bandaged. Great. Well, at least I was left-handed, although, I thought, shifting my gaze back, that one wasn't looking quite how it started the day, with its perfectly manicured nails and hand creamed to within an inch of its life in preparation for my big interview. The nail polish had been re-moved and my whole arm was a mish-mash of blue, green and purple bruises. Attractive.

'Are who OK?' Henry asked, softly.

'Mum and Dad.'

'They're fine,' Henry reassured me as a sudden wave of emotion rolled in and took me by surprise, welling in my eyes. 'They're fine, Mils,' he said again, reaching over to the tray table and grabbing a tissue from the box that sat there, before gently mopping the tears that had escaped onto my cheeks.

'Why are you upset? What are you not telling me?' I asked. My voice was still croaky and my throat was sore.

'Well, good morning, Milly.' A tall, attractive man entered the room, followed by a male nurse wheeling a machine. The doctor wore a dark blue, three-piece suit and a smile. 'Hello, Henry,' he said, nodding at my brother, before raising an eyebrow. 'Sleep here again, did you?'

I frowned at them both. Morning? Sleep here again? Just what exactly was going on?

'I'm Dr Sands. How are you feeling?' the doctor asked as the nurse bustled the machine around to the side of the bed, and Henry moved the chair out of the doctor's way.

'OK... I guess,' I said, feeling a little unsure now.

'We're just going to take some observations, temperature, blood pressure and the like, and then we can have a little chat. I'm sure you have questions.'

I did have questions. One of which was whether I had any chance of getting another interview scheduled. My intuition said probably not, but I had to try. I mean, it wasn't like I just didn't show up. OK, it was exactly like that, but being hit by a bus had to be a pretty good excuse, didn't it? But this was *Vogue*, so possibly not. The nurse seemed to have finished and, having completed writing things down on a chart, handed it back to the doctor. He looked over them, nodded and thanked the nurse. He smiled at me, gave Henry a brief raised hand wave and pushed the machine back out of the room, leaving the three of us alone.

'Where's my phone?' I asked Henry.

Henry looked across at me, his expression suddenly tight. He looked almost angry.

'Really?' he snapped. 'Really, Milly? You spend over a week in a coma and the first thing you say is, "Where's my phone?"' He stared at me for a moment. 'Jesus, Milly. What's it going to take?'

Childishly, I wanted to point out that wasn't the first thing I'd said. I'd asked if Mum and Dad were OK first but my mind was getting hooked on the initial bit of his sentence. Over a week in a coma? That's ridiculous. I'd got knocked over by a bus earlier today... hadn't I?

The doctor put a hand on Henry's shoulder. Henry looked round at him and seemed to be calmed by the gesture. He still looked mad at me, though.

'Let's just take this one step at a time, shall we, Milly? First off, there's just a couple of tests I'd like to do. Can you follow my finger if I hold it up like this?'

A few minutes later and I'd completed the set of hoops the doctor wanted me to jump through with apparently flying colours. Henry looked slightly less cross and definitely relieved.

'Do you know what day it is?' the doctor asked.

I pulled a face. I could hardly forget. The date had been circled and highlighted on every calendar I had. 'Of course. It's the twenty-seventh of January.'

'No, Milly. It's the fifth of February.'

I heard the words but they didn't make sense. Obviously, I had misheard. That was the only explanation... although Henry's retort... *over a week in a coma...*

'How is...' I didn't really know what the question was I wanted to pose. All at once, a hundred different ones came to mind, all screaming to be asked. I put my hand up to head, as if by doing that I could quieten them. My hand touched something fuzzy. I moved it around a little. Rough bits over fuzzy. My hand moved some more. Henry and the doctor waited for the inevitable.

'What happened to my hair?' I cried, a floodgate of emotions now opened by that one touch.

Henry moved quickly and caught my hand, as he pulled the chair back to the bed with his other. 'It's just a patch, Mils. Just a couple of little patches. It's fine. The rest of it is all still there.' He lifted my hand within his own and guided it to show me by touch that what he said was true.

'I'm afraid we had to shave a little bit, Milly. You took quite a bump to your head and we needed to get to it to stitch things up.' The doctor let that sink in for a moment. Henry shuffled closer. He didn't look cross any more, which I was glad of, but actually this was worse – now he was looking at me like he had that time I'd bet him I could climb to the top of the frame of our swing when I was nine years old. Henry had scoffed that of course I couldn't, and I'd set about proving him wrong. Which I did. Thankfully, I hadn't bet him that I would be able to climb down again and had instead taken a much quicker route to the ground as I slipped and landed with a thump on the lawn, baked hard by a hot summer. Henry had stood staring at me for a moment before hollering for Mum. The fall had knocked all the wind out of me and I'd lain there, staring back up at him, unblinking as my body tried to find a way to breathe that didn't hurt. Henry, he later admitted, was convinced he'd killed me by challenging me to the bet, knowing I wouldn't back down. And now he was looking at me like that again.

'Am I going to die?' I squeaked out.

Henry squeezed my hand as hard as he dared without hurting me. 'No, Mils. Of course you're not. But you gave us all a bloody good scare.' He leaned over and brushed a stray hair back from my forehead. 'Please don't do that again.'

I shook my head gently, as I was still unconvinced and unclear on the whole situation and didn't want to risk my brain rolling about. Or out!

'You're very lucky, Milly. Thankfully the bus wasn't going fast but it's still a lot bigger than you are and I wouldn't, in general, advise a person taking on a bus. Any vehicle, really.' Dr Sands sat on the corner of my bed and proceeded to tell me how I'd been rushed in, having lost consciousness and a certain amount of blood whilst lying on a London street. My right wrist was broken in two places and had needed pinning. It would depend on how it healed as to whether that metalwork stayed in or if I would be setting off airport scanners for the rest of my life. I'd broken two ribs and suffered some internal bleeding which, thankfully, they had managed to stem quickly once I was in the trauma department. The rest of it was mostly severe bruising, and some cuts and grazes. I also had a cut on my face, having managed to somehow break the bus's headlight with it. My brother had rolled his eyes at me when the doctor stated this part.

'Only you, Mils.' But he'd given that gentle squeeze again before reassuring me. 'They've done a good job. You'll barely notice the scar once it's healed.' And his words made me want to cry for all sorts of reasons.

'You really were quite lucky,' Dr Sands reiterated.

I tried to nod but it didn't really happen.

'I'm sure you don't feel like it at the moment, but trust me. You are.'

'You didn't mention the coma,' I forced out.

'I was just about to. And that's what I mean about you being lucky. The bump you took to your head resulted in some brain swelling.'

I felt weak and listless but at these words I found strength from the grip of Henry's hand.

'Sometimes when this happens, the best thing, and what we decided the best thing was for you, was to induce a coma. This lets the body rest and recover and hopefully allows the swelling to go down before it can do any, or at least too much, damage.'

He paused for a moment, letting me absorb this. I looked at Henry. Now I understood why he looked like he hadn't slept for over a week. He very likely hadn't. Because of me.

'Obviously, we can never give any guarantees that this will work or that there won't be longer-term damage.'

Oh, God, poor Henry. He'd obviously been told all this last week and had sat there waiting all these days, waiting to see if it would work, and if it did, to what extent.

'But we've been monitoring you throughout and your body responded very well, I'm happy to say. The paramedic team were excellent and got you here very quickly, which helped enormously. You've been for a few scans and the last one was a perfect score. You responded well to the basic tests I did earlier. We'll give you a few more but, from everything we've seen, I'm pretty confident you'll make a very good recovery.'

My throat felt tight and sore and like I'd swallowed a tennis ball so I just gave him as much of a smile as I could muster. I'd thank him properly later.

Dr Sands nodded at me, his expression showing he understood completely. 'Right. I'll leave you in peace for a while, but I'll send someone in to see about a drink and perhaps a little something light to eat.'

I wasn't sure if I could face any food right now but I didn't object. My mind was too busy spinning with all the information I'd just been given. I understood now why Henry had snapped at me earlier when I'd asked for my phone. Blurry images were drifting around in my mind. A chill, January day, the traffic busy, me heading to the interview I'd waited my whole life for, dashing across the road, checking my phone as I did so...

3

I'd become rather immune to the phrase, 'Will you stop looking at the damn phone!' and variants on this theme over the years. Mostly it was Henry who'd said this. My parents were a bit caught in the middle as I'd explained that I needed to keep up with everything, know the latest gossip, releases, up and coming names, if I wanted to make a success of my career. They too, occasionally suggested I get my face out of whatever device I was looking at, at the time, but they also understood how much I wanted to succeed. Henry had always been more blunt. Mostly in a good way.

I think my folks were probably a little relieved

to no longer be in the middle of it when they finally decided to sell the house, pack everything they needed in a luxury camper van and set off on the grand adventure they'd talked about for decades. Henry had been made to promise by my parents to check on me, I was mortified to learn – making sure I was eating properly and not working myself to death. Being the sort of decent bloke he is, he'd kept his promise.

Not that we wouldn't have seen each other anyway, even without the regular meet-ups at my parents' that would now no longer be happening. I am blessed to have the most amazing sister-in-law, Ava, who is the sweetest, kindest person, plus a niece and nephew whom I adore more than anything. I wish I did get to see them a bit more, I admit, but work kept me pretty busy. Being freelance, I always found it hard to say no to people. It was all extra money, which God knew I needed if I was ever going to get out of that poky flat and away from my sullen flat mate. 'Mate' being employed loosely in these circumstances. Plus, the world of fashion is all about networking and you never know who knows who and what might just be the job that leads on to bigger and better things. Hence the reason I was regularly to be found with my nose in a screen. Henry's requests to 'look up for five minutes' (which of course I did – he always exaggerated), in the end, sort of became white noise.

But I did get it. I really did. I knew that spending as much time as I did on screens probably wasn't the healthiest way to live my life, and that I should put them away sometimes and take notice of... stuff. I still felt like a horrible person for missing my nephew's one line of dialogue in his school play two years ago because I'd sneaked a quick look at my phone. But it was New York fashion week and, as I hadn't been able to persuade anyone to actually send me on their behalf, and certainly couldn't afford to fund a trip myself, I'd had to keep up online as much as possible and garner all the news and gossip for the columns I'd managed to secure commissions for. It was just a sneak peek – but it was at the worst time possible.

Of course, then Alfie had asked me what I'd thought of his performance, his little face shining with excitement and pride. My brother had looked round after Alfie had delivered his line, his own face alight with joy, and caught me looking up from my phone. The joy had immediately turned to disgust and disappointment, both of which I fully deserved and which had been reflected again in the look he gave as my nephew awaited my reply. I had, of course, lied through my teeth and told Alfie just how wonderful he'd been. Even if he'd fluffed the line completely, I'd have still thought that. So, it was true – that's what counts, right? I tried to convince myself that, but I still felt like the worst aunt in the world for missing that moment. Henry had definitely not been convinced and even Ava, who was pretty easy going and always the one to calm the waters, had remained silent on that particular occasion.

'You're going to have to get that bloody phone surgically removed from your hand one day,' Henry had snapped at me once the children were ensconced in the car that night and the doors shut to prevent little ears overhearing. I'd apologised but I knew Henry was right. I'd missed a moment I would never get back.

He'd been right about the other bit too, as it turned out. Dr Sands had returned on his rounds

later, and seeing I had absorbed the information
he'd given me to a large extent, thought I'd be interested to see the X-ray of my arm. In the midst of
bouncing off the bus and making rather a mess of
my arm, I'd become even more attached to my
phone than I'd thought possible. The doctor had
pointed out the various pieces of glass, metal and
plastic that had become embedded in my hand and
wrist during the accident. Henry slid his gaze to me
and I met it, practically able to see the words *I told
you so* dancing in neon letters above his head. I
would never live this down. On the plus side,
though, I would live – which, as trade-offs go, was a
pretty good one.

4

'Auntie Milly!' Rosie and Alfie's excited voices took the pain away more effectively than any of the drugs I'd been given, and I held them as close as I could as they knelt on the bed, one each side of me, their arms snaked around me, resting my head on their soft hair that smelled of baby shampoo and home.

'Don't forget, Auntie Milly is very bruised so you have to be careful.' Ava's soft, melodic voice drifted into the room. I looked up from the sweet smell to meet Ava's eyes. She tilted her head and I saw the tears in her eyes. I thought back to Henry's exhausted face. I'd done this to them. To all of them. And, right now, I had no idea how to ever make up for it.

'Come on, kids. We don't want to tire Auntie Milly out, do we?' Henry said, following Ava through the door the following evening and looking, thank goodness, like he'd actually caught up on some of the sleep he'd missed.

The children climbed down off the bed and I missed their warmth immediately. Rosie held my fingers where they peeped out from the end of the bandage. Big blue eyes haloed by a mass of golden curls looked up at me, and she blinked, suddenly serious.

'Does it hurt?'

'Not too badly, sweetheart,' I lied.

Alfie came around the bed to stand next to his sister and took her other hand. She shuffled a little closer to her big brother. 'Daddy said you were very poorly but we wanted to see you so he brought us,' Alfie said. I shifted my eyes quickly to Henry and Ava.

Henry shrugged.

'Rosie was a bit upset at first but the doctor

came and said you were just very tired so they were helping you sleep so that you would get better quicker.'

'I wanted you to get better quicker.' Rosie nodded.

'And here I am!' I said, forcing the biggest smile I could onto my face.

'We're glad you're awake again now.'

'Me too,' I said, trying to inject a lightness into my tone. 'You must have lots to tell me. What have you been up to?'

As the children began telling me all about school and their friends and what they'd been doing, I realised Ava must have run herself ragged trying to make this as normal a week as possible for them, as Henry spent most of the time at the hospital by my bedside while she, no doubt, worried about both of us. When Henry eventually managed to persuade the children away with the help of some home-made flapjack, Ava came up to the bed and gently took hold of my hand. The nurse had removed the drip earlier but they'd left the cannula in for ease of facilitating extra pain medication or anything else my battered body might need some help with.

She bent and dropped a kiss on my forehead and stroked away a flyaway hair, her look gentle.

'Henry tells us that the doctors are very pleased with your progress,' she said, sounding proud of me, as if I'd had something to do with the luck I'd been handed. Ava was always good at saying the right thing, and I was never more grateful than now. She hadn't asked me how I was feeling because it was probably pretty obvious how I was feeling. I felt like I'd been hit by a bus.

'Thank you,' I said, glancing over at where the children were now squished together on an arm-chair, playing a word game with Henry on his tablet. 'I'm so sorry I've put you all through this.'

'Oh, tsh,' Ava flapped her hand as she snagged a tissue from the box and tidied up my watery eyes. 'They're fine. They knew something was up as Henry was working from home that day. Typically, their school had chosen to have an inset day that particular day so they were in the room when he got the news. It was obvious from his face there was something very wrong.'

'Oh, Ava—'

'Now, don't apologise again or I shall get cross. You didn't ask to be knocked down. Accidents happen.'

Of course, they were more likely to happen when the person involved had her nose in her phone rather than concentrating on her surroundings, but that was left unsaid by both of us.

'There was no point trying to pretend there was nothing wrong so we told them as much truth as we knew – up to a point. That you'd had an accident and were in hospital. Rosie was a bit upset she couldn't wake you up but that lovely doctor, Dr Sands, is it? He stepped forward and was so kind and good with them. They were much more relaxed once they'd seen you, even though you were a bit bruised.'

'But what if...'

'There's no need for any what-ifs. You're here and safe and recovering. That's all we – you – need to think about.'

I met her gaze and gave a small nod. She was right. Thankfully. There was work to deal with yet but not tonight. Tonight was for my family. Tonight,

I didn't want to feel any more overwhelmed than I already did.

There was a knock at the door and a couple of seconds later, Jed Matthews walked into my room and back into my life.

5

My brain was still a little tired from all I'd put it through in the last week but right now it felt more scrambled than ever. But then Jedidiah Brenton Matthews had had that effect on me from the first day I'd met him. Six foot four, broad shouldered with dirty blonde hair worn short and the most piercing ice blue eyes I'd ever seen, he was kind of hard to miss. Except, that first day, I'd done exactly that and spilled my just-purchased latte all over him as I turned in such a hurry in the coffee shop, my feet couldn't keep up and I'd tripped over absolutely nothing and flung my drink all over his clean white t-shirt for good measure.

There'd been an immediate pouring forth of a colourful collection of expletives from both sides and I'd begun making an effort to apologise profusely, adding in, I remembered, cringing, that at least I hadn't ordered it extra hot. Judging by the look he gave me, that hadn't been helpful. It had apparently been quite hot enough, and then I'd stopped talking as he'd stripped the t-shirt off, before quickly pulling on the shirt he'd had tied around his waist. It must have been seconds but a quick glance around had told me I wasn't the only person in the shop who momentarily lost the ability to speak at the sight of a man that gorgeous with a body that good half naked. I was kind of sorry I didn't have another coffee to throw at his jeans but I was pretty sure he'd have had me up for assault if I tried that.

I'd stumbled getting myself up off the floor, sliding on the coffee I'd just wasted and, graciously, he'd put his hand down to help me up. As I'd stood and looked up to say thank you, he was smiling. I was stunned by two things at that moment. Firstly, how damn good that smile was and, secondly, the fact it seemed to be aimed at me after I'd just done a good job of trying to inflict bodily injury on him, albeit accidentally. The following two years had been amazing, and happy, but the one after that was when everything began to craze and crack, and at the beginning of the fourth, finally shatter.

That had been four years ago and now here he was, filling the doorway, face serious, ice blue eyes wary. And, if it were possible, looking even better than he had before. Bloody hell. So much for not feeling overwhelmed.

'Jed!' Henry stood, striding to the door quickly and gesturing him in before exchanging a brief man hug. Jed gave Henry a couple of pats on the back. Luckily Henry was a decent size himself as anyone slightly built might have been burped instead.

What the hell was he doing here? I looked to Ava for an answer but she merely squeezed my fingers gently and headed over herself for a hug. Jed managed this whilst Alfie hugged one solid, jeans-clad leg and Rosie clung on like a small chimp around his neck. I looked on. I knew they'd all become friends when I was seeing him and Henry was also Jed's most trusted business advisor, a role

Henry had been reluctant to take on. Mixing business and pleasure didn't always have the best results but, from the look of things, they'd only built upon their friendship. Something they'd clearly failed to mention to me.

There should be a law that you're not allowed to run into exes unless you are looking at your utmost fabulous, successful and glowing with happiness. If there's a drool-inspiring god or goddess with their arm draped casually around you, this means extra bonus points. If you absolutely must run into an ex, this is the only acceptable scenario.

Except it would seem that the universe hadn't quite got that memo because what inevitably happens is that instead you actually bump into them when you're buying a meal for one at your local Tesco Express, having dashed out in your 'at home' clothes (i.e. ones you would never ordinarily wear out in public) because you are, after all, only nipping to the local shop. And there they are. The Ex. They are, of course, looking just as fabulous as you yourself had planned to, casting their eyes over the meal for one in your basket, as it loiters next to the chocolate cake which apparently serves eight. (This is a blatant lie, by the way. It serves four. At the very most.)

And now there he was. My ex. Jed Matthews. A man whom a self-confessed 'cougar' friend of his mum's had once stated with absolute certainty that God had definitely spent a little more time on. I wasn't sure I believed in God, but the rest was pretty spot on. Standing in my hospital room, looking, somehow, even better than ever and who was now, like he didn't have enough going for him, also a tech billionaire.

Although I wasn't partaking of a meal for one, I was a million miles from the 'hey, look how fabulous I'm doing and how gorgeous I look' scenario I'd planned on, should I ever have to see him again.

For a start, I was sporting one of those enormously unflattering hospital gowns with the built-in air vent at the back. (Seriously, what was the point?) In films, gorgeous actresses manage to pull off the beautifully vulnerable look in these items but I had my suspicions that theirs must be made to measure because that was definitely not the look I was rocking right this moment. Not only was this my #ootd, I had odd-looking bald/tufty bits around

the stitches holding my bonce together and accessorising the entire ensemble was a pair of anti-
thrombosis socks with a hole in them through
which my big toe was now peeping. What is it with
all the weird gaps and holes in medical type clothing? I'd bought anti-DVT socks for a flight once and
they were nicely complete. No weird holes for body
parts to say hello through. Somewhere I guessed
there was a reason but right now, I couldn't fathom
it. I also couldn't fathom how this, of all times, was
what God, the universe or whoever was in charge
thought would be the optimum time for me to see
my undeniably effortlessly hot ex-boyfriend. I
mean, seriously? Had I not had enough bad luck?
Just exactly what had I done to piss the powers that
be off *that* much?

Ava stepped back and peeled the two reluctant
children off Jed. He stood for a moment, hesitantly.
It was unlike him. Or at least unlike how I'd known
him and, from what I saw in all the gossip magazines, he hadn't changed that much.

'Hey.'

'Hello,' I replied, trying to shove myself up a
little more in the bed, which suddenly proved to be

more difficult than I'd anticipated, with only one arm to do the pushing. A sharp intake of breath hissed from me as the broken ribs made themselves known with my movements.

'Here, let me help.' The deep voice was gentle, its soft American South accent still noticeable even after all these years of living back in his dad's homeland.

'I'm fine,' I said, preparing to push him away just as the pain in my ribs dug at me again, making my eyes water.

'Please, Mils.' He didn't wade in, wasn't overbearing, but we both knew it was going to happen.

I swallowed and briefly flicked my gaze to meet his, an acceptance given and received. And then gently, carefully, he helped me shift into a better position, adjusting the pillows and handing me the bed's remote so that I could tip the head up a little more.

'Better?' he asked.

'Yes. Thank you,' I replied, overly polite and not entirely sure how to act... or feel. 'Jed? Why—'

We were interrupted by a quick knock at the

door followed by a nurse pushing the obs machine in.

'Just need to take your blood pressure,' she said cheerfully before catching sight of Jed and driving the machine straight into the door frame.

I dreaded to think what my blood pressure was at that moment, bearing in mind a man I never expected to talk to again, a man I'd shared my dreams, my bed, my life with now stood a couple of feet away. The nurse wrapped the cuff around my arm as Jed turned and began talking to Henry, his broad shoulders relaxing. God, I really shouldn't have thought of Jed in bed... I watched the numbers counting up as the cuff got tighter on my arm. I was going to give it a short circuit – if I didn't give myself one first.

'Ooh, a little high,' the nurse said as she noted down the numbers.

'Really?' Henry turned, concern in his voice. 'Is that OK? Why would that be?'

I exchanged a glance with Ava. She rolled her eyes.

Perhaps because you invited my ex nearly-fiancé into my hospital room, brother dear?

'Nothing to worry about, I'm sure,' the nurse re-assured Henry. 'These things happen.' She flicked her glance to me, then to Jed, then back to me. 'I'll be back later to check them again.' And, with that, she and her machine exited the room.

'Do you feel all right?' Henry asked, his eyes scanning my face.

'I'm fine, Henry,' I said, reaching out for his hand and once again feeling guilty that my normally calm, collected brother was getting agitated this easily.

'I'm guessing the higher reading probably has something to do with me showing up.' Everyone looked at him then at me. Jed had always been sharp and he'd always been one to say what he meant.

'Yes, I expect it has,' I replied, catching the snippiness in my voice. 'A little warning might have been nice.' I directed my gaze at Henry and Ava, who at least had the decency to blush. 'And, you know, maybe an explanation as to why the hell he's here?'

'You need to calm down a bit, Mils,' Henry said,

as I felt my breathing quicken and winced as my ribs reacted.

'I was perfectly calm before...' I waved a hand in Jed's direction.

'Milly.' It was Ava. She glanced over to the children but they were wrapped up in a game on their dad's tablet and not listening. She lowered her voice a little anyway. 'Henry was worried out of his mind and Jed has been marvellous to us all this past week.'

I flicked a glance up at my ex but he was looking towards the window, uncomfortable at the praise. He might be one of the world's richest and most eligible bachelors these days – assuming he was still a bachelor – but he clearly still had that humble thing going on.

'I know you two have a lot of history but he's been worried sick about you too and when he asked if you'd let him see you, I knew you'd say no. So, I'm afraid I took matters into my own hands.'

Jed looked round sharply. It was obvious he'd been in the dark too.

'I thought you said she said it would be OK?' he

asked, his voice low so that little ears didn't pick up on anything.

Ava shrugged.

Jed shifted his weight.

'I did what I thought was best.' She turned to me. 'Remember what I said about the children wanting to see you?'

I gave her a look. 'That's different.'

'Not really,' she said. 'It all comes down to people who care very much about you wanting to make sure you're OK.'

I gave her another look, then switched my gaze to Henry. He looked totally befuddled. Clearly this had been solely Ava's plan.

'Maybe I should go.' Jed's voice broke the moment of silence.

'You're here now. You may as well stay for a while. Henry and I can take the children for a walk around and get us all some coffees. Apart from you, obviously, Mils. The doctor has already said you drink far too much caffeine. Something else that needs to change.' With that, she gathered up the children and a still slightly confused looking husband and hurried them all out the door. It clicked closed behind them and Jed and I were left in the silence.

'I had no idea,' he began.

'Clearly none of us did.'

'If you want me to go, I will.'

I really had no clue what I wanted right now but just knowing that he'd helped hold my family together this past week was enough for me to make the immediate decision to let him stay, even if it was just long enough to thank him.

'What Ava said about you being there for them...'

'Don't.'

'What?'

'Thank me.'

'Why not?'

'Because I just did what any friend would do.'

There was no arguing with Jed when he was like this. It wouldn't have occurred to him to do any less than put his life on hold to help someone out and, even though he'd had evidence to the contrary, he still believed in the innate goodness of people, especially those he chose to call friends.

'Well, I hope someone is there for you like that should you ever need it, to repay that faith.'

He shrugged. 'Henry and Ava already were.'

'When? Did something happen?'

He turned that glacier gaze on me. 'Yes, Mils. You left.'

6

I didn't know what to say, so I said nothing.

Jed let out a sigh. 'They picked me up from that, so I owed them.'

'Henry isn't someone who keeps score like that.'

'No.' He glanced back at the window. Darkness had fallen and, several floors below me, the lights of London projected an orangey haze across the sky. 'I know he doesn't. He's a good guy. They're good people. You want this blind closed?' He changed the subject.

'Umm, I don't really mind.'

'I'll close it,' he said striding across and shutting out the city. The lights in the room had been dimmed a little and it felt strangely intimate. And incredibly awkward. Something I could have predicted, had anyone bothered to ask me first. But he was here now so I should make some sort of effort, if only to please Ava.

'You look...' *So good.* 'well,' I started, a little lamely.

He turned then and smiled that smile. 'Thanks. You kinda look like you got hit by a bus.'

I laughed, letting out some of the tension, and winced. Jed moved closer, immediately apologising.

'Sorry.'

I waved it away with my good-ish hand. 'No, don't be. I think we probably both needed that pressure valve released.'

He sucked in a deep breath. 'Yeah. Ava's a lot more sneaky than she looks, huh?'

'It would appear so.'

'I didn't mean to...' he rubbed three fingers across his forehead a couple of times. 'I just... when I heard what happened, and Henry was, man, he was a mess.'

I watched Jed for a moment and suddenly his gaze shifted and locked onto mine. A fire I had thought long extinguished began to smoulder as my stomach fluttered. Hurriedly, I mentally sent three fire engines out to well and truly douse any hint of re-ignition. That ship had most definitely sailed and I'd chosen not to be on it. Which was fine. Exactly how it needed to be. How I wanted it to be. That feeling – not even a feeling really – that hint of reaction I'd just had was just all part of my recovery. Nerves and muscles healing. That sort of stuff. And nothing to do with the fact that Jed Matthews only seemed to improve with age.

'I'm not making a whole lot of sense, am I?'

I gave a small smile. 'Not really. To be honest, you're the last person I ever expected to see walk in that door.'

'Yeah,' he grinned. 'I kinda got that from the look on your face when I did.'

'Oh, you did not. I have an excellent poker face.'

His laugh rippled around the room. 'Oh, honey, you have a terrible poker face. I can read you like a book.'

The laugh died away. 'Sorry. I didn't mean to be quite so... familiar.' He shrugged. 'Old habits, I guess.'

It had been a long time since someone had called me honey. I'd forgotten how much I'd liked it. The mental fire engines turned up the hoses to full power.

'Why are you here, Jed?' I asked, genuinely curious. He shifted his weight again. 'Maybe if you sat you'd feel less out of place.'

He gave me a brief glance that seemed to indicate he didn't think his position was going to make much of a difference at this point, but he took the chair beside the bed anyway.

'I wanted to see you,' he answered simply.

'Why?'

A small shake of his head accompanied his briefly raised brows. 'I don't know. I guess I needed to see for myself you were OK. I mean, Henry told me you were. That you'd pulled through. You were kind of still beaten up, but you were going to be OK. And that was one heck of a relief. But... sometimes you've just got to see things for yourself. You know?'

I thought back to what Ava had said about the children. I did understand. To an extent.

'Don't take this the wrong way...'

'Uh oh. This doesn't sound like it's going to be good.' There was a glimmer of smile.

'It's just that... I don't understand why you'd care.' I saw him swallow and he turned his head away, towards the shuttered blind. I tried to word it better. 'I mean, I know you care about Henry and Ava and the kids. Clearly, they've become closer to you than they let on to me, which is fine. And I'm glad you've got such good friends, obviously, but I'm... we're not...'

'We're not what, Mils?' His eyes were back on me, looking like they could see straight through me.

'Together.'

There was a beat before he shook his head. 'Nope. We're not. But just because we split up doesn't mean I don't care what happens to you. I can't just erase everything we had from my mind, even if you can.' His voice was quiet and steady.

'Of course I can't,' I replied, stung. 'But we both know you've not exactly been a monk since we broke up.'

'Nope. I haven't. And I don't suppose you've been a nun either.' His Adam's apple bobbed. I hadn't been a nun – but the truth was I hadn't been far off it. I'd thrown myself even harder into work, proving to myself, and everyone else, that I'd been the one in the right. And although I met a lot of people, very few of them held much romantic interest. There'd been a nice guy I'd seen a few times. We'd dated for a month or so but, in the end, he told me that he wanted someone to spend time with and I didn't seem to have a lot of that available. He'd also mentioned that, when I was with him, I'd still spent a lot of time scrolling and he just didn't feel we were the right fit. And he was probably right. The fact that I didn't miss him when I was no longer seeing him told me all I needed to know.

'I didn't come here to fight with you, Milly. I came to see, with my own eyes, that you were OK.'

'I'm just peachy,' I replied, feeling quite the opposite.

'Is there anything I can get you?'

I rolled my head on the pillow slowly, from side to side. 'No. But thank you.' Jed was looking at me. 'What?' I raised my hand up to the fuzzy patch. 'If you laugh, I'll get the nurse to put laxative in your coffee.'

He smiled. 'Then I'm definitely not laughing.'

'Good. Because, from the way she was looking at you, I don't think she'd do it anyway. Annoyingly.'

He gave a small, self-deprecating head shake and caught my hand as it made exploratory movements around my head. 'Stop poking at it. It's just fine.'

'It's not just fine. I've got bald spots! How would you like it?'

'I'd like it a whole lot more than the other options God was offering you at the time.'

I rolled my eyes at him. Me and Jed and God didn't always see eye to eye but it was part of his upbringing, and I got that. He had his beliefs, which he moulded to suit as most people did, and that was fine. But he had kept the faith his mama had instilled in him growing up. It was part of him and I had to admire, and admit to sometimes feeling a little bit jealous, that he had this belief that there was some purpose to things that didn't always make a whole lot of sense. Even second hand, it had been comforting at times. To be honest, I could have done with some of that comfort right now. But even thinking about getting any sort of comfort from Jed

Matthews was a bad idea because I knew that he was very, very good at comforting – in all sorts of ways.

'Do you want me to get you some ice chips or something? Do they have those here? You look a little flushed.'

'You say the nicest things,' I said, trying to snake my hand back up to my head.

Jed caught it again. 'Leave it alone. It won't heal if you keep poking at it.'

I let out a sigh as he released my hand. 'I forgot how bossy you were.'

That brought a smile. 'I am not bossy.'

Actually, he was more than capable of being bossy when he – and I – had wanted him to be but that was a whole other story. One that ended long ago.

'I'm advising you not to keep poking around at your wound. That's offering sensible advice. Two completely different things.'

'Is that so?'

'Uh huh,' he replied, settling back in the chair a little, one brow slightly raised as if daring me to challenge him. Unfortunately, I couldn't think of a pithy remark so I stuck my tongue out at him and had to settle for that.

'Kinda hard to argue with that erudite comeback.'

'Oh, bugger off,' I replied, as I concentrated on not smiling.

'Good to see that smile again.'

I met his gaze.

'You scared the shit out of me, Mils. You looked so...'

My mind span as he searched for a word.

'When?'

'I was here when they brought you in. Someone found that next of kin card in your purse and called me. Henry's number was busy initially, apparently, so they came to me. I called Henry from here.'

'You were here?'

'Yeah.' Tension had tightened the muscles in his face, making the hard planes of it sharp enough to slice with.

'You had everyone pretty worried.' He tried to smile but it didn't quite work.

'I'm so sorry they called you. I... had no idea I still had that card in there. I've been meaning to sort out that purse for, well, years clearly. I'll take it out now. Obviously.'

He laid one large cool hand across my fingers. 'I'm not upset they called me. I'm glad they did. If you'd have woken up, I'd have wanted you to have a friendly face there.' He gave a little head wobble. 'Well, sort of a friendly face.'

'Your face is OK.'

His face was so much more than OK but I wasn't about to go there.

'Gee. Thanks. You say the nicest things,' he quipped my own line back at me.

I smiled.

'I happened to be doing a mentor session just down the road from here. A new start-up venture. My phone rang, which was odd because I usually switch it off when I'm doing these things so it doesn't distract me.' I knew he hadn't said it as a dig at me. He was good like that. When Jed was with you, he was present. He gave you his full attention and I didn't doubt that he would turn his phone off in a situation like that. 'It was weird I'd forgotten but I just grabbed it, ready to shut it off, but it has this automatic business number recognition thing, and the screen was showing the caller as this hospital so obviously I answered, but honestly? I expected it to be a wrong number. But better I told them that than have them leave a message on the wrong person's phone and somebody miss something important.'

Oh, bloody hell. Did he have to be this kind and good? I'd held on to all the arguments and bickering that had marked our final year together. Those kept me going. Kept me clear that Jed was not The One, and not where my future lay. I'd put away all the good memories of him and held on to the stuff that helped me get through the day. And now here he was, inconveniently reminding me of everything I'd tried to forget.

'Anyway, they told me you'd been in an accident. I don't even know what I said to the guys I was with but I'm pretty sure they thought I'd lost a marble or two. I ran down here and they said you were on your way in the ambulance and sent me off to wait in the waiting room.'

'Which you didn't.'

He flicked that blue gaze to me and shrugged. 'I went back outside to wait instead. Couple of minutes later, an ambulance came in, lights blazing. I just knew.'

'Could have been anything. London's a pretty busy place.'

He locked eyes with me. 'I knew.' He gave a small clear of his throat before carrying on. 'Anyway, I'm sure I pissed a few people off, trying to ask questions when I should have just got out of the way but... jeez, Mils. I know we parted not seeing eye to eye, but never do that again, OK?'

I gave him a watery smile. 'I didn't really plan on doing it this time.' I shook my head. 'You shouldn't have come,' I said, softly.

'Yeah. I should.'

'No. It wasn't your responsibility.' I put a hand to my head. 'I can't believe that damn card was still in there. I'm so sorry, Jed.'

'What are you sorry about?'

I looked up. 'You know what.'

'My dad?'

My look gave him the answer.

'No one's a fan of hospitals, Milly.'

'Yes, but I'm sure this was too much of a reminder.'

'Dad's gone. You're here. That's all that matters.'

I tried to swallow the lump in my throat, reaching for the glass of water on my trolley to help. Jed passed it to me, and I took a couple of sips.

'Anyway. I just wanted to try to explain. I mean, I know we didn't part on the best of terms but we...' He sighed, searching for the right phrase. 'We have history. And Henry and Ava are good friends, and you're his sister and... anyway. I needed to see you. I needed to make sure you were OK, and maybe you're right, maybe that's a hang-up from Dad's accident. So, I hope you'll forgive me for asking to see you in the week and for Ava inviting me over tonight. I know it was probably the last thing you expected or wanted but, man, it's good to see you sitting up and talking sass again.'

'I do not talk sass.'

'Yeah. You do. But you wouldn't be you if you didn't.'

I touched my face, suddenly a little overwhelmed. 'I'm a mess.'

'You're not a mess, hon.'

'I have a big scar on my face and bald patches and my whole body is purple! And I...' Exhausted, the emotions washed over me, my breath hitching as I started to sob. 'I lost the biggest opportunity I'll ever have!'

Jed turned as the door opened and Henry and the troop filed back in. My brother stopped short at the sight of me sobbing. He turned to Jed.

'What did you do?'

'He didn't do anything,' I managed to get out between sobs and hitches. 'He was just... nice!' Which set me off again.

'I think she needs some rest.' Ava had put Henry in charge of the kids and was now bustling around me, adjusting the bed back to a sleeping position and rearranging my pillows.

'I'm fine,' I sobbed.

'Is Auntie Milly sad?' Alfie asked, holding an unsure looking Rosie's hand.

'No, darling. She's just tired. Come and give her a goodnight kiss so she can get some sleep.'

'I'll go,' Jed said, moving the chair away.

'Probably best. Take Henry with you. Why don't you all go and get some ice cream at Ginelli's?'

'Ice cream!' The children cheered as they clambered up to hug me.

I pulled them close and kissed the top of their heads as they wrapped their arms around the bits of me they could.

'OK, now say goodnight and go with Daddy and Uncle Jed.'

They slid off the bed, Rosie with a little help from Jed, before lifting her arms up to him.

'Rosie, you're too big to be carried around,' Ava admonished as she fussed around me.

'She's OK, aren't you, sweetheart?'

'Uncle Jed looks sad too. I'm cuddling him to make him feel better. I can do it better from here.'

A smile at Rosie's comment found its way through my tears and I met Jed's eyes. He returned it but I couldn't read what was behind it. He moved closer again and, with his free hand, held mine a moment. 'It was good to see you, Milly.' His hand moved and he gently brushed a rogue tear away with his thumb. 'I didn't mean to make you cry.' He looked pained.

I shook my head. 'You didn't.'

Disbelief showed on his face.

'You didn't. I'm just tired. And I want some of that ice cream.'

His face cleared and that killer smile broke through. 'I'm pretty sure you're going to be out like a light soon. How about a rain check?'

'Deal.'

'Caramel swirl, right?'

'Is there any other flavour?'

'There are lots of flavours, Auntie Milly!' Rosie piped up and Jed grinned, resting his head against her blonde curls for a moment.

'Get some rest, Mils.'

A few minutes later and the room was quiet, the only light coming from Ava's Paperwhite Kindle as she read quietly, having ensured I was comfortable for the night. I was pretty sure there'd be another nurse's round at some point but whether I'd be awake enough to notice was another matter.

'When I'm feeling better, remind me I need to have a talk with you about bringing Jed Matthews back into my life.'

'Um hmm,' Ava replied, completely un-concerned.

Closing my eyes, I let sleep overtake me.

7

'Henry, can you get me a phone? My credit card should be in my purse.' I looked around. 'Wherever that ended up.'

My brother's head had snapped up at what I had thought was a perfectly reasonable request.

'A phone?'

I frowned. 'Yes.'

He gave me an exasperated, disbelieving look.

'What?' I asked.

'You.'

'What about me?' I asked, genuinely confused.

'You seriously think I'm going to get you a phone after everything that's happened?'

'I need one!' I said, getting annoyed and trying to push myself up in the bed. 'It's been over two weeks now I've been offline.'

'I'm not buying you a phone.' Henry was adamant.

'What is your problem?'

'My problem,' Henry's voice rose, 'is that you can't be trusted with one!'

'I'm not five, Henry! Don't be so ridiculous.'

'No, but Rosie has more road sense than you do! She knows to wait until the lights change, and to keep looking around when she crosses the bloody road, unlike you, apparently!'

'It was an accident! I needed to be somewhere and those traffic lights were broken.'

'They weren't broken, you were just impatient.'

'I wasn't the only one!' I retorted, defensively.

'You were the only one with your face glued to your phone instead of on your surroundings! So much so that you didn't see a bus coming! I mean, it was a bus, Milly! They're pretty hard to miss in general.'

'It must be nice being so perfect,' I snapped, upset now.

Henry pushed his hands back through hair the same colour as mine. 'I'm not perfect, Milly, and I'm not claiming to be.'

'Just acting like it.'

He let out a sigh. 'I'm sorry. I just... we know you have a tendency to stick your face in that thing and that's the last anyone sees of you for hours. This time it could have been the last anyone saw of you at all.'

'I do know that. It was an accident,' I repeated.

'I know, Mils,' he said, calmer now. 'Look, what is it you need to do?'

'Erm, work?' I said, raising my hands, one complete with cast. My brother's eyes lingered on it a moment. I glanced at it momentarily. 'I'll manage.'

'You need time to recover. You could have died, Milly.'

'Yes, but I didn't. And, consequently, I need to get back to work.'

He shoved his fingers back through his hair again, his brow creased. 'OK. How about a compromise?'

'What sort of compromise?'

'We'll get you connected but just so you can get

in touch with people and let them know you'll be out of action for a while. It's not like you don't have a decent excuse. They'll understand.'

Henry didn't get how the fashion industry worked, and I had a feeling he was overestimating their generosity, but I had to have faith. I'd built myself a good reputation – good enough to get an interview with *Vogue,* although I was pretty sure that was a chance long gone. I planned to contact them anyway and explain. Maybe I'd catch them on a good day.

'Perhaps you could use this time as an opportunity?'

'An opportunity?'

'Yes.'

'For what?'

He spread his hands. 'I don't know. Take stock of your life. Make some changes. Decide what it is you really want.'

'I already know what I want, Henry. Because I had it. Or, at least, I was on my way to having it.'

'Really? That life is what you really want? Spending all your time with your face in a screen, writing about clothes that are so ridiculously priced you could never have them yourself. Bending over backwards for people who don't appreciate you and leaving yourself very little time for family and even less for friends or relationships. That's what you want?'

'It won't always be like that,' I defended my choices, although, if I was honest, he'd hit a nerve. Sometimes, when I sat back, it did feel exactly like that. But it was just temporary. Once I got the editorial position I was after...

'Won't it?' Henry asked, his tone genuine. 'Are you sure about that?'

'It's nice to know you have so much faith in me.' I tried not to be stung but he was my brother and, like Jed, could see my emotions all over my face.

'I do have faith in you, Mils. And I know you'll get to where you want to. But then what? And at what cost? Ava said you told her you were only rushing because the magazine changed the interview time right at the last minute.'

'It's *Vogue*.'

'I don't care if it's the Pope! You give someone a time, you stick to it. You don't change it at the last minute, assuming everyone will jump for you. How arrogant is that?'

'People do jump for them though. You kind of have to.' I did a small, one-shouldered shrug that I'd discovered was less strain on my ribs.

'You don't have to jump in front of a bus, though.'

I gave him a look.

'You don't get how it works.'

'I get exactly how it works and I do respect what you do and know you're very good at it. But all I see is you getting a raw deal. That upsets me.' He fiddled with the blind pull. 'And it really upsets me when it lands you in hospital. Nothing's worth that, Milly.'

'It was—'

'An accident. I know. I'm just saying you need to look after yourself, and maybe this is a chance to think about whether you're actually doing that or not.'

'I know you're trying to look out for me, Henry, and I really do appreciate that, but this is what I've worked for. This is what I know how to do.'

'You can do anything you want, Milly. If something isn't working for you, it's never too late to change things. You used to talk about writing a book.'

'And I'd still like to. I just haven't really had the time yet. But I will.'

'Not if you carry on going the way you were going. It was bad enough before, but once you split up with Jed you stepped it up to a whole other level.'

'I had to.' My voice was quiet.

'Because of money?'

'No. Because he was no longer in my life and that left a big hole. A massive hole. I needed to fill it with something. I wasn't interested in meeting anyone else so that something became work.'

'He'd have come back if you'd asked him. You know that, right?'

I shook my head. 'No. It was beyond that. We were going in different directions.'

'He was just worried about you even way back then. If he knew the hours you put in now...'

'Well, it doesn't affect him now, does it, so none of that matters.'

Henry didn't reply.

'Why didn't you tell me you'd stayed close to him?'

'Because you'd have huffed and been a diva and demanded that we take your side and not see him.'

'I'm not a diva.'

'You've been known to be on the very odd occasion. Most people have a bit of a diva streak somewhere.'

'Still...'

'See? This is what I mean.'

I rolled my eyes.

'He is our friend, and he was a mess. It didn't seem fair to just jettison him because things hadn't worked out between you. It would have been different if he'd cheated on you or something but he didn't. He was trying to look after you.'

'I didn't need looking after. And I still don't.' I didn't miss the irony in the fact that I was saying this from a hospital bed, but I held my ground.

'Well, I don't think he has any intention of trying that again so you don't need to worry on that front. He's hardly short of offers.'

I tried not to let Henry's words bother me. I didn't want Jed back. Of course I didn't. There was a reason things didn't work out. It wasn't that he didn't support me. I'd have been doing him a disservice if I claimed that, but the amount of time I ended up spending on work, admittedly not always for a lot of reward, began featuring more and more in our arguments, which themselves had increased from almost nothing to at least weekly and sometimes more often. He felt I was being taken advantage of, and that I was missing out on my family and on him because I gave all my time to other people, who didn't necessarily deserve it.

When Dad had a funny turn, they'd initially thought he might have had a mini stroke. It turned out to be an allergic reaction to an antibiotic he'd been given for an eye infection, but the end result was the same in that it gave Jed an opportunity to try to make me see that I had to make the most of people while they were there. His dad had been taken from him far too early and he'd missed out on a lot of stuff that he shouldn't have. My parents had loved Jed, of course, and I was thankful that he'd got a little bit of that back with the time he'd spent with Dad. I knew it wasn't the same and nothing would ever make up for the loss of his own father but it was always evident how much it meant to him, spending time with my parents. A thought popped into my head.

'Do Mum and Dad still see Jed, too?'

Henry straightened the items on my trolley table, avoiding my eye.

'Right. So, basically, no one took my side!'

'It wasn't about taking sides, Milly.'

'Of course it was!'

'No, it wasn't. We were all there for both of you. He'd built a life here. A business here. He couldn't just walk away from it all and fly back to the States.'

'I thought that was exactly what he did.'

'For a few weeks he did. He went and stayed with his mum down in New Orleans but he had to come back, and we were his friends. We were all his friends. Both of you were in a mess. It was hard to watch.'

'I was fine,' I said, the automatic response still popping up.

'You were very far from fine but you pretended you were, which made it a lot harder to be there for you – on the odd occasion we did see you. Jed, on the other hand, freely admitted he was a mess, which made it easier to help him.'

'Well, it looks like you did a great job, if the bevy of women I've seen in the gossip mags lining up to date him is anything to go by.'

Henry grinned. 'If I didn't know better, I'd have said I just saw a little glimpse of a green-eyed monster.'

I fixed my brother with a look. 'Then it's a good thing you do know better.'

He nodded slowly a few times. 'Yeah. Can't see what all these women see in a disgustingly good-looking, super-rich tech entrepreneur myself.'

'You're hilarious, and they're welcome to him. Now, can we please get back to a far more important matter? I.e., that of me earning a living.'

'I'm afraid I can't recommend you return to work any time soon, Milly.' Dr Sands caught the end of our conversation as he entered on his rounds.

'I'm self-employed. I don't get paid if I'm not working.'

'I understand. Really. I do. And while I'm pleased with how you're healing, even when you're up and about, you'll still need to be careful. Your body has been through a lot of trauma. You have stitches inside as well as on the outside and all that takes time to heal. You'll probably find you get tired more easily for a while. You'll need to hold off attempting to dive straight back into the hectic lifestyle it sounds like you were living.'

'I can do more from home,' I said.

'That's a good start but long days at home won't be good for you either. You really will need to take care of yourself for a while, Milly. You've been making a good recovery but it's not an overnight thing. As much as I wish I could flick a switch to make everyone better immediately, unfortunately it doesn't work like that.'

'Well, that's disappointing,' I replied, a half-smile on my lips, as I tried to ignore the scrambling my brain was doing as it absorbed what the doctor had said. But then, if I cut the extra work I did on top of the columns, that wouldn't be so bad. And it would only be temporary. Just until I healed more fully. I could still pay the rent and live, albeit even more frugally, on what those brought in.

'I'm working on it, and you'll be the first to

know,' he smiled as he made a note on my paperwork, before heading off to his next patient.

Henry pulled up the chair beside the bed and
rested his phone on the bedcovers before looking at
me. 'You will listen to what he said, won't you?'

I read the unease in his face.

'I know you're worried about money and stuff,
but there are ways around that. There's no way
round your health.'

'It's OK, Henry,' I promised, feeling my stomach
twist at his concern, only able to imagine how
much worse it had been when Jed had called to tell
him the news. He was right, I was worried about the
money but I could manage. I had no wish to end up
back in here once I left and I'd already put my
family through enough. A few extra weeks rest was
manageable for the sake of that.

He studied me for a moment, seemed satisfied
and pressed the icon for the internet browser on his
phone. 'Right, so do you know what phone you
want?'

8

I looked at the clock, trying to work out whether the battery in it had died or whether time really was going that slowly. The trouble with hospitals is that the days are so long because they start so early. Ordinarily, so did I but as I had nowhere to be – or at least nowhere I was allowed to be right now – clock watching had become my new favourite hobby.

Jed hadn't returned since that first night and I assumed, from his parting request for me to take care of myself, he had no plans to. Which was fine. Obviously. And for the best. Although... once I'd got over the shock of actually seeing him again, it had been nice. Henry and Ava had been absolutely brilliant, of course, and been trying to keep me amused. I knew that, had we told them, or even been able to tell them, Mum and Dad would have come back straight away and been at my bedside as much as possible to keep me from getting bored. But, thankfully, they were in some remote meditation centre in the middle of... was it Greece? I couldn't remember. Henry would remember. I should have paid more attention to the rough itinerary they had given me. It wasn't that I wasn't interested, I was just busy. The more I thought about it, the more I realised I had used that phrase an awful lot.

But as it was, my parents were out of contact at the moment. Dad hadn't been keen on this bit of the tour but Mum was keen to try it and had persuaded him it might be good to switch off entirely for a few weeks. All outside communication was banned and they had initially worried about that but we'd all persuaded them to go ahead. Nothing would be that urgent. Obviously that had ended up being a bit of a fib but hopefully, by the time they chugged their motor home out of the wellness centre and got back on the grid, I'd be in a better state in which to give them an overview of my recent exploits.

There was no way I wanted them to know now anyway. The trip had been such a dream of theirs, exploring like this. It was always 'when the kids have left home'. But it had still taken a while for them to actually do it. Henry and I tried to encourage them but it just never quite happened. They talked about it, and maps would be brought out, destinations researched, but that was the extent of it. I guessed that so many 'I'd love to' plans never came to anything because it never seemed the right time. But sometimes you just have to take that step. And Mum and Dad finally had. In the end, the swiftness of the whole plan coming together had been a bit of a shock. And the 'travelling around Europe for a few months' morphed into 'travelling the world, possibly for a year or so'. When my parents finally got their bums in gear, they didn't mess around.

It had taken Dad's funny turn to get those gears to shift. Although it had turned out to be nothing, it seemed to be a reminder that they weren't getting any younger (although I steadfastly refused to acknowledge that fact) and that if they didn't do this now, they might never do it. They had the opportunity, and the means. Actually, they had a lot more means than Henry and I expected when they announced they'd sold the house too and would get themselves an easy-to-manage flat once they returned. There were definitely no half measures once they'd got some momentum. The thought of them dropping everything and coming back, having waited so long to do it, just wasn't an option.

Just after lunch, there was a knock at the door and I was surprised to see my flatmate peer into the room.

'Hi!' I said, surprised. We didn't exactly have a pally relationship. It wasn't strained either, it was just... nothing, really. I rented her spare room and that was it. We'd never become friends as such so it was a pleasant surprise that she'd taken the time to come and visit me.

'Your brother says you get better now.' The eastern European accent hadn't lessened in all the time I'd known her – basically, a few months after moving out of the flat I'd shared with Jed. It wasn't the most desirable address in the world but it was convenient and the price was doable.

'Yes, thanks,' I replied, smiling.

'That's good.' She didn't smile but then Xenia wasn't really the smiling type. She had those high, Slavic cheekbones that people paid plastic surgeons a lot of money to fake and a perpetually bored, slightly pouty expression that, by the number of men I'd awkwardly bumped into in the shared kitchen of the flat of a morning, obviously held a certain appeal.

'Thanks for taking the time to come and see me.' I felt the need to fill the awkward silence that had drifted on following her reply.

She gave a shrug. 'No problem.'

More silence.

'So, how have—'

'I need your rent money,' she cut across me.

'I... er... what?'

'The rent.' She shrugged again. 'Is due. I need your money. Is already two days late.'

I frowned. 'I've been kind of busy, Xenia. You know, trying not to die!' OK, so that was a bit dramatic but she'd taken me by surprise.

The bored expression remained.

'If you are here, you are not working. That means I don't get rent money next month, perhaps?'

'I'll get you the money, Xenia. Thanks for the concern, though.'

She let out a sigh. 'I have a friend who wants your room.'

'What? Well, they can't have my room! I'm using it.'

'Not at the moment. And maybe you can't pay me soon, so...' she held up her hands, the long fingernails covered in intricate designs. 'I have someone who will be reliable.'

'I'm reliable!' I cried. 'And you can't do that. You have to give someone proper notice.'

'I give you notice now. Elena is moving in at end of month. But I still need rent for this month.'

'As you pointed out, I'm not using it at present so maybe I should just hold on to that rent.'

She gave an unconcerned look. 'OK. Tell your brother to collect your things. I leave them on the landing this evening. Seven o'clock. Not sure how long they will stay there, though.' And with that she pulled open the door.

'Xenia. You can't...' But she had already gone. Looks like she could. And she definitely would. Shit.

'I need a bloody phone!' I shouted to no one in particular before flopping back onto the bed. 'Owww!'

9

'Good to see your smiling face.' Henry raised one brow as he entered the door, one hand holding Rosie's and the other holding a bag from a large electronics retailer in which I really hoped was my new phone.

'Auntie Milly!' Rosie and Alfie ran in and gave me some much-needed hugs, which made the world slightly brighter. I was still in a fix with my living arrangements but I did have these two, which made up for a lot. Ava followed, giving me a kiss and a concerned frown at my sour expression, before unpacking a delicious-looking cake.

'What's up with you?' Henry asked, as he pulled back from dropping a kiss on my forehead.

'Apart from all this?' I mumbled.

'Yep.'

'Xenia.'

'Xenia?'

A tap at the door interrupted us. 'OK to come in?' Jed's unfairly good-looking face peeped around the door.

'Of course!' Henry waved him in.

'This is my room, you know,' I said, giving my brother a look.

'Yes. Paid for by the insurance company you're covered by thanks to me, so I guess we have joint say on who visits.'

I had no reply to that.

Jed approached the bed. 'Hey.'

'Hello.'

Henry had bustled off to fix a rogue wheel on the toy car Alfie had brought, and Ava was getting Rosie settled with a book for a little while, leaving Jed alone beside the bed.

'I can go if you want. Henry means well but you're right. It is up to you and if you don't want me here, I totally get that. I didn't plan to come, actually. Just so you know.'

'Oh.'

'I had to meet Henry to give him some paperwork. They were on their way here and asked if I wanted to come.'

'I'm surprised you don't have far better options for your evening than this.'

Jed glanced around, smiled at Rosie giggling at something in her book then brought his gaze back to me. 'Nope.'

'No glamorous gala or swanky restaurant opening tonight?'

'Nope,' he said, again. 'You know that's not really my thing anyway.'

'But you still go to them.'

'I have to eat.'

'And having a beautiful model on your arm is an aid to digestion, I guess?'

Jed said nothing but gave me a head tilt.

I tried not to blush but was pretty sure I missed the mark.

'Sorry.' I shook my head.

He blinked in acceptance as Henry caught the last of the exchange.

'What's up with you? The nurse put itching powder on your gown or something this morning?'

'No. I told you. It's Xenia.'

'Oh. Right. Your flatmate? What's she got to do with anything?'

'She visited today.'

'Oh! That was nice.' Ava smiled over.

I smiled back, a little tighter. 'It would have been, had she not demanded my rent and then proceeded to say that as it was likely, in her opinion, that I wouldn't be earning enough to cover the rent going forward, she's decided to give my room to one of her friends.'

'From when?'

'Seven o'clock this evening.'

'What?' Henry and Ava both cried together, causing the children to look up.

'She can't do that, Milly.' Jed, as ever, was calm in a crisis. 'She has to give you notice.'

'That little,' Henry lowered his voice, 'cow! You said you lent her money to cover her own rent payment the other month!'

'I've done that more than once, actually.'

'And this is how she repays you? Little...' He didn't say anything but all of us adults could fill in the blank. 'Anyway, as Jed says, she can't just evict you like that. She has to give proper notice. What are the terms in your contract?'

I scratched a fingernail on the cotton sheet, concentrating hard on it.

'Milly?' Jed asked.

'Hmm?' I still didn't look up.

'What does the contract say about termination period?'

I slowly raised my eyes to his. He met them and knew. 'You don't have a contract, do you?'

I gave the tiniest of head shakes. Jed let out a breath that was half disbelief and half exasperated laugh.

'You don't have one?' Henry asked, in a tone that had absolutely no humour in it.

'No.'

'Why not?'

'I meant to!' I said. And I had. I really had meant to.

'But, let me guess, you were too busy.' He ran a hand through his hair. 'Milly!'

'I know! All right? I know! But I was busy and I wasn't exactly in the best place mentally when I moved there, was I?'

Henry's eyes flicked to Jed then back to me.

'I know I've screwed up and I should have got it sorted but the time went by and then I'd been there so long I actually forgot I didn't have anything in writing. I never thought she'd do anything like this, though. And, to be honest, Henry, I feel like enough of an idiot without you making me feel a bigger one. I couldn't even arrange for someone to collect my stuff because I don't have a bloody phone so not only am I now homeless, I'm going to have nothing left to put in a home even if I could find one because she's just going to dump my stuff on the landing this evening. It won't last five minutes in that place!'

Jed laid his hand on mine. 'Hey, calm down.'

'Don't bloody tell me to calm down. It's all right for—'

'I'm going to go and get your stuff.' He curled

his fingers around mine. 'OK? Will it fit in my car? Or is there furniture?'

I took a deep breath. 'No. No furniture. There isn't that much, really. Just my clothes, laptop and a few photos.' I paused. 'Sounds a bit pathetic put like that, actually.'

'No, it doesn't.' He squeezed my fingers.

'Oh. There's a blue silk throw that I had on my bed. Xenia's always had her eye on it. If you happened to get a moment to check...'

'I'll make sure it's there. The one from Agra?'

He remembered.

I nodded. 'Yes.'

'I'll get it.'

I gave him the address and he plugged the destination into his phone's map. 'I'll head off now before she can just dump it.'

'Wait,' Ava said, 'I'll come with you. You have a few very nice pieces in your wardrobe. I'm going to make sure she hasn't liberated any of them. If she's doing this, and she's been coveting your throw, I'm not putting anything past her. I can direct you then.' She waved Jed's phone away. 'I know a quicker way.'

'How are you going to find out?' I asked, grinning at Ava's woman-on-a-mission demeanour.

Ava looked at me. 'I have two small children. I'm pretty good at sniffing out fibs. I'll ask her. To start with.'

Henry turned and gave me an even look. 'Oh, she'll find out, don't worry. Never try to plan a surprise birthday party for this woman.'

Ava grinned and gave him a big kiss. 'Come on, Jedidiah! We have work to do.'

Jed threw me a look and I laughed. He hated his full name but he loved Ava so she was one of the few to get away with using it.

'We'll be back soon.' Ava waved and the door closed behind them.

'Right.' Henry said, glancing around. After the sudden flurry of activity, the room was now strangely quiet. Both children were happily occupied with books, Rosie reading quietly to the cuddly toy elephant, Eric, that went everywhere with her while Alfie absentmindedly drove a small car back and forth over the arm of the chair as he read his own book.

'Well, they seem happy enough. Let's get this

phone of yours set up, shall we? I got you a new sim card as the old one is in goodness knows how many pieces, including those that ended up embedded in you, but I asked them to put your old number on it. They quoted twenty-four hours but it's often far quicker than that.'

'Thanks, Henry. I really do appreciate this. Everything.'

He looked up from where he was emptying the bag over my bed. 'I know. And I'm sorry I got cross earlier. I know you were in a difficult place when you went to that flat, having not that long broken up with Jed. I should have realised that back then and checked everything was in order.'

'I'm a grown up, Henry. You don't need to check everything for me. It was my mess up.'

He looked at me. 'You're my little sister, Mils. I want to do it... Oh no, you're not going to cry, are you?'

'No.'

Maybe.

'Come on. Here, let me help. That arm needs to be rested, and I'll never find that tiny sim card if we drop it.'

10

A little over an hour later, Jed and Ava were back.

'Well, she's quite the delight, isn't she?' Ava said, pulling a face at me as she entered.

'Is she?' Henry asked, looking up from seeing if my phone had been connected yet.

'Oh, yes. Took quite a shine to our Jed here, though, which I think helped things along enormously. She was distinctly frosty until he unleashed that secret weapon of his.'

My eyebrows raised as did Henry's. 'Ava!' and he gave a nod of his head towards the children.

Ava gave a wink then rolled her eyes. 'His smile. She practically melted on the spot.'

Jed was standing behind her, looking away from us and rubbing his hand back and forth over his recently trimmed crop.

'Hardly,' he mumbled.

'Oh, please,' she dismissed. 'Honestly. I was right, though. She actually had one of your tops on! Can you believe it?'

'She did?'

'How did you know it wasn't her own? I mean, the same as Milly's?' Henry asked.

'Because it was something Milly had made in a back street in India,' Jed filled in. 'She designed it and drew it for the guy, sat out on a street with this old Singer sewing machine.'

I smiled at the memory. 'He didn't speak English and I didn't speak Hindi but we got there.'

'It turned out great.' Jed looked a little more relaxed now the spotlight had been turned away from him.

'So, I was looking at this top as we got the other stuff together and I was sure it looked like yours. Jed hadn't taken much notice of her, much to her disgust, I might add. But when I whispered to him about the top he looked and he was absolutely sure it was Milly's. So, I asked her.'

Jed came and sat down near the bed as Ava continued the story.

'First, she denied it and then, when Mr Charm here switched it on, and said so endearingly about how he was pretty sure he recognised it from your trip, she changed tack. After she'd finished interrogating him as to whether you two were an item, obviously.'

'Obviously,' I agreed, sliding a look to Jed who returned a patient one.

'She said that you'd given it to her.'

'I bloody well did not!'

'No, well, exactly. I knew you two were hardly BFFs so I didn't think that was likely. Anyway, she was all defensive until dream boat here said that it held sentimental value to him.'

'You did?' I couldn't keep the surprise out of my voice.

Jed gave a shrug. 'The fact you still had it must mean you wanted to keep it. She was... kind of flirty.'

Ava coughed.

'So, I thought trying to work with those tactics might have more luck than Ava was having.'

'Then she's like, "Well, you could see a lot more of it if you take me to dinner and I wear it,"' Ava added.

'So, when are you taking her?' I raised a brow.

Jed returned a sarcastic smile. 'Your top is in one of the bags.'

'And probably covered with make-up, by the looks of her. She wasn't exactly careful about taking it off.'

'How do you know?'

'Oh. She did that in front of us. I think I was just a lucky bystander, though. The show was all for him.' Ava sat down and repositioned Rosie on her lap.

'She... took it off in front of you?'

'Umm... yeah. Didn't see that one coming, I gotta admit.'

'And yet still no dinner date? I'm surprised.'

'Not really my type.'

'I'm pretty sure she'd make herself any type you wanted,' Ava opined.

'I'm not into people changing for me either. I prefer to know what I'm getting.'

I had a good idea as to what Xenia would have given him and tried not to think about it. She'd never been friendly, but her true nature had really shown itself today with one thing and another.

'And you were right about the silk throw too. That was on the couch. I got it, though. Hopefully, between us, all your stuff is there.'

'Thank you. Both of you. I don't know what I would have done without you.'

'Not something you have to worry about,' Ava said, smiling, and blew me a kiss over the top of her daughter's head.

'No, all I have to worry about is that I don't have a place to live.' I looked around. 'I wonder how long I can eke this place out for?'

'Don't worry about that for the moment. We'll sort something out before you're discharged,' Henry said, glancing at Ava who nodded her agreement. 'You just concentrate on getting better.'

'Where's all my stuff now?'

'It's in the back of my car at the moment. I'll

take it home tonight and put it in the spare room until you decide what to do.'

'Thanks, Jed. I really appreciate that. And your help today.'

'No problem. Anyone would have done the same.'

I doubted that but remained silent. Jed was one of the good guys. He just wasn't meant to be my good guy. Been there. Tried that. And it sounded as if Xenia had fancied a try too. It didn't particularly surprise me that she'd stripped off in front of Jed – he was the kind of man who could easily have that effect on women and, from the many times I'd exited my bedroom and got an eyeful of her prancing around the flat in the smallest underwear known to man, or woman, she wasn't exactly shy about her body. Not that there was anything to be shy about. Xenia had a hot body and she knew it. Jed turning her down must have come as quite the surprise. The fact that she'd evicted me and tried to steal some of my stuff took the edge off any female solidarity I might have ordinarily felt.

'I brought your laptop, though, so you can check anything you need to.'

'You did?' I felt my eyes light up.

'Yep. But I've set up some software on it so it turns itself off after fifteen minutes so you can't over do it.'

My mouth dropped open. 'You did not.'

Jed placed the device in front of me. 'I guess we'll see.'

I narrowed my eyes. He'd made his money from tech and was a demon with computers. There had been many a time when we were together that he'd saved me from launching an expensive bit of kit out of a window. There was absolutely no doubt he could have done what he said he had. The question was, had he?

'You wouldn't dare.'

His face was blank. 'You do have a habit of being a workaholic. And this,' he pointed at my cast, 'needs to be rested. As does the rest of you.'

'I need to just let people know I haven't fallen off the face of the earth and explain why I'm a bit late with a couple of things.'

'That's fair,' Jed said, watching me struggle to open the laptop. 'You need some help with that?'

'Nope. I've got it.' I so obviously didn't have it as

the damn thing flapped up and down while I tried to get a purchase on the thin edges.

'Man,' he blew out a sigh. 'Give it here.'

'I've got it,' I said, trying to push his hand away.

'You so don't got it. And it's going to end up on the floor in a minute and give you something else to stress about. Here.' Jed quickly opened the laptop with ease and set it in front of me, casting me an exasperated look as he did so.

'What?'

'You.' He sat back and crossed muscled fore-arms over his broad chest, the fabric of the t-shirt he wore pulling tighter across it.

'What about me?' I asked, pressing the start button on my computer.

'You don't change, do you?'

'I don't know what you mean.' I did, in fact, have more than an inkling as to what he meant but it wasn't good so I went with denial instead.

'Pretty sure you do.'

'Nope,' I said, stabbing at my keyboard with one hand to enter the password.

'Insisting on doing everything yourself.'

'It's called emancipation, Jed. I don't need

people to do things for me. It's not the 1950s any more. And even then, women were quite capable. They just had to pretend they weren't.'

'Really?' He tilted his chin down. 'You're going to accuse me of being misogynistic?' There was a hint of 'pissed off' in his voice.

I slid my gaze sideways to him. He really wasn't. His mum was a strong, sassy woman and he'd grown up under no illusions that women couldn't do anything they put their minds to. The last thing I'd read, two thirds of his executive boardroom were women. Jed was always focused on getting the best person for the job. And, quite often, that was a woman.

But he was also the kind of man who wanted to take care of people, especially women. Not because he thought they couldn't do it themselves, but because he felt they deserved it. It could be quite a heady combination when you were in the mix of it all. But I wasn't any more. And, therefore, I didn't need his help. Except to go and get my stuff. And apparently open the damn laptop. I'd have to look into a workaround for that.

'No.'

'Good.'

'This is connected now, by the looks of it,' Henry said, handing the phone across to Jed, who was nearest, as he sat with Alfie and his book.

Jed took it and laid it next to my laptop. I quickly picked it up.

'I guess that's the last conversation any of us are going to get out of you for a while.' He sat up, ready to make a move.

'What's that supposed to mean?'

'Well,' he said, standing and stretching, the bottom of his t-shirt riding up and exposing a narrow band of toned stomach. 'You've got everything you need there now, don't you?' He nodded at my devices.

'Oh my God! This is the first time I've looked at anything in weeks. Give me a break!'

'Yeah. And the only reason for that is that for the first week you were in a damn coma purely due to the fact that you're more attached to your phone than you are, or ever could be, to anything else.'

His voice was low, in deference to the children, but from the corner of my eye, I saw Henry and Ava exchange a look.

'That's unfair and you know it.'

'Do I?' One large hand did a spread, taking in my laptop and phone. 'You could have died, Milly. You're still weak – and I don't mean that in a derogatory way before you climb up on that high horse of yours. I mean medically. Physically. Mentally.' He shook his head. 'You got hit by a bus, for God's sake! You should be resting and recovering.'

'I've been doing that for the last three weeks!'

'It's going to take a lot more than three weeks to get over this, Milly. You need to understand that!'

'I do know that!'

'Do you?' he asked, scrubbing his hands over his hair for a moment. 'Because, right now, it doesn't look like it. Right now, it looks like you're about to dive straight back into how you've been for years. Choosing this,' he pointed at the tech, 'over anything real in your life.'

'Oh, don't be so dramatic, Jed.'

I looked over at Henry and Ava. They were watching now, as were the children.

'I'm being dramatic?' he asked, a jaw muscle flickering in the shade of a five o'clock shadow. 'I wasn't the one who got knocked down by a bus! Now that's what you call being dramatic.'

As he said this, his accent had got thicker and a distinct drawl now accompanied his words. His face was all hard planes anyway but there was an openness to it. Usually. Right now though, those angles were sharp and edgy and the thickening of his accent told everyone he was even more pissed off than he looked. And he didn't exactly look cheery to start with. Ava and Henry remained silent.

'Why do you even care?' I asked, suddenly feeling upset and tired. The screen had lit up and already hurt my eyes. My words were supposed to come out strong but, even to my own ears they sounded weary. Exhausted. I closed the screen without opening any programmes and lay back on the pillow. I rested my hand across my eyes. The room wasn't overly bright but it was still too much all of a sudden.

Jed hadn't answered. I heard movement and a few moments later, the door to the room open and close. Even without looking, I knew he'd gone and wouldn't be back.

'Nicely done, Mils,' Henry said with a sigh a few

moments later, with all the natural tact of a brother. Ava shooshed him and came over to unnecessarily straighten the bed sheets.

'You OK?' she asked, quietly.

I nodded. My hand still over my eyes.

'It's just because he cares about you.'

I wasn't sure if she was talking about Henry or Jed but either way it didn't matter. I didn't want to think about it any more tonight. Maybe ever. Jed's words were still flouncing their way around my brain. I knew I'd missed out on things – Alfie's first ever acting dialogue was just one of many examples. One of many moments I'd missed and wouldn't get the chance to redo. But I was trying to forge a career in a hugely competitive world. I'd put years and years into it. If I stopped now, even if I wanted to, what would have been the point of all those missed moments? The broken friendships? The broken relationships? Leaving Jed? It would all have been for nothing. I couldn't face that. It had to have been for something. Walking out on the man who had made me the happiest, best version of myself had to have been for something.

I'd barely noticed my family leave last night. After the drama of Xenia's eviction notice followed by relief at Jed and Ava rescuing my possessions, I was already tired. I should have rested then. But at the sight of my laptop, I hadn't been able to wait to sign in. Jed had known that. I had a pretty good idea now that he'd been testing me. Seeing if the events of the past few weeks had changed anything. I guess he'd got his answer. But I hadn't got my answer. Why did he even care? I knew he didn't have feelings for me. Not like that. I'd done a pretty thorough job of squelching those in our last few months together as I focused more and more on work, seven days a week.

But it was obvious he cared deeply about my family. Henry was known to chatter on when he'd had a few drinks and it wouldn't have surprised me to learn that he'd told Jed about my inattention at Alfie's play, along with a list of other examples I'm sure he and Ava could compile, given five minutes. A swirl of discomfort washed around me. I didn't do it on purpose. It wasn't like I wanted to miss out on anything. But I wasn't superwoman. I just couldn't do it all. If he or anyone else couldn't understand that, then that was their problem, not mine.

I leant over and picked up the phone from the bedside and switched it on. Having eagerly waited for it to connect yesterday, I couldn't face looking at it in the end and it had been put aside. But today was a new day. Time to start getting back on track. I had no plans to overdo it. Despite what Jed said, I was quite capable of being sensible in my approach to getting back to work. I already had a plan. Concentrate on the columns to bring money in – although I still needed to work out that whole living arrangement thing – and then start doing extra only as and when I was up to it. See, Jed? Whatever you think, you're wrong. I totally had this.

* * *

'Oh my God.'

Three days later, I dropped my head into my hands, elbows resting on the table. I'd been through a whole range of emotions this morning, running the gamut from rage through to despair. There was probably a good dollop of hurt in there too but I was avoiding that for the time being in order to avoid complete and utter overwhelm.

The plan of action I'd been so confident in initially had been strafed to pieces on the first day I plugged back in by a barrage of emails and texts plus a handful of voicemails. I'd spent the last three days desperately trying to salvage things but nothing had worked. I'd made calls and sent emails but all to no avail.

What each incoming message had essentially had in common was the accusation that, as they hadn't received my copy at the promised date, it had left them in a very difficult position. Had I called them to let them know there was a problem, perhaps they might have been more understanding. I'd worked with most of these people for a long time, and I could pretty much guarantee it wouldn't have made the slightest bit of difference, but I suppose they had to be seen to be magnanimous. As it was, the general consensus was that they would be unable to accept any further work from me as reliability was key to them maintaining the schedule for their publication. Like I didn't know that! And, of course, I totally understood the position. Had I been let down randomly in the way I appeared to have let them down, I'd be annoyed too. But, to be fair, I'd had a pretty good excuse and accidents do happen. Quite literally, in my case. I'd hoped that, once I'd explained the situation, they would realise this was a completely unavoidable one-off, and for many of the publications involved, take into account the years I'd worked with them, never once missing a deadline, realising that a lack of reliability was not something they'd ever had to worry about with me.

That had been the plan. The hope. The expectation, really. Except it hadn't gone like that. Instead of understanding, I'd received cold, dismissive emails advising that they were unable to change their mind on this but 'wished me the best in placing my work elsewhere'. On the flip side of this was the total ghosting I'd received from other contacts. Contacts I'd built up relationships with over many years with hard work, good time-keeping and that all-important reliability. But now none of them wanted anything to do with me. I'd received notice from three outlets that, due to non-delivery of my last columns, my services would no longer be required. The other messages and texts for one-off pieces that had been due to be submitted in the last couple of weeks said much the same thing.

I'd done my best to rectify things. Explained that this really had been a most unusual situation and that I had no plans to get hit by another bus any time in the foreseeable future – obviously I'd worded it far more eloquently and, yes, I admit, more grovelly than that. But nothing changed. Those that did bother to reply just sent the same form email as they would to any unwanted submission, despite the fact I knew these people. Many I had even been out for drinks and dinner with. Now I was reduced to receiving the same treatment as all the hopefuls knocking on the door for their first opportunity. Having no luck with emails, I'd tried calling a few but that got me even fewer results. From pretty much always taking my calls, now either a message was taken – and obviously discarded – or there was no answer at all. I knew nearly everyone screened their calls so the choice not to answer was being actively made – a situation reiterated by the fact that none of the voicemails I'd left had issued any type of response either. I'd gone from valued contributor, the person they all turned to when they suddenly had a gap that needed filling, or the copy they'd been sent by someone else hadn't come up to scratch, to a nobody. To someone who didn't even earn the right to have their call taken.

'Wow. That's a face,' my brother said considerately when he walked through the door to my room later that day. I had neither the energy nor the inclination to think up a retort. That in itself made him throw me a second look as the children rushed to the bed to clamber up and smoosh kisses on me. I hugged them to me, absorbing their love and warmth and innocence. You knew where you were with kids. They showed you love or they had a paddy and sulked. Their feelings were communicated pretty much in black and white. Unlike adults, who could quite easily look you in the eye and say one thing while doing or thinking something completely different.

'What's the matter, sweetheart?' Ava asked once the kids had settled down with the toys they'd brought.

I shook my head. I didn't even know where to start.

'Mils? What's up?' Henry pulled up another chair next to the bed. The laptop was closed and stacked, along with the phone, on the trolley table. 'Have you been overdoing it already?'

I gave a hollow laugh. 'Chance would be a fine thing.'

'What do you mean?'

'They've all dumped me,' I said, looking up finally. 'All of them. None of my contacts want anything to do with me. They say, the ones who actually deigned to reply, that I let them down so they won't be using me again.'

'You were under a bus!' Henry exclaimed. 'That's a pretty bloody good excuse for not turning up for work.'

'Apparently not good enough,' I replied as I slumped back against my pillow then winced.

'Surely they're not all of that opinion.'

'Unfortunately, that seems to be the general consensus.'

'But you've worked your arse off for years for these people! Who the hell do they think they are, treating you like that?'

Ava reached over and took my hand. 'I'm so sorry, Milly. It's an awful way for them to behave.'

I gave the one-shouldered shrug that appeared to be becoming my trademark.

'Did you have any luck rescheduling the interview you missed?'

I shook my head.

'No. I did finally get someone to reply to me but they just told me the position had been filled.'

'Did you explain what happened?'

'I started to try but it was pretty obvious they

weren't really listening and when it comes down to it, it doesn't really matter, does it? The fact is the position is taken. As far as they're concerned, I didn't show up so they went with another applicant.'

'Yes, but it wasn't because you didn't want to show up. It was them moving the appointment time forward that made you rush across the road in the first place!' Ava said, defensive on my behalf. 'The least they could do is to give you a chance.'

I'd been turning that thought over in my own mind most of the day as I looked down at the plaster cast on my arm, the bruises almost everywhere that were at least beginning to fade a little, and felt the aches throughout my body. As hard as it was to admit, I knew I had to accept that even if they had given me another chance to show them what they'd be getting if they chose to hire me, right now, I wouldn't be able to keep up with the frantic pace required for such a position.

'It's all right, Ava.'

She opened her mouth to say something else, paused, then closed it again before kissing me on the forehead. 'They didn't deserve you, anyway.'

'Exactly,' I agreed, doing my best to add conviction to the words. By the look on Henry and Ava's faces I was a little off the mark but at least I was trying.

'What will you do?'

'I've got some emergency funds set aside that will tide me over for a bit but I need to find some work sooner rather than later.'

The concern was evident on my brother's face and I saw him glance at Ava. Something was definitely going on.

'What?'

'We've been talking.' He lowered his voice a little, although the kids were busy playing a game on Ava's iPad and completely zoned out of any adult conversation. But you could never be too careful with children. They had an uncanny tendency to zone back in just at a critical point. 'We think you should move in with us for a while. Just until you're back on your feet again.' Henry glanced down the bed. 'Both literally and figuratively.'

'Oh, no, I couldn't do that.' I smiled at them and tried to blink back the tears prickling at my eyes. I wasn't especially a big crier. At least I hadn't been but my eyes had a definite propensity to fill up a little more often since the accident. Apparently anaesthetic could make you feel a bit weepy for a while, one of the nurses had said kindly when I'd had another teary moment. Hopefully it was just that. It wasn't that I was against showing emotion, I'd just got used to being that way. I worked in a tough industry and definitely not one that showed mercy. At least I *had* worked in it.

'Of course you could!' Ava took my hand. 'We'd love to have you, you know that. It's really no problem. The guest room is always made up anyway and you could make it your own for as long as you like.'

'It's really kind of you but you have enough going on.' I tilted my head towards the children. 'Plus aren't they supposed to be starting work on your kitchen extension any time soon?'

Henry shifted his weight. 'Monday. But,' he added quickly, 'that doesn't change anything. The kids would be thrilled to have you there and I know it won't be ideal for you with the noise and stuff going on, but we'll make it work.'

'I thought you were supposed to be moving into Ava's parents' holiday flat while it was being done.' Ava was from an old, wealthy family from Lancashire, even though her accent had long been drummed from her at the private schools she'd attended. Although they'd never leave their beloved Lancashire, her parents had bought a swanky riverside apartment in London once the grandchildren were born so that they could stay for longer visits and have them round.

'Well,' Ava began, 'we were but this way we can all be together.'

'And covered in dust, and trying to cook for a family on a camping gas ring in the living room?'

She covered it well but the momentary flash of horror on Ava's face spoke volumes.

'We'll just eat out.'

'That's a big job you're having done. You can't eat out all that time.' I reached out and took a hand of each of them. 'Thank you so, so much for the lovely offer but you need to stick with the plans you made.'

'Maybe we could ask the builders to reschedule?' she suggested, looking at Henry.

'No, Ava. You can't. They'll have planned other work around this just as you've made your own plans. Really. I'm fine. I've been looking online at places to rent and, as soon as they sign me out of here, I can go and view them.'

'Where are they?'

'Where are what?'

'The places you're looking at,' Henry clarified.

'Oh, there's a few I've found. Different areas,' I answered as casually as I could, walking the fine line between non-committal and suspicious. The fact was all of the places were in areas that wouldn't exactly be described as 'desirable', but the other fact was I didn't have many options. My budget was incredibly limited. I could fund a few months if I found something cheap and pretty much ate nothing but pasta but after that I was out on the street. I knew Henry would never let that happen but I'd never relied on anyone to bail me out before and I wasn't about to start now. Besides, the media always exaggerated the worst aspects of anything. Sure, it wasn't exactly Chelsea or Kensington I was looking to rent in (sadly!) but it wasn't exactly like I'd been living in the Shard before. It would be just fine.

12

It was so not fine. Really, really not fine. In fact, it was pretty much the opposite of fine but I'd just finished viewing the third and last property on my list and, rather incredibly, this was the best of them. I'd been discharged earlier this morning, although I still had to return for check-ups fairly frequently for a while. After that, I'd proceeded to drag myself around London to look at my housing choices, becoming more exhausted and more dejected with every step. With little other option, I'd just signed a lease on a gloomy, damp flat on the sixth floor of one of the ugliest Brutalist style buildings I'd ever seen, with a lift that didn't look like it had worked since the day the place was thrown up. God knew how I was going to get my stuff up to the flat. It had been enough of a trial dragging my own behind up and down the stairs, especially while holding my breath against the pungent odour emitting from the stairwell. But it was, for the moment, the place I was about to call home.

I pushed down a wave of nausea that might have been caused by exhaustion or just as easily by the thought of living in the dark, dank place I'd just handed over a deposit on. I sank down on the outside step of the building, aware I'd probably just incurred a large dry cleaning bill for my coat but my body overrode my brain and sense of clothing preservation. The wind was cold and I shivered as it funnelled through the corridor made by the surrounding blocks of similar style to the one I sat outside. Grey, faceless blocks that had been built with good intentions but had, over the years, lost their way and now looked tired and abused.

I thought again about how to get my stuff up the stairs. In a way it was lucky I didn't have a lot. When we'd split up, I'd refused to take anything Jed and I had bought together. Perhaps that hadn't been the wisest decision looking back. I'd contributed as much as possible to the living expenses when we'd moved in together, even though Jed's business had already begun taking off and his income was far in excess of mine. And that was small fry to where he was now. But he'd never made a thing of it either way and I was grateful for that. He'd just treated us as monetary equals even though we both knew that was far from the case. A wave of nostalgia washed over me at the happy times we'd had in that apartment, making it our own, making it a home. But as I'd taken on more and more work, determined to get to the position I wanted, fighting for the jobs I wanted, I'd had less time to devote to it. I'd barely even noticed it sometimes, being so wrapped up in a new season or trend that I wanted to study so I could write about it with authority.

The cracks began to show and after Jed pointed out that he'd painted the living room a completely different colour a week prior and I hadn't even commented, it had become impossible to keep papering over those cracks. The sad thing was, once I noticed – once I took the time to notice – I absolutely loved what he'd done. Apparently, he'd tried to talk to me about colours and I'd made sounds of agreement but clearly hadn't listened as I didn't remember that either. We'd both known that day it was over but had spent more months trying to make it work. Or at least pretending to. I couldn't slow down. Surely Jed could understand that? I was trying to make my mark, just like he was.

In the end, we stopped arguing about things and there was just silence which, in a way, was so much worse. Then I'd left, leaving everything behind. Except the memories. Those I'd buried away as deep as possible as I got on with my life, reassuring myself that I was happier this way anyway as I could now devote myself to my career full time without any guilt. And that philosophy had worked – for the most part. As Jed's star rose, the gossip columns showed that he had certainly moved on if the starlets and models with legs up to their armpits were anything to go by, so there was absolutely no reason to feel in the slightest bit bad about the part I'd played in the failure of our relationship. It might have felt right to start with – and yes, I admit, I'd never known anything to feel as right and as natural as being with Jed, even from that first day. But some things aren't made to last and we were obviously one of those things.

I pushed all thoughts of Jed Matthews out of my mind and dialled Henry. I could get by with the stuff I had with me for the moment but I'd need the rest of my gear, such as it was, at some point. I knew Henry and Ava were up to their elbows trying to sort things out for the start of the building work, plus getting themselves and the kids ready for a temporary move to her parents' flat, so I didn't want to ask them. They'd already done so much for me since me and my life had been almost literally turned upside down that I really didn't want to ask them to do more. I needed another option. Perhaps a man and a van? That would do it. I thought of my possessions. A very small van would be sufficient. If Jed could just let Henry know when it would be convenient to pick up the stuff he and Ava had collected from Xenia's, I'd arrange the rest. It was the ideal solution.

From the way he'd stalked out of my hospital room several days ago, once he realised I wasn't about to shuffle off my mortal coil just yet, I got the impression that Jed had satisfied that nostalgic sensibility for the times we'd had together, and now his memory had reminded him of all the things that had led to us splitting in the first place. Seeing me again would most definitely not be top of his 'to do' list. So, having an independent intermediary shuttling my worldly possessions from his place to mine seemed the perfect solution. I thought of what his place was probably like and then glanced behind me at the dark oblong of the flats looming above me, silhouetted by the orange haze of streetlights that floated over the city. I hope my things hadn't got used to the luxury because they were in for one heck of a disappointment.

Darkness had fallen and there was a definite change in the atmosphere. I shivered, although whether that was from the cold seeping through my coat from the cold, dirty concrete I'd sunk down onto, or from the discomfort that had begun to grow within me at my surroundings, I couldn't be sure. I dialled Henry and gave him a quick rundown of the situation.

'I'll bring the stuff over myself. It won't take long and that way you'll have your things tonight rather than waiting for them, trying to organise something else. A van would be a waste of money when I can do it easily anyway.'

In the background my niece sounded like she was having a meltdown of such proportions, it was likely registering on the Richter scale.

'Really, I don't mind!' Henry added quickly, his voice jumping half an octave as the words flew out. 'Text me the address and I'll be there as soon as I can.'

'Henry!' Ava's summons broke through the tantrum.

'Got to go. See you in a bit.'

'Henry, I—' He was gone. Now I felt even worse. Clearly, I'd be providing Henry with an escape plan, which was fine. He was my brother, after all. But Ava sounded like she needed all hands on deck right now and although we might not share blood, I loved her just as much, and felt awful that I might be enabling her being left to deal with the Fukushima-scale crisis going on in their house right now.

I messaged Henry.

It doesn't sound like it's the best time for you right now. Perhaps we can arrange something tomorrow?

Henry's message came back swiftly.

It's fine. Just send me the address.

I chewed my lip for a moment and wrapped my coat tighter as the strengthening wind funnelled between the buildings. As soon as Henry took one look at the place, I feared there would be another crisis. Taking a deep breath, I let it out slowly. That was one situation I would deal with. The choice of where to live was, after all, mine. Admittedly, this was most definitely not where I'd choose to live but out of the available options, it was still my choice and Henry would just have to deal with it. Hopefully it wouldn't be for long anyway. I messaged the address and waited.

About a quarter of an hour later, I'd moved from the step to try to find some shelter in the lee of a wall, which had sort of worked, but one look from a woman also doing the same thing indicated that this wasn't such a good plan after all. The skirt she had on was so short I'd have been worried about frostbite on my unmentionables and the heels on her shoes could easily fall into the category of lethal weaponry. I'd made an apologetic nod of my head and shuffled off, every part of my body aching and complaining against the work I'd put it through today. Admittedly that work had only been a few Tube rides, some walking and viewing of three dingy flats, but it was way more than it was used to compared to the last few weeks, and clearly way more than it wanted to deal with.

I swallowed down the wave of nausea swirling around, unsure as to whether that was caused by exhaustion or pain, or just the fact that I knew I'd been used to doing ten times the amount I'd done today for years without a thought. Discharging me, Dr Sands had reiterated that rest and recuperation were absolutely vital, and I'd nodded and agreed and promised. With my fingers crossed behind my back, obviously. They said that to everyone, didn't they? Especially those who'd come into close contact with a large motor vehicle. It was probably standard doctor discharge speak. But it was suddenly becoming clear that, actually, he'd meant it. Really meant it. When he said it would take time to get back to where I'd been at the time of my accident, he'd been speaking from the experience of putting many others back together, and an understanding of bodily trauma that I, in a state of both ignorance and denial, had arrogantly dismissed as not applying to me. But it did apply to me. As I found another step to sink down onto, in full exposure to the wind but hopefully away from anyone's 'patch', I realised it applied to me big time.

My phone rang, making me jump. My brother's name showed on the screen.

'Hi.'

'Hi, look, sorry. Bit of a change of plan.'

'Red, Henry! The lights are red!' Ava's voice came over through his car's hands-free. Both of them had that 'we're perfectly calm' tense tone going on.

'What's up?'

'Oh. Nothing to worry about. Alfie's had a little mishap. We're on the way to hospital now.'

The wave of nausea reared up. 'What do you mean, mishap? What's wrong? Is he OK? What can I do?' My words ran together in a torrent.

'He's fine. Nothing to worry about.'

I wasn't reassured.

'There's loads of blood!' Rosie's voice shouted in over the mic and I could hear Ava trying to sort her out although admittedly the little girl had sounded more thrilled than upset at the fact she had just imparted.

'Blood?' I squeaked. 'Why is there loads of blood?'

'Oh, they were both having a paddy in the kitchen and Alfie turned to stomp off and, in his haste to make a dramatic exit, managed to clock himself on the corner of the cabinet and cut his forehead. I don't think it's as bad as it looks but he might need a couple of stitches so we're taking him to A&E now.'

'OK. Will you let me know as soon as you know anything?'

'Of course. Don't worry, sis. He's fine. Really. Although we may need a crime scene clean-up team in the kitchen.' Henry did actually sound a bit calmer now. I tried to settle my stomach.

'I'm OK, Auntie Milly.' Alfie's little chirpy voice

came over the phone and tears flowed immediately down my face.

'I'm glad to hear it!' I said, trying to sound as if I wasn't sat in a cold concrete entranceway in a dodgy area, bawling my eyes out.

'Mummy said I'm being very brave.'

'It sounds like you are, my darling.' I pushed a smile into my voice.

'So, obviously, bit of a change of plan.' Henry picked up the conversation. 'But don't worry. I've spoken to Jed and he's going to bring your stuff over to you instead.'

I groaned.

'What?'

'What?'

'You groaned.'

'Oh. Sorry. That wasn't supposed to be out loud.'

'Oh.'

'I just can't imagine that news was greeted terribly gleefully.'

'You know what Jed's like. He's happy to help out. Even when it's for a pain in the arse ex-girlfriend.'

'Language, Henry!' Ava scolded.

'Sorry,' he mumbled, contritely. 'Look, I've messaged Jed the address and he's said he'll bring your stuff so try to be a bit more gracious than that when he turns up, will you? He did bother to check you hadn't died a few weeks ago, after all.'

'I'm sure that was more out of respect and love for you and Ava than anything he felt for me.'

'Probably. You did a real number on him so that makes sense.'

'Thanks for that.'

'What? I'm agreeing with you.'

'You don't have to be quite so blunt.'

'Of course, I do. I'm your brother. It's in the contract.'

I smiled, relieved to hear the tension easing from his voice, even if it did involve a dig at perhaps not my finest hour.

'It takes two to make things work or fail, you know.'

'Yep, I know. No one's saying he's an angel. But he's helping us both out tonight so just try to be nice, OK?'

'I'm always nice.'

Silence.

'Funny.'

'We're at the hospital. I'll call you later when Al-fie's been seen, OK?'

'Don't forget. I love you all!' I raised my voice a little to get the message across before ending the call. Looking up, I saw a group of shadows in the flickering light of the stairwell opposite my block. I pulled my coat closer again and shoved the phone back in my handbag. The coat was made for aesthetics rather than warmth and the handbag was probably worth more than some people, myself included, made in a month. I'd used what I had with me at the hospital, and things that Ava had kindly collected for me but suddenly, as the group began moving slowly, but confidently, towards me neither seemed like such a great choice. They moved as one collective swagger and I tried to seem uninterested and unconcerned, but over the sounds of a screaming baby and rap music with lyrics that left a small blue cloud in its wake, I was pretty sure the entire estate could hear my heart hammering against my still sore ribs.

13

Bright headlights cut through the early evening mist. They flashed twice and the shiny off roader pulled to a halt in front of me. Jed. I felt the breath I didn't even realise I'd been holding whoosh out from me. He glanced through the side window at me momentarily, one eye slightly squinting as it always did when he was thinking, or puzzling something out. I knew what he was trying to work out and raised a thumb in a move that made me feel a little foolish, not helped by the big smile I'd plastered on to my face. I looked and felt like an idiot, but Jed was doing me a favour and I appreciated that. Plus, my brother had requested I be nice. Jed wasn't the type to tell tales but I had a feeling Henry would find out if I wasn't. Jed squinted a little more before pulling the car across the broken tarmac and into a space. He pushed open the door, got out and beeped the locks before walking over to where I was standing. His expression was serious. Clearly, he was less thrilled about having to help out than he'd let on to Henry.

'Hey.'

'Hi. Thanks for this. It's really kind of you. I'm really sorry to put you out but I really had no idea I'd be lucky enough to find a place today.' I stopped and looked up at Jed. For the first time in what felt like years, I was wearing flats and he suddenly seemed a lot taller.

'I've said "really" too much.'

'You OK?' The serious expression remained.

'Umhmm!' I said, again a little too brightly.

Jed gave me a suspicious look then glanced around. The group that had been advancing had stopped, and were now milling about, the lighted ends of cigarettes occasionally illuminating, along with the ever-present blue glow of phones. His eyes scanned the area, taking in the buildings, the grounds (which really was far too grand a word for what was concrete and a scrubby patch of spindly, dying trees that had clearly been a half-hearted effort to bring some greenery to the spot). His gaze rested on the street lamp I stood close to.

'I guess the bulb went.'

He gave me a look that was part patience, part pity and a healthy dash of exasperation. But, to be fair, I'd got used to the last expression during the final part of our relationship, which is probably why I recognised it so easily.

'What's that look for?' I said, trying to keep any trace of annoyance out of my voice. *Be nice!*

Jed gestured with his chin towards a collection of rubbish and dirt around the bottom of the street lamp. 'I'm pretty sure those helped the bulb go.'

'What?'

He nudged a few with his toe. 'They're air gun pellets.'

'Oh. Right. Yes. I...'

He waited for an ending to the sentence but I didn't have one so after a few moments he looked up at the building.

'This the place?' His tone was flat, giving nothing away.

'Yes, sixth floor, but the lift is broken.'

'The elevators are always broken in a place like this.'

'You haven't even been inside yet. Don't you think you ought to wait until you start judging it?' I asked, trying to keep an even expression on my face.

Jed looked down at me.

'Yes, all right, fine,' I said, feeling my shoulders sag. 'It's not exactly the most salubrious address, I agree. But it was the best of the three I saw today and it's all I can afford, so can we just get on and get my stuff in. Maybe it will feel a bit more homely then.'

'Yep. Maybe,' Jed replied. I met his eyes and we knew we were both lying.

'The agent did say the lift is due to be fixed shortly.'

'Yeah, I bet that's been his standard line since the damn thing broke,' Jed returned.

'Maybe it only just broke,' I said, trying to be positive.

Jed looked down, studied me for a moment before smiling gently. 'Yep, sure. You could be right. I've just seen quite a few of these type of places in my time and guess I'm a bit jaded. Sorry.'

'Nothing to apologise for,' I smiled back. We both knew he was more than likely right. The lift probably hadn't worked since 1983 but I appreciated him going along with my charade of 'perhaps things aren't really that bad'.

'OK, you want to show me this place then?'

I shook my head. That was really the last thing I wanted to do. 'No, you don't need to actually see it. I'm sure you're pretty busy so if we can just get my stuff out of your car and stack it here, I'll take it up. There's nothing that heavy. I'll be fine.'

Jed blew out a sigh slowly and adjusted the baseball cap he wore (thankfully, with the peak facing forward. I'd never have even dated him had he ever worn it backwards).

'I hate to say it, but I've kinda got several issues with that statement.'

'Yes, your face rather told me that.' I spread my hands. 'Let's have them, then.'

'OK, one, you've literally just got out of hospital

after a traumatic accident and some serious surgery, so carrying anything more than a toothbrush is pretty much off the cards for you for a while. I've a feeling the doc probably told you that already, though.'

I was suddenly glad of the shot-out street light as it meant he couldn't see my guilty blush. I shifted my feet.

'I might not be able to see you blushing although I imagine you are, but you still do that little foot shuffle when you're nervous or uncomfortable so I'm guessing I'm pretty near the mark with point one.'

'I'm just chilly. Nothing more.'

Jed grinned and I saw his perfect white teeth against the gloom.

'Don't be a smart arse. It's not attractive.'

'I wasn't going for attractive.'

'No, well... obviously not. I didn't mean... anything.' *Shit.*

'Point two. Even if you were up to lifting anything, apparently you've been scooting all over London today looking at places to rent which, again with having literally just left hospital, must mean you're already dead on your feet. And I imagine none of those lifts worked either.'

'And point three? I'm assuming there's a point three?' I said, glossing over point two mainly because he'd been accurate in every aspect.

'Point three,' he began, 'is that if I put any of your stuff down here, it's going to be gone the moment we turn around. Probably before. We've had an audience since I got here.' He didn't move his head but I knew the group he was talking about, still milling and hovering in the shadows of the buildings.

'They've been there the entire time I was waiting. I'm sure they're just bored,' I said, trying to inject a tone of airiness into my declaration. 'There can't be a lot to do around here. The facilities list was pretty short.' Try non-existent.

'Boredom can lead to trouble.' He inclined his head fractionally towards the scattering of air gun pellets around the bottom of the light pole.

'At least that's better than real bullets,' I said, scrabbling for a bright side.

Jed studied me for a moment then looked back down and toed something from the pile with his front of his boot. The clouds were clearing now, leaving a cold crisp night in their wake and a full moon slid from behind one of the remaining banks of cloud, catching the item by Jed's foot in its light. It glinted slightly and I swallowed hard. I didn't know much about guns – my total experience came from TV and films. I'd refused to go to the range when Jed had taken me to New Orleans and instead opted to sit and stuff beignets at Café du Monde with his mum. But I'd watched enough telly to give me a clue about the thing he was gesturing to and it looked disturbingly like a spent bullet case. Not an air gun. A real, proper, scary-shit gun. And there it was, a spent casing, right outside the place I'd just signed up to live in.

I looked up at Jed.

'Handgun. Small calibre.'

'Oh, because that makes it better,' I replied, trying to keep it together.

'It doesn't,' Jed countered, his laid back, melodic tones serious now. 'That's my point. They're more easily concealed. And disposed of.'

I felt a bit sick. Actually, a lot sick. But what was I supposed to do? I'd evaluated my situation and my finances and this was the solution. So now I just had to get on with it.

'Well, it's not like I'm planning to be sitting out here all the time anyway. At all, even. So, it'll be fine.'

Jed gave me a look that suggested he didn't entirely agree but said nothing.

'Show me this apartment, then.'

Calling it an apartment made it sound so much better than the more accurate description of 'dingy flat'. But apparently, I wasn't going to get my stuff before he saw the damn place so I acquiesced and headed into the stairwell, past the broken lift.

'Have you paid up front?'

'No, the guy's letting me have it for a trial period, free of charge,' I snapped, then stopped and turned back to face Jed. 'I'm sorry.' I ran a hand back over my hair, which I knew was in need of a wash. I felt crappy and probably looked worse and the fact was, Jed could easily have said no to Henry's request. Right now, he looked like he wished he had, and I couldn't blame him.

'Maybe I should just leave your stuff on the kerb and let you take your chances,' he said, the twang in his voice twangier than ever, which meant the calm way he delivered that sentence belied his level of pissed off-ness.

'Honestly, I wouldn't blame you. If I were you, I probably would.' All the fight had gone out of me and I leant against the metal banister. It moved in its fixings and my blood rushed cold through me as I lost a little balance. Jed's arms were around me before I realised.

'You OK?'

'Umm... yeah. The railing was just a little less secure than I was expecting. Made me jump.'

He nodded and, sure that I was back in balance, dropped his hands and I was sorry to lose the warmth of them, if not the awkwardness of the situation.

'It's probably on the list of things to be fixed.'

I gave a half-hearted smile. 'You're probably right. Look, Jed. I really am sorry about snapping at you. I'm just a little tired. I do appreciate you coming out here to bring my stuff.'

'As I'm guessing "a little tired" is one of your famous understatements, I'm going to let it slide. Come on, only three more flights.'

I nodded and began puffing my way up the rest of the stairs, trying not to think about how enjoyable lugging groceries up here was going to be. Although, unless I got some work back quickly, I was going to be living on Lidl super noodles for the foreseeable future and they didn't weigh much, so maybe there was a silver lining there.

'You OK?'

'Yep,' I puffed out, feeling pretty much the opposite of OK.

'Liar.'

I could hear the smile in his voice. Right now, I could do without Jed Matthews knowing me quite so well. I ignored him and tried not to breathe a sigh of relief as we reached the sixth floor and the door to my new 'apartment'.

'Here we are!' I said, trying to force enthusiasm into my voice as we stood beneath a dodgy fluorescent light strip with no cover that flickered intermittently like the lighting at a low budget rave. The rave was probably for the rats. I'd definitely heard scuffling noises but I was doing my best not to think about that.

Jed pointed upwards. 'I'm guessing he said that was due to be fixed too?'

'You're very cynical these days,' I said, trying to deflect the question.

'No, I just like to know the details about things. It helps me make decisions.'

I pushed my hair back from my face and avoided his gaze.

'Yeah. That's what I thought.'

I let out a sigh, put the key into the lock and tried to turn it. Nothing. I gave it a wiggle. Still nothing. Taking it out, I plugged it back in and tried again just as the door to the next flat opened.

A large, sweaty man peered out at us from behind the security chain and stared, saying nothing. He wore a once white vest that a whole vat of Vanish now couldn't save and a pair of grey jogging bottoms that apparently also doubled as a food diary.

'Hey, buddy,' Jed said after a few more moments of awkwardness. The man stared a little longer at him before giving the briefest of acknowledging nods.

'The door sticks. Leonie's pimp kicked it in last year. Never been the same. She always had to slam it after that. Kind of annoying bearing in mind some of the hours she kept.'

Excuse me. Pimp?

'Leonie moved out?' Jed asked, apparently

nowhere near as mentally hung up on the exchange as I was. But then he wasn't going to be living here.

The sweaty man shrugged. 'One day she was there. The next?' Another shrug. This was not comforting.

'You moving in?'

Jed shook his head. The neighbour's gaze slid to me. 'You?'

'Ummhmm.'

'You a sex worker, too?'

'No.'

'Leonie used to give me—'

Oh God, I really didn't want to hear the rest of this sentence.

'A discount.'

Oh.

'Uh huh. That's... umm... nice. Neighbourly of her.'

'I'm a really good... neighbour.' There was a definite leer in his expression now. What the hell was up with this door?

'Was it open when you got here earlier?' Jed asked.

'Yes. The agent was waiting inside.'

'Figures.'

'You her boyfriend?'

Jed didn't answer, instead taking the key from me and giving it another good wiggle in the lock. The man seemed to take this lack of reply as a yes.

'I hope you're not a screamer,' he said. 'The walls are really thin here.' Unsubtly, he adjusted his downstairs equipment.

Jed put one muscled upper arm against the door, and with a combination of heft and twist, managed to align things enough to open it. He stood back, allowing me to enter first, before closing the door behind him.

'Looks like there's a knack to it,' I said, motioning towards the door, scrabbling around for any upbeat glimmer I could find in my head. It was taking some serious searching. What I actually wanted to do was burst into tears, take some painkillers and sleep for about a week but I wasn't about to let Jed see that. He was glancing around.

'It obviously needs a bit of a clean.' This was an understatement akin to saying that it can get 'a little chilly' on the top of Everest but I had dignity to maintain. 'But I can do that tomorrow.'

'It needs a hell of a lot more than a bit of a clean, Milly. A crime scene clean-up crew would be more appropriate.'

'Oh, stop exaggerating.'

He relented. A little. His face still showed that he wasn't exactly in love with my new abode, but that made two of us. He was right in as far as it looked like the place hadn't seen a can of Pledge in a long time, but it had a roof, four walls and a door. It was basically furnished, which I needed, having no furniture of my own, and the rent was affordable in my current circumstances, which was saying something for London. Jed took himself on a walking tour of the place which lasted all of thirty seconds before returning to where he'd started.

'You might want to get a tetanus shot before you use that mattress.'

'Funny.'

'Not a joke.'

'I'm up to date on tetanus. I already checked.'

'Was that before or after you viewed this place?'

I wrapped my arms around my middle, exhausted. 'Look, what do you want me to say? No, of course it's not my first choice of places to live but sadly not all of us possess the resources to live somewhere swanky.'

He ignored the dig and continued. 'Your parents will flip if they find out where you are, especially on top of everything else, and Henry's already commented that he didn't think it was the greatest of areas.'

'Oh, so he sent you to be his informant?'

Jed pulled a face. 'Probably not a word you want to bandy about around here but no, I'm not here for Henry.'

I wasn't sure what he was here for then.

'Well, neither my parents nor Henry will be living here, so it doesn't really matter, does it?'

'You know they won't bring the kids here, don't you? And frankly I wouldn't blame them. I wouldn't either.'

I looked up to meet his eyes. I wouldn't blame them either. In fact, I'd insist none of them came anywhere near the place. Last year, a seven-year-old girl had been caught in the literal crossfire of a gang war. She'd died about four hundred yards from where we were now standing.

'I need to get my stuff.'

Jed caught my hand as I turned to leave. 'Milly. You can't live here.'

I shook his hand off. 'I have to. Now could you just let me in the car and you can be on your way. I'm sure you have plenty you'd rather be doing this evening.'

A noise from next door caught our attention. The television had been getting progressively louder and now seemed to be reaching a rather climactic scene – in every sense of the word. All this was accompanied by my new neighbour who, let's say, seemed very enthusiastic about his viewing choices. And he'd definitely been right on one thing. The walls were really, *really*, thin.

I sank down on the edge of the saggy sofa, whose springs had long ago lost all pretension of springiness, reluctant to touch very much of it, but knowing I had little choice. Right now, I just needed to sit. Even without looking up, I could feel Jed's eyes on me.

'Is this really what you want?' he asked, softly.

'Of course it's not what I bloody want.' There was no fight left now. 'I doubt it was what Leonie or any of the previous occupants wanted but when choices are limited you have to take what you can get. Most of my income sources have suddenly dried up, and I haven't a hope in hell of getting another interview with *Vogue*, so right now, it's not what I want but it's what I've got.'

'Come home with me.'

I looked up. 'What?'

'Come home with me.'

I dropped my gaze back down, shaking my head. 'That's a bad idea.'

'Why?'

'Because we already tried that once and it didn't work.'

In front of me, Jed's feet shifted their weight. 'I didn't mean anything like that. God knows I remember how much that didn't work.' I looked back up to see him adjusting the cap again on his head, discomfort on his face. 'I meant the guest room. Sorry. I guess I should have been more clear.'

Well, this was awkward.

'No, of course. I mean... obviously.' I scooped my hair round over one shoulder and then immediately pulled it back again. 'I mean I didn't think you meant... you know.'

Shut up, Milly. Please?

He gave a broad-shouldered shrug. 'No. I know.'

How was he so bloody casual? Not a hint of pink about his cheeks, while I felt as red as a beetroot. Was it an American thing? I thought for a moment. No. It was a Jed thing. And, right now, it was a super annoying thing.

'I think we both know that isn't a path we ever want to try walking again.'

'Yes, all right,' I snapped, feeling sore, tired, uncomfortable and, stupidly, a tiny bit rejected. All these emotions rushed and tumbled through me to the accompaniment of ever louder porn from next door.

'Just to clarify,' Jed began. 'Yes, all right to getting out of this place or to acknowledging—'

'Both.'

'Really?'

'Yes,' I replied quietly, and tried to surreptitiously wipe a tear of frustration from the corner of my eye with one hand while scratching my leg with the other. 'I think this sofa has fleas.' I stood and eyed it suspiciously. 'It's probably best if I don't get in your car. How do I get rid of fleas? Do I need...' I looked up at him. 'What do I need?' My words were getting faster and higher.

Jed placed his hands on my shoulders, firm and warm. 'You need to get out of here, then you need a hot shower, some food and a good night's sleep. That'll do for a start.'

'What about my clothes?' I asked, scratching again but now I wasn't sure if I was actually itchy or if it was in my head. Like when someone starts talking about nits and suddenly it feels like your head is alive with the damn things.

'How attached to them are you?'

'That probably depends on whether they're crawling with fleas!'

'They're not but let's get out of here before we both are.'

'I'll find somewhere else.'

Jed scooped an arm around me and guided me towards the door. 'Not tonight you won't. You look fit to drop on the spot which isn't exactly what the doctor ordered.'

'How do you know what the doctor ordered?'

'Henry told me.'

I rolled my eyes. 'Henry is such a tattle tale.'

'No, he's not. I asked.'

'Why?'

'Because I'm nosy. You ready to go?'

I'd stopped walking. 'My deposit. And I had to pay six months up front. They'll want to keep all that! I can't afford to find somewhere else.'

Calm as ever, Jed began guiding me again. 'We'll deal with that. Come on.'

We exited the dank space and Jed gave the door a good few slams, getting it to catch on the third go. As he did, the neighbour's door opened again. He was just as sweaty and more red-faced.

'I hope you're not going to be one of those noisy neighbours,' he said, with no trace of irony.

I turned to face him, a torrent of words filling my head. As I opened my mouth, the lightest of touches on the small of my back made me pause.

'You know how long the elevator here's been broken?'

Sweaty Porn Man stared at Jed.

'The lift?' Jed tried again, jabbing his thumb in the direction of the graffitied metal doors.

'Oh,' he shrugged his pudgy shoulders. 'Don't remember it ever working.'

'How long you been here?'

'About five years.'

'And this?' Jed pointed to the strobing fluorescent strip light.

'Since before Christmas.'

'Right. Cheers.' It had always made me smile when Jed spoke traditionally British words in that soft, melodic accent of his. It had always been a mix, his accent. A mid-Atlantic twist of British and Deep South, a reflection of his parentage and upbringing, although it always leaned towards the other side of the pond when he got cross. Or passionate. I hastily pushed the latter thought out of my mind before anything unhelpful turned up in there.

The neighbour stared at us again for a moment and then closed the door.

'That's how we get your money back,' said Jed. 'False description.'

I gave a groan, inadvertently audible.

'Don't worry about it for now. You can ring them tomorrow. You need to get some rest first.' He tilted his head at me. 'Have you eaten at all today?'

Had I? I had to think. Actually, no. I knew I'd

meant to but I guess I never actually got around to it.

'I'm taking that silence as a no.'

'I was thinking.'

'The fact that you had to think about it at all probably was a hint.'

He might have a point.

'They'll never go for that, though.'

'Huh?'

We were nearing the bottom of the stairs now, thank goodness, although the shadows of the stair-well didn't exactly look reassuring. Jed fell into step beside me.

'They're not going to give me my money back because of a dodgy lightbulb.'

'It's not just the light, and they will if you advise them your lawyer has fully explained your rights.'

I snorted. 'Yeah, they're really going to buy that I've got a lawyer. If I could afford one of those, I'd hardly be living in a place like this, would I?'

'I have a lawyer and I know exactly what he'd say.'

'Yes, so do I. He'd say hi, that'll be a grand just for me picking up the phone.'

'He owes me.'

'Well, he doesn't owe me, so we're still back to square one.'

'You want out of this contract or not?'

I took in the surroundings once more as we headed back towards the car which, thankfully was still there, and didn't look like it had had a respray or donated its wheels during the time we'd been gone. I did want out of the contract. I had no idea what to do next or what the best option was, just that there had to be one. One that was a little less... everything.

'I do.'

'OK then. You can speak to them tomorrow and go from there.' He looked down as we reached the car and opened the door for me. It probably went against some feminist creed but I'd always loved and appreciated Jed's manners in moments like this. I never felt that they undermined me. In fact, it felt quite the opposite. He'd been brought up to value and respect others and this was one of the ways he showed that respect. And frankly, coming off the back of having just been taken for a sex worker and asked for mates' rates, it made a nice and far more preferable contrast.

His voice softened as he stood close. 'Don't look so worried. It's going to be fine.'

I pulled a face but tried to believe him.

'Come on, let's get you home.'

I looked in at the plush interior, made to move and hesitated. Stealing a glance at Jed, I saw that smile. The one that brought back so many memories.

'You don't have fleas.'

He could still read me like a book.

'I might have!'

'Mils, just get in the damn car while it still has some wheels.'

He had a point and I clambered in, with only minor assistance, as he shut the door behind me.

15

'You OK? You're pretty quiet.'

We'd been driving along for about twenty minutes and had barely exchanged a word. Traffic was solid and we crawled along in the caterpillar of head and tail lights.

'Sorry about all this.' I waved at the traffic with my cast.

'No problem. You didn't create the jam.'

'No. But I helped put you right in the middle of it.'

'Actually, I made the decision to do it. I could have said no. I didn't. And here we are.'

'Thanks to me.'

'I don't have anywhere else to be,' he said, his manner relaxed. I glanced across in the low lights of the car's interior. Jed was a man happy in his own skin. He always had been, from the moment I met him. Even covered in scalding hot extra tall, extra skinny mocha choca latte, he'd – after the moment of shock dissipated – been chilled. Right now, he was sitting back, accepting of the traffic, knowing he could do nothing about it, and therefore not getting worked up about it. I looked across at the other lane, where a driver was tapping the steering wheel in frustration at a pace that was bordering on psychotic. He suddenly flung his head back against the seat and bumped it a couple of times, his mouth moving, and from the shapes it was making, letting loose a tirade of expletives. A rush of gratitude flooded over me that I was in Jed's car and not with someone like that. He might be a perfectly nice man in most situations but he could definitely learn a few things from Jed. I slid my glance back inside and across to my ex. He was as relaxed as if he was sitting at his favourite bar in New Orleans, feet resting on a battered stool as he listened to one of the many talented locals playing the blues. His head turned and I was caught. One brow slowly raised.

'You know it's rude to stare, right? I'm pretty sure your mama taught you that.' His even white teeth showed in a smile.

'I wasn't staring.'

I'd totally been staring, and Jed knew it.

'OK, I was, but not in a creepy way.'

The brow raised a little higher.

I pulled a face. 'And not in that way either. Don't worry. I've no plans to beg you take me back.'

He let out a puff of laughter on a breath. 'Believe me, that particular scenario had never crossed my mind. I'm pretty sure I know you well enough to know that it never crossed yours either. Not really your style.' His eyes turned back to the road and we moved. About a foot and a half. This was London rush hour after all, but it was at least progress.

'What's that supposed to mean?' I felt a ripple of unease.

'Doesn't mean anything. Just a statement of fact.'

'Well, obviously it means something. It's the way you said it. Like it meant something.'

Jed let out a sigh. 'Milly, it meant nothing other than begging isn't exactly your style. You're a go-getter. You make things happen. You don't beg people for them.'

'Oh... right.' Put like that, it didn't sound so bad. I chewed the inside of my lip for a moment. 'Sorry. I thought you were... you know. Sort of having a dig.'

He let out another sigh. 'Nope. It's ancient history, Mils. No point raking over the past.'

'Yes. I mean, no.' Classic FM played quietly in the background as we sat cosily in the car. 'I'd have probably begged them for that *Vogue* job though. In fact, I sort of begged them for another interview, not that they were having any of that of course. So maybe I do have it in me, after all.'

Jed inched the car forward a tiny bit and stopped again before looking over at me. 'You don't need to beg, Milly. If they can't see what they've missed out on, they're the ones that will regret it, not you.'

'I think, right now, I'm definitely the one with the biggest regrets on that front.'

'Yep, right now, I expect that's true. But right now isn't forever. Right now is just right now.'

I giggled. 'OK, grasshopper.' He laughed. 'Did that one come out of Mr Chang's special fortune cookies?'

'He died.'

'What?'

'Joe Chang. Died last year.'

'Oh... Jed. I'm really sorry. I know you were friends with them.'

'Still am. Turns out he was ninety-six years old.'

My head spun to face him. 'He was not!'

Jed pulled a face. 'I know, right? And he was still working in the restaurant pretty much up to the last.'

'Bloody hell.'

'Yep, that's kind of what I said. I knew he wasn't exactly a spring chicken but damn, he aged well.'

'Did they check his attic for paintings?'

He grinned. 'Remember if he ever found out one of us was sick, he'd send some magic potion over with the order?'

I smiled at the memory. 'I do. I don't know whether it was some sort of placebo effect or just coincidence, but I usually felt better the next day.'

'Me too. Maybe there was more to those herbs and potions than we knew.'

'Maybe.' We sat there for a few moments, each lost in our own thoughts. 'I am sorry, though. He was your friend.'

'Thanks. He always asked after you.'

I grimaced. 'Sorry.'

He smiled and rolled his head slightly against the headrest. 'Don't be. Joe used to laugh about it. Say that he knew he wasn't being very tactful but that he had a reason for asking.'

'Which was?'

'I have no idea,' Jed laughed. 'He never would tell me. And I guess I'll never know now.'

'I guess not. I am sorry if it made you uncomfortable though. I know you probably thought I was a complete cow by that point so the last thing you wanted was someone bringing me up in conversation.'

'It was only momentarily. He'd ask. I'd say you were fine as far as I knew and we'd move on. It was just a routine in the end. I didn't even think about it.'

'Right. Good. That's good.' *I think.* 'So, is the restaurant still going?'

'Uh huh,' he nodded, moving the car further than it had gone in ages as we edged our way closer to his apartment. 'But in answer to your original question, no. That particular gem of wisdom was all my very own.'

'Perhaps that's another possible string to your bow? Fortune cookie writer. All these business gurus say about how important it is to diversify.' I tapped my chin for a second. 'In fact, I'm pretty sure you even did a keynote speech on that very thing at some tech expo or something, didn't you?'

'You remember that?'

'Most of it.'

'Surprising.'

'Hey, it'd been a late night. I only nodded off right at the end.'

'You went about a foot up off the chair when the applause woke you.' He was chuckling at the memory.

'I thought I covered that up pretty well.'

'For anyone who hadn't heard your cute little snores, I guess you did.'

'I was not snoring!'

'OK. No, you probably weren't.'

'Thank you.'

'Just drooling a little.'

'You're such a wit.'

'So they tell me.'

I smiled, then turned to look out of the window up at the beautiful Edwardian building Jed was approaching. The warm brick glowed in the light from the streetlamps, and squares of yellow were dotted evenly across its façade as residents relaxed in the opulent surroundings of the luxury conversion.

'You live here?' I'd seen the apartment complex featured in some of the high-end magazines and drooled over the gorgeous architecture combined with the modern, lavish but tasteful finish.

Jed nodded.

'Wow.'

16

He pulled into the entrance of a covered parking structure and beeped a control button. The metal door rolled open like a big grey mouth and he drove in, lights inside it flicking on as they sensed movement. Finding a space, he tucked the four by four into it, and stopped the engine.

'What about all my stuff? Is it safe in here?' I asked as we met at the back of the car.

'Promise not to get mad?'

'No. Why?'

'I don't know why I even asked that. OK. So I didn't exactly bring your stuff.'

I looked up at him, then peered into the back of

the car, then back up. 'What do you mean you didn't "exactly" bring it? Surely there's no grey area in this particular situation. Either you did or you didn't.'

He shrugged. 'OK. Then I didn't.'

I frowned, then shook my head. 'Why not? What was the point of you driving all the way over there if you didn't even have my stuff?'

'Because I invest in property, Mils. I know the good areas, and I know the bad and that's a bad area. I mean, a really bad area. I get chills thinking you've been traipsing about these places today anyway – and not in a good way. But the thought of you living there was just...' He adjusted the baseball cap. 'I don't know. I know it's none of my business and you can live wherever the hell you like. But I still want you to be safe and happy. And as soon as Henry gave me the address, I knew that you wouldn't be either in that place.' He looked down at me and held out his hands. 'OK, so now's the part when you get all mad and yell at me for being so arrogant and presumptuous and probably a few other words. I've likely been all those things so give me what you got.'

He was right. I should be mad. Yes, he had my best interests at heart and it was in his nature to look out for people. He'd dealt with bullies at school and been part of a mentoring scheme in college and, from what I fuzzily remembered from something Ava said after his first visit to the hospital, was still doing something similar now. It was who he was. He wanted the best for people and he did want them to be safe and happy, especially if he'd once cared for them. Or if they were the sister of his closest friends. But the deal had been to bring my stuff. So yes, I should be mad. He'd made assumptions that weren't his to make.

'If you've changed your mind, we can go back tomorrow and I'll get your stuff to that place. But at least stay tonight. Once you've yelled at me, obviously. I know there's got to be something brewing in there.'

I shook my head. 'No. You're right. It was kind of presumptuous but, at the end of a very long day, you're right. I hated it. My anxiety levels were about eleven out of ten from the moment I got there until the block of flats was well in your tail lights. I knew it wasn't a great area but I hadn't realised quite how not great. And, whatever you think of me nowadays, I do see that you were looking out for me, and for your friends by doing what you did and I'm not quite awful enough to be entirely ungrateful or un-appreciative of that.'

Jed stared at me and remained silent.

'Wow. By your lack of contradiction, it's apparent you actually did expect me to be quite that ungrateful after all. It seems that in your eyes, and in your vernacular, I was a "real piece of work".' I nodded. 'That's good to know.'

'No, Milly. That's not what I meant by—'

'It doesn't matter. As you say, ancient history. I probably had my moments.' I thought back. 'Quite a few moments. But I can't change that and, right now, I really, really need the bathroom.'

'Oh! Shit. Yeah, right. Come on.' He led the way to the front of the building, and scanned an entry card, unlocking a heavy glass door. This led in to a muted, tasteful reception area decorated with blonde wood and subtle, matt gold accessories. A female concierge dressed in an expensive business suit sat behind the desk.

'Good evening, Mr Matthews.' Her smile was

gracious and wide. She turned it on me. 'Good evening, madam.' I smiled back as I tried not to start doing the I-need-a-wee dance.

'Evening, Angelique. How are you?' Jed replied, nodding me in the direction of the lift.

'Fine, thank you.'

'Great.' The easy smile was back. 'I'll be back down in a minute to collect my mail.'

'Very good.'

The doors slid open, almost silently, and admitted us. Inside there was more of the blonde wood interspersed with mirrored glass.

'Oh, God!'

'What's wrong?' Jed asked, resting his knuckle briefly on the button for the penthouse.

'The penthouse?' I asked, distracted for a moment.

Jed shrugged. 'Mom was over when I was looking for a new place. She liked the view.'

'I bet she didn't like the price.' Jed's mum was lovely. Grounded, honest, funny and from a hardworking background. As her son's star began to rise in the world of technology, she'd worried about him when he spent large amounts of money. But Jed was savvy. He knew things could change and, as far as I'd seen, was always wise with his investments, spreading them around in different markets and different industries so that if one aspect went pop, hopefully the rest would be able to take the hit.

'I didn't tell her the price and she didn't ask.'

'Probably better that way.'

'Yep. Probably. So, what's wrong?'

'Huh?'

'Or is this a new thing? Exclaiming "oh, God" every time you step in an elevator?'

'Oh.' I looked away from him and my eyes met my own reflection once again. 'No. Although it might become a new thing. I just caught sight of myself in the mirror.'

The lift announced its arrival with an almost apologetically soft ding. The ride had been so smooth it had barely felt like we'd been moving at all. It opened on to a small, private foyer which led to a solid charcoal door with a slim steel horizontal bar-style handle. Jed swiped another key card and a lock clicked softly. He pushed the door with one arm and ushered me in.

'First on the left.'

'Thanks,' I said, as I quickly kicked off my shoes and scooted as fast as I could to my desired destination.

Washing my hands, and now feeling much more relieved, I took time to study the bathroom. No detail had been missed. All the fittings were of the highest quality. Subtle but expensive. Class rather than crass. I hadn't even had to put a light on. The moment I entered, a gentle glow enveloped the room, having sensed my presence. It certainly beat stumbling about in the dark in the middle of the night, or alternatively, blinding yourself at three o'clock in the morning with full-on bright light. The walls, tiled with something matt and no doubt expensive, were also charcoal, contrasting beautifully against the white suite. A wooden-edged circular mirror hung above the sink, its gentle lines and natural material softening the feel of the room. I dried my hands on a towel that was so thick it could double as a duvet and headed back out at a more leisurely speed.

Noises guided me towards the kitchen where I found Jed pottering about.

'Hey.'

'Hi.'

'Better?'

I pulled a face. 'Much. Nice bathroom.'

'You always did like a swanky bathroom.'

'Still do, although, to be honest, it's a while since I've seen one.'

Jed glanced over at me as he pulled a stack of takeaway menus from a drawer. 'Budgets for accommodation been shrinking?'

'Try non-existent.' I let out a sigh and lowered myself on to one of the dining chairs surrounding a beautiful oak table in the kitchen diner. Jed sat next to me and spread the menus out. 'You OK with ordering something in?'

'Of course.'

'Great, then pick what you want and I'll get it done.' He tilted his head at me. 'You need food and rest.'

I waved him off. 'I'm fine.'

'You're definitely not fine but now's not the time to argue. Come on, what do you fancy?' I looked at the options. Thai, Chinese, Korean, Fusion, Italian, French, Lebanese. Sometimes there was just too much choice. I moved them about a little in the vague hope that might help me make a decision.

'Or there's always pizza.'

I looked round at him, exhaustion wrapping itself around my body. 'Pizza sounds great.'

He smiled, reaching for his phone and choosing a number from his contacts. 'This place is great. I'll tell them it's an emergency and they'll get some food round as soon as possible.'

'Where's the menu?'

'They don't exactly have a takeaway menu. What do you want?'

'Whatever. I really don't mind.' I've never been a fussy eater and definitely not when it came to pizza. I even eat anchovies which I'm aware makes me a little more unusual, but pizza is pizza.

Jed gave a short nod and turned his attention to the phone. 'Hey, Carlo. It's Jed Matthews.' There was a pause, some laughter and Jed agreeing with whatever was being said. 'Any chance of a delivery tonight? Kinda as soon as possible. Just an extra-large totally loaded pizza and some of that cheese-topped garlic bread?' Another pause. 'You're the best, Carlo. Tell the others I said hi, and I'll be in again soon.' Another laugh and a warm sign-off ended the call.

I peered at him.

'What?'

'You didn't pay.'

'They'll send the bill with the food and I'll put the money across tonight.'

'They send out food that people might not pay for?'

'Not usually, no.'

'But you're special.'

He flashed that grin as he pushed the chair back. 'I guess I am.'

I rolled my eyes but right now, as my stomach grumbled and I felt decidedly weak and weird, I was incredibly glad he was special, although I had a feeling we could replace the word special there with 'unfeasibly rich' and still come to the same conclusion. But if it meant I was going to get good food as soon as possible, then that suited me just perfectly.

'They're good but it's still going to take time to cook. You want to take a shower or bath or something before the food arrives?'

'Oh, God, the fleas!'

Jed laughed, soft, warm and rich. His laugh had always been a good one. It wrapped itself around you like a warm blanket and drifted through your veins like the golden aged Irish whisky he'd sometimes sit down with at the end of a long day.

'There are no fleas here.' Jed's voice, thankfully, broke into the memories.

'I hope that's true. But I'd feel better getting out of these clothes as soon as possible.'

'You'll feel more human once you've washed and eaten.'

'I'm getting the feeling I must pong,' I said, giving an unsubtle sniff. 'That's the second time you've hinted I need to bathe!'

'No, but, as much as you probably hate it, I know you and I know what makes you feel better.' He gave a shrug. 'At least I did, unless you've changed more than I know.'

I shook my head. 'No. You're right. It's just what I need.'

He met my eyes briefly before turning away. 'Your stuff's in the guest room up here. Ava put a load of your clothes in cases but I don't know where your night stuff is.' He opened the door to another beautiful room that looked like a high-end hotel room but with more soul. The only thing spoiling it was the boxes piled up, and several suitcases, containing my entire worldly possessions. All of it. Everything I owned was there, staring back at me. Mocking me. I'd worked my arse off for five boxes and four suitcases. When it came down to it, that was the hard truth. And suddenly it felt a little too hard.

17

'Milly?' Jed's voice was soft, his hand touching my arm in concern.

'I'm fine,' I said, turning away and trying to pretend I didn't in fact have tears streaming down my face. I've never been a pretty crier and, having glanced at my reflection earlier, which was already a little disappointing, I doubted things were improving.

'It's going to be OK, you know.' There was no question mark to his comment. It was a statement and I knew he believed it. Positivity was one of his best qualities. But right now, I didn't agree. Things were most definitely not OK, and I had no idea how I was going to make them that way.

'No, I don't know, Jed,' I said, flinging my arms out. 'It's not OK. It's an absolute bloody mess and I have no idea how to even begin to get out of it. I don't even know how I got into it. Apart from the bus bit, of course! I remember that. But all the stuff before? What did I do wrong?' I'd given up on any semblance of trying to maintain my dignity now. The tears were racing down my face and dripping off my chin and I was sniffing, incredibly unattractively, and topped that off by wiping my nose with my sleeve. In a haze, I realised the jumper I was wearing had cost me nearly three hundred quid and I'd just wiped snot on it.

'What do you mean?' Jed asked. 'Why do you think you did something wrong?'

I stared at him, amazed that for someone of his intelligence I had to spell this out. 'Because this,' I waved my arm in a mad, Kermit style flap towards the pile of stuff, 'is all I have to show for my life! For all the hours I've put in, for all the money I've spent, the networking, the late nights, the jibes, the lost friendships, the broken relationships. This is all I have.' I sank down on the floor. 'This isn't how it was supposed to be. I was supposed to be a top editor by now in a big office with an amazing view, working in an industry I loved, with people who respect me. And instead, I'm nothing.'

'Don't say that.' Jed's voice was harder now. I looked up at him, met the hypnotic eyes with my own. 'Don't ever say that, Milly.'

I looked away. 'Nobody wants me, Jed. Despite all the times I've filled in for them, helped them out, done favours, it's all been for nothing. They're never returned, those favours. The reason I've not seen a swanky bathroom in years is because no one wants what I'm offering any more and so they don't send writers like me to the shows, or to cover events. A degree in fashion history and a Master's in creative writing counts for squat. Nobody cares about it. You know who they send? Who even get front row seats, sometimes?'

Jed shook his head, concern still clear on his face. Probably concern that he'd ever met me in the first place but definitely concern that he'd agreed to Henry's favour, which meant I was now on the floor of his swanky apartment, with a tear-stained, puffy-eyed face, not smelling my best, in a possibly flea-ridden, snot-covered jumper having a full-on melt down.

'Influencers.'

Jed said nothing.

'Influencers!' I said again. 'According to pretty much everyone, it seems that spending years studying the greats of fashion counts for nothing against someone who's barely out of their teens but is like "really into fashion"' – I did the quote marks – 'and gets a ridiculous amount of hits on their social media for just unpacking some huge haul from Primark!' I sat back against the bed. 'I was stupid.'

'Milly...'

'No, I was. I should have seen the writing on the wall years ago. I obviously got into the whole social media thing but I can't compete with those girls. Stupidly, I thought I didn't have to. Not like that. I'd thought that my knowledge and writing skills would be enough of a draw for people to keep using me.'

'And they have been.'

'Once maybe, but not any more.' I blew a strand

of overlong fringe from my eyes. 'Why do you think I was living with Xenia?'

'I'm guessing it wasn't because of her warm and fuzzy personality.'

'I had my own tiny flat for a few months, but as the work dropped off I couldn't afford the rent on my own. More and more of the space I'd filled for these places before has been given over to these flippin' influencers. We've all been losing out to them and the last spot in a magazine I lost, I'd been doing a bloody good job on for the last three and a half years.'

'What explanation do they give?'

'Oh, this is the best bit!' I laughed but it came out as a sort of painful, strangulated noise instead. 'I was told,' I put my fingers up and made quote marks in the air again, 'that "while we really love what you do, we have to cater to the new generation". Like I'm some stuck in the mud, old fuddy-duddy writing out of the 1950s! Half these so-called talents wouldn't know a new trend or a hot designer if it bit them on their twenty-year-old, pert bloody arses! I've dedicated my whole life to making sure I can cater to every generation, writing so that no one feels left out of fashion or that they're not on trend enough. But now I'm apparently an old hag who's completely out of touch!'

'That's not what they're saying, Mils.' Jed folded his long legs up as he sat down on the floor next to me.

I rested my head on my knees. 'They may as well have been.' I blew out a sigh, the tears slowing a little now. 'I get that everyone's fighting for their place in the market, desperate to catch those readers, be the place where people stop scrolling for a few minutes, but I can help them do that if they just give me the chances they're giving these others. I can't afford to fund my own trips to the shows and don't have any sponsors to send me like they do, and suddenly that means I have nothing of value to offer. Because I'm not getting vapid, empty Likes!'

Jed let out a long breath. 'So many people put a hell of a lot of importance on those things.'

'I know...' I said, my voice calmer. But I wasn't calm, I was just entirely depleted. 'I do get it, and I don't even blame them. It's just... I had a lot of time to think in hospital and I can't help but wonder what it was all for. I gave up so much for this career.

I thought that I had to do that. That was the compromise I had to make. I dedicated all my time, all my energy to making that work, missing moments that I'll never get back. Losing people that I'll never get back.' I didn't look at him when I said this and although there were others covered by this statement, we both knew that my determination, the singlemindedness I had held onto to pursue what I thought was the ultimate goal at the expense of all others, had been a major factor in the breakdown of our relationship.

'Things change, Milly. New people come along.'

I swallowed. For him they had. I'd never stopped long enough to give anyone much of a chance.

'I'll never get Alfie's first line of dialogue in his school play back, for instance. Or any of those other moments where I thought something else was far more important. Something that I thought might just be that last stepping stone.'

'No. That's true. But knowing you made a mistake missing out means you'll make sure you never do it again.'

'But I did, didn't I? I did it again and again and

again. And look where it's got me! On your guest bedroom floor, looking like a shrieking banshee from the wilds with no prospects and no friends and no real life.'

'That's not true and you know it.'

'No, I don't. And the only reason I'm sat on my arse on wonderfully soft carpet that probably cost more per square metre than six months' rent at Xenia's is the fact that, despite how I treated you and everyone else, you still have enough charity in your heart to not let me stay in some gang controlled, filthy flat with a neighbour who wanted mates' rates for a shag! Honest to God, the way things are going, I might have to consider that as a career choice.'

'Well, I'd better get mates' rates then.'

I rolled my face to the side as I rested my head on my knees. 'Hilarious.'

'It's only fair. Tit for tat. No pun intended.'

I giggled, despite everything. 'That pun was definitely intended.'

'OK. Yeah. I'm quite proud of that one, actually.' He pushed himself up from the floor and then bent, helping me up too, his arms under mine, gently easing my sore and tired body into a standing position. 'Come on. Just forget about it all for tonight. The food will be here shortly. Don't worry about your clothes for now. I'll leave you a clean t-shirt in here and there's a dressing gown on the back of the door in the en suite through there. Just use those tonight and start again in the morning. You going to be all right in the shower? You're not going to fall down or anything?'

'I wasn't planning on it.'

'I'm assuming you weren't planning on walking in front of a bus and yet here we are.'

'Smart arse.'

'Ass.'

'Arse. And I'll be fine.'

'Go on, then. I'm under no obligation these days to save you any food if you don't get a move on. And I don't need to impress you with manners either so, if you're not out, I'm inhaling it all. Just laying it out there.'

I bobbed my head slowly. 'Sounds fair. How long have I got?'

Jed glanced at the face of a simple but clearly

expensive watch. What was it with men and watches? 'I'd guess about ten minutes, give or take.'

'I can do that. If you don't mind leaving.'

'Already gone.' Jed began walking away. 'Hey.' He stopped, his hand resting on the door handle as he began pulling it closed behind him.

I popped my head back through the neck of my jumper I'd been about to wrestle off.

'Hmm?'

'I was only kidding about the food. Don't rush. You were in a hospital bed this morning, remember.'

'That seems a long time ago!'

'You've had a long day. Just be careful.'

'I guess a strange woman being stretchered out of your apartment might raise some questions in the media, too?'

'I don't much give a monkey's nuts about what the media write about me.' His face was suddenly serious. 'It's often inaccurate, anyway. See you in a minute.' Jed closed the door behind him.

As the rainfall shower head washed away some of the aches and all of the grime I felt I was smothered with, I thought about what Jed had said. *It's often inaccurate, anyway...* I mean, not that that surprised me. The media in general, but especially the tabloids, weren't exactly the most reliable sources of information. It was partly why I preferred to think of myself as a writer rather than a journalist because, although there were some amazing ones out there, the bad ones had stolen and tarnished the title. I rinsed out the conditioner from my hair, feeling the soap run down my body as I thought about what he said.

I never searched for articles about Jed, not even when drunk, which was something I was quite proud of, actually. But because of his wealth and philanthropy, not to mention that face and that body, he generated media interest, and so it could be hard to avoid seeing pieces about him. I'd even seen him a couple of times at events I'd managed to somehow wangle an invite to cover. Not that I'd ever approached him at them. I didn't want him thinking I was using him to try to get something better, or access to someone who would otherwise have no inclination to speak to me. Maybe that had been dumb. After all, I did it with everyone else. That was the whole point of networking. But with

Jed it was different. He was in a different compartment in my life and it had just never felt right. Believe me, I wished I'd been able to overcome that. God knew if I'd dropped in a mention of his name, I'd have had a lot more doors open, rather than slam, in my face. But I wanted to do this on my own.

I got out of the shower and wrapped myself in one of the duvet-thick towels, warm from the towel rail, and blissfully absorbed the soft touch of it on my skin. My own towels had definitely seen better days and although they were pretty good as an exfoliation tool, they certainly didn't offer this level of comfort. On the other hand, they also didn't come with a multimillion-pound penthouse, so I guess it was all relative. I began to dry myself and thought again about what Jed had said about the media. According to the papers, he'd been linked with some American heiress most recently and things were getting serious between them. The tabloid in question had a photo of them walking together, obviously taken right at the extent of the telephoto lens's capabilities, judging by the fuzziness of detail. Around her left hand was a red circle, apparently suggesting she was now sporting a rock. It was pretty hard to see much but there was definitely a ring there, and, unsurprisingly, it looked to be a good size. If you're heiress to a massive fortune, you're not likely to settle for something from Argos. Especially not if you're dating a tech billionaire. Was this one of the inaccuracies? Or was this one of the things they'd got right?

18

I wandered back into the bedroom just as an internal phone rang. Jed's deep tones rumbled through for a moment before the receiver was replaced.

'Milly. Food's here.'

'Just coming.'

I dropped the towel and reached for the neatly folded t-shirt he'd left on the end of the bed.

'Thanks, Anthony,' Jed was just waving someone off and closing the front door as I padded into the main living area, cosy in the borrowed t-shirt that reached halfway down my thighs and dressing gown that reached all the way to my ankles. 'Hey. Feel better?' Jed asked, turning and seeing me as he took the boxes of food to the kitchen island.

'Yes. Much. Thanks.'

'Good. Where do you want to eat?'

I shrugged. 'Don't mind, so long as we eat.'

'Couch?' He looked at me.

'Perfect.'

'Grab those.' He indicated a couple of glasses and a bottle of sparkling elderflower cordial.

I peered at the bottle as I made my way in. 'I wasn't sure what meds you were still on so went for a soft drink. There's wine and fizz if you want it,' Jed said, glancing up as he unpacked the delicious smelling food from the bags.

I shook my head. 'This is perfect, thanks. Besides, I think champagne would be a little inappropriate, don't you?' I asked as I snuggled into the deep cushions of the sofa and made myself comfy.

'Help yourself.' Jed handed me a plate. 'Why inappropriate?'

'Because there's not exactly a lot to celebrate right at this moment, is there?' I asked, concentrating on loading up my plate with cheesy garlic bread, the like of which I had never seen, the smell of it divine. My stomach sounded a long, low growl in anticipation.

'Oh, I don't know,' Jed replied, loading his plate in a similar way.

'Seriously?' I asked through a mouthful of cheese. 'You were there today, right?'

'Yeah. So?'

I looked across at him, then around at his beautiful home. 'Never mind. You wouldn't understand.'

Jed put his plate down. 'Try me.'

'No. Just... forget it.' I helped myself to another slice of the delicious bread and could practically see the calories doing the rhumba on top of the cheese. But right now, I didn't care.

'Nope. Tell me why I wouldn't understand.' He poured two glasses of elderflower and placed one close to me.

'Thanks.' I looked up. 'What?'

'I'm waiting.'

'For what?'

He raised a brow.

'Fine. How could you possibly understand? Look at you! If someone looked up "success" in the dictionary, there'd be a picture of you there with your winning smile, sat on a bank vault accompanied by at least one unfeasibly beautiful woman with legs up to her armpits.'

'You knew me before, Milly. I haven't changed. And just because one person is in a different position to another, doesn't mean they can't empathise with a situation.'

'No, but...' I tailed off, not sure of how to word it without sounding snarky.

'But what?' He'd yet to pick his plate back up and was waiting, watching.

'We should eat this before it gets cold.' I didn't look at him but moved on to the pizza, loading a slice on to my plate. 'Do you want a piece?'

Jed picked up his plate and held it out towards me. 'Thanks. And nicely avoided. But then I guess I shouldn't have expected anything different. Some things never change.'

I sat back and narrowed my eyes at him. 'And just what is that supposed to mean?'

'You. Never answering a question you didn't want to. Pretty good at asking them in your job but not so keen at being on the receiving end.'

'That's not fair.'

'And it's fair assuming that because I've done OK, I can no longer understand other people's struggles or don't give a shit about them?' There was a ripple of hurt in his voice under the steady, controlled anger. I knew it of old and it twisted something deep inside me.

'That's not what I meant.'

'I'm pretty sure that's exactly what you meant when you asked how I could possibly understand.'

I put my plate down and pushed it away.

'What's the matter?'

'I'm not very hungry any more.'

'Mils, you have to eat. You've barely eaten all day.' His voice was softer now.

I shook my head. I'd gone from ravenous to nothing in the space of a few sentences, the tension dredging up memories I didn't want to think about.

'Come on, please eat something. You need to build your strength up. There's even less of you than there was before.'

'There's still more of me than some of those models you've been seeing.' I glanced up at him and tried a smile.

He returned one, almost as tentative. 'Been checking up on me?'

I snorted. 'Hardly. Unfortunately, I have to follow a lot of them on social media to keep up with everything and make sure I don't miss out on anything they're doing.'

He picked up my plate and held it out to me, a peace offering. I took it and tried a bite of the pizza. Oh, my God. That was so good. My appetite opened one eye again and began to take an interest.

'From my experience, you're not missing out on much if you didn't follow them.'

'Is that so?'

'Yep.' He gave a shrug. 'I guess it's what floats your boat but parties where the only aim is to be seen there don't really do it for me.'

'Looks like you forced yourself a certain amount.'

'Gotta try new things sometimes.' He took a slice. 'I'd still rather be sat up here, with a cold bottle of beer looking out on the city.'

I laughed. 'I'm pretty sure a lot of people would rather be sat on the balcony of a multimillion-pound penthouse too.'

'I felt the same way with the tiny balcony we had at our apartment.'

That definitely hadn't been a luxury pad like this, but we'd made it home. For a while.

'I think calling it an apartment is giving it airs and graces.'

'I don't know. A ratty apartment at home is still an apartment.'

'Did I teach you nothing? It's a flat until it gets to a certain level of value and desirability. Then it steps up to being an apartment and the agent can bulk up the price.'

'That's how it works, huh?' he asked, loading another slice on to my plate.

'Absolutely. It's probably written down in a rule book somewhere.'

'Always good to write these things down.'

We ate in silence for a few moments. Low in the background, Jed had some soft jazz playing, although I couldn't see anything that resembled a speaker so where it was coming from I couldn't say. Jed might be half-British but he had New Orleans in his blood.

'What did you mean about me having something to celebrate?'

He smiled over his pizza. 'I'm from New Orleans. We always have something to celebrate.'

'That's true,' I smiled, remembering the first time he'd taken me to visit his mum and 'his city' and how I'd watched, fascinated, as a funeral cortège passed, the mourners joyful and celebratory. What a contrast it had painted to our sombre, gloomy equivalent. 'So, what do you think your city would find in my current predicament to rejoice in?'

Jed shook his head. 'Maybe that's something you need to work out for yourself.'

I rolled my eyes and he laughed.

'I'm too tired. Can I have a clue?' I looked back at him over the rim of my glass.

'Nope. You got to figure this one out yourself.'

I let out a sigh that a teenager would have been in awe of.

'That was a good one. Been working on that?'

'I worked around a lot of divas. You pick up tips and tricks.'

He grinned and I tried not to remember what

that grin had once done to me. Thankfully, it no longer had the same effect. But I was still a human and it was still one of the best grins I'd ever seen.

'I guess so.' His soft drawl became a little more pronounced as the day wound down and I noticed the signs of tiredness.

'You're really not going to help me out.'

'You've never needed anyone's help to get where you're going, Milly.'

My head snapped up and he held his hands up before I could say anything. 'And that wasn't a jibe, or anything. The past is the past. We already decided that. All I meant was you can do anything you want to. Everything you need is in you.'

19

Dinner finished, I scooted down a bit, cuddling into the soft blanket that had been draped across one arm of the sofa.

'I give up. There. So now you can tell me.'

'You give up?'

'Yep.'

'Since when did Milly Finch ever give up?'

'Now. I'm turning over a new leaf. Not giving up hasn't exactly got me very far, has it?'

'Your journey isn't over yet.'

'Yes, it is. I'm done. I give up.'

'No, you don't. You couldn't even if you wanted to.'

'Watch me.'

'I watched you not give up having taken on a bus.' Jed's smile had faded now and his expression was hard to read. 'Milly, you shouldn't even be here...'

'Oh!' I suddenly pushed myself up from where I'd slipped into blissful comfort. 'Do you have a guest coming? Of course! I'm totally in the way. I mean, not that I'd be—'

He caught my hands to catch my attention as I flailed about trying to extricate myself from the blanket. I'm sure it hadn't started out this big.

'That's not what I meant.'

'Oh...'

'Milly, you could have died. They were worried about you. I mean, really worried. Putting you into that coma was a difficult decision for the doctors but it was also the only decision. That was your best chance. Kind of your only chance really. But they had no idea if it would work or if you would come out of it, or how well.'

'Poor Henry.'

'Yeah. He was trying to hold it together but he was terrified. You may annoy the shit out of him sometimes but he loves you so much. The thought of losing you nearly broke him.'

I swallowed hard.

'Thank you.'

'For what?'

'Being there for Henry. He always takes care of others and likes to do everything and thinks he needs to be in control all the time.'

'He does. When the crappy, scary stuff happens, that's when you show what sort of person you are. Henry's shown what sort of person he is when I needed him. This time it was my turn to be there for him.'

'And I'll never be able to repay you for that.' I flapped the blanket around me lamely. 'Or this.'

He tilted his head. 'Life isn't about keeping count, Milly.'

'I guess it depends what sort of world you operate in.'

'Well, if that's the kind of world you're in, it doesn't sound all that great.'

I didn't answer. The truth was, it wasn't. But it was the one I knew. The one where I fitted in. At least I'd thought I had. Now I wasn't sure I fitted anywhere.

'Come here, I want to show you something.' Jed was standing now and held out his hand, helping to haul me up. The heavy blanket slid back to the sofa and puddled in an opulent pile. 'Wrap this around you.' He laid a smaller version of the blanket I'd been swaddled in around my shoulders. 'That coat didn't look like it was doing much of a job at keeping out the cold earlier.'

'No. It's not actually all that effective.' I followed him out of some glass doors next to the kitchen. 'Looks fabulous, though, right?'

He let out a small laugh. 'It does. But then you always did look great.'

'Thanks,' I said, feeling like all that was a world away now. Right now, I was wearing an ex-boyfriend's t-shirt and a cuddly dressing gown topped off with a blanket. I was the opposite of stylish and I was the most comfortable I'd been in years. 'Pretty sure it's ruined now, though.' The coat was cream and I'd been sitting on a variety of public transport all day, which was bad enough. But I'd topped it off by sliding down onto my backside when my legs would no longer hold my weight on a filthy step in the back end of London. I'd perform a small farewell ceremony for the coat when I had more energy and find a way to move on.

'I've got some dry cleaning to go tomorrow. I can just send it down with that if you like.'

'I think it's beyond that.'

'Why don't we give it a try? My dry cleaner has got skills.'

'I appreciate the thought, but I'm not really sure I can spend out on cleaning for a purely impractical coat right now.'

'It's going on a tab. You can just pay me back when you're ready.'

'I don't want to owe you any more than is strictly necessary.' I held up a hand. 'And don't take that personally.'

He gave a slow shake of his head from side to side once. 'I don't. For a woman who operates in a world dominated by who owes whom what, you've never been one to like owing anyone anything.'

'No. I know. Maybe that's my problem.'

'Don't you have a store of favours of your own you could call in now you need to?'

'I never really kept count like that. Maybe I should have done. I know people and places that I've done favours for but I never tallied them like a lot of people do.'

We were outside now, up on the roof of Jed's building. The lighting was soft and subtle and perfect. He smiled down at me. 'I think that says a lot about both you and them. And you come out of it way better.'

'But definitely not better off. I mean...' My words died on my tongue. 'Wow.' I glanced back at him. 'Oh my God! Is it heated?'

'Damn straight it's heated. You kidding me? This ain't New Orleans.'

I laughed, bending down at the side of the endless pool and drifting my fingers gently through the warm water. Under the artful lights, it sparkled and glinted invitingly.

'I thought, when you're ready, it might help with your recovery. Good exercise, but gentle on your joints and limbs. The docs did say swimming could be a good option.'

'How do you know that?'

'Told you, I'm nosy.'

I pulled a face.

'I asked one of the doctors.'

'What about patient confidentiality?'

'I told them I wanted to help and asked what would be most beneficial.'

'I don't need looking after any more, Jed,' I said, quietly, withdrawing my hand from the water and shaking off the droplets as it suddenly felt cold in the chill night air.

'You never did need looking after, Milly, even when I wanted to do that for you.' His voice hardened a little. 'But this isn't about that. This is about getting you back to where you need to be.'

'Then I'll go to a gym.'

'Gyms cost money. This is free. And nicer.'

'Don't be smug.'

'I'm not. And you know it. You hate gyms. And you hate public swimming pools because they're bright and loud and never warm enough for you.'

'Oh, stop being so annoyingly accurate about everything. It's very unsettling. What am I supposed to do? Interrupt your romantic evening by trudging through the house with my swimsuit and towel tucked under my arm saying, "Don't mind me!"'

'What romantic evening?'

'Any romantic evening!' I said, flinging my arm out and losing the blanket off my shoulder.

'I don't do romantic evenings very often and generally not here.' He tucked the blanket back around me.

'Oh, got another pad especially for those?'

'Smart ass. I just generally do dinner and go to my date's place. That way I can leave when I need to. And don't look at me like that. It's what works for both parties.'

'It just... seems a little cool on your part. I guess I'm surprised.'

'I have other priorities. Romantic relationships aren't at the top of my list right now.'

'What about the heiress?'

Damn. That sort of slipped out.

'Christine?'

I shrugged, going for nonchalant. I didn't want him thinking I'd been following his love life, which I definitely hadn't. It was just hard to avoid.

'You have been checking up on me.' A half grin

slid on to his face, the day's stubble softening the hard planes of his jaw and cheekbone.

'I have not! You're just annoyingly hard to avoid for someone who works in the media. Anyone would think you enjoyed the publicity.'

'We both know that's not true.'

'Which bit?'

'The publicity bit. I'm undecided about the checking up bit.'

'Oh, hilarious. I think I cracked a rib.' I winced as I fake laughed, reminding me that I had indeed cracked a rib. Two, actually.

'As you say, it can be hard to avoid. I try to use it for good rather than just accept the evil. As for the other part of your question, if you're alluding to the article I think you are, that was a ring on her finger, but it wasn't from me.'

'Oh? So she is engaged?'

'Nope. She just thinks it's fun to play with the media sometimes. The rock she had on was one of the various family heirlooms she has kicking around.'

'Blimey. Nice things to have lying around to play dress up with.'

'She lives in a different world.'

'You can say that again.' I'd watched that different world from the sidelines for all of my working life and still couldn't get my head around it most days. 'Don't you mind?'

'Mind what?'

'Her playing like that? Surely, it's dragging you into gossip which, unless you're a completely different person from the man I knew, isn't exactly up your street.'

'I am a different person from the man you knew.' He paused and threw a glance at me. 'But on that front, you're right. I have asked her to find other games to play but Christine isn't really used to being told what to do. She promised she wouldn't pull that particular stunt any more but time will tell.'

Which meant he was still seeing her. I thought about that for a moment. They seem pretty well matched in terms of status, although Jed wouldn't be a fan of her apparent propensity to drama, but I guess when a person is used to getting everything they want, that could come with the territory.

I pulled the blanket around me and moved

across to the glass-edged balcony. London was spread all around us, dots and clusters of lights in all directions, mixing with the inky blackness of the night far in the distance away from the artificial light's reach. A couple of clouds scooted across the midnight sky, their edges picking up a hint of streetlight, mixing orange with their illuminated white fluffiness.

'This is beautiful, Jed.'

'Exactly what Mama said.'

I stared out longer, not turning my head when I spoke again. 'How is she?'

'Doing good. She misses you.'

Tears pricked at my eyes unexpectedly and I blinked them away. When I split with Jed, I'd lost his mum too, and that had been almost as painful as losing him. From the moment he'd taken me home to New Orleans to meet her, we'd hit it off. I felt as if I'd known her for years and it had been im-mediately clear where he'd got his ease and warmth from. She'd become like a second mum to me and then, as things got worse between her son and me, I stopped calling her too, reasoning with myself that it was only natural she'd be on his side.

She'd tried to talk to me but I'd always excused myself or let the phone ring off. I hated myself for doing it but the truth was, I didn't know what to say. I knew, deep down, that I just didn't want to hear the disappointment in her voice that I was convinced would be there. So, it was easier not to hear it at all. Except it wasn't. Not really.

'I miss her, too.'

'I'll let her know.'

I nodded a couple of times, fixing my eyes on a patch of London that was dark and unlit, one of the parks. I was too tired, and now too emotional, to try and work out which. I didn't really know which way was up in my life right now, let alone which way north was.

'You should get some rest. You look beat.'

I let out a sigh and tilted my head up to meet his eyes. 'I am beat.'

His soft smile threatened my tears again and I kept my eyes averted as he held out his hand to me. I took it, grateful for the steadiness of it as we made our way back down the steps to the main apartment. At the door to the guest room, Jed stopped and turned to face me.

'Sleep well, Milly.'

'Thanks, Jed. For everything. I know I probably don't deserve—'

'Don't.'

'What?'

'Don't say it. Let's just focus on the now. OK?'

'OK.'

'What?' he asked, as I paused.

'You were right earlier. About the champagne.'

'I was?'

'Yes.'

'You thought of something to celebrate? Even amongst all the gloom and doom.' He widened his eyes dramatically and I felt a smile on my exhausted face.

'I did. I got to see that view tonight. That's something to celebrate.'

His smile was soft. 'There could be hope for you yet, Milly Finch.'

20

'Holy shit!' I shook the phone on my bedside as if that would change the time. But nope. It was resolutely staying at ten past two in the afternoon. I pushed back the covers and pulled back the curtains. Solid blackout blinds lay behind them, fitted into channels at the side of the windows, ensuring not a smidgen of light entered. No wonder I'd slept for so long. The only question now was how to open the damn things. I looked for cords but found nothing, then prodded the bottom to see if that released something. Not a dickie bird. I padded back to the bed and sat down in the dark. Really? I may not be in a great place in life but I was an intelligent, mostly independent woman – stepping in front of buses aside. Surely, I could work a bloody bedroom blind. A recessed switch next to the bedroom light caught my eye. Hmm... Pressing the button, slivers of light began entering the room from the floor up as the full-length windows were slowly revealed, the blackout blinds slotting discreetly back into position at the top of the window, blending with the surround.

'Snazzy.'

Now that I could see what I was doing, I rummaged in the top of one of my suitcases, found something comfortable, if not especially chic, and did a quick set of ablutions in the bathroom before peeking my head out of the guest bedroom door. Silence.

'Hello?' I called, tentatively.

I shuffled along in a pair of swanky hotel type guest slippers and made my way into the living room.

'Wow.'

Last night I'd been exhausted, half asleep, and although I'd been aware of London spread below and even dug deep to find some gratitude for seeing that view, seeing it in daylight was another matter. It seemed that most of the walls in this room were floor to ceiling glass, the run of windows halted only occasionally by supporting pillars. A balcony wrapped round the outside, and even in the cold depths of March, Jed had green things growing out there. I had no idea what. That had never really been my area of expertise. He'd once asked me to get a particular herb from the tiny window box we'd had and I'd stared at it for a while, having no clue as to which was which. In the end I'd cut a bit of everything and covered all the bases.

I perched on the edge of one of the sofas and looked out at the view, then around at my surroundings, feeling a tiny bit lost. I couldn't remember the last time I got up with literally nothing to do. Not that I had nothing to do. Find a job. Find somewhere to live. Tiny chores like that sprang to mind, but for as long as I could remember, I was up early and on it. Checking emails, catching up with the fashion world's gossip, writing columns, writing articles, heading off to interview someone or meet up with someone else. Never a dull moment and all that. At least, never a spare moment. But now I had that spare moment. I had all the spare moments in the world, and I wasn't entirely sure what to do with them. The thought of trawling through the 'to let' ads filled me with dread, and frankly I still hadn't got my head around where to start trying to find work just yet, now that every door had slammed in my face. A ripple of anger trickled through my spine, chased closely by something that felt remarkably like sadness. It wasn't like I'd intentionally let anyone down. But there were no second chances in this world. Walked in front of a bus? Too bad. Next!

'You look deep in thought.'

I jumped as Jed's honey-rich voice broke into my thoughts.

'Sorry, didn't mean to startle you. Sleep OK?'

I nodded. 'Yes. Thanks. Where did you come from?'

'A run, via the bakery.'

'Doesn't that cancel the run out?' I asked, trying not to sway with the delicious smells wafting up from the two brown paper bags he'd just placed on the worktop.

'No. Not if you share. Doesn't count then.' He

grinned and bent to untie the laces on his trainers. By the look of him, it definitely didn't look like calories had been settling on him anywhere they shouldn't. I guess he'd been doing a certain amount of sharing. Good for him.

'Here.' He tipped the contents of the bags out on to two plates. One was full of various savouries – mini quiches in a few different flavours, little cheesy bites wrapped in mouth-meltingly soft puff pastry, bite-size sausage rolls, and some herby-type bread. 'That's olive and rosemary. Grab a slice because once I get at it, it'll be gone.' He came back from washing his hands and grabbed a bread knife from the magnetic strip holding a selection against the wall behind us, and an olive wood breadboard that looked like a piece of art.

'That's lovely,' I said, running my hand along the side of the wood as he put it down.

'Thanks. An Italian friend took me to their family's olive farm a couple of years ago. It's on the edge of a tiny village so they came up with this scheme to make items like this as a sideline, employing some of the villagers and running it as a sort of co-op thing to pump money back into the village itself.'

'That sounds like a great idea.'

'It is. Although I could spend a fortune in the little shop there.' He placed the bread on the board and began cutting slices from it, the delicious waft tantalising my tastebuds and making my stomach growl. 'Actually, I did. Needless to say, lots of people got olive wood something or others for Christmas that year. Whether they wanted them or not.'

I smiled as I stole a corner of bread that had broken off before pouring two glasses of fresh juice from a bottle with a fancy label retrieved from the fridge.

'This looks posh. Squeezed by a silent order of monks from a monastery perched high on a mountain in another remote corner of Italy?'

Jed's gaze flicked up to see what I was referring to.

'Close. Aldi.'

'Oh.' I took a sip. It was sweet and delicious and had he agreed with the monk provenance, I'd totally have bought into it. 'This is yum.'

'Good, isn't it?' He took a large swig himself. 'Of course, there are those that won't actually touch it knowing where I bought it.'

'That's ridiculous. But I get it. I know quite a few people that have that sort of attitude too. Personally, I think you ought to try things before you dismiss them.'

'Well, you always were more adventurous.'

I felt myself blush but a quick check showed Jed to be focused on his food – not a surprise. He'd always been a total foodie and it had occasionally been sickening to watch the stuff he could put away and still keep *that* body. A surreptitious glance told me that whatever the secret was, he still had the knack. I sloshed down some more orange juice, hoping it would cool my blood. Of course, he hadn't meant anything other than in a culinary manner. I was adventurous in a lot of aspects, but food especially. How could you say you didn't like something if you didn't try it? Obviously, I had a limit – I was never going to try monkey brain or anything that tipped into the downright-weird-you've-got-to-be-kidding-me department but, as for the rest, I could never be classed as picky. It was just that the last few years I probably hadn't eaten as well as I should have. Between a lack of time, or inclination to cook after a knackering day and keeping weird hours, not to mention the slightly dodgy and not terribly inviting area that had been Xenia's kitchen, my love of food had waned. And, of course, half the people I associated with seemed to barely eat.

Even on the odd occasions I was called to a ritzy restaurant for an interview over food, lunch often seemed to be the smallest salad possible and a lot of mineral water. Meanwhile, swirls of delicious smells would waft past, rising from piles of pasta generously covered with parmesan, thick steaks sliced artfully showing the perfect pink inside, and warm, oozing chocolate puddings, drenched in custard. I'd look down at the five salad leaves I'd felt obliged to order in line with my interviewee and try to tell myself it was healthy and doing me good. It never once stopped me from wanting to mug one of the passing waiters and dive face first into one of those chocolate puds.

'Did you have any luck with the letting agency?' Jed asked, brushing crumbs from the sides of his mouth with his finger and thumb. 'Tea?'

'Yes, please. And no. Not yet.'

Jed filled a bone-china mug with boiling water from some fancy tap – nothing so mundane as a kettle here, I noticed – then sloshed a big glug of milk in, just the way I like it. Placing it in front of me, he took the glass jug of rich, dark coffee from the stand and poured himself a large mugful. The scent of it wafted up, tantalising me, despite the fact I couldn't stand the stuff. How could something that smelled so good taste so revolting? But then Jed wasn't a huge fan of tea, and only drank it on certain occasions. Oddly, though, he did enjoy that strange phenomena of iced tea so beloved by many Americans and something that, when I was queen of the world, was near the top of my list for abolishing. Tea should be hot. Cold tea accidentally was a horror. Doing that on purpose? Just wrong.

'Huh?' I sipped my lovely hot tea as Jed repeated himself.

'You didn't call yet?'

'Oh. No.' I pulled a face and gave my hair an awkward scratch. 'I haven't quite got around to doing it yet. I sort of got up late.' Late for me was about half eight. That, before the accident, felt like half the day had already been wasted so bearing in mind I hadn't seen daylight today until gone two in the afternoon, was to put it mildly, an under-statement.

'You were shattered. You needed the rest.'

'Not that much.'

Jed gave a shrug as he indicated for me to take the last mini quiche. I shook my head and pushed it towards him.

'Apparently your body had a different opinion to that and, right now, that's probably what you should listen to.'

I wasn't as sure as he was but still, I had to admit I did feel better for the long sleep. The perfect bed and thousand thread count sheets probably didn't do me any harm either. I scrubbed my hands back through my hair.

'Better have a go at wriggling out of this contract then, I guess.'

'There's no wriggling. There was clear misrepresentation. The law's on your side.'

'I'm glad somebody is,' I mumbled grumpily and caught the end of Jed's eye roll. I let it go because he was right and I was just feeling anxious at the task. I knew I was lucky, I mean, putting the whole getting whacked by a bus thing aside. I had a great family and, glancing at Jed's back, friends I wasn't entirely sure I deserved.

I got up and retrieved my phone from the side where I'd left it yesterday. There was a message from Henry, just checking in. Jed had obviously filled him in on the temporary arrangements and, from the smiley faces accompanying the text, this was an arrangement that suited Henry much better than me living in the vicinity of a drug den. Funny, that. A follow-up message let me know that my parents should be venturing back into civilisation at some point this evening and, assuming they called him first, did I want him to take the lead in explaining the events of the past few weeks in an effort to keep things as calm as possible. I couldn't get the affirmative reply back soon enough. Henry dealt with all sorts of disasters at work in his calm, collected, we-can-sort-this way so him taking the initial heat from Mum and Dad, with regards to the barrage of questions and immediate panic I knew would come his way, was incredibly appreciated.

I owe you one.

The ticks went blue and I could see he was typing.

You owe me bloody loads. Not that I'm counting...

A pause.

I'm totally counting.

He followed this with that slightly deranged looking emoticon face with one winking eye and its tongue hanging out.

You're an accountant so that doesn't surprise me.

I returned the same face, smiling as I did so. Henry had a thing about being called an accountant. I knew he did far more than just tax returns and so on. The fact that Jed was a client said a lot. People with lots of money generally don't like to lose it. So, of course, I regularly called Henry an accountant. We're brother and sister. It's in the rules that we take every opportunity we can to push each other's buttons. Thankfully with us two, it was pretty much only ever done in fun.

This bean counter just added another bean to your pile.

Sounds fair. Love you all lots. Xxx

Love you too. Will give you a heads-up if the parentals ring later xx

I sent a hug and then turned to my emails and messages. Both inboxes were empty apart from the usual promise of hot girls, a cure for a flaccid willy and a truly altruistic offer from some Nigerian prince offering to hand over a bunch of money if I could just help him out. Seriously? Were people really not onto that scam yet? Did it still work? Had it ever worked? Sadly, I expected the answer to the last question at least was probably yes.

Going to recent contacts, I sucked in a deep breath and let it out as I pressed the one for the letting agent and put it on speaker. It answered on the fourth ring.

21

'Oh... hi, um, it's Milly Finch here. I viewed... well, sort of took a place from you yesterday.' I rubbed my hand across my forehead. I'd spent years speaking to people I didn't know, getting people who didn't really want to talk to me to actually talk to me. I was comfortable on the phone. Me and my phone were like best buddies. But now it felt like we'd had a massive, irreparable falling out. To be fair, it had been instrumental in the accident that had sent my world spiralling, but still, I didn't like it. This wasn't me. I sounded timid and insecure and completely unlike the woman I knew I was. Or at least the woman I thought I'd been before both me and my world had been turned upside down by a London bus.

'Oh, yes?' the agent was clearly only half listening. I could hear him shuffling papers as he spoke and the disinterested note in his voice told me now he'd got my money, he had little concern for anything else I had to say.

'It's just that... well. I didn't stay there last night. It sort of didn't really feel... umm... as safe as you suggested.'

'Right. OK,' came the bored, automatic reply.

I felt irritation prickle through my veins.

'Yes, so I jumped in a rocket and shacked up with a Martian on the dark side of the moon.'

Jed gave a snort and I waved at him to shoosh.

'Uh huh,' came the agent's reply. OK, so definitely not listening.

'Excuse me? Did you hear what I just said?'

There was a pause. 'Is there a problem?'

'Yes. There is a problem,' I pushed myself a little straighter in the chair. 'Actually, there's several. The first one is your lack of attention.'

'I can assure you, Miss...' He'd not even listened to my name and now clearly had nowhere to go with that so stuck with 'miss'. 'You have my full attention.'

'Good,' I replied, digging deep to find an inkling of the confidence I'd once relied upon. 'Because I have a certain amount to say, beginning with the fact that you misrepresented several aspects of the let that I took on yesterday. And when I say "misrepresented", believe me, I'm being kind.'

'I don't know what you mean. We're always transparent with our clients and do our best to advise them to the best of our knowledge. If there are any aspects of the flat you're not happy with, I can liaise with the landlord to try to get them rectified, but other than that, I'm afraid it's rather out of my hands.' There was a smug satisfaction to his tone and I got the feeling this was a standard spiel. It probably worked 99 per cent of the time too. By the sounds of him, he was confident it was going to do so again this time. Except it wasn't.

'Wrong. I made the agreement through you and it was you to whom I addressed the questions, and you who reassured me the light on the landing had only just become faulty. Apparently, it's been that way since before Christmas.'

'Now, I can assure you it was fine when I visited the week before.'

'And I can assure you I spoke to some neighbours who say quite the contrary.'

He went silent for a moment.

'They also told me that the lift which you advised me is due to be fixed any time now has in fact been broken for at least the last five years. Of course, if you have confirmation that a repair is scheduled and the name of the company involved...'

'I... erm... I'm not sure I have that information to hand just at the moment.'

Shocker.

'You also met me in the flat, with the door already open, and failed to mention that since it was damaged by the previous tenant's...' I hesitated. I didn't like to say pimp as I'd only had that information from the sweaty neighbour, although he'd seemed to be free with his information and, right now, I was more inclined to believe him than the squirmy letting agent. Still, with respect to Leonie, I chose my words carefully. '... acquaintance, the door no longer fits well and has to be slammed several times to try and get it to even catch.'

'I never had a problem,' he snapped, apparently getting bored with this conversation. 'We never pretended it was the Ritz. What did you expect?'

'I expected some civility from you for a start. Do you have a manager?'

'I am the manager.'

'Well, that explains quite a lot.'

'Look. I'm really busy. What is it that you want?'

'I want my deposit back and the letting agreement cancelled.'

'Sorry. Can't do that. You signed it. It's a legally binding document.' He said the last few words slower. 'It means no backsies.'

Did he really just say no backsies? The prickling of irritation had now grown into full-blown wrath.

Across the table, Jed's brows had shot up at the comment. He mouthed the word 'wow' at me. I knew exactly what he meant.

'Firstly, I would appreciate it if you didn't treat me, or any client, as if they are an idiot. It's an incredibly disrespectful and ignorant attitude to take and although you are, apparently, the manager, I'm sure your governing body would be interested to hear how you speak to your clients, alongside the fact that you are, shall we say, economical with the truth, when it comes to the properties you're showing them.'

'There's nothing wrong with the property.'

'There are several things wrong, as I've explained, and these were either misrepresented or downright lied about. I'm giving you the benefit of the doubt here for the former although, from your attitude, I'm edging towards the latter. The place also needs a visit from a pest controller.'

'The lease is signed. Stay there or don't, but you don't get your money back.'

'I beg to differ. You lied, which invalidates the agreement. It clearly states that the information given was true to the best of your knowledge.'

'Which it was.'

'You'll forgive me if I am unconvinced.'

'Your choice. If there's nothing else, I have work to do.'

'Yes, and I imagine refunding me and cancelling that lease is the first of your tasks.'

'No. I just told you—'

'If you'd prefer to hear all this from my solicitor instead, that's fine with me.'

The agent made a snort of derision. 'Right.'

'Yes. Absolutely right.'

'If you're talking about that tin pot little place on the corner of the block, you'll forgive me if I don't quake in my shoes.'

I'm not, and never have been, a violent person. I abhor violence, in fact. And yet, just occasionally, you meet someone whom you'd happily beat about the head with a large, wet fish. This weaselly little agent was exactly that person.

'Mr Benson, firstly, I do not appreciate your continued derogatory tone. Just because people can't afford more expensive housing options does not give you the right to treat them as though they are unworthy of respect. If you were in their shoes, I'm sure you wouldn't appreciate it either.'

'Yeah, but I'm not, am I?'

'Not today, no. But who's to say what another day might bring.'

He went silent for a moment before blustering on. 'The answer's still no. And if you think I'm going to believe you can afford a shit-hot lawyer when you're looking at poxy rentals like that—'

'I'm an investigative journalist, Mr Benson. That was my purpose in viewing the place yesterday. And I have to say, it, and our conversation today, have been quite a revelation. I do expect my money back and confirmation, in writing, of that plus that the lease is cancelled emailed over to me within the next hour. If you do wish to waste more of both our time, I would refer to you my solicitor.'

Jed slid a card across the table to me. I met his eyes and he nodded encouragingly.

'His name is Rupert Mason-Smythe, and the firm's name is Mason-Smythe, Ludlow, Braithwaite and Bregman. Their office is in Mayfair.' I paused. 'Have you got that?'

There was silence on the other end of the line for a few moments.

'Fine. I'll refund you the monies before the end of the day. You should have said who you were. That's taking advantage, what you did.'

'Had I told you who I was and what I was doing, I imagine things would have been rather different, wouldn't they, and it would be less of realistic report, wouldn't it?'

'Where's this report going to be?'

I'd previously had no intention of writing a report but his attitude to those less fortunate in their circumstances was making me want to write one anyway.

'I look forward to receiving the above confirmation within the hour and all monies by the end of play today, Mr Benson. Should I need any further information, we'll be in touch.' Quickly, I pressed the hang up button on the phone in front of me on the pale oak table.

'Oh, God.' I folded my arms in front of me and rested my head down on them. I felt sweaty and sticky and boiling hot. All of the adrenaline and energy had immediately drained the moment I'd hung up.

'That was brilliant!'

I lifted my head a little. 'Was it?'

'Yes!' Jed grinned and then pulled a face. 'I'm surprised you don't look more pleased.'

'I'm knackered!'

'He was hard work, I'm not surprised.'

'He was a doddle compared to some of the people I've dealt with over the years and I'd have a day full of those sometimes.'

'No wonder you're burned out.'

'I'm not burned out!'

'OK. Bad choice of words. You know what I mean.'

'Not really, no.'

He gave me a look that suggested he thought I was just being argumentative for the sake of it. 'You've worked your ass off for years, and you've been through a traumatic experience. Give yourself a break. You did great.'

'He was a shit, wasn't he?'

'Total and utter.'

'Maybe I should try to do something about it. I mean, write about it?'

Jed was tossing a teabag into a cup and filling it from his fancy tap again. 'Maybe you should. You can do anything you want, you know.' He placed the tea in front of me. 'You look like you need that.'

I took a sip then let out a sigh. 'Could you stop being so perfect and helpful, please?'

Jed let out a low rumble of a laugh that years

ago had done things to parts of me that now probably had cobwebs on.

'You, more than anyone, know I'm not perfect.'

'I do.'

'You certainly told me often enough.'

I flicked a glance at him. 'Thanks.'

'What?'

'I know I wasn't exactly my best self towards the end of our relationship but you don't need to remind me you think I'm a total moo.'

He smiled at my terminology. 'I don't think you're a total moo. If I did, I wouldn't have offered you a bed for the night, would I?'

'Probably. You have that big-hearted, philanthropic playboy image to keep up. Plus you'd never upset Ava.'

'Both of those statements are true, although I think playboy is pushing it a little.'

I shrugged.

'And, for clarification, I didn't think you were a total moo back then either. I don't think either of us were our best selves by that point.' He echoed my shrug. 'We just ended up bringing out the worst in each other.'

I looked past him to the London skyline outside the wall of glass, my stomach knotting uncomfortably.

'What's the matter?'

'Nothing.' I flashed what I aimed to be a smile briefly at him.

'I know you better than that, Mils. Come on. Tell me.'

'No. Really, it's nothing,'

He moved and blocked my line of vision. Being a big guy, he did this quite easily and while, from a totally independent viewpoint, it was certainly not a bad view, it was also forcing me to talk about things I didn't particularly want to. He took the seat opposite, still blocking the view. I could have peered up over his head but even I had to admit that would have been slightly ridiculous.

'Were you always this annoying?'

'Yep. I'm surprised you don't remember.'

'I must have blocked it out. Too traumatic.'

A smile flickered, crinkling the corners of his eyes.

'So?'

My breath came out in one long sigh. 'Fine. It's

just that, ideally, I guess we all want to think we bring out the best in people. I'm not sure I do that. Well, judging by what you just said and having the history to back it up, I clearly don't do that. And to be honest, that just feels a bit... crap.'

'I didn't say you did that for everyone. And I wasn't any better. It was just one of those things. It doesn't mean you're a bad person because one relationship fell apart.'

I dropped my gaze and took a big mouthful of tea, grateful for the large mug that effectively hid a good proportion of my face while I pondered his reply and the fact that it wasn't just one relationship. It was nearly all my relationships. How I'd managed to keep my family's love and support was frankly a miracle I was eternally grateful for.

'It wasn't always bad, anyway. Focus on the good stuff.'

'A good mantra for life.'

'Yep.'

'Except right now I need to focus on finding somewhere to live and a job to pay the bills.'

'I was thinking on my run earlier.'

'That was always when you had your best ideas, you used to say.'

'Still is.'

'So, what gem did you come up with today? Finally going for the whole world domination thing?'

'Not just yet. That one's still on the back burner. All in good time.' His features remained deadpan but the striking eyes twinkled with the joke. 'But I do think you should stay here a little longer.'

Having just gulped the last of my tea, I suddenly had to make a concerted effort to stop it exiting through my nose. I swallowed, coughed, tried not to choke, wiped my eyes with my sleeve and looked back at Jed who seemed entirely unperturbed.

'Pardon?'

'I think you should stay here,' he said again, the words sounding calm and reasonable in his soft drawl. 'Just until you decide what you want to do.'

I threw my hands up. 'Why is everyone saying that? I know what I want to do, and I was doing it until all this mess happened.' I dropped my arms down and bumped the cast on my arm a little harder than intended, making me wince. Jed's eyes switched between my arm and my face, a question in his eyes.

'It's fine. Honestly,' I lied, feeling the arm throb.

'Yep. Looks it,' he replied, clearly not fooled in the least. He let out a breath between his teeth. 'Look, Mils. People are concerned about you, that's all. We all know how hard you work. But is this how you want your life to be? Working your ass off day and night, jumping through higher and higher hoops for people who don't appreciate you? Missing out on friendships?' he paused. 'Missing out on relationships?'

'I have friends!' I replied, forcing a conviction into my voice that I didn't feel. At least I thought I had friends.

He rubbed his forehead briefly with an open palm. 'And how many of them came to see you in hospital? How many were bothered enough to even come and check you were still breathing?' His voice had risen a little now, the accent stronger.

'Xenia came!' I blurted out, purely because I had no other answer.

'To evict you! You'd just woken up from a coma

and she came to evict you! Is that really what you class as friendship?'

'People are busy,' I said, still determined to win the argument.

'You're never too busy for the people that matter to you.'

I pushed my chair back from the table and went to stand next to the window, looking down on London, on the millions of people within it, wondering if they managed their lives better than me. I guessed the answer for a lot of them was probably yes. Jed had always managed to balance the whole friends, family, work, life thing pretty damn well, even from the other side of the Atlantic, and I envied him that. I always had. It seemed to come naturally to him. He knew where to draw the line and I didn't. And it had been that line where the fractures in our relationship had emanated from because I had no idea where the line was. In fact, by the time I stopped and looked back, I couldn't even see a line. All there was instead was a pile of hurt feelings, and empty space.

'Milly, I—'

A mobile began to ring, shattering the stillness

and the atmosphere that suddenly engulfed the room, swallowing up the airy feel of the apartment. It rang a couple more times.

'You should get that,' I said, quietly.

Jed rubbed his forehead again and then snatched up the phone. 'Shit. I do have to take this. Look, we'll talk again after, OK?'

He waited for a moment but I didn't answer. The phone stopped mid-ring as Jed put it to his ear. 'Hey, Mike. Thanks for calling back...' The words faded as he headed off to another room that he'd made into a home office.

22

I pushed open the heavy glass door from the foyer and exited on to the street. The air was damp with the promise of rain. Clouds struggled to contain it all and the odd raindrop would plop down, as if testing the way for the rest of the deluge. A cold wind whisked its way through the streets, wrapping itself around the pedestrians as it went. Coats were tightened, hats were adjusted and pulled a little lower and collars were raised as the chilly tentacles of cold sent shivers via the slightest hint of bare skin. I wandered slowly along the road, not having a destination in mind, just needing fresh air. Admittedly, I was in the middle of London so the concept of fresh air was a fluid one, but still. The walk would do me good. Gentle exercise? Hadn't that been one of the doc's recommendations? There seemed to have been quite a list and, although I'd really tried to listen, I'd zoned out halfway through. Concentration seemed to be a bit of an issue at the moment. Which was weird as I'd never had a problem with it before. Concentration and focus had been my thing – apparently to the detriment of everything else – so the fact they had up and buggered off now was a bit discombobulating to say the least. What was I left with? If I didn't have a USP any more, what was I? Who was I?

'Oh!' I bounced off someone. 'I'm so sor—'

'Look where you're bloody going!' The woman snapped at me as she strode on. I tucked my plastered arm closer to my body and tried to ignore the increased throbbing. My cast had collided with her bag, not her body, so her reaction seemed a bit intense. Maybe she was just in a bad mood because she was hauling around a breeze block in her damn handbag. At least, that's what it had felt like. I moved closer to a shop doorway, concentrating on keeping out of the way as much as possible. Ahead, a rush of people poured out of a pub after what looked like a liquid fuelled business meeting and were heading my way. Panicking, I pushed open the nearest shop door and practically fell in.

'You OK?'

I looked up from where I was clinging to the door handle with my sort of good hand and met a pair of concerned dark brown eyes.

'Umm... yes. Thanks. Just... missed my step.'

The man nodded then smiled. 'Welcome to Ravi's Bookshop.'

I glanced around, enveloped in that peaceful sense of calm you only ever get from a bookshop. 'It's beautiful.'

'I'm Ravi,' he said, extending his hand.

I held my left out and apologised, gesturing to my plastered up right one. Ravi took the left one and shook it, smiling widely.

'This is yours?'

'Yep. Well, pretty much. My grandmother invested in it and said if I didn't make it a success she'd never speak to me again.'

'No pressure, then,' I smiled, running my fingers lightly across the spines of a set of Charles Dickens.

'None at all. Thankfully, it's doing well so I'm still her favourite grandchild at the moment.'

'I didn't think they're supposed to have favourites.'

'They're not but we all know they do.' He winked. 'So long as it's me, I don't mind.' He pointed to my arm. 'What happened there?'

'Got hit by a bus.'

Ravi began to laugh then stopped. 'Oh! Blimey. You're serious?'

I laughed then too. I wasn't even sure why, but it felt good. 'Yep. Afraid so.'

'Wow. That was a crap day at the office.'

'Didn't even get to the office.'

'Time off work now, then? I've not seen you in here before so either you've just never had time to read because you work so much or you've never re-alised we're here because you work too much.' He raised a dark brow, the smile hovering permanently.

'Probably both. But I was living somewhere else before. I'm... staying with a friend for a couple of nights. Just until I... you know...' I made a vague gesture. I wasn't sure if he did know. I sure as hell didn't.

'And you didn't bring any books.'

I wasn't sure I really owned any books. Well, I did but they were stored at my parents', and I guess now they were in the storage unit with the rest of the stuff they'd chosen to keep. Beautiful books about fashion, and designers and their history. They'd been with me briefly when I'd lived with Jed. Jed didn't think a home was really a home unless it had books in it and I had to agree. I just hadn't really had a home in which to put them for a while.

'Something like that.' He was so chirpy and friendly it seemed cruel to tell him I'd only come in to avoid getting mown down by a group of well-lubricated office workers.

'Do you need any help or shall I leave you to browse?'

'Umm... I'll just browse if that's alright?'

'Of course. Shout if there's anything you need.'

I nodded my thanks and smiled. Crap. Now I was going to have to buy something because he was so nice. I couldn't just leave. He had such lovely

books... But I didn't really have any disposable income to spend on them.

The next forty minutes were spent in a blissful
state of perusal. The shop was like a TARDIS,
seemingly a quaint little shop from the outside but
going back deceptively far with another level above.
It was stuffed with everything from the chart top-
pers to the classics and covered pretty much every
genre you could want. I was thrilled to see a romance section.

'Very popular section, that,' Ravi said as he
passed, a stack of books in his hand.

I was reading the back of a romcom and smiling
at the blurb. At his comment, I looked up. 'To be
honest, I was a little surprised to find it here.'

Ravi waved his free hand. 'Can't be doing with
any of that literary snobbery. Books are books. And
these make people happy. Why would I not want to
sell them? Frankly, some of our most loyal customers shop in this section. Crime and thrillers are
all very well but they're not for everyone. Some
readers just want to escape and be ensured of a
happy ending. People who put romance writing
down are the ones who've likely never even read

one. It takes skill to make people feel emotion and care for characters.' He leaned over to see what I was looking at. 'That's a good one. My sister was raving about it.'

'That sounds like a good enough recommendation to me. I'll take it.' My own happy ending hadn't yet materialised and the signs for it weren't exactly great, but between these pages I was absolutely guaranteed of one and could escape into it for a few hours. Right now, that sounded just about perfect.

By the time I waved goodbye to Ravi and headed back out onto the street, most of the shops were closing up for the day. Darkness had fallen and the pavements were now shining with rain, reflecting the streetlights, whitish clouds within the small puddles now forming on the ground. I held my little parcel close to me, protecting it from the weather, as I tried to get some warmth from my coat but it proved to be a pointless exercise. I'd need to find something in my wardrobe that was warmer than this. Plus it really did need a clean. Where once the coat had looked smart and sharp, now the cream had a distinctly grubby tinge to it and it both felt and looked decidedly second hand. But not in a cool, vintage or opportunistic-look-at-this-bargain kind of way. More in a musty old these-should-probably-have-gone-for-recycling-as-no-one-is-going-to-ever-buy-them way.

I felt uncomfortable. Not just because I'd always taken pride in my appearance, even before I felt it was part of my job to look on trend, but because of the amount of money I'd spent on trying to do that. Money I hadn't really had. I'd thought it was an investment piece but, as I picked up my pace, as far as I was able, battling against the exhaustion and aches, and shivered again, it didn't seem like such a great investment after all. There was no doubt it was a gorgeous coat – at least it had been until I'd swept the steps of the grotty block of flats with my bottom yesterday, but, in all honesty, a winter coat that didn't actually keep you warm was a little bit pointless, wasn't it?

I guess it was like 'dinner shoes'. You know the kind. They're soooo beautiful that you just have to have them even though you couldn't walk more than ten steps in them without your feet threatening to go on strike entirely, but if you're only going to get dropped off outside a restaurant, walk to a table and then do the reverse at the end of the night, the fact they're not exactly made for walking in is a little less important, isn't it? Well, no. Not really. But that's the logic that gets applied.

Arriving at the penthouse, I rang the bell. Within seconds, Jed pulled the door open, his brow creased with worry. 'Hey, you OK? Jesus, you look frozen!' He bustled me in and closed the door. I stood for a moment, absorbing the lovely comforting warmth of the flat. Xenia's place had rarely been warm. She had a fan heater in her own room and kept that toasty in the winter, but the rest of the flat had been left to fend for itself, the heating barely ticking over. I'd once asked about the possibility of turning it up a bit and she'd begun talking about how she'd have to raise the rent. When I suggested I might get a heater like hers, she began the same refrain, quoting rising fuel rates so I'd never mentioned it again and made do. This, however, was like a different planet, and utter bliss.

Jed helped me off with my coat, gently helping me ease my cast out from the sleeve, which turned out to be harder than it looked. I knew it had been a bit tight going in but had I swelled up in the rain or something? Surely it shouldn't be this difficult. As he wiggled it some more, being careful not to hurt me, I gave up.

'Honestly, Jed, just cut it off. I don't even care any more.'

'Won't be a minute. We're nearly there.'

He had said this several minutes ago as well, so my belief was waning.

'It's just clinging a bit more because the fabric's wet.'

'It's ruined anyway,' I said, sounding a little sad and a lot pathetic.

'No, it's not,' he replied in his calm, patient tone. 'It just needs a clean and it'll be as good as new. Told you, I know a guy.'

'Someone else who owes you a favour?' I asked, remembering what he'd said about the lawyer.

'Nope. I'm just a good customer.'

'I didn't think jeans and t-shirts needed that much dry cleaning.'

'They do a laundry service.'

I smiled. 'And what does your mum think about that?'

'Someone else doing my laundry when she taught me how to look after myself?'

'Exactly.'

'Pretty horrified initially, but when I explained it was just a case of time, plus it's supporting another small family business, she came round.'

'You could sell snow to penguins.' I frowned at the sleeve still clinging to my wrist.

'Maybe, but I still can't fool my mom.'

'Good point.'

'There!' He finally released my arm from its coat prison and hung it on a hook.

'Thanks.'

'You look frozen. Here.' He reached out for a fleece-backed hoody hanging on a separate hook and handed it to me.

'Oh... no, really. I'm OK.'

'You're super pale, your nose is red and your lips are practically blue. Don't read into it. Just put it on and warm up. Your body is already dealing with quite enough.'

'Bossy boots,' I mumbled from inside the hoody. Jed ignored me. The jumper slid down over me, with plenty of room to spare, and settled mid-thigh.

'Where did you go?' he asked, gesturing us through to the kitchen where he plopped a teabag from a wooden box into a bone-china mug and began filling it with hot water. 'I was worried about you.' He didn't turn round immediately but when he did I saw the concern.

'You don't need to worry about me, Jed. It's not your job any more.'

'I never saw it as a job.'

'No, I know. But you still don't need to worry about me. I'm just a bit off balance at the moment and I know you feel beholden to Henry to make sure I don't end up in some gang-run dodgy block but you don't—'

'I don't feel beholden.' He placed the drink in front of me. 'Here, that'll warm you up.'

'Then what is it?'

'Turmeric herbal tea. Sounds revolting, I know, but it's surprisingly good.'

'Oh. Thanks.' I eyed the drink a little suspiciously but I'd give it a whirl. 'But that wasn't what I meant.'

'Then what did you mean?'

I sighed. 'Why are you doing this? We didn't exactly part on the friendliest of terms and I know you're close with my family still but that doesn't mean you have to put yourself out.'

'Stop analysing things to within an inch of their lives. If you're worried there's an agenda here, you don't need to be. I don't have one. You need a safe place to stay, I have the space. That's it. Sometimes people just want to be nice. To help out when they can, if they can.' He spread his hands. 'That's all this is, Milly. If it makes you feel uncomfortable for whatever reason you've concocted in your head, then the company has several apartments for visiting guests. I'm sure one of those is probably free.' He shoved his hands in the back pockets of his jeans and waited.

23

I took a sip of the drink. It smelled oddly like curry but tasted, as he'd said, surprisingly good. 'It's not that I think you have an agenda. I know you're not like that.' His willingness to lend a hand, an innate goodness that shone out of him was one of the things I'd fallen for all those years ago. So why was I having such a hard time dealing with it now? Maybe because I wasn't used to asking for help. I wasn't used to needing help. It felt alien to me and... weak. But it wasn't really, was it? When I saw someone in need, I didn't automatically think they were weak and dismiss them for not trying hard enough. So why did I continually do that to myself?

The other part of it, I knew, was the world I'd been wrapped up in until recently. A world that counted every favour, remembered every debt and had no compunction about calling them in, whether it was convenient or not. I'd done my best not to become that way. I'd always help out a publication or an editor when I could, but not to store up a jar of you-owe-mes. Although, looking back, perhaps I should have.

'Sorry. I know I sound incredibly ungrateful.'

He gave a small shake of his head. 'Nope. Not really. You just sound like you're kinda lost.'

'Oh, God!' I groaned and slumped onto a kitchen stool, before resting my head on the countertop. 'That sounds so pathetic.'

'Hey.'

'What?' I asked, not moving.

'I refuse to talk to the back of your head.'

I dragged myself up and turned to face where he'd now taken the seat next to me, and wrapped my hands around the mug, absorbing the heat.

'That's better.'

I gave him a look that suggested we had differing opinions on this particular point.

'Answer me this. If a friend came to you and said they were feeling a little lost, would you turn around and call them pathetic?'

'No! Of course not.'

'So why do it to yourself?'

I frowned. This was the same conversation I'd just been having with myself. Had his billions allowed him to buy some secret mindreading technology? Or was that something his company was quietly working on, with the highest level of secrecy? How much would governments pay for that sort of capability?

'Are you working on some sort of mind reading technology?' I blurted out.

The ice blue eyes narrowed. 'Huh?'

'Never mind.'

He quirked a brow and was clearly worried my head injury might be causing longer-term side effects.

'It's just that I was sort of having that same conversation with myself a minute ago. And then you said something very similar. And you work in tech development and...'

He was trying really hard not to smile.

'Don't think I can't see that.'

He gave in. 'Sorry. I'd just forgotten the weird tangents your mind sometimes shoots off on.'

'They're not weird. I'm sure someone somewhere is looking into it!'

'Scarily, you're probably right. But I can assure you, it's not us.'

'Maybe it would be better if it was. You're more likely to use your powers for good rather than evil.'

'Thanks.'

I shrugged and was reminded that particular action still hurt.

'Still sore?'

Jed didn't miss much.

'A little.'

'Fibber.'

'Do you really not think I'm pathetic?'

'I really don't. No one does. You've just had a tough break. Happens to lots of people, and often through no fault of their own.'

'This was entirely my own fault though, wasn't it? If I'd have looked up from my phone, I'd have seen the damn bus.'

'If they hadn't changed the interview time at the

last minute, you wouldn't have been rushing. Mils, you can't go through all the what-ifs. The situation is what it is. And you just have to find your way forward.'

'Easier said than done.'

'You'll get there.'

I nodded. Although still unconvinced, I was grateful that someone had that belief for me. In me.

'Where did you go earlier?'

'Just out.' I caught the look that skittered across his features. 'What?'

'Nothing.'

'Fibber,' I repeated back.

'I thought for a minute you'd left. As in gone.'

'Without saying either thank you or goodbye. That would be lovely manners.' I felt a twist in my stomach. 'I really did leave a great lasting impression on you, didn't I?'

'It's not that...' he started but then stopped. An awkward silence drifted around us. 'So, where did you go?'

'Just for a walk and some fresh air. Although admittedly I should probably have checked the weather.'

'Warmer now?'

'Yes. Thanks.'

'Feel better for getting out?'

'I do, actually. You have some lovely little independent shops around here. It's so nice to see a change in line-up from the standard names.'

'Yep. It's a nice area like that. Gives it a bit more character.'

'A bit like home?'

'Something like that. Although I kind of think of London as home too now. I guess I finally fell in love with it, just as you said I would.'

'Well, I have to admit I never thought I'd hear that from you. When did that happen?'

'A few years ago, I guess,' he replied, vaguely. I waited for more but apparently that was it.

'It's different from New Orleans, for sure,' I picked up, 'but they're both special in their own way. And like you say, each have a character that's all their own.'

'What's that?' Jed nodded at the parcel I'd kept protected from the rain.

'It's a book.' I chewed my lip for a moment. 'I feel a bit bad for buying it bearing in mind my current situation, but the man in the shop was so nice, and the cover is so pretty and—'

'Milly, you don't need to justify buying a book to me, or to yourself. It's put a smile on your face. That's enough reason for anything.'

Jed had always been like this. I was always searching for reason, for justification, for a purpose. He, on the other hand, had a much more go-with-the-flow, do-it-if-it-makes-you-happy attitude to life. I'd loved that about him but I'd struggled to shift my mental attitude from its path and try another way. I liked plans, goals, timescales. That way I could see how far ahead or behind I was in my schedule for the life I had planned out. Except that hadn't really worked. I was always behind, and every time I'd looked at my five, ten and fifteen year plan I had a burst of anxiety because I wasn't on schedule and it had fuelled me into working even harder, taking on more, in the hope that this job or that contact would propel me into my neatly mapped out future. But it hadn't.

Was it really as simple as Jed made it out to be, though, either? In truth, I guessed it was probably more a mixture of both. Jed had worked hard to become the success he was, but it still made him happy and that success had allowed him to do more things that made him even more happy, like mentoring others. I'd spent so long focusing on the end result, doing what others wanted, trying to fit into this perceived mould of what my life should be and look like, and what I should be and look like, that it was entirely possible I'd lost sight of what it was about my chosen career that actually brought me joy.

'Oh, God...' The realisation hit me. They were right. All of them. I'd been striving for what I thought I wanted. Or rather what I thought I *should* want from my career. But the truth was, this afternoon in that bookshop, I'd lost myself for a little while. Chatting to Ravi about books and his family and sheltering from the weather in the warm snug of the welcoming shop, I'd forgotten that I was unemployed and that no one in my professional life had taken the slightest bit of interest in my plight or felt either inclined or indebted to give me a hand back up. It was just friendly conversation, peace and books. And it'd been perfect.

24

'What's the matter? Are you in pain? Is something wrong?' Jed moved towards me and I felt something tear deep inside. I'd found a good man that day in that café, quite by accident, someone who'd still sent me a smile from heaven and wanted to see me even though I'd just chucked hot coffee over him. And I'd let him go. Worse than that. I'd pushed him away until we got to the point where neither of us could see why we'd ever got together in the first place. I'd thought he was holding me back. What he had actually been doing was trying to hold me together, but my eyes were on a bigger prize. One

I'd felt was more important than anything. Including him.

I pulled the little package towards me and hugged it as though by doing so I could gain a little of that happy-ever-after by some sort of magical, literary osmosis.

'I'm fine,' I said quietly, as everything I thought I knew crashed to the ground in my head.

'You don't look fine.' His voice was soft, brows drawn together, tension in his jaw. Tension that I'd put there. Again.

Delving down into the very root of my being, I dragged out a smile. 'No, really I am.'

'Mils, that smile might fool all those fancy editors and fashion types but it doesn't fool me, and it won't fool your brother. What's wrong?'

I shook my head and frowned, feeling the now-familiar trickle of tears dampening my cheeks.

'OK, now I know something's really wrong. Please, tell me. I might be able to help.'

'You can't!' I replied sadly, in between sniffs as the tears flowed faster. 'You can't. No one can. I've messed it all up! Everyone was right and I had no idea, and now I think I do but it's too late, and I don't even know where to start and...' The words rushed out in a torrent to match the tears and I had to stop to take a breath which turned into a hitch. Jed sat there, looking uncomfortable. 'I'm sorry.'

'Don't be sorry. I want to help. Let's go through to the living room. It's more comfortable there. And you can tell me about it. Or not. Whatever you want.'

'Please don't be so nice to me.'

Jed stopped, halfway up from his kitchen stool. 'Excuse me?'

'You. You're being so helpful and nice and it's making it worse.'

He rubbed a hand over his short hair, then pulled it back forwards again.

'OK, we clearly need to talk about something so let's go and do that.'

'There's nothing to talk about. I've made a huge mistake. It's not fixable. That's it! Done.'

'Milly. Most things are fixable.'

'We weren't,' I shot back, taking us both by surprise. 'I'm sorry,' I hurriedly added. 'I don't know where that even came from. I'm just a bit... emotional.'

'Which is a little unusual in itself, hence my concern.'

I'd pushed myself off of the kitchen stool and had taken a step towards the living room but, at his words, I stopped.

Jed raised his hands. 'That came out wrong.'

'You think I'm a total cold-hearted fish, don't you?'

'No.'

'You do.' I plodded away from him, still hugging my book like some sort of comforter. 'And I don't blame you.' I turned suddenly and he bumped into me and quickly steadied us both.

'You OK?'

'Yes. I'm not china, Jed.'

'No, but you're not stone either, whatever you're thinking. And no one thinks you're a cold-hearted fish.' He blinked. 'Whatever that is.'

'It's like a cold fish. But worse.'

'Right. I see. Well, I can confirm that's not the case. Here.' He moved a couple of cushions and then sat beside me. 'What's going on, Milly? I can't help unless you talk to me.'

I remained silent, watching the rain being

blown into the large windows and streaming down in channels as the bamboo plants on the balcony bent and danced with the wind.

'If you don't want to talk to me, is there someone else I can call for you? Ava?' He hesitated. 'Someone from work?'

I turned and lifted my eyes to his. 'I think we both know no one I worked with gives a shit.'

Thankfully he didn't disagree or try and put a spin on it. I knew it and he knew it. In fact, I was beginning to think he knew it a hell of a long time before I did. I'd kept the rose (or whatever colour was in that season) tinted spectacles on for so long they were almost a part of me. But they'd become dislodged during the accident and then today, somewhere between here and the bookshop, I'd lost them completely. And right now I was trying to figure out what that meant and whether I could now see clearly without them.

'Do you want me to call Ava?'

I shook my head. 'Ava has enough to deal with.'

'She's never too busy for—'

'People she cares about.' I finished off the sentence and turned to face him. 'I was, though, wasn't I?'

He shifted position. 'It wasn't that.'

'What was it, then?' I asked sadly, already knowing the answer. As he did. 'I had my eyes so firmly fixed on the future, on what I thought I wanted that I didn't see what I was missing out on right in front of me. And now it's too late. I've wasted so much time and hurt so many people and it's all been for nothing.'

'People understand. You were ambitious.'

'You're ambitious! And you didn't miss your nephew's first ever line of dialogue in a play because you were too busy looking at your phone, checking to see what you might have missed. I ended up missing the most important thing of all!'

Jed squinted one eye. 'I don't have a nephew.'

I gave him a look. 'You know what I mean.'

A brief hint of smile shadowed his lips. 'I do. And yes, we have different approaches to getting what we want in life. But everyone's different, Milly. What works for one person doesn't necessarily work for someone else.'

'That's what I'm trying to say, though. I did all

that, missed important things that I'll never, ever get back, let friendships drop by the wayside because I was too busy to put the effort in to maintain them, messed up relationships for the same reason or because I deemed my five or ten year plan more important. And look where it's got me. Scrounging a bed off my ex-boyfriend.'

'Not exactly scrounging.'

'You know very few exes would do this. Most would slam the door right in my face.'

'If you say so.' He paused. 'So, what exactly are you saying? You don't want to do fashion any more?'

'I don't really know. I know I don't want to go back onto that same hamster wheel though. If I'd died that day—' I began.

'Don't say that.' A streak of pain shot across his features.

Automatically I reached out and touched his arm. 'I'm sorry. I didn't mean to bring up painful memories of your dad. I didn't think.' I removed my hand and covered my eyes with it. 'See? This is what I mean. I *am* a cold fish. Even when I don't mean to be. And that's probably being polite.'

'No, it's not Dad. I know we're not... us... any

more and no, you're right, we didn't part on the best of terms, but I still don't like to think about what could have happened that day and can only thank God, the universe, or whoever the heck was in charge that day for the fact that you're sitting here now.'

I sniffed. 'Do you mean that?'

Jed squinted. 'Of course I mean it. You think just because we broke up I wanted you to get hit by a bus? Looks like we both left each other with some interesting impressions.'

'Well, no... when you put it like that...'

'So, what happens now?'

'I don't know.' I looked back up. 'I really don't know. If that's not what I want to do, what else do I do? I need money and a place to live and the only thing I know is fashion and writing!' My voice was rising in panic as the reality started to swim around me. I was, to put it mildly, a bit buggered.

'I think the first thing you need to do is recover from the accident. Properly. You have metal holding your arm together, for God's sake, and you gave that brain of yours a pretty good shake around. Everything is easier one step at a time. Something will turn up. Don't worry.'

'That's easy for you to say. I have the small issue of no income. I've got my gran's money that will last me for a bit but not that long and definitely not in London.' I screwed up my nose. 'Where's the cheapest place to live in the country.'

Jed gave an eye roll. 'OK. Remember that whole one step thing?'

'I am. The first step is to find somewhere cheap to live.'

'While taking yourself away from your support network at a time of vulnerability.'

I flinched and he saw it.

'Being vulnerable is not being weak, Milly. We all need help sometimes. When Dad died, my mom, who is the strongest woman I know, was vulnerable. She was in pain and she needed people around her that loved her. It didn't make her weak.'

'No, of course it didn't.'

'And this doesn't make you weak, either. The doctors on your case are here, your family are here. And, if we can rub along somehow, I'm here.'

'What do you mean?'

'Just stay with me,' he began, pushing himself up from the sofa and moving across to the window, watching the rain streak down the panes before turning back to face me. 'But only if you feel comfortable with that. I know you're independent and would rather be doing this on your own but there's no strings attached here. I'm not asking... or suggesting... anything. I'd do this for anyone in the same situation.' He gave what I assumed was meant to be a casual shrug, although it was so stiff he looked a bit like he was made out of LEGO, then shoved his hands in his back pockets.

'No. Obviously. I didn't think that you were... that this was... I mean, that you thought...' For someone who wrote for a living I was suddenly finding it impossible to string a coherent sentence together. I cleared my throat and took a moment to let my brain and mouth get back into sync. Outside the rain was beginning to ease, the droplets chasing slower down the panes. I looked up at Jed.

'I know this isn't an ideal situation for either of us and I wouldn't want to be in your way.'

'You wouldn't be.'

'I mean if you...'

'I know what you mean. And the answer is still the same.'

'Oh. Right. OK.' On the plus side, I imagined Jed's bed was a lot more expensive than Xenia's and therefore hopefully had far less audible bed springs. Also, the place itself was a tonne bigger and the guest bedroom he'd given me was the one furthest away from the main one. I wondered whether that had been deliberate and then told myself to stop overthinking it all.

'I'd obviously keep out of your way.'

'It's fine.'

'I mean, you know, if you were having, umm, company.'

Was that a smile?

'I mean I could go out. I'm sure there are places I could—'

'Milly?'

'Yes?'

'Let's get you unpacked.'

'Oh! Right. Yes.. But I can do that.'

His glance slid to the plaster cast covering the best proportion of my arm.

'Sure?'

'Absolutely.'

'OK. Well, I'll be in my office if you want me.'

'Bit late, isn't it?'

His laugh was warm and rich and wrapped itself around me. 'Well, there's some words I never thought I'd hear from you. I didn't think it was ever too late for work in your eyes.'

I swallowed hard and felt the sting. Quickly, Jed moved back across the room, the smile gone from his face now. 'I didn't mean that the way your face is telling me you took it.'

'It's OK. You were probably right.'

'Even so.'

Without thinking, I laid my hand on his briefly. 'I'm fine. I'm sure I deserve that and more.'

'It wasn't meant like that.' He reiterated his statement.

I looked up and met his eyes and I could see the truth. It wasn't a dig. It was just an observation.

'I know,' I replied. 'I just don't like to think of you doing the same stupid hours I used to.'

'I don't. And I won't.'

'Good.'

'It's great to hear you say that, Milly.'

I pulled a face. 'Maybe that bump on the head did me some good after all.' My hand went automatically to the still-tufty patches they'd had to shave and stitch and I automatically pulled some hair over them. Jed's hand on mine stilled the movement.

'Don't worry about those.'

'They look a bit ridiculous.'

'They helped save your life. And it will grow. It's already growing.'

'Oh, crikey, I forgot you saw me at the beginning. God. Try to wipe that image from your memory or something, can you?'

One side of his mouth curved. 'Memory doesn't really work like that.'

'No, I guess not. Unfortunately.'

'You think it looks worse than it does.'

I stood and moved to the mirror hanging on the wall. Most of the bruising was gone from my face and he was right, the tufty bits had grown a little, but there was no denying there were definite tufts and, whatever I did with the rest of my hair, they soon exposed themselves.

'Looks like it's going to be hat season, then.'

Jed shook his head. 'Or you could just embrace the fact that you're alive.' He stood and headed to the door. 'Just a thought,' he added as he walked out, padding along the polished wood in his socks until I heard a door close.

I fiddled with the tufts again for a moment, blew out a sigh then headed off to the guest bedroom to begin unpacking.

25

An hour later I was pretty much done, which was both pleasing and a little bit sad. The task had been made more difficult by the fact one arm was pretty much out of action and yet I'd still finished in under an hour. A lifetime's possessions in a few suitcases and a handful of boxes. I could sell it as minimalism. That I only kept what I loved and needed and what, to coin a phrase, 'brought me joy', but even if I told that to others, I'd be lying to myself. I tried not to think about the fact that despite everything, this was it. That I'd worked my arse off for years and still didn't actually have a place to call home. A place I could make my own.

Somewhere I could come to at the end of a crappy day, or even a good day, and close the door on the world outside. That had been the plan. That had even been on the plan! But the plan most definitely hadn't gone to plan.

A knock at the door brought me out of my thoughts before they could begin spiralling.

'Come in.'

The door opened and Jed peeked his head in.

'It seems very odd to be saying "come in" to you in your own house.'

He leant against the door frame, almost filling it, relaxed and ridiculously sexy. Not that he knew it. Not that it had that effect on me now. Nope. Not in the slightest. Was it fair for a man to look that good in jeans?

'This is your space now. How'd you get on?'

I looked around from my position on the floor, next to the floor to ceiling windows that looked out on the city. 'Pretty much done. Except this one.' I nudged a small, bulging case with my toe. 'I think the catches are jammed. I've spent twenty minutes and a month's worth of expletives trying to get the damn thing open.'

I had no idea what was in there as Ava had obviously just grabbed my stuff as quickly as possible and things had been mixed in different cases and boxes. Which was good, actually, as at least I knew what I had now. There were a couple of things that needed mending so I'd set them aside to deal with later, i.e., when I had some money to pay someone to do it.

'Want me to try?'

'That'd be helpful, thanks.'

'You should have called me.'

'You're here now and you were busy.'

He shot me a quick look before picking up the case but I caught it.

'What was that look for?'

'Nothing.'

I toed his leg where he'd sat on the thick rug next to me and balanced the case on his thighs. 'Fibber.'

He smiled without looking, working on the latches. 'OK. It's just that you aren't exactly known for your patience.'

'Waiting four hours for a fashion show to start can take a lot of patience, actually.'

'Fair point. Let me rephrase. If you wanted something done, you wanted it done then and there.'

I couldn't argue with that. Before The Day Of The Bus, I'd have spent two minutes wrangling with it then probably stomped along to the kitchen to find something heavy to hit the latches with. Yes, OK. Patience, unless it was forced, as in the example I'd given him, hadn't exactly been my strong suit.

'I think we're nearly there.' He leaned forward a bit more, still working on the latches. Suddenly they freed, the lid flew open, catching Jed on the chin as the case spewed its contents of underwear all over his legs and the surrounding floor.

'Oh, God! Are you all right?' I asked, as Jed rubbed his chin and I hurriedly tried to scoop up the spilled contents with one hand and stuff them back in the treacherous case that I'd now slid off his legs and onto the floor in front of me.

'Yep.'

'You're bleeding!' I said, catching sight of a drop of blood pooling on the day's stubble on the end of his chin.

'Am I?' He began laughing.

'Why is that funny?' I asked, rummaging in front of me for a hanky, which I then pressed to his chin.

'I didn't know women's underwear could be quite so dangerous.' He chuckled again before his eyes drifted downwards to the mess surrounding him. I'd stopped collecting it up as his injury distracted me but was suddenly spurred into renewed action. 'Want some help?'

'No!' I replied, a little louder than I'd planned.

Jed's brows flickered.

'I mean, no thank you. I'm nearly done.' I was now on all fours scrabbling about. Damn my broken arm and damn the crappy suitcase. It had never worked properly but charity shops don't tend to have a strong returns policy so I'd made the best of it.

'It's not like I've not seen lingerie before.'

'Yes, but this is my lingerie.'

'Well, let's be honest, it's not like I've not seen your lingerie before either.'

I put the last bits in and shoved the lid closed.

'Not in a long time!'

He grinned, still apparently finding the whole thing highly amusing.

'You're such a boy!'

'Last time I checked,' he chuckled again, his accent soft, drawly and relaxed, a reflection of his body. I, on the other hand was wearing my shoulders as earrings. It wasn't that I was prudish. It was only underwear, after all, and as he had pointed out, it wasn't like he hadn't seen it before. He'd seen that, and a whole lot more! I snapped that thought shut quicker than I had the lid of the case.

'What's up?'

'Nothing,' I said, finding a corner in the wardrobe and manhandling the case in there with one arm and keeping my face turned away. Silence descended.

'OK,' Jed said eventually as he pushed himself up off the floor and then put a hand down towards me, which I took. 'I don't believe you, but OK.' I looked up from where I was now level with his chest. His tone wasn't accusatory. He was just letting me know he'd called bullshit. Something else I'd liked about him and something I knew had helped him get where he was today. People knew where they stood with Jed Matthews, and in a world full of yes men and back stabbers, it was good to know who the decent guys were. The ones you could trust. He let go of my hand and left the room.

I padded over to the bed, sat down, and stared out of the window at the lights of London. Everyone going about their evenings, getting ready for bed. Did they all know where they were heading? What their life plan was? Did they care or were they just living in the moment and appreciating it like I knew I should be doing? After all, having a life plan hadn't worked out for me, so maybe I did need to try a different approach. But what? And why the hell did it have to be all so scary? I'd been told before that my approach to work and life had been fearless. Now I wasn't sure if that had been quite the compliment I'd taken it to be. I certainly didn't feel fearless now. I felt... I didn't even know what I felt. I wasn't sure I even knew who I was.

I pushed myself off the bed and headed back out to the living room. Jed was sitting near a lamp, a book open on his lap. His feet rested on what my parents called a pouffe. I didn't know what they were called now, but doubted it was that. He looked up as I entered and took the reading glasses off.

'I didn't know you wore glasses.'

'I got them a few months ago. Just for reading.'

'They suit you.'

'Thanks. Still feels a bit weird and I'm always forgetting them.'

'You'll get used to it. It's just because it's different.'

'Yep.'

'How's your chin?'

'It's fine.'

'I just wanted to say thanks for the help. With the case, I mean. Sorry if I was snappy.'

'You weren't.' He paused. 'Well, maybe a bit.'

'I was and I'm sorry. I was embarrassed.'

'Told you. No need to be. It's just underwear,' he shrugged, not understanding the big deal.

'Not exactly the type you're used to seeing.'

'I don't follow.'

'Jed, even as a bloke you can't have missed the state of it! Even I'm embarrassed by it. God knows what they thought when they had to cut my clothes in the hospital. Probably that the bin was the best place for them! My mum always told me to make sure I wore clean underwear in case I got hit by a bus. Of course, I don't imagine she thought I'd ever *actually* get hit by a bus. And perhaps it was a good thing I didn't see the bus coming after all because that might have been a different conversation. Anyway.'

He was still sat there, patiently waiting for me to say whatever it was I'd planned on saying. A few moments passed before he realised I was actually done.

'I think I must have missed something.'

'What?'

'I still don't get it. What you were so upset about? The state of what?'

'My underwear! Or lingerie, as you so grandly called it, and I think we both know that pile of greying pants and bras with fraying straps definitely isn't deserving of such a grand term as lingerie!'

I stopped for breath. Jed opened his mouth but I ploughed on. Apparently now once I'd decided to say something, I couldn't stop.

'And I'm sure you're used to seeing La Perla, and

Agent Provocateur and so on. Not years old, grey-ing, washed-way-too-many-times-should-be-in-the-bin stuff! The thing is, I had to try and look good on the outside, so that people would take me seriously. At least I thought I had to. And I liked it, I mean you know I enjoy clothes, but trying to keep up with it all was a nightmare and it wasn't like I could even scour charity shops. Not that anyone donates designer goods there now with all the sell your stuff websites. But the thing is, it wasn't enough to wear a designer name, it had to be the right season. Which cost me a fortune! I mean it's ridiculous. Does it really matter if it's last season or even three years ago?' I paused.

Jed started, realising that I was, this time, awaiting an answer.

'No?' he ventured, clearly unsure both about the answer and, probably now, the wisdom of asking me what was wrong in the first place.

'No. Exactly. You're right.'

He looked relieved. 'Great.'

'Except it does.'

'It does?' The frown was back.

'Totally.'

'But you said it didn't.' The poor man looked thoroughly confused now and I couldn't blame him.

'It doesn't. I mean, it shouldn't. But it does. To the people I was trying to impress, it was of the utmost importance. So, I spent the money I made on the things people could see. The outside. They didn't see I lived in one room in a tiny, shared flat. And they didn't see my grotty, misshapen, horrible underwear. I kept it hidden from everyone. Even on the very odd time there might be a chance of someone seeing it...' For some reason, I felt myself flushing. Jed scratched his cheek and glanced away for a moment. 'I made sure it was dark... or whatever. And then you, of all people, are sat staring at it all sprawled across your lap.'

'It doesn't matter, Mils,' Jed said, softly. 'Really. It doesn't.'

'It does!'

'Why?'

'Because I'm a fraud!'

His brow wrinkled. 'How on earth does not having brand new underwear make you a fraud?'

'Because I spent all that time pretending to be

something I'm not! The underwear is just like a... a metaphor for my whole life! Don't you see?'

The look on his face told me that no, he didn't see at all.

'On the outside, I'm this go-getting, super-styled, on-top-of-everything woman when underneath I'm just an out-of-shape, greying pair of old pants!'

I plopped down on the sofa, exhausted by my revelation. Jed still hadn't spoken. I rested my head in my hands – well, one of them, the elbow resting on my knee – and looked round at him. 'And now you're looking at me like you wished you'd just dropped my stuff off at that place and left me to it.'

'Nope. I'm just trying to think of the right thing to say, and to be honest, honey, I have no idea what that is.'

'It's OK,' I said. 'Thanks for trying, though.'

'I do know I'm not wishing I'd left you at that place, though. And while I'm still a little foggy on the whole metaphor thing, I'm pretty sure I don't think you're an old pair of knickers.'

I gave a snort. It came from nowhere but for no reason, or perhaps for all the reasons the last month or so had sent my way, hearing Jed say knickers tickled me. I mean, it's kind of a funny word anyway, isn't it? But so much nicer than 'panties', which would have been his go to word as an American, but he'd obviously remembered how much I hated it. I have no idea what it is about the word. It's just a bit... naff. Knickers is far better. But was also suddenly hilarious.

The giggles started small and began to build. I saw Jed watching me, smiling warily as though trying to decide whether to join in or get on the phone immediately to book me in to a nice, cosy room for one with the latest look in padded walls.

'What's so funny?' he asked, his eyes crinkling with amusement once he had, thankfully, decided on the former.

'You. Knickers!' was the most I could get out before setting off again, my arm wrapping around my still sore ribs.

'You hate the word panties! What was I supposed to say?' he giggled along with me.

I made an 'eew' face at the word 'panties', which made him giggle even more.

'I don't even know why I'm laughing. My life is a

disaster and I am the human equivalent of pants that should have been thrown out years ago. I should in fact be hysterical,' I said, the laughter subsiding now as reality crept back around me.

'Hey.' Jed scooched up the sofa next to me and put an arm around my shoulders and pulled me into a sort of buddy-style side hug. 'Disaster is a strong word. Sure, things haven't quite gone to plan but that just means you make a new one.'

'I'm thinking of giving up on planning altogether.'

'That's an option too. Plan to give up on planning. As for the other thing, sometimes our oldest clothes are our most favourite, comfortable ones.'

I turned a little on the seat and his arm dropped on to a cushion, resting behind me at the small of my back. 'That's for things like well-worn jeans or that check shirt you love. It's all soft and just gets better the older it is.'

'Exactly!'

'Pants don't get better! They get grey and old and saggy!'

Jed tilted his head. 'Hey, I'm trying with this whole metaphor thing, all right? Suffice to say, A, you ain't an old pair of jocks and B, if this is an is-sue, we really need to get you some new underwear.'

'We?'

'You.'

'I can't afford any.'

'I will buy you them if it's going to help you feel better!' He stopped. 'Well, not me personally. I mean, you buy them and then just, you know, pay me back if you want.'

'Of course I'd want!'

'Yep. I know. Not sure why I said that.'

I rested my head on his shoulder. I didn't mean to, but for that moment, it felt right. There was nothing in it but the need for comfort and a drawing of strength from someone when it felt like all my own had disappeared down a large, bus-sized hole. In turn he rested his head against mine.

'What am I going to do?' I asked.

'Take it easy.'

'I don't really do taking it easy.'

'You do now.'

'I can't afford to.'

Gently, Jed sat back up and turned me so that

he could look directly at me. Even in the low light those eyes were almost hypnotic.

'You can't afford not to, Mils. Something will turn up. Yeah, it seems rough now but every storm runs out of rain at some point. Something will come along that's better than what you wanted before. But you have to be in a position to take advantage of it...' He let the sentence drift off but I got his meaning.

26

His gaze slid to the wall clock. 'It's getting late and I've got an early meeting tomorrow but just help yourself to anything in the cupboard. Marie will be along around eleven in the morning.'

'Marie?'

'Housekeeper.'

'You have a housekeeper?'

'A friend of a friend's mom needed a job.'

'So you created one.'

'Not really. It saves me from doing chores I don't enjoy and if it provides a job for someone who needs it, we both win. Although with Marie, I'm pretty sure I get the better deal. She's amazing. The doc said about you needing to build your strength up, didn't he?'

I rolled my eyes. 'Did you have the place bugged?'

'Yeah, it's a great device, nicknamed the Ava.'

I would be having words with my sister-in-law.

'So, anyway, I know that's a yes and believe me, Marie will help you with that, whether you want to or not.'

'She cooks for you?'

'She's not supposed to. I mean, it's not in her contract but inevitably there's a dish or two here in the week ready to heat up or stick in the fridge for another day. I tried to ask her not to but she enjoys cooking and I think, now her children have left home, she misses cooking for other people.'

'So you let her have free rein in your fancy kitchen.'

'Pretty much.'

I smiled.

'Goodnight then, Mils. Sleep well.' He began to move from the kitchen.

'Jed?'

He turned. 'Yep?'

'What if I can't change? What if that person from before actually is the real me? That that drive within me that made me push everything and everyone to the sidelines is still there?'

Jed took a deep, slow breath, his broad chest expanding, momentarily stretching the t-shirt and highlighting the definition of his muscles. 'Change rarely happens overnight and it's usually something we have to work at. But if you want it enough, you can do it. And sometimes it can happen without you even trying.'

'What do you mean?'

'You haven't looked at your phone for hours.' He nodded at the sideboard. I must have put my phone there when I got up earlier but I hadn't looked at it all day. 'You didn't take it with you when you went out. It rang while you were gone. Several times. Turned out to be Henry as he rang me after, panicking that you weren't answering or even reading messages and didn't pick up. He's spoken to your parents now. They were apparently all for flying back tonight but he's managed to persuade them you're doing good and that you'll video call them as soon as possible so they can see you're in one piece.

Sorry, I should have told you earlier. I got distracted when I thought you'd gone... permanently.'

'It's OK. Thanks. I'll message them now and set up a time to call them tomorrow.'

'Gotta say, when I told Henry you'd gone out without your phone, I'm pretty sure he had to call for the office first aider to treat him for shock.'

'Oh, hilarious.' I pulled a face as I picked up the phone. All the messages were from Henry. No emails, other than the usual spam.

'Anything?' Jed read my mind.

I shook my head. 'No. I no longer exist, it would seem, in that world.'

'Then perhaps it's time to create a new world where you feel more at home and more authentic.'

'Maybe it is. Sounds easy, put like that.'

'Few things worth having come easy. Doesn't mean it's not worth trying for them.'

'You know, you should try doing one of those TED talks. Might be worth a shot. I mean, you might be rubbish but a few people would probably watch. You never know.'

Jed had, in fact, done several TED talks now and always pulled in record viewing figures. Apparently. I hadn't actually watched any myself. I hadn't had time.

'Maybe I'll give it a go sometime.'

'Who knows? A new string to your bow?'

'Maybe.' He grinned before placing one large, warm hand on my shoulder. 'But give yourself some time and some credit. Considering everything you've been through, you're doing great.'

'Thanks to you and Henry and Ava.'

'And you.' He smiled, his eyes tired.

'Get to bed, you. Hope the meeting goes well.'

'Thanks. See you tomorrow.'

'Night, Jed.'

'Night, Milly.' And then he was gone.

* * *

I'd heard the front door close quietly a couple of hours before and then had opened the blinds on the world below and snuggled into the warm, comfortable bed. Picking up the package I'd bought the day before, I fluffed the luxury pillows, opened the book and lost myself in another world for the next hour. And it had been wonderful.

I couldn't remember the last time I'd read something for pleasure. I'd always loved to read but for years the only thing I ever seemed to have time for were fashion magazines and those books that I'd been reviewing for a publication. And while I enjoyed them, I was never just reading for pleasure, reading for the sake of reading, as an escape. Now I was loving the romance I had bought from Ravi – both the book and the experience. And, let's face it, I might as well indulge in love between the pages as there was very little hope of me finding it anywhere else.

A little later, after my leisurely start, I was showered, dressed and waiting at the bus stop. The electric bus sidled up quietly. I know it's better for the environment than all those fumes chugging out but I was still struggling to get used to the lack of noise I'd grown accustomed to from childhood. I was tempted to blame the quiet technology for my accident, but if I was honest, the rest of the London hubbub had made up for the lack of bus chugging and I'd been so engrossed in my phone, as always, that in all likelihood a jet could have swooped by me and I still wouldn't have looked up.

The bus inched along in the traffic as I stared out of the window. In years past, I wouldn't have seen any of what surrounded me. Who got on, who got off, the quirky shop there, the spray-painted mural here. All I'd have seen was a screen. As I took in the people and scenery around me, streets I'd travelled countless times and yet never really seen, I wondered what else I'd missed.

'Mind if we sit here?' A jolly voice popped into my bubble of thought and I looked up. An older lady, elegantly dressed with classic make-up, well applied (some habits were easier to turn off than others), was smiling down at me. In her arms she carried a small, fluffy dog whose face looked as friendly as its owner's.

'No, of course not. Sorry.' I hoisted my bag slightly awkwardly onto my lap with my good arm and made room for them both.

'Thanks.' She smiled again as she sat and made them both comfortable. I smiled back and turned to the window.

'Lovely day out there today,' my new companion began.

I hesitated for a moment. Was she talking to the

dog? I mean, this was London after all and people didn't generally exchange pleasantries, least of all on public transport. Although that could be partly down to the fact that everyone these days generally had their face in some sort of screen and was plugged in to whatever they were engrossed in. Or, even more annoying, not plugged in and just oblivious to the fact that no one else wanted to hear their video call/film dialogue/football commentary. When did that become a thing anyway? Was it just another sign of how disconnected we were becoming as a society that it literally didn't occur to people that that might be incredibly annoying to everyone else? I guessed not. Either that or they didn't care. Whatever the reason, it was kind of sad.

'I thought it wasn't going to ever stop raining the other night.' The voice came again and I turned. My companion was looking directly at me, not the dog. I was about to open my mouth and then suddenly realised she might be on the phone. Wireless earbuds were useful but it had led to more than one awkward situation in the past when I'd begun to reply to a work colleague and been waved away, one perfectly manicured finger pointing at an ear. But she was looking at me...

'Umm, yes it was a bit damp, wasn't it?' I groaned a little internally at what seemed like a bit of a lame reply. But this was small talk. I didn't really do it. I'd never had to. Work small talk I had the knack for, although that had usually just involved listening to one person, or several, bitching about someone else and trying not to get drawn into the bitch-fest, at the same time as keeping in favour with those involved in it. I'd hated that side of the business, especially when the person they'd been sniping about joined the party and they were then all the best of friends. It had made my stomach knot and twist, not to mention being exhausting. I dreaded to think what they'd said about me behind my back when I'd excused myself. Probably best not to think about it. Or perhaps they didn't even notice I'd gone. I wasn't sure which was worse. Either way, it didn't really matter now.

'Sun's out now, though,' the woman beamed at me. 'Gus and I are just going into town to do a little shopping and have a nice walk around.'

'That sounds nice.' My conversation was sparkling.

'Are you off anywhere exciting?' she asked, actually seeming genuinely interested.

'Oh... umm... no, not really.' I pulled my sleeve back a little to expose a bit more of the plaster cast on my right arm. 'I'm going to the hospital to have this taken off, with a bit of luck.'

Her face had fallen and I suddenly felt a need to bring back her lovely warm smile.

'But that's good, though. It'll be great to have it off.'

'I'm sure.' Her smile was back and I was pleased to see it. 'How did you do that?'

'I got hit by a bus.'

She stared at me for a moment as if trying to assess if I was pulling her leg. 'Really?'

'Yep.'

'Goodness.' Clearly, she wasn't quite sure what to say. That was fair enough. I'm not sure I'd know what to say in the same situation.

'Can I stroke your dog?' I asked, suddenly keen to continue the conversation.

'Of course!' she beamed again. 'Gus just loves

a good fuss, don't you, boy?' She shuffled round a little on the seat so I could reach with my good arm and tickle the fluffy pooch under his chin. I laughed as he pressed his chin down into my hand and made contented little noises as I continued.

'Oh, he likes you!'

'Is he fussy with people, then?' I said, feeling a bit special.

'Not really,' she admitted. 'If a burglar gave him a fuss, he'd probably show him round the house and point out where all the best pieces are.' She chuckled and gave the dog's back a little scratch.

'It's nice to have someone to talk to,' she said. 'Most people these days aren't interested in anything an old biddy like me has got to say, and everyone has their face pressed to their phone anyway.' We both glanced around the bus. Barely anyone was talking and the majority did indeed have their phones in front of them. Some held them so close I feared for their eyesight.

'I'm afraid that used to be me, too.' It seemed hypocritical to criticise my fellow passengers when I had once been exactly the same.

'But not now?' She raised an enquiring eyebrow, as if sensing a story.

'I'm trying not to be. And honestly, it's easier than I thought.'

'What changed?'

'Remember the bus thing I mentioned?'

'Yes.'

'I didn't see it because I had my head down, buried in my phone.'

'Oh, I see.'

'I was very lucky.' It felt strange saying that out loud. But I was. I knew that now. Even if I didn't know where life went from here. I knew I was lucky that it was still going on for me at all.

'It's good to appreciate what you have,' my new friend agreed and I smiled.

'It is,' I said, smiling and glancing away momentarily from my fussing with the dog to the view outside. 'Oh shit!' I immediately apologised to the lady. 'I mean, sorry. This is my stop. I didn't realise we were here already.'

She patted my arm, or rather my cast, and rang the bell for the driver.

'Good luck, dear. Although I'm not sure you

need it. I have a good feeling about you.' She gave me a wink as I got up and made my way to the front as the bus slowed. Turning back, I waved and stepped off onto the crowded pavement. The bus pulled away, and the lady smiled and waved one of Gus's little paws as they passed. And then they were gone. I stood there for a moment, knowing I would never forget that conversation, even though it had been about something and nothing. It had felt real. Authentic. Just as the one with Ravi at the bookshop had. All the time I had spent over the past years with people I professed to know and yet it felt like nothing had been real. It was all careful, constructed, adjusted to sound right. What the hell had I been doing with my life when the most real I could be was with complete strangers?

27

Having had my X-ray, been directed to the consultant area waiting room and slightly clumsily managed to make myself a coffee, I aimlessly flicked through the magazines spread on the low table in front of the sofa I was currently perched on. The latest copy of *Her* caught my eye. Half of me wanted to pick it up, and half of me didn't. Unfortunately, I'd always been too curious for my own good so I plopped it onto my lap and began leafing through the pages until I got to the page where my column had once been. There was still a column but it was now bylined by someone called 'Minty'. That was it. No second name. Just Minty. I started reading.

Hi guys!

Really? I thought of the editor's face had I ever even considered handing in a piece that began 'Hi guys'. The expression 'chewing a wasp' sprang to mind, although it would have been more like the whole nest. I guess things really had changed. And, frankly, I still didn't think I could start a piece in that way but then I also wasn't – I squinted at the byline photo – oh, God. I was probably old enough to be her mother. OK. Not really. But not far off. If I'd started really early. I continued reading.

> So, you won't believe where I was this week! Paris! The hotel was like, so amazing (check out my Instagram @minty for all the gorge pics and goss). And oh my God, you would not believe how unbelievable the inside of Gucci's workshop...

I tossed the magazine back on the table. This? This is what I had been replaced by? This is what people wanted to read? Picking up my phone, I opened Instagram and looked up the handle, then scrolled. There were an awful lot of duck faces, and an awful lot of Minty herself, admittedly looking great in every single one. And, as promised, there were plenty of Paris, and Gucci as well as Milan, Rome and the south of France. Seemingly all at someone else's expense. My eyes drifted to the top of the screen and then I understood the reason. This girl had well over a million followers. A million! And, from what I could see, she didn't actually do anything, which was apparently enough. The world I'd been striving for didn't even exist any more. If this was the future, it definitely wasn't mine.

'Milly?' Dr Michaels, the orthopaedic surgeon from the team that had worked on me, came out of one of the consulting rooms nearby and smiled before standing back to let me in and closing the door behind me. 'You're looking well. Not rushing about?'

'No. I promise.' I'd barely done anything in the past week except sleep and wander down the roads near Jed's place and drop in on Ravi a couple of times for a browse amongst the peace of the bookshelves. That and have about ten video calls with Mum and Dad to convince them that I really was fine and that they most definitely didn't need to cut their trip short, and that them doing so would, in fact, just make me feel a whole lot worse.

'Good to hear. Now, I've got your X-ray here.' He pulled it up on the screen in front of him. 'Everything is looking like it's healed really well. As I said before, the pins will have to stay in there as you did rather a good job on that one, but the cast can definitely come off today.'

I felt a smile break. 'That's brilliant. I can hardly remember what it's like without it.'

'You still have to be careful. No heavy lifting for a while. You know, just common sense stuff.'

'Of course. No plans to take up body building just yet. Maybe next week.'

He gave me a look.

'I was joking!'

The doc looked relieved. 'That's good. I say "use your common sense" to all my patients. But I do wonder sometimes if such a thing exists any more.'

'He says to a woman who didn't have enough to

know crossing a road with her face attached to a screen could end badly.'

'I'm imagining that was a one-off.'

'I bloody hope so. I mean... sorry. Yes.'

He laughed. 'Believe me, I've heard, and used, far worse.'

'I promise I've learned my lesson.'

His smile was kind. 'That's what life's all about. It's good to see you doing so well, Milly. I'll put you down for a three-month check-up but if you have any queries or any pain, just give my secretary a ring and we'll get you in.'

'Thanks ever so much, Doctor.'

'It was a pleasure,' he said, shaking my free hand. 'Now, just pop yourself down in the waiting area and I'll get someone to come and take you over to get that cast off.'

About ten minutes later, I was sitting in another room, about to drop several pounds in weight.

The technician looked at my cast, up at me, and then back at the cast.

'I have a small niece and nephew.' She nodded.

I looked down at the pretty, childlike flowers adorning some of my cast. These decorated, and oddly highlighted, my nephew's contribution of words such as 'willy' and 'bum'. I'd been talking to Ava while they decorated my cast and neither of us had taken much notice of the direction his artistic expression had taken until it was a bit late.

'Could have been worse,' I offered.

'Believe me, I've seen way worse,' she grinned as she leant over and picked up the saw that would release me from my plaster of Paris prison. 'Now, keep still.'

Watching the blade begin to spin, this was not an instruction I needed telling twice. The technician paused.

'It's OK to breathe, though. Actually, it's kind of advisable.'

'Right,' I said, on a whoosh of air. 'Right. Yes. Good.' And then held my breath again.

* * *

Walking back down to the bus stop, I felt oddly lighter. Well, I was physically, no longer having a large lump of plaster attached to me, but there was something else. It felt like a step forward.

Seeing my column given over to a twenty-two-year-old influencer with a rich daddy (I did a search. I couldn't help it. Like I said, way too curious for my own good) hadn't exactly given me the warm fuzzies, but for some reason I wasn't as devastated as I thought I'd be. Perhaps I'd already done my grieving for that part of my life. Perhaps I'd finally dropped the Prada rose-tinted spectacles for good. Perhaps I felt she was welcome to it all.

The bus dropped me not far from Jed's apartment and I walked slowly back towards it, peering in the windows of the nearby shops. My stomach rumbled, reminding me that I hadn't had lunch. It was nearly three now. I pondered waiting until dinner but my stomach intercepted that thought and gave a loud growl of disapproval.

'Fine. I'll feed you,' I said, aloud. A man glanced my way briefly, his eyes shifting back immediately as I met them. With my hair tied back, exposing the fact I had no earbuds tucked in my ears, I couldn't even pretend I was on the phone. I was just a woman talking aloud to her own stomach. 'This looks nice,' I said to it as I came upon an Italian deli. Hell, I'd started the conversation. I may as well continue it now.

The place was stocked to the rafters with every Italian drop of goodness you could think of. There was bread, meats, cheese, pastries, puddings (hello cannoli!), olives, crackers, pesto. If you wanted Italian, it looked like they had it. Tucked to the side were a few tables, dressed in checked cloths, a small vase sporting a frilly headed rose decorating each one.

'Signorina, 'ow may I help you?'

'Are you still serving food?' I pointed at the tables and the man laughed.

'We are Italian. It is always time for food. Please, please sit.' His smile was warm as he directed me to one of the small tables and swooped a menu in front of me. 'Can I get you a drink to begin?'

'Umm... yes, just an orange juice or something, please.'

'Orange juice coming up,' he smiled again and headed off, leaving me to study the menu. When he returned a short time later, I could easily have ordered one of everything from the menu but I restrained myself and stuck with a cheesy pasta dish made with capers and sundried tomatoes, picked from the starter menu.

'And for main?' he asked.

'Oh! I was just going to have that, if that's all right?'

'Of course,' he nodded, taking the menu. 'But you will not grow up big and strong if you only eat the antipasti.' He gave me a big wink and laughed. It wasn't exactly the most appropriate thing to say but I loved that he didn't care. Across the room, a younger man was giving him an even look. My server pulled a face. 'My nephew says I should not be saying such things. It is not correct, apparently.' He put his hand on his chest. 'I apologise.' And he did actually look sorry. From the corner of my eye, his nephew's expression was somewhere between exasperation and forgiveness, but there was no mistaking the love in it.

'Really.' I laid my hand gently on the man's arm. 'It's fine. I'm not offended. I just don't want to spoil my dinner.'

His hand rested on mine for a moment. 'A wise woman. Thank you.' His eyes danced, accompanying the warm smile. 'Your lunch will not be long, but it is cooked from scratch so...' He made a gesture with his hands.

'I'm in no rush.'

'Now, that is something good to hear! Everyone these days, they rush, rush, rush! No one takes time.'

'Well,' I sat back, smiling. 'Right now, I have all the time in the world.'

My reply seemed to please him and he sauntered off, singing something in Italian and disappeared through a pair of double swinging doors at the back of the shop. I reached down and pulled my phone from my bag for the first time that day. There was an unread message from my brother from an hour or so ago.

How'd it go?

I felt a wash of guilt. Had the shoe been on the other foot, or more pertinently, the cast been on the other arm, would I have remembered what day, let alone what time, he'd have had his follow-up and removal booked for? I had a horrible feeling that the answer would not show me in my best light.

I snapped a photo of my cast-free arm and sent it to Henry, adding the words 'Ta Dah' beneath it.

A row of three smiley faces came back as a reply. Across the shop, I saw the uncle and nephew engaged in a conversation, peppered with laughter. Suddenly I missed my family. Pressing Henry's contact, it rang once before he picked up.

'Hi, everything OK?'

'Yep. I just thought I'd call you. Haven't spoken to you in a few days.'

'Aww, did you miss me?' he asked, putting on a silly voice.

'Yes.'

There was a pause. 'Oh.'

'Wow. I really was a terrible sister, wasn't I?'

'What? No! I'm just... I don't think I've heard you say it so flatly before.'

'Sorry.'

'Not at all. It's nice to hear.'

'No, I mean for not saying it before.'

'It's all right. We all know you mean it, even if you don't get around to saying it.'

'I'm planning to get around to saying more things more often.'

Henry paused. 'You OK, Mils?'

'Yes. Why?'

'You just sound different.'

'In what way?'

'In a good way.'

'You should be pleased, then.'

'I am. It's just taking some getting used to.'

'I know the feeling,' I replied, honestly.

'What have you been doing since you left hospital?'

'Not a lot, if I'm honest.'

'That's great!'

'As you say, it's taking some getting used to. I do need to think about work at some point. Nana's money isn't going to last forever and it was really supposed to be for a house deposit.'

'I know.'

Actually, we both knew that with the way house prices in London were, I'd have needed a score of grandmothers to leave me a generous bequest before I had a hope in hell of putting a down payment on anything bigger than someone's box room. But that wasn't really the point.

'I've been reading.'

'You have?'

'Yep. I found a gorgeous little bookshop near Jed's place. The owner is lovely and he recommended me a book his sister really enjoyed. I'm loving it.'

'That's great, Mils. You always used to love reading, but I can't remember the last time I saw you with anything other than a fashion magazine in your hand. It's great to hear you're enjoying it.'

'Yeah, well. I've been avoiding the magazines for the moment.'

'Probably not a bad idea.'

'Although I did see *Her* earlier at the hospital.'

'Who?'

'*Her*. The magazine.'

'Oh! Is that one you wrote for?'

'Yep. I had a column. A twenty-two-year-old influencer has it now.'

'I bet it's awful,' Henry replied immediately and loyally, and I wanted to hug him.

'It's different.'

'It *is* awful. I knew it.'

'I love you,' I laughed.

'Love you too,' he replied and I smiled at both

his reply and the steaming dish winging its way towards me on the arm of my friendly waiter.

'I'd better go. I'm in this fabulous little Italian
deli place and my pasta has just arrived.'

'The one near Jed's?'

'Yes. Do you know it?'

'Yeah. It's brilliant, isn't it? I spend a fortune in
there every time we visit.'

'I may have to not come in too often.'

'One day at a time, sis.'

'True. OK. Better go. Speak to you soon.'

'Will do. Eat your late lunch or early dinner or
whatever it is and enjoy.'

'Thanks, Henry.'

'Bye, Mils.'

'*Buon appetito!*' the waiter said, placing the dish
down before me.

'Thank you!' I said, almost drooling at the
aromas swirling up from the plate.

'My pleasure. Enjoy!'

I certainly did. As I savoured the food, rather
than bolting it as I'd been known to in the past, the
next task always on my mind, I watched the world
passing by on the street outside. London was a

melting pot of creed, colour, age and gender, and every one with their own story to tell. But, right now, I was happy not to know them. I was just enjoying noticing them, and everything else around me, for the first time in what seemed like forever.

28

'Hey, Mom, how are you?'

Jed's deep, chocolatey voice reached my ears as I hung up my coat and entered the living room. I made a gesture that I'd go to the other room but he waved a reply indicating there was no need and that I was welcome to stay.

'Oh, I'm just dandy, honey. How are you? How's London?'

'Colder than there, by the looks of it,' he laughed. I could see the screen from the angle it sat at on his lap and saw his mum relaxing on a porch swing, surrounded by pots of lush foliage, shaded from the sun, a tall glass of something cool in her hand as she rested the tablet on a table. Her head was down for a moment, fussing with the fluffy mutt of a rescue dog she'd recently acquired, which meant Jed was able to interact with me without alerting his mum to the fact he had a house guest. I worried she may not approve of me staying. If what Henry had said at the hospital about Jed being a mess after the break-up was true, I probably wasn't flavour of the month, even all this time on. Mothers could be champion grudge-holders when it came to their sons.

Outside the apartment window, the skies were already past dusk and drizzle now sheened on the deck, highlighted by strategically positioned out-side lighting.

Jed chatted to his mum about this and that, catching up on all the gossip about people they knew, his accent gradually thickening as he spoke to her. It always happened the moment he dropped back into his old life. He'd never lost his accent, but it was softer in general until he met up with family or friends from the States or travelled home. And then a switch flicked and he was pure Louisiana again. Albeit a half-British Louisianan.

I did my best not to listen, burying myself in my book, but I couldn't help my ears perking up the moment the conversation turned to how his week had gone.

'Yeah, good,' he said. 'The start-up I'm mentoring is doing really well so that's great.'

'That's wonderful, honey. I hope they know how lucky they are to have you taking an interest.' The pride in her voice was palpable.

Jed deflected the compliment with a comment about how there are lots of great people out there doing the same thing. I could imagine the look his mum gave him before moving on.

'And have you heard any more about Milly? I know you said she was due out of the hospital soon. That's great news.'

'Oh... umm, yeah. She's out.'

'That's great. I hope she's not going to overdo it. She always did push herself far too hard, that girl.'

I chewed my lip.

'No, I think she's going to be OK now.'

I only wish I had Jed's confidence.

His mum tilted her head at him. 'What are you hiding from me?' Suddenly her warm, open face clouded. 'She is all right, isn't she? You're not trying to protect me from something? I know she broke your heart...'

Oh, God. Why is there never a hole in the ground handy when you need one?

'But you know I think that was a combination of things. She'll always have a special place in my heart.'

'Mom—' Jed scratched his cheek.

I was pretty sure I didn't deserve to be so valued by a woman whose son's heart I had well and truly stomped over in a pair of overpriced Chanel boots.

'You need to tell me if something's happened,' she continued, sitting up now, closer to the screen.

'There's nothing.'

'Jedidiah Brenton Matthews,' she warned.

I gave a smirk. She only rolled out his full name when he was in trouble. Jed gave me a side eye.

'Mom. Milly is fine. I promise. Actually...'

Without warning, he turned his screen to face me. I shot him a look of panic. *Oh, touché, Jed.*

'Milly!' His mum's face burst into a smile that was as bright as the sunshine that surrounded her. 'Darling girl!'

'Hi, Bea.' I waved with one hand and kicked Jed with my foot. He shot me a glance and shrugged.

'Oh, my goodness, I can't tell you how good it is to see you! When Jed said you'd had an accident, oh, my Lord, I was so worried. I went to church that very moment and I've been praying for you the whole time.'

'Umm... thanks. That's really kind.' I wasn't sure what else to say. Personally, I thought the fact that I was sitting here right at this moment was more to do with the skill of the emergency services, great doctors and a massive dollop of luck, rather than the influence of any higher power, but who's to say? It was beginning to feel like I'd been wrong about a lot of things so there was no guarantee I wasn't wrong about this too. Either way, I was grateful for Bea's kindness.

'Oh, honey! It's so good to see you. I had no idea that you and Jed were back together,' she beamed and Jed's face fell as he slowly put a hand across his eyes and rubbed his forehead with the tips of his fingers. My own face felt frozen in a rictus expression that was somewhere between a smile and panic, and slathered in embarrassment.

Jed pulled the screen back towards him. I rubbed my nose.

'We're not, Mom. Milly's flatmate evicted her when she was in the hospital and the place she was going to go into wasn't safe so she's... staying here for a bit. Just until she gets back on her feet.'

'You're not?' Neither of us missed the disappointment in Bea's reply, although we both did Oscar worthy performances of pretending to.

'Nope.'

'Are you sure?'

Jed laughed, the deep, melodic sound breaking the tension. 'Yeah, Mom. We're sure.'

'Well, now that *is* a shame.'

'Not really,' he said, quickly. 'So, how's the latest quilt going?' He gave a monumental heave of the conversational steering wheel in the opposite direction.

'Oh, it's fine. The weather's been so lovely this week, though, I've been out in my garden more than in front of the sewing machine to be honest.'

'That's fair enough, whatever makes you happy. What have you been doing in the garden?'

Jed's conversation was a bit like a swan. On the

surface he was calm and laid back but underneath, his feet were paddling like the clappers. Almost literally. His right leg, out of sight of his mum, was jiggling up and down. I watched him for a moment, sorry to be the cause of the discomfort. As though sensing my gaze, he turned and I had no chance to look away.

'Sorry,' I mouthed.

There was a pause and the leg slowed then stopped and his look softened. The tiniest of head-shakes accompanied the change.

'Jed?'

'Huh? Yes?' His head spun back to the screen and I giggled.

'I said did you say Milly's flatmate evicted her when she was in the hospital?'

'Yeah. Kind of a shitty move, huh?'

'Jedidiah.'

'Sorry, Mama.' He grinned that grin that made most women forgive him most things. His mum raised a brow and moved on.

'But yes, it wasn't a kind or gracious thing to do at such a time.'

'Mils has bailed her out with the rent in the

past, never paid her own late and that was the thanks she got.'

'What an unpleasant person. She'll have to answer for that in time.'

'Yeah. Maybe.'

From the angle I was sitting at, I could just see his mum give Jed the brow again and he moved on swiftly.

'Anyway, Henry and Ava are having their kitchen ripped out and an extension built so they're staying in a flat her parents own, otherwise she would have stayed with them.' He seemed desperate to get across to his mum that there was most definitely and absolutely no chance of anything going on between us. I could see why. If she'd been upset when we broke up before, he wouldn't want her upset again. His mum meant the world to him and he'd protect her in any way he could. Including from me. 'I've got the space, so it's fine. We won't be in each other's way. Probably hardly see each other to be honest, between one thing and another.'

All right, I think she gets the point, Jed.

'Is she still there? Are you still working too hard, Milly?' she called across the miles, without waiting for an answer from her son. Jed looked across at me, a silent message in his eyes. Pushing myself up, I shuffled up the sofa until I was next to him. He adjusted the screen so that his mum could see both of us.

'Hi,' I said, feeling a little self-conscious. Obviously, she didn't hate me as I'd expected, but I wasn't sure I felt I deserved her kindness either. I couldn't help loving the feel of it though. I'd missed her so much.

'Hi there, darling. Now, are you still putting in those crazy hours?'

'Nope, definitely not.'

'It's good to hear you finally saw the light on that. It's not healthy for a body to work as many hours as you do.'

'I'm not actually working any hours at the moment. I obviously went a bit quiet with the accident and now no one wants to work with me.'

'Honey, you were in the hospital in a coma. Did they somehow expect you to respond to their emails from there?'

I pulled a face. 'Probably. These sort of people don't really do excuses.'

'If Jed's face was anything to go by, they were pretty worried about you there for a while. Surely these fashion people understand that sometimes things happen in life?'

I ignored the bit about Jed's face and he'd suddenly found the pattern on a scatter cushion of phenomenal interest, so I focused on the other bit of her question.

'I'm not sure they really do, Bea. They want things done and they want them when they want them. I missed some deadlines, and I missed an important job interview. When it comes down to it, that's all that matters.'

'Well, then you're better off without them,' Bea said, determination written across her attractive face.

'You're probably right. My bank balance would disagree, but I'm sure something will come along.' I was working on convincing myself of this fact, so saying it out loud seemed a good step in the right direction. Like repeating a mantra or something.

'It sure will and it will be so much better. You'll see.' She beamed a warm, comforting smile across the miles, full of sunshine, as she gently moved the swing back and forth with one bare foot.

'I hope so,' I smiled back. 'And now, I should let you get back to Jed, and stop hogging you.'

'Oh, not at all, he can talk just as well with you there, I'm sure, and it's so nice to see you.'

'Thank you. It's lovely to see you too but I'd better get on and... do some dinner.'

'Maria left a casserole earlier so there's not much to do.' Jed glanced at me.

'Well, I can put that in the oven.'

'It's in one of those cast-iron things. It's heavy.'

'I'm not incapable.'

'No, but you did just have your arm out of plaster this morning and I imagine the doc told you not to go lifting anything heavy?'

My eyes widened. 'Seriously. Do you actually have me bugged?'

He grinned. 'Nope. But I had a friend who busted his arm and had it pinned. I was with him when they took the cast off and heard what he was told about it.'

'They might have said something different to

me. Techniques move on.' I gave him a look with just the tiniest hint of smug.

'Techniques might but bones pretty much act the same as they always did.'

I said nothing.

'So, did the doc tell you not to overdo it?' he paused. 'Again?'

I will not blush.

'I'm guessing the blush means yes.'

I turned back to the screen. 'Has he always been this impossible?'

His mother laughed and raised her glass of iced tea in a toast towards me. I gave her a wave and went off to find something to do. I wanted to be useful but felt quite the opposite. Wandering back towards my room, the conversation picked up again.

29

'Are you still seeing that Christine girl?'

'Kind of.'

'Kind of?' Jed's mum repeated. 'What does that mean? Surely either you are or you aren't?' There was no verbal reply so I'm guessing he gave her a shrug.

'I don't understand you sometimes, Jed. She doesn't even seem your type. I mean, that whole stunt with the engagement ring?'

'I don't have a type, Mama. And that was just a joke to wind the press up.'

'Most decent people try to avoid the media attention. This girl seems to do whatever she can to court it. Pretending to be engaged to you? Honestly, whatever next?'

I wasn't trying to listen. It was just kind of hard not to. Admittedly, I could have shut my door, but that would have made the conversation a little harder to follow. OK, yes. I was being nosy. But let's face it, I didn't have a lot going on in my own life right now so it made sense I'd be more interested in others'. Although, as my stomach began to swirl, I wasn't entirely sure I was comfortable listening in on a conversation about the state of my ex's current love life after all.

Some conversations should be private, and this was one of them. So if I closed the door now, would he hear, and therefore know I'd been listening? I got up from the end of the bed and moved the door to close it. It let out an apologetic squeak and I jumped back. Crap. I didn't remember it squeaking before! How can a door in an apartment this expensive squeak? I stood by it trying to decide what to do.

'She wasn't pretending to be engaged to me, Mama. We've been through this.'

'How do you think I felt seeing that? Thinking

my boy had got engaged without telling me. And to someone I've never even met.'

'I know, and like I said before, I'd never do that. She was just playing for the cameras. It wasn't that she was pretending to be with me.'

'Honey, she's already with you, so she knew exactly what the press and everyone would think. You're one of the world's most eligible bachelors, so the girls at the salon tell me. You ask me, that girl knew exactly what she was doing.' Bea was pretty laid back as a rule, a trait she'd passed on to her son, but there was a definite edge to her voice now.

'Can we talk about something else, please?'

'Am I ever going to meet her?'

'That's the same topic, Mama.'

'So, give me an answer, and I'll switch.'

'I don't know. That's the only answer I can give you. Now, can we change the subject?'

'Sure.' Her voice took on a lighter tone. She definitely didn't sound a fan of Christine, and it was hard to tell how much of one Jed was. He didn't exactly give much away. Not that it was any of my business.

'What would you like to talk about?' his mum

continued, gaily. 'I know. How about the fact you're living with Milly again?'

I snatched my noise-cancelling headphones from the bedside table and shoved them on my head. I might be nosy but I wasn't a masochist. Jed had taken me in because he'd felt it was his duty to his friend. Sweetly, and surprisingly, his mum still had a soft spot for me, it appeared, but I didn't need to hear him explaining his act of charity to her. I was already finding the situation of having to rely on others a little unfamiliar so hearing that rubbed in, even unintentionally, was more than I'd be able to deal with right now. I cranked up the audio book, laid back on the bed and closed my eyes.

A while later, Jed cautiously poked his head around the door. I pulled the headphones off, pressing pause on my audio book as I did so.

'Hi,' he said, 'I did knock.'

I shook my head. 'It's your house.'

'Your room.'

'Temporarily.'

'So long as you need it.'

I nodded and wondered how Christine would feel about the arrangement now that I knew he was definitely 'kind of' seeing her. A woman who was used to getting her way, I imagined it might not go down well. Then again, she could take one look at me, realise I was in absolutely no way a threat – Jed himself had been at pains to explain how much of a non-possibility 'us' was – and carry on as usual. I wasn't sure which I preferred.

'Dinner's ready.'

I followed him through to the kitchen diner.

'It is? I thought you were going to call me to help.'

'There was literally nothing to do. Like I said, Maria spoils me. All I had to do was put it in the oven.'

'Can you ask her to put it in a lighter dish next time? Then at least I won't feel quite so useless.'

'I can do that.' He grinned and I looked back to the table and adjusted a fork.

'Smells good. Shall I start dishing up? I'm pretty sure the doctor didn't rule out spoons.'

He handed me the carved ladle and I set about the task, a strange feeling of comfort and familiarity, overlaid with a fine layer of something I couldn't put my finger on. A feeling that told me it *shouldn't* feel this easy. This right. Pushing it to the back of my mind, I placed the two bowls on the table, added a wooden bowl full of sliced artisanal bread and sat down opposite Jed.

'Wine?'

'No, I'm fine with water, thanks.'

He nodded and poured two glasses.

'You should have some if you want.' I nodded to the bottle of wine.

'Nah. Not really in the mood. I was just being polite.' The low light didn't hide the amusement in those striking blue eyes or the lazy half-smile on his mouth. I did my best to ignore both.

'Your mum looks well.'

'Yep, she's doing good. Thrilled to see you, of course.'

I pulled a face, mouth full of casserole.

He laughed, shovelling in another forkful himself. 'Don't worry about it. I think she was more upset than I was when we broke up.'

I nodded, trying to ignore the sting.

'That came out wrong.'

I tried to laugh it off. 'It's OK, Jed. It was all a long time ago and, having had some time to think about things, I can imagine you were pretty pleased to see the back of me by then.'

'Not at all.' His tone was serious and when I looked up, his expression matched it.

'Anyway, I am sorry your mum was upset. And I'm sorry that I hurt you. I'm not sure if I ever said that, or if you believe me, but it's true.'

'I do believe you.'

'Frankly, I'm still stunned you let me back into your home.'

'Luckily I'm not the kind of guy to hold a grudge.' The half-smile was back and the atmosphere lightened.

'Besides, the thought of that guy getting mates' rates...'

I threw a piece of bread at him, which bounced off his forehead. Classy, I know. Jed, however, burst into laughter and put it on the side of his plate.

'What you up to tomorrow?'

* * *

When Jed had asked what I would be up to tomorrow, I'd had no idea but, as I lay in bed, having pressed the button to open the blinds, I turned on my side and looked out at the view. The sky was blue with a few splodges of white cloud bumbling along on a gentle breeze, and the clock told me the temperature was heading for one of those 'hint of early spring' days when you still needed a jacket but with a definite promise of warmer days to come. I pushed off the duvet and the new blanket that had appeared a couple of days after Jed had questioned how I was sleeping, commenting that I'd looked tired. For once I hadn't taken offence – another step forward – recognising the enquiry as concern and not criticism and just said I'd been having trouble over the last few evenings.

The next thing I knew, a box had appeared for me. Inside was a plush blanket, and the paperwork advised it was something called a 'weighted blanket', which was supposed to be good for those suffering from poor sleep, especially stemming from anxiety. I'd heard of them, of course. Any latest fad seemed to find its way to the fashion set pretty quickly, but I wasn't always convinced of the sincerity of their opinions, I had to admit. Let's face it, I wasn't always convinced of their sincerity full stop, having seen it, or the lack of it, in action, so I'd not taken a lot of notice. But Jed's thought was kind and having had a few rough nights, I was happy to give it a go.

What a revelation! I'd rushed out – well, as quickly as I rushed anywhere these days – the next day once I heard Jed in the kitchen. He'd never been the quietest, even when he thought he was. It was a quirk and kind of funny – unless you had a raging hangover or had been out far too late the night before attempting to network in a desperate effort to gain favour. Then it had been less funny. But, looking back, life had gradually become less funny back then. Or at least I had missed the opportunities for laughter I'd been offered. Thankfully, I had neither been out late nor guzzled too much wine and had instead had the best night's sleep I'd had in years. Aside from that whole coma thing, but that didn't really count.

'You *have* to get one!' I had said, bursting into the kitchen that morning.

'Good morning to you too, ma'am.'

I grinned. It always made me laugh when he'd called me that. 'Hi. But you have to get one!'

'One of what, exactly?'

'The blanket you got. It's amazing!'

'Really? I didn't know if it was a bit of a gimmick but thought it might be worth a try.'

'Honestly, so did I, but I slept like a baby.' I paused. 'The kind that sleep through, not the ones that scream half the night and make their parents into living zombies. Obviously.'

'Good to have the distinction. Want a tea?'

'Yes, please.'

'Peppermint?'

How did he remember this stuff?

'Lovely, thanks.'

'I'm glad it's helped. You certainly look better rested.' His back was to me and I saw his hand pause momentarily as he reached for the mug. He was waiting for me to question what exactly he'd meant by that and I felt that uncomfortable twist again. The more I looked back on who I'd become in the past, the less I liked it. But I wasn't that person any more. I'd never really been her, not truly, but somehow she had taken over and all the time I'd been fighting for what I thought I wanted, I'd actually been losing more, including my true self. But I was on another path now. All right, it was a path with no income at the moment but so long as I kept putting one foot in front of the other, hopefully that would come along too. I crossed my fingers for an extra boost and replied.

'Thanks. I feel it.'

Jed picked up the mug he'd been reaching for, glanced over his checked shirt-clad shoulder and smiled.

* * *

A few days later, I smiled down at London and up at the clear blue sky from my bedroom vantage point and then picked up the empty cup from the peppermint tea I'd made myself earlier that morning.

'Oh! I thought you were at work,' I said, padding into the open plan kitchen and finding Jed perched on a stool at the breakfast bar.

'You saying it was quiet so you assumed I wasn't here?'

'Kind of.'

He laughed and took a sip of the thick black coffee he favoured. 'I've got a mentoring session in a while and didn't feel like going into the office today so I'll just go straight there.'

'How come? I mean, not going in.'

He shrugged. 'No reason. It's a beautiful day and I'd rather be here, gazing out of the window. I pay enough people enough money to allow me to do that if I so choose, so why not take advantage of it?'

'Good point.' I plopped down on to the bar stool next to him. 'How did you figure that out?'

'What's that?' he asked, turning a little in his seat to face me more.

'The whole balance thing. You've always been really good at it. You always knew when to work and when to play, and how to never go crazy on either. And look where it's got you. I mean, I know you worked really hard to build what you have. I'm not saying it's come easy or anything, but you just knew... I don't know, how to balance things.' I met his eyes. 'I should have learned from you.'

'We all have to find our own path, Mils, and what works for us.'

'I wish I'd found a better way of seeing that

mine wasn't working for me, rather than leaving it to a bus to knock some sense into me.'

He finished his coffee and gave a couple of small, thoughtful nods. 'Admittedly, that was a fairly drastic route to take and one that, frankly, scared the absolute shit out of all of us, but then the one thing you never were, Milly, was boring.'

'That's something, I guess.'

He took my cup and put it alongside his own in the dishwasher and I placed a book I'd liberated from his bookshelves last night on the counter. Jed stood behind me and looked over my shoulder as he tucked his stool back beneath the worktop.

'What's that?' I could feel the nearness of him and his warmth. It felt like a long time since I'd had that feeling. It wasn't anything sexual, it was closeness. Suddenly it struck me again, almost as hard as that bus – and almost as painfully. I'd spent the past years surrounded by people, at parties, at network events, at offices, even with my family, when I spared the time, but I'd never been present. I'd never been there with my whole self. Even on the odd, very odd, occasions I'd met someone, it was like the main part of me was somewhere else. Until now.

'You OK?' Jed leaned round a little more.

'Uh huh.'

He did a small head tilt, his brow wrinkling as he studied me for a moment. 'You seemed miles away.'

I smiled at the irony. 'Nope. Right here.'

'You going exploring?' He leaned his hip against the counter, nodding at the book.

'I thought I might. I hope you don't mind me borrowing the book?'

'Of course not. I told you before. Just make yourself at home. I want you to recuperate and for that you have to, you know, actually relax.'

'I know. I'm working on it. I just don't want to be in the way.' His comment to his mum about him 'kind of' still seeing Christine had lodged in my brain and occasionally poked itself out to remind me I was merely a guest, no matter how comfortable things felt.

'You're not.'

'But...'

'But what?' he slid the book over from me and flicked through it as he asked.

'Christine?'

Jed looked up. 'What about her?'

'I just, well, you know, don't want to be in the way when she...'

'You're not in the way. Thought of where you might go?' he asked, dropping that bright gaze back to the book and effectively firmly closing the door on the other subject. I was allowed to make myself at home in his place, but his personal business most definitely had a 'no entry' sign hung on the door.

'I've got a couple of ideas.' I had marked the pages of the *Hidden London* book with slips of paper and he nosed at a couple of them. 'I haven't decided yet.'

'Just see how you feel.'

'Yep, that's what I thought.'

'Don't overdo it.'

'No, doctor.'

He grinned, gave my shoulder a brief but gentle squeeze and headed off to his home office.

30

An hour later and I was exiting St Pancras station into the bright sun of the early spring day. Heading away from the main station, I wandered towards my destination and turned into the green space, the peace immediately surrounding me. As I slowly made my way towards the church, occasionally the announcements from the international rail station so close by drifted on the soft breeze towards the churchyard, before being swept away by the unfurling leaves of the spring branches.

I gazed up at the bell tower and ran my hand across the intricate stone carving of the doorway, both apparently remodelled in the nineteenth century, according to the book I'd borrowed, after the church had fallen into disrepair. The work had attempted to hark back to its supposed Norman roots. All I could see was the beauty and detail as a gentle, weak sun warmed my skin and the soft breeze ran its fingers through my hair, tossing it playfully in front of my face until I pushed it back. I checked the door, expecting it to be locked, but to my surprise the large handle twisted beneath my hand and I stepped a little hesitantly into the hushed surroundings.

Gazing around at the small church, I was pleased to find it light and bright and welcoming. For some reason, I'd expected dark walls, and a stark, foreboding atmosphere but this was neither of those things. Chairs were lined up in place of pews that had, perhaps, been lost during the time the building had been left to rot, and it was obvious that the place was used for other purposes as well as worship. I ran my fingers over posters on the small noticeboard advertising lectures and musical concerts. Stepping further, I noticed grave slabs fixed in the floor and read the inscriptions. Moving to the side of them, I squeezed my way past. It was silly, I knew. It wasn't like the people were directly under the slab and, judging by the dates on them, little would remain by now anyway, but it still felt disrespectful to trample straight over them. Taking a seat on one of the hard, wooden chairs I absorbed the stillness, looking around, looking up, and just peacefully noticing things.

'Hello, dear.' The voice shot me out of my seat and a throaty laugh followed as I turned to see the owner of it. A woman I'd guess to be in her late sixties was approaching me, a basket hooked over one arm and a huge bouquet of freshly cut flowers resting over the other. She had a pile of dark hair streaked heavily with grey piled on the top of her head, and an aura of faded glamour. 'Sorry, love. Didn't mean to make you jump.'

'That's OK,' I smiled, trying to pretend my heartrate hadn't just doubled. 'Umm... it's OK for me to be here, isn't it?'

'Of course, of course!' She waggled her head as both her hands were full and the loose bun on her head followed at a slightly slower pace. 'You sit there as long as you like, duckie. I'm just going to do the flowers.'

'They're very beautiful,' I said, admiring the large bunch, recognising lilies and roses but unable to name many of the others.

'They are, aren't they? Hopefully I'll do them justice.' She gave me a wink as if to say there was no doubt about it.

'Have you been doing the flowers here long?' I shuffled up a few rows to watch the process closer, encouraged by the woman tilting her head at me.

'I do a few of the churches around here.'

'You're religious, then?' The question was out before I thought about it. 'I'm sorry. That's none of my business. I'm... was a writer. I guess I'm a bit too used to asking questions.'

She flapped a hand that held a soft yellow rose and I inhaled its scent as she wafted it around in her reply. 'Oh, don't you worry about that. I don't have anything to hide. I've been coming to churches around here since I was a little girl, depending on where I lived and I sup-pose I'd say I am religious. Although I have my moments of doubt, like a lot of people, especially when you see such awful things happening on the news. But I try to keep my faith and find some comfort in that. We all have to find a way forward, don't we?'

'We do. It's whatever works, isn't it?'

'Are you? Religious, I mean?' she asked, artfully poking some flowers into a large vase.

I shook my head. 'No. Not really. Although I think maybe someone, or something, was looking out for me a little while ago.'

'Oh?' she asked, glancing back, curious now. She was waiting for an answer and being mysterious now seemed a bit rude. And, like the lady on the bus with her dog, just talking to this stranger felt natural. There was no agenda. Just conversation.

'I got knocked down by a bus and it was all a bit touch and go for a while. Apparently.'

'Well, I'm glad to see you here then.'

I smiled. 'I'm glad to be here.' I leant forward and rested my chin on my hands, balancing my elbows on my knees. 'I didn't feel that way initially. It felt like everything fell apart after that.'

'And now?'

'Maybe everything was supposed to fall apart.

Maybe that needed to happen for me to realise something.'

'And have you?'

I smiled. 'I'm working on it.'

She returned the smile. 'Glad to hear it, love.'

I shook my head. 'I'm sorry. I don't know why I just told you all that.'

She smiled wider. 'I have one of those faces. People love to divulge their deepest, darkest secrets to me.'

Laughing, I listened to the soft echo. 'Maybe you should be the writer.'

'Maybe I should. And what did you mean about that? You used to be one. What are you now?'

'I'm not really anything now. Things got... complicated following the accident and the opportunities I had weren't there any more.'

'There are always more opportunities, duckie. Sometimes you just have to look in a different place.'

Something about her words comforted me and suddenly I wasn't so scared any more. Finally, there was an inkling of belief behind the words I'd told

Jed's mum about how something would come along.

'Have you been around the churchyard?'

'No, I was going to do that next.'

She gave me a long look, a white lily poised in her fingers, its large white head bobbing from the movement. 'I think you'll enjoy it. There's a peacefulness about it. Like in here but an atmosphere, too. Not ominous,' she said quickly, 'just a feeling. There's centuries of history and you can feel it there better than anywhere. You're a creative type. You'll see what I mean.'

'Thank you. I'm Milly,' I held out my hand. The lady wiped her hand on her swishy, burnt umber skirt and took it. 'Rose. Pleasure to meet you, Milly. And don't forget. Opportunities are everywhere. You just have to look up and see them.'

Look up. The words danced around my head. I'd been so busy looking down at my phone or computer, or embracing the tunnel vision of where I thought I should be going, I'd stopped looking anywhere else. It had cost me in a myriad of ways. But I was looking up now, I said to myself, as I closed the door behind me and stepped back into the sunshine, dappled by the mature trees scattered around the graveyard.

Having explored the tombs, famous and mundane, I came back to the Hardy Tree with its circle of gravestones surrounding it. I'd read up on this in Jed's book, as the Tube had brought me from Islington to St Pancras, and was now keen to see it in person. In the 1860s, with the expansion of the railways, space was needed for more lines and so the graveyard was disturbed to make way for them. Thousands of bodies were moved and reinterred within a mass grave in a different area of the churchyard, the bones all muddled and tumbled together. It seemed a little sad and undignified and, again, according to the book, this mass grave was more subject to graverobbers than individual ones, as once the villains were in, it was easy pickings. Being a quieter area, the thieves were also freer to move around as the churchyard wasn't guarded as some others closer to the city were. I wondered if, as Bea would have it, those people who took such disrespectful liberties had been made to answer for such actions when their own time came. Who knew? I wasn't a vengeful person but I kind of hoped so. Some things were just plain wrong, whatever your beliefs.

The Hardy Tree was a mature specimen and all around the trunk, like the spokes of a wheel, were gravestones from those whose bones had been moved. At the time all this was being done, the architect of the plan to remodel the graveyard, which had by now become a public park, had a young assistant by the name of Thomas Hardy. Years before he became the literary giant who penned some of the most depressing English literature (honestly, Tom, really? Why does nearly everyone have to die?), he was instrumental in creating the scene I saw before me. Plants and moss now wound their way around some of the headstones and the leaves were beginning to unfurl above them, preparing to shade them from a warm summer. Uprooting all those resting places seemed wrong, although in a crowded and growing city I supposed it was inevitable. It was still happening today. At least Hardy had done something artful that helped visitors remember and investigate the stories behind the stones. I wandered around a little more, listening to the breeze, and the birds perched high in the branches, singing their songs as loud as they could, irrespective of whether anyone was listening or not. But this time I was. I smiled at the sound as I watched soft-edged clouds tumble gently across the deep blue sky above. It was calming and my heartrate, already slower these days than it had been in years, seemed to slow a little more. We spent so much money on things to help us calm down, gadgets, gyms, headphones, retreats. And yet one of the best methods was here, all around us. Even in a city like London. Nature was here. Waiting. Ready to help. You just had to notice it.

As I left the churchyard and walked past its walls, high above the current pavement, testament to the years of burial as the ground had been piled up and up, I realised I'd walked this way before. More than once. But I'd never looked past the end of my nose. Or, more likely, past the end of my phone. All that history right there beside me and I'd never even noticed. I'd just focused on the next job. The next meeting. The next possible big thing. I looked up at the high wall and thought about what Rose had said about opportunities being all around. I just had to see them. I crossed my fingers and hoped she was right.

Wandering back, I checked the timetable and hopped on a bus, deciding to take an overland route back to the apartment. Changing part way, I stepped onto the one that would drop me closest.

'Hello, again!'

I looked up from tapping my Oyster card and saw the lady I'd sat beside before.

'Hi!' I waved and took the seat next to her, tickling under Gus's chin as I did so, which by the wiggle of his tail he seemed to appreciate.

'How are you?' She looked at the hand now fussing the dog. 'I see the cast is off. Bet that's pleased you?'

'More than you know,' I confessed. 'I felt so clumsy with it on. It was hard to remember what it was like before so it's great getting used to that again. Have you been shopping?'

'Well, just for a few little treats.' She gave me a girlish grin under her lashes, having glanced at the collection of bags beside her. Liberty, Selfridges and the classic blue of Fortnum and Mason. Treats indeed!

'Why not?' I grinned.

She wrinkled her nose in pleasure and patted my hand. 'That's exactly what I think. I might get hit by a bus tomorrow!' She laughed then immediately stopped. 'Oh, my dear! I didn't mean... that was so thoughtless of me. I'm so sorry.'

But I was already laughing and squeezed the hand she'd patted my own with. 'It's fine, really. And it's absolutely true. You need to live your life while you can. Who knows what's around the corner for any of us.' She still looked a bit unsure. 'Honestly, I mean it. I'm absolutely fine.'

In a world where people said the most vile things from behind a screen, unable to see the impact their cruel words could have, and perhaps not caring anyway, this lady's absolute mortification at what was, at the most, a faux pas was refreshing, sweet and funny.

'I'm Milly, by the way.' I held out my now uncast hand.

'Eleanor. It's a pleasure. Do you take this bus often?'

'No, not really. I'm just staying with a friend for

a bit but that's temporary.' I thought about Christine. 'Very temporary.'

'Oh. That's a shame. It's so nice to see a friendly face.'

I looked up to where my stop was coming up. 'It is. Hopefully I'll see you again before I move off,' I said, standing to make my way to the front.

'I hope so, dear. Now you take care!'

'I will. And you.' I smiled down at her before giving Gus a final fuss and a quick wave to them both before disembarking.

31

I waved at the concierge and headed into the lift that would take me up to the penthouse. Unlocking the door, I listened out for any sounds. Apparently, Christine was out of the country so I knew Jed wouldn't be 'entertaining', which was a relief but still. I know he'd told me to treat his place as my own, and although I felt incredibly, and surprisingly, comfortable with him again now already – something I tried not to think about as it brought up way too many thoughts, feelings and questions – I was still aware this was not my home. Its price tag was a big enough clue for a start. Movement caught my eye as I hung my coat on a hanger in the hallway closet.

'Hi, how are—' I stopped, taking in the expression on Jed's face, the blue eyes, ordinarily bright, now highlighted by red rims around them. 'Jed, whatever's the matter? Is it your mum?' I asked, worry pitching my voice up a little. I checked my phone. It was in my pocket. And switched off. I'd gone from one extreme to the other. There had to be a happy balance.

He shook his head and I felt a cold seep into my blood. 'Not Henry or...' I couldn't even finish the sentence, bile threatening to rise at my throat, tears springing to my eyes. Was this how Henry had felt? Was this what I had put people through by the simple act of not looking where I was going?

'No, no.' He pulled me into his chest quickly and dropped a kiss on my forehead before standing me gently back, looking directly at me. Making sure I understood. 'They're all fine. I promise.'

'Oh. OK. Good. Thank you.' I wasn't sure what I was thanking him for but it seemed the right thing to do. His hands still rested lightly on my arms as I looked up to meet the sad eyes. 'So, what's wrong?'

He shook his head and moved away from me, folding himself on the corner seat of the sofa. I followed and took the space next to him.

'Please tell me. I don't suppose I can help but I'd like to try if I can.'

He looked across as I sat down and his sad smile made me feel even worse than the serious expression he'd had prior to it. His hand moved to mine, resting on the couch.

'Did you have a nice trip out?'

I nodded. 'Yes. Thank you.' I waited. If he wanted to tell me, he would.

'Where did you go?'

'To Old St Pancras church.' He nodded at my words, still not talking. 'I chatted to a nice lady called Rose who was doing the flowers, and then I wandered around the churchyard and saw the Hardy Tree.'

'The one with all the gravestones around it?'

'Yes, that's the one.' It didn't surprise me that Jed knew about this. He'd always been curious about everything. Unlike me, he'd spent much of his life looking up.

'My friend died,' he said simply.

'Oh, Jed. I'm so sorry.'

He looked up and met my eyes. 'Thank you.'

'Had you known him long?'

'About three years. I mean, he was an old guy but, I don't know, he still seemed like he had a lot of life left in him. A lot more to offer, you know?'

'I do. I'm so sorry,' I said again. 'Is there anything I can do?'

He shook his head.

'I could make you a drink?'

'You don't have to do that.'

'I know, but it might make you feel better.'

A faint smile, like the weakest winter sunbeam, crossed his face.

'Thanks. That'd be nice.'

I got up and busied myself making tea. He wasn't a huge tea drinker but when he'd been upset in the past, I'd done the British thing and made tea and he'd never complained. Although time had passed between then and now. 'Is tea all right?' I asked, suddenly feeling I ought to check.

'Perfect,' he said, following me into the kitchen area.

'What was his name?'

'Bert. I met him at the park. His dog had got himself lost and ended up trotting beside me while I was out for a run. When I realised he was staying put, I looked around for a possible owner but there was no one around. It was getting dark by then and I didn't take my phone on the run so I took the pooch home with me and gave the number on the tag a call from there. This guy answered and when I said I had his dog, he just burst into tears.'

'Oh no!' I pushed the mug of steaming tea towards Jed.

'I know. Thanks, Mils.'

'So, what happened?'

'He said he'd come and get him but I could tell he wasn't the sprightliest of chickens so I said I could drive him over tomorrow or meet him first thing in the park tomorrow. The dog by this time had had some leftovers and was happily curled up on the end of my couch, completely unaware of the trauma he'd put his poor owner through. Although Bert said he'd been missing for hours so it might have been that the dog was just as exhausted and had picked me to throw his trust onto.'

'Must have good instincts.'

Jed smiled a thanks.

'So we arranged a meet-up the next morning at the park and as soon as Hector, that's the dog, saw Bert standing there, he took off like a rocket, practically bowled the poor guy down like a nine pin.'

'Aww, that's kind of sweet.'

'It was very sweet.'

I nudged him. 'Big softie.'

'Don't tell everyone.'

I made a zipping motion across my lips.

'So, you became friends?

'Bert wanted to reward me somehow, tried to give me money.'

'Which obviously you didn't take.' Jed could have been on his last quid and he wouldn't have taken money for what he saw was just doing the right thing.

'Nope. I said he could buy me a coffee. He said he could do better than that and took me to this tiny little mom and pop café and bought me the best breakfast I've ever had!'

'Don't let your mum hear you say that,' I laughed.

'OK, let me rephrase. Bought me the best

British breakfast I've ever had. We just kind of hit it off, and sat there for the next two hours, swapping stories.'

'Where was the dog all this time?'

'Just sat there, sprawled out beneath the table, happy as a clam to be back with his owner.'

'You did a good thing.'

'Maybe it was meant to happen. Bert ended up becoming one of my closest friends. It can be good to have friends from different generations, don't you think? I think I learned more than I ever realised from him. Plus, we just had a great time whenever we met up.'

'Was that often?'

'Pretty often. Hector was an unofficial PAT dog, you know?'

'Like a therapy dog?'

'Yeah. Bert took him into the local old folks' home. I think it was the highlight of their week. I ended up going along a few times when I could after Bert talked me into it once. Actually, it was great fun and then, a couple of times when Bert couldn't make it, they let me take Hector in. He knew me so well by then that the staff were more than happy for me to do it so their residents could still have that four-pawed ray of sunshine trot in.'

'I guess they have to be sure the dog's comfortable and reliable with someone other than his owner being there?'

'Exactly. But Hector had taken to me and he'd had a few sleepovers when Bert had to have the odd trip to hospital or some other appointment, so they could see we worked pretty well as a team too.'

'I bet it was nice having Hector stay? Having the company, I mean. Not that you're short of company,' I babbled, 'but you know, there's something about a pet.'

He, thankfully, ignored the babble bit and just replied to the rest. 'Yeah. It was great. And you're right, there is. I've thought about getting one myself but I'd want it to be right for the dog, too.'

I thought for a moment about how some fluffy company would have been welcome over the past few years as I shut myself away writing the next article that I hoped would be the breakthrough piece, the one that really got me noticed. But that would have been impossible.

'I don't think I could have even been a good

hamster parent.' Jed half smiled but didn't disagree. He was at least honest. 'But you'd make it work. Whatever you wanted to do, you'd find a way to do it that was the best for everyone.'

'Thanks, Milly. I appreciate that.'

'So, what happened?' I asked.

'Heart attack. Died in his sleep.'

'Oh Jed, I'm so sorry. At least he wasn't in pain...' I twiddled the ring on my finger. 'I'm never sure if that's the right thing to say. It's not like it makes the loss of your friend any easier, I know. I'm sorry. I don't really know what to say.'

Jed took the hand I was worrying and held it within his own large, lightly tanned one. 'You don't need to say anything. You're here and that's enough.' He tilted his head at me. 'Bert would have loved you.'

'I think I would have loved him too by the sounds of it. I'm sorry I didn't get to meet him.'

'Me too.'

'When did he pass away? Last night?'

'No,' Jed frowned. 'About ten days ago. Unfortunately, his family had moved away and weren't always the best at keeping up with him, but his friends started noticing him not showing up, and then when he didn't turn up for his weekly visit with Hector, alarm bells started ringing and they called the police. He'd never missed one without letting them know.' He shook his head. 'I hate to think of him just lying there.'

'Then try not to think about it.' I placed my other hand over his. 'What about the dog?'

'Apparently, Hector was just lying beside him, his head on his chest. Those police and emergency crews have seen a lot, I'm sure, but from what I heard from Charlie, Bert's friend, who went in after them, there wasn't a dry eye in the house.'

'I'm surprised they let him go in with them. Charlie, I mean.'

'Oh. They didn't. But Charlie wasn't having any of that nonsense.'

'So, where's Hector now?'

'The family were informed and said they'd take care of him.'

'I see. And the funeral? I take it you're going.'

'Yes. It's tomorrow. I just found out. His friends assumed the family had contacted me already.'

'Didn't you say something about a big meeting tomorrow?'

'Some things are more important. Ira is going to take my place. He's just as capable, and I can read the minutes later.'

'Right.'

Jed quirked a brow at me. 'I can almost hear the cogs. What's up?'

'Nothing.'

'I don't believe you. Come on.'

He was right. There was a thought spinning around in my mind but I was too ashamed to voice it to him. I was ashamed to even acknowledge it myself.

'So?' he prompted.

'I wasn't a great person, was I? I mean, I'm really trying to improve but...' I turned to face him and looked directly into his eyes. 'OK, you're like this superstar billionaire guy but you are happy to blow off a meeting with no warning so that you can go to a friend's funeral. Which is as it should be.'

'So, what's the issue?'

'The issue is that I don't know for certain, even though I was waaaaay further down the ladder of importance than you, that I'd have done that. I'd have probably found an excuse and thought the flowers I sent instead made up for it. But they wouldn't have. There wouldn't have been any excuse, and yet I can't say I wouldn't have tried to find one.'

'And you feel bad about that?'

'I feel entirely shitty about that!' I said, pulling back.

'But you wouldn't do that now?'

'No, of course not.'

'Then, what's the problem?'

'I was a bad human being. That's the problem. No wonder you left.'

Shit.

'That last bit wasn't supposed to come out.'

'We both know there was more to it than that.'

'You're generous, but we both know there wasn't.'

'Of course there was. I don't think I appreciated just how much you wanted it. All I saw was that you never had time for me. I understood you working hard but I don't think I realised just what a competitive world you were fighting in. And that's on me.'

'Oh.' I didn't have a lot else to say to that but it did make me feel a tiny bit better. A tiny bit.

'As for the rest, we all do things we wished we hadn't done and not done things we wished we had. All we can do is hope to learn and have a better go at it next time round.'

'If there's a next time round.'

'Well, that's true. And in that case, all we can do is hope to learn from it full stop. Don't beat yourself up too much. Sometimes, the higher up the ladder you are, the easier it can be to do things. I don't answer to anyone. Yes, the client probably won't be best pleased but I've emailed and told him I have a funeral and my second in command will be there. If they can't or won't understand that a funeral of a friend takes precedence, then that's probably not someone I want to work with in the first place.

'You, on the other hand, were trying to make your mark, get that deserved notice, network that particular person and the timings were out of your control. It's not such an easy decision from that perspective.'

'But that's what I mean. It should be, shouldn't

it? It should be an easy decision. In fact, it shouldn't be a decision at all.'

'Don't beat yourself up, Mils. We're human. We all mess up at times. Like I say, all we can do is learn as we go along.'

'What time is the funeral?'

'Eleven.'

'Is it far?'

'Not too far, no.'

I pondered for a moment, unsure whether to ask the next question.

'What is it?'

'Oh, stop reading my face. That's not fair.'

'You're more of an open book these days. Besides, it's good practice for my poker games.' He flashed a grin and I was happy to see the sadness recede for a moment. 'Also, never play poker. You'll lose your shirt.' He gave a grin that would have got him in trouble with his mother and got a lot of other women in trouble. 'And possibly a lot more, depending on what version you're playing.'

'Oh, funny,' I said, attempting to take the higher ground. 'I have never nor do I intend to indulge in poker, strip or any other kind.'

'Probably a good choice.' He paused. 'For you, at least. Others may be a little more put out.'

'Ha! I doubt it.' He opened his mouth to say something else but I cut him off. 'So, what I was going to say was would you like some company tomorrow? I don't want to intrude and I can just wait outside or in the car if you're driving or whatever but...' I rambled on until I had to draw a breath.

'That'd be really great, Milly. If you're sure you don't mind?'

I shook my head. 'After everything you've done for me, it's the least I can do.'

'I'm not counting favours, and you shouldn't be either.'

'I know you're not. I just meant it'd be nice to be able to do something in return, however small.'

'It might seem small to you, but it means a lot.' He gently squeezed the hand I rested near him and I nodded, keeping my eyes averted.

32

It was a clear night and the bright, sunny day had melted into a warm evening. The door to the balcony was ajar, sounds from the street floors below occasionally drifting up. The phone rang and as Jed had his hands full cooking a stir fry which he wouldn't let me help with, he put it on speaker. To be fair, I probably still didn't have enough reliable strength and control to be wielding a knife near anyone, including myself, just yet, although I was working on the exercises I'd been given by the physio.

'Hey.'

I was sitting at the table, typing something

mostly one handed, just a rough draft of an idea I'd had floating around in my brain. There was no pressure and no agenda. This was just for me.

'Sweetie, do be a darling and pick me up from the airport tomorrow morning, won't you? The plane lands at nine thirty.'

'Hi, Christine, how are you?'

'Fine, darling,' she huffed out, completely missing the thread of sarcasm in his tone that there'd been no greeting, just the request. I got the feeling here that request was just a polite name for demand. 'But my damn chauffeur's wife is having a baby and he's insisting on being at the birth, just when I need him.'

My head was down but my eyebrows were raised. I was inordinately proud of myself for not actually having gone 'Wow' out loud. Of course, there was still time but I was keeping a lid on it for the moment.

'I'm pretty sure his wife needs him more than you at the moment.'

'Oh, don't be so silly. Of course she doesn't! It's not like he can actually do anything, is it? Whereas he could actually be driving me, like he's paid to!'

'It's a special moment. His child is being born, Christine.' Jed shook his head as he stirred the vegetables.

'They're bound to have more.'

'Wow.' Immediately, I clapped my hand over my mouth. Thankfully, it had come out quietly and I hoped I was the only one who'd heard. Slowly Jed turned his head. I opened my mouth to apologise but his eyes were crinkled with laughter. With his free hand, he lifted a finger to his lips.

I pulled my most genuinely apologetic face. 'Sorry,' I mouthed.

He shook the apology away with a grin and a small roll of his eyes.

'That's not really the point, Christine. Just call a car.'

'You're not coming to get me?'

'I can't.'

'Oh, this is getting ridiculous! Is there some sort of plot against me getting home? Why not?'

'There's no plot, Christine. Your driver is having a child and I have to attend a funeral.'

'Oh. Whose?'

'My friend Bert.'

Silence.

'The one with the dog?'

'The old guy?'

'Yes, the older gentleman. That's right.'

'Well, he was old.'

'And?'

'He'd have been anticipating it. I doubt he'll be expecting someone like you to take time out to go to the funeral.'

'And yet I'd swap that time to come to the airport to get you?'

'Of course. I'm still alive! Although what all this is doing to my nerves, I don't know. I'll have to call my kinesiologist and my herbalist once I hang up.'

'I can't pick you up, Christine. I'm sorry. You'll have to call a car. I'm not missing my friend's funeral.'

'Fine.'

Uh oh. That was the kind of fine that didn't bode well but Jed didn't seem bothered.

'I'll call you when I'm home. Assuming I ever get there!' she added, dramatically.

'OK,' Jed replied, not rising to the bait. 'Have a

safe flight.' The call was ended and I risked raising my eyes.

'What?' his expression was half amusement, half intrigue.

'Is that a fire you need to ring back and put out?'

'Nah. That's just how she is. Loves a bit of drama, does Christine.'

'Yeah, I kind of got that impression.'

He gave a small enquiring head tilt and I lifted my left hand up and wiggled my ring finger.

'Oh jeez, yeah, that.' He gave a roll of his eyes. It was apparent that Jed and Christine did not share a similar view on that particular stunt. 'You ready for dinner, or was that rumble I just heard a storm building outside?'

'More than ready and nope, that was all me. I was rather proud of that one.'

His laugh surrounded me and I was happy to hear it, happy to see the laughter in his eyes especially as I had a feeling tomorrow was going to be difficult for him. From the little he'd said, it was clear that he and Bert had been good friends and saying goodbye was never easy.

* * *

'Oh Jed, he'd be so happy you came!' A lady in a blue floral dress hurried towards us and enveloped Jed in a huge hug. Well as much as it was possible to envelop him in one of those when you were about half his size, but she had a good go. He hugged her back, retaining hold of one hand for a moment as she stood back and dabbed at her eyes with a delicate hanky with the other.

'Carol, this is my friend, Milly.' I shook her hand as Jed continued the introduction. 'Carol runs the home Bert and Hector visited.'

'It's lovely to meet you. Jed was telling me all about the visits last night.'

There was an almost imperceptible flicker of Carol's eyes between me and Jed and I ran the conversation back over in my head. *Last night.* Yeah. Probably not the best choice of words but oh, well. Jed didn't seem worried and really there were bigger things to think about today.

'Do you know where Hector is?' Carol asked him.

'No, I only know what you told me. That the

family are taking care of him. Have you managed to find out any more?'

She pulled a face. 'Not really. They're not the most talkative lot. Do you know they weren't even going to have a wake after? Said "Bert wouldn't have wanted it". What a load of hooey. Bert was up for any chance of people getting together for a chinwag. I think he enjoyed his visits to the home just as much as the residents enjoyed seeing him.'

'No doubt about it,' Jed agreed. 'So,' he frowned. 'Is there a wake?'

'Absolutely! At the King's Arms, just down the road. I arranged it myself. Of course, now they're saying they feel they ought to come and show their faces. Cheeky... wotsits.'

I liked Carol.

'So, you paid for it too?' Jed asked.

'They're going to invoice me and it wasn't much anyway.' Carol waved the enquiry away and made to change the subject.

Jed exchanged a look with me. He was totally paying that bill. No way was he going to let Carol take that hit. I nodded and gave a tiny squeeze of his arm.

'I can see why Bert didn't have much to do with them to be honest,' another man who'd now joined us offered, glancing back at the group that seemed to comprise of Bert's family. 'Don't know how the old codger was even related to them! What a bunch of stuck up—'

'Charlie, this is Jed's friend, Milly,' Carol interjected at an opportune moment.

Charlie's rant halted and he beamed a smile at me as I held out a hand. 'Hello.'

'Pleased to meet you.'

'Jed says you and Bert have been friends for some time.'

'Oooh,' he rubbed his chin, 'Long as I can remember.'

I gave him a sad smile, unsure what to say. 'It seems like he picked some great friends.'

Charlie studied me a moment and I wondered what I'd done.

'Much prefer this one to that Barbie doll you were running around with, young Jed.' Jed opened his mouth to reply but Charlie continued. 'Met her once. Barely looked at me, she did. Looked at her watch often enough and tapped her foot, but guess people like me are below the notice of an heiress.' He dragged the last word out and pulled a face. 'Yes, much prefer this one. Far more suitable.'

Suitable for what exactly I wasn't entirely sure but I think it was a compliment, so I took it as one and just smiled to myself.

'Milly is just a friend, Charlie. An old friend.'

'You don't have to put quite so much emphasis on old, thank you,' I nudged him. I was well aware that Christine was younger and perkier and almost everything else more than me, but he didn't have to rub it in.

'Well, maybe she should be a new friend.' Charlie shook his head at Jed as if he was being forced to explain something in words of one syllable to someone who really wasn't getting it.

'Not an option.' I patted Charlie's arm. 'But thanks for the vote of confidence.'

'Not your... type?' He indicated Jed with a quick nod of his head.

'He's all right,' I said, completely aware that Charlie was basically asking if I batted for the other team. 'But like he says, we're just friends. He's very happy with his current girlfriend.'

Charlie made a huff of disbelief and when I turned to Jed he was staring off into the middle distance. Carol met my gaze and gave me a shrug. I was almost relieved when, in the next moment, there was movement and we were summoned into the chapel for the funeral service.

Jed was quiet during the service. He didn't sing any of the songs, even though I knew from experience he could hold a tune. He said 'Amen' when he had to but for the most part, he kept his head down, listened to the words being spoken and occasionally let his gaze drift up and land on the coffin. A spray of flowers lay on top of it in the colours of Bert's old regiment, arranged by an old comrade. It appeared his family had not bothered with an arrangement of their own. I let my thoughts drift to my own family and how lucky I was that we were still so close, despite me having pushed things to the limit with my single-minded determination that the only thing that mattered was my career trajectory. I could have lost them. I could have been left alone like Bert – except Bert, thankfully, had some wonderful friends, judging by the pews filled with people dabbing their eyes.

My glance slid to his family. There were four of them and not one of them looked in the slightest bit emotional. One man was gazing round the chapel, up at the plaques on the walls. Another woman was studying her nails and a younger member was... no she couldn't be. Yep, she was. She was looking at her phone. It was tucked under the bag on her lap but there was definite scrolling going on. I felt eyes on me and looked back, meeting Jed's bright gaze square on. It was filled with thunder as he glanced quickly at the family before returning his gaze to me. I'd hoped he hadn't noticed, caught up in his own memories. Not much rattled Jed but this blatant disrespect to his friend was hitting the button. His jaw was set, a muscle pulsing to the side of it as he gritted his teeth. Without thinking, I took his hand and gave the tiniest shake of my head. We couldn't fix this. All we could do was honour Bert ourselves and be thankful that so many others felt the same. Jed looked at me for a long moment as I tried to telepath that message to him. His hand tightened around mine, warm and firm, and he turned his face back to the celebrant.

The day was sunny and the brightness made us squint as we exited the chapel. Murmurs of 'lovely service', and tales of fond memories were exchanged as we walked slowly past the row of flower arrangements sent for Bert. My hand was still within Jed's and I made no attempt to withdraw it. He'd drop it when he was ready. Yes, he was six foot four, two hundred odd pounds and had muscles that rippled like a lake in the breeze, but he also had a big heart. And right now that heart was in pain, a situation that had only been increased by the attitude of the family. He'd helped me out of a miserable situation and I was more than happy to do what I could to repay that generosity and kindness.

'Ready for the pub, then, Carol?' another lady, resting on a walker, asked.

'Just heading there now, Phyllis. Do you need a lift?'

'No, I'm all right, dear, thanks. Hello, Jed, love. You all right?'

'Hey, Phyllis,' Jed said, bending to place a kiss on the papery cheek. 'You holding up?'

'Yes,' she nodded, but tears filled her eyes. 'He was a grand lad, was our Bert.'

'He was certainly that,' Jed agreed and his hand squeezed my own almost imperceptibly before we headed back to the car and on to the pub.

* * *

An hour later, Jed got about his sixth enquiry as to whether Hector would still be coming to visit the home.

'I really don't know. I was told someone in the family has taken him. I guess it just depends on them.'

'Right. Yes, of course.' The man who'd asked did his best to put on a brave face but it had clearly been an emotional day, and both Bert and Hector had meant a lot to all of these friends. 'Hang on, let me see what I can find out?' He clapped the old man gently on his shoulder. 'You OK here for a minute?' Jed asked.

'Absolutely,' I smiled and turned to the man who'd enquired about the dog. 'I'm Milly.'

'Gerald.' He held out a hand to me. 'Everyone calls me Gerry.'

'Hello, Gerry. I take it you're fond of Hector's visits then?'

'Oh, that dog is such a bright spot in our week. It can get a bit dull, you know. I'm sure you young things probably think we don't need a lot of excitement in our lives, but I tell you, everything can get a bit samey when you're just sat there day after day.'

'I don't think that at all, and I'm sure it can. I think that's true of anyone, whatever your age. Did you ever have your own dog?' I asked, trying to draw him out some more.

'Years ago. Before the home. Mutley, I called him. Could be a little bugger at times. Stubborn as a rock but loving as anything.' He let out a sigh. 'I had to rehome him when I had to go into the home. Broke my heart.'

'Oh, Gerry. I'm so sorry. I can see why Hector's visits mean so much.'

He nodded and gave a smile. 'Jed'll sort it. He's a good lad. You've found yourself a good one there.'

'Oh... no, we're not... a thing.'

'A thing?'

Probably not the best choice of words.

'You're not courting, you mean?'

'No. Exactly. We're just friends. Old friends.'

'Right.' There was something in the way he said it that made me think he didn't believe a word of it. But then perhaps it was just a generation thing. Now men and women being friends was far more normal, but when Gerry and the others were our age, it probably wasn't quite so common. I looked over to where Jed was now standing with the small huddle of family. They'd all filled their plates from the spread Carol had organised with the pub and had busily demolished the offerings that they'd initially 'felt no need for'. Right now, however, it was easy to see the tension vibrating from Jed and the defensive stance of the others. Apart from the young woman who'd been on her phone during the service. She was just looking up at Jed from under thick false lashes and blatantly undressing him with her eyes. If anyone needed signing up for lessons on how to behave appropriately at a funeral, it was this one.

Jed ran his hand back over his hair and spoke some more, his hands moving more rapidly as they often did on the odd occasion he got worked up. I wondered whether I should go over but, as I pondered this, he gave a quick shake of his head and turned on his heel and strode back towards us. I couldn't remember the last time I'd seen him this angry. Actually, I could. And when I'd got back that night he'd booked himself into a hotel so that I could clear my stuff from the flat in peace.

33

'We have to go,' he said, his eyes blazing into me.

'OK,' I said, lifting my coat from the chair behind me and slipping my arms in. 'Where are we going?'

'Jed?' Carol asked, hurrying over, having apparently also seen the exchange. 'What's wrong?' Charlie, Gerry and a few others had now gathered around.

'I need to find Hector.' His muscles were taut, and his normally mischievous eyes were stern and determined.

'Find him? But I thought the family were taking care of him? And Charlie always said he'd made arrangements for him should he go before Hector.'

'Yep. Well, they seem to have ignored that. I need to get on to my solicitor and see what we can do to find out what he did about that.'

'So, where is he?'

'I don't know.'

The look of shock and upset on the faces of those around me sliced through my heart.

'This family's idea of looking after Hector was to tell the police to take him to a shelter.'

'A shelter?' There was a distinct wobble in Carol's voice. 'Which one?'

'I don't know. The police asked if they wanted to know where he'd been taken and they said no. Right now, I don't have a lot to go on. I need to make some calls.'

'Go, go!' Charlie and Carol hurried him out towards the door.

'Look after him.' Gerry patted my arm as we left.

By the time we'd got to the car, Jed had put out three calls to various contacts, and sent several messages.

'How do you know where to start?' I asked.

'I don't. I'm just starting somewhere.'

That seemed as good a plan as any.

'Is there anything I can do?'

'Not at the moment, thanks,' he said, distract-edly, as he wound his way through the traffic. 'Maybe just offer up a few prayers.'

'Your mum might be the better one to do that. I think she has more of a direct line than me.'

He glanced over and smiled. At least that was something.

Two hours later we'd tried various shelters in the vicinity of Charlie's place but no one had received a dog answering Hector's description. Jed was more agitated than I'd seen him in years. This dog meant a lot to him and I had a feeling it was more than that. It was the connection to Bert. The memories. He'd lost a friend. An older man he'd been able to relate to, share jokes and wisdom with. Perhaps a kind of father figure. And now he'd lost the one thing that tied them together. Hector.

He stabbed at the answer button when the phone in the car rang again.

'Jed? It's Jakob from Battersea.'

'Hey, Jakob. How you doing, buddy?'

'Not so bad. I hear you're looking for a dog?'

'A particular dog.'

'I think we might have him. Airedale, right? Between three and four years old?'

'Yes!' Jed's face lit up. 'You have him?'

'Yeah. Looks like he was dropped off by the police about ten days ago.'

'He's not on the website. I checked already.'

'No. He's not really in any state to be rehomed at the moment.'

'What? Why not? He was fine.' Jed's jaw was clenched and his fingers had tightened on the wheel.

'He's not taken to kennels well. Seems pretty depressed and is barely eating. The staff are taking it in turns to sit with him but he's not really responding. I think he's a bit confused about what's going on. It's kind of sad.'

'Can I come over now?'

'If you think it will help.'

'If it's Hector, he knows me. Can I at least try?'

'Of course, anything that might help. It's kind of

heartbreaking. Seems like a great guy if we just get him out of this depression.'

'And then what?'

'If we can get him out of this, then we'll do some behaviour tests and assuming he passes all those...'

'He will. He's been an unofficial therapy dog for the last couple of years.'

'Then he'll go up for rehoming. If he's as good as you say, I can't think it will be long before he finds a home.'

Jed looked across at me momentarily. 'OK. I'll be there as soon as I can.'

'See you then, Jed.'

Jed pressed a button on the steering wheel to hang up the call and flexed his fingers on the wheel, releasing a little of the tension.

'Poor guy must be so stressed out. He's got no idea what's happening. And those... people,' he almost spat the words, restraining himself, although why I've no idea.

'Let's just get there first. One step at a time. Have you had any luck in finding out Bert's wishes for his dog, legally, I mean?'

'No. I've got a call in with my solicitor and he's

on it. There's absolutely no way Bert would have let this happen. Jesus!'

'You'll sort it. Don't worry.' My tone was definite. Sure.

We pulled up at a red light and he looked across at me, absorbing the words. 'Yep. We will.'

As we entered the doors at Battersea, various people said hello and waved. Jed was obviously popular around here.

'You come here a lot?' I asked.

'I've done some volunteering and fundraising for them.' He said it casually and I knew that meant there was a whole lot more to it than that. It wouldn't surprise me if Jed and his firm were a large donor to the worthy cause.

'Hey, Jed!' A stocky man of medium height with an eastern European accent and a blue Battersea t-shirt came striding towards us, hand extended, which Jed took, shaking it warmly.

'Hey, Jakob. Thanks for this. This is my friend, Milly.' We shook hands before Jakob waved us to follow him. After a few twists and turns, towards the end of a corridor, Jakob stopped outside a ken-nel. No sound came from inside, no dog bouncing as some others had as we'd passed. Curled up in the tightest of balls, his face to the wall, toys untouched around him, was a large pile of fur.

'Hey, Hector,' Jakob called softly. There was no response. Jed's shoulders sagged and the concern on his face was evident to anyone. 'Got a visitor for you.'

Still nothing.

'Hey, buddy,' Jed whispered softly.

At this, there was a twitch of ears. Jakob nudged Jed to try again.

'Hector, boy?'

The dog lifted his head and turned towards the sound. All of a sudden, there was a flurry of movement as he pushed himself up, tripping over his own paws, a crying, howly sort of noise emanating from him as he propelled himself towards the kennel door.

'Oh, my God. That's the most he's moved the whole time he's been here. Even getting him to go out for the necessaries was an effort.' Jakob was busy opening the kennel door and Jed slipped in, laughing as the dog shoved himself against him, as though he couldn't get close enough, still making the same sounds. It was as though Hector was talking to him, telling Jed what had happened and how sad he was. Jed hugged him close, words of re-assurance pouring from him, the smile on his face clear to see. As he turned towards me for a moment, the tears in his eyes were just as clear. I knew that look. Whatever he had to do, there was no way that dog was spending another night in this kennel. As brilliant as Battersea were, Hector was suffering. He'd lost his owner, his home and his way of life and he definitely wasn't coping. If he carried on not eating, he was going to lose even more weight than he must have done already, staying with Bert after he'd passed away with no one to feed him and then being so depressed and confused that he didn't want to eat.

'Can I take him home?' Jed sat back on the floor of the kennel in a bespoke suit that likely cost thousands. Hector clambered around him and sat as close as he could without being directly on top of him. 'Milly, come in.'

I hesitated. 'He might not like me.' The bond between the two was obvious and I didn't want to ruin anything now. 'I used to work for this editor sometimes and she had a chihuahua. It growled and snapped at me every time I went near it!'

'Don't take it personally,' Jed laughed. 'Chihuahuas don't like anyone.'

'I guarantee, this dog will like you.' Jakob, sitting opposite Jed in far more suitable clothes, waved me in, reaching over to open the door so I could enter.

'Hector, this is Milly,' Jed said.

Hector tilted his head at him before looking back at me.

'Come sit by me.'

I did so, Hector watching me, his fuzzy eyebrows twitching and raising as Jed told him how I was staying with him at the moment because I'd had an accident. The dog seemed to absorb all this and then, when I was seated as comfortably as I could manage, he clambered onto Jed, flopped himself down with his body on Jed and his head resting on my thigh. I reached out gently and stroked the soft fur. It was the colour of champagne with a black saddle shape over his back. His tail, curly at the end, flopped contentedly from side to side as his eyes gradually began to close.

Jed touched my head with his own. 'I think we can safely say he likes you.'

I looked up, feeling a warmth and a happiness I hadn't felt in years. It filled my entire being and for the first time in as long as I could remember I felt something else. Whole.

'So, can we take him?'

'There's paperwork that needs to be signed and I'd feel happier if he had a vet check before we released him to you,' said Jakob. 'It can really only be on a foster basis though. I can't just let you have him permanently today.'

'But he's clearly happy?' I said, concerned that this dog would be forced to suffer any more.

'I'll do what I can. But a foster placement is a good start.'

'I'll take what I can get,' Jed said. 'Thanks.'

34

Three quarters of an hour later, the three of us were sitting in the front of Jed's car. Hector had started off in the back but then scooted through the gap to the front once the door was shut, his soulful brown eyes searching us out as we prepared to climb in, apparently worried we were going to leave him.

'OK, just this once,' Jed told him as Hector settled himself into a curly ball of fluff on my knee. 'You all right?' He looked up from the dog to me. 'He's not the lightest of guys.'

'I'm fine.' To be fair, he was pretty heavy, getting on for thirty kilos from what Jed had said but, despite the fact I was slowly losing feeling in my legs, there was something comforting about the snuggly weight of his big, furry body squished up against me as Jed secured us both in and set off at a steady pace back across London.

'I assume they do let you have pets in your building?' I asked as I stroked Hector's now sleeping head about fifteen minutes later.

Jed flashed a look and a grin at me. 'When you pay that much money for a place, people generally don't like being told what they can and can't do in it.'

'Fair point.'

'But yes. I'm allowed pets. Just to put your mind at ease.'

'I wasn't worried. It's not my flat or my dog.'

Jed threw a quick glance over at Hector, who was snuggled up to me like an enormous teddy, and me contentedly cuddling him back. 'No, I can see you're not attached to him at all.'

'Oh, shoosh up and drive.'

It wasn't my flat and it wasn't my dog but for a moment, just the slightest, fleeting moment, I wondered how things might have been if they were.

We unloaded ourselves, let Hector water a

nearby tree then grabbed all the paraphernalia and goodies Jed had bought at the Battersea shop. He hooked the lead loosely over his wrist and took the heaviest stuff from the back of the car. Hector stood patiently, watching us as we prepared, then Jed called his name and we all made our way to the reception area.

'Evening, Mr Matthews,' the concierge nodded. 'Hello, Hector! It's nice to see you again.' He came out from behind the desk and gave the dog a quick fuss, which Hector showed his appreciation of by whipping his tail from side to side in a frenzy. 'You coming for a visit again?'

'Bit of a longer one, with luck,' Jed explained, hefting the gear he was carrying a little higher. 'Unfortunately, his owner passed away. I'm going to take care of him until we find out what provisions Bert made for him.'

The concierge tilted his head up to meet Jed's eyes. 'I have a feeling you won't mind if that particular process takes a while.'

Jed gave what he thought was a non-committal shrug but his face told another story. The older man nodded and smiled.

'Well, I'm happy to see him, although I am sorry about your friend.'

'Thanks. I'll see you later, Eamon.' I wondered briefly if everyone in that building took the time to find out the names of all the concierges and exchange conversation. Somehow, I doubted it.

We made our way to the lifts and wedged ourselves and the dog bed, food, toys, etc inside and I pressed the button for the penthouse.

'Remind me to call Carol when I've fed Hector.' Jed looked down at the dog. 'He's so much skinnier than he should be. I really hope he's going to eat.' The vet had given him a clean bill of health, apart from the fact he wasn't eating. Hector was allowed to come with us on the basis that that side of things improved. If it didn't, they'd have to have another think about what could be done.

'I'm sure he will,' I said, trying to think positively. Positivity had always been Jed's forte and the fact it wavered showed just how much he cared and was concerned. 'The vet said it's likely that he was just so unsettled with poor Bert passing away and Hector not being able to wake him up. Then he's taken away by people he doesn't know to a place he doesn't know. It must have been pretty overwhelming. He's somewhere familiar now and with you who he obviously has quite a thing for.' Hector was, at this point, sitting with one hip slouched a little against Jed's right foot. 'I can see this is quite the bromance.'

The lift made its soft, almost apologetic ping to let us know we were at our destination, like some incredibly tactful butler from a country house.

'I'm not ashamed to admit it. How about you, boy?'

The dog looked up at his new, if temporary, master, the tail wagging once again.

'No shame there, by the looks of it,' I smiled, bending to give the dog another fuss. Jed was right. Despite the thick fuzzy pale tan and black coat, you could feel Hector's ribs. I didn't know that much about dogs but listening to Jed and the vet talk, this was clearly not the breed's natural build. Catching the concern on Jed's face as he unpacked his new pet's things, I only hoped Hector would relax enough to begin eating. They'd both lost a good friend. It seemed right for them to be together now, comforting each other.

'Anything I can do to help?' I asked as Hector took off round the apartment for a good old sniff inspection.

'No.' Jed looked down at me. The dark charcoal of the suit with the faintest of faint window pane check woven into the fabric contrasted sharply with the ice blue of his eyes. He looked great in jeans but this suit definitely did good things for him. It was doing things for me too but I knew that probably was less good so I moved on. 'You've done more than enough today.'

'I haven't really done anything.' I thought back over the day. I'd mainly stood or sat around for most of it.

'Not many people would volunteer to come to a funeral.'

'Was that weird?' I pulled a face. 'It wasn't meant to be weird.'

'No,' he laughed, softly, a gentle melodic sound with a hint of sadness wrapped within it. 'It wasn't weird. It was just what I needed. Thank you.' He hugged me to him and I felt his warmth, both physical and spiritual melt through me.

'You're welcome,' I said, somewhat muffled by the expanse of body I was pressed against.

He pulled back and when I raised my eyes, he was looking at me. The glance lasted what seemed like a moment too long as he suddenly pulled the mobile from his inner pocket. 'I'd better call Carol and apologise for rushing out of Bert's wake after she worked so hard to arrange it.'

'Yep.' That was about all I could manage for the moment. I reminded myself that it had been an emotional day – and I hadn't even known Bert. For Jed it had been so much harder, dealing with both the loss of his friend and the possible loss of another four-legged one. The hug was just friendship and gratitude and the look... the look had meant nothing.

As Jed spoke to Carol, Hector had apparently finished inspecting the place and was now sitting contentedly at the window, watching a pigeon strutting around, pecking occasionally at the ground. He slid down into a lying position, his head now resting on his front paws, which he'd crossed. A large sigh emanated from him. He seemed calmer than he had at the kennels, taking in the world about him, no longer clinging to Jed's side as he had in there. He knew this place. He knew he was safe here and was able to relax into it. Perhaps I could learn something from this dog, I thought.

I'd fought with the thoughts of whether I'd been following the wrong path all this time, as others had hinted at. And when I gave in to the idea of being able to slow down, it felt like a knot unfurled in me. But then, if I really did give up on it all now, was everything I'd done, worked for... I glanced at Jed, still in conversation with Carol but now crouched down next to the dog, stroking his head... given up... Would it all have been for nothing? Was that time, that energy, those burned bridges, all wasted for absolutely no return?

Jed had finished his conversation with Carol, who had suitably berated him for paying for the wake behind her back, but gratefully. He'd shucked his jacket now and was preparing Hector's dinner. On tenterhooks, we both waited as the dog sensed something and came over from where he'd been patiently watching the same pigeon and took an interest in what his friend was doing. As the kibble hit the metal bowl with a ting and a ding, Hector's ears pricked up, and although he sat beside Jed, his bum was barely on the floor as his tail whizzed from side to side. Jed looked over at me, hesitantly but with hope shining in those ice blue eyes. This definitely looked promising. Mixing a little warm water and some of the meat from a dog food tin, Jed looked a natural. He'd clearly done this before and knew how to make it just right. And despite what the kennels had said, Hector seemed excited to get to it.

Bending, Jed placed the bowl next to one of water in a stand that lifted them off the floor a little, making it easier for taller dogs' digestion. To my surprise, Hector waited, his eyes switching from the food to Jed and back again.

'Go on then,' Jed said gently and Hector immediately began hoovering up the food, surprisingly daintily. We both watched him for a moment, almost holding our breaths in case he stopped as quickly as he'd started, but he continued, engrossed in his dinner. Jed snagged a charcoal biscuit from a selection of boxes on the work top and came and sat next to me. He didn't speak but his eyes said it all. Relief. Absolute relief.

Hector, unaware of all this drama, was now licking his bowl thoroughly clean. Once satisfied he'd done that, he had a quick drink then toddled over to Jed, his chin dripping a little trail as he did so. I pulled a spare hanky from my pocket, having gone prepared earlier to the funeral, and quickly mopped the dog's chin before he could drip all over Jed's highly expensive trousers. Bearing in mind he'd been on the floor of a kennel in them earlier, I knew Jed wasn't precious about the suit, but still. Hector seemed happy to let me tidy him up then plopped his bottom down and looked at us expectantly.

'What's he doing?' I whispered, with no idea why I was whispering.

'Waiting for his dessert.'

'Oh?'

Jed held out the bone-shaped charcoal biscuit. The dog reached out with his mouth, taking the biscuit so gently it made my heart melt. Once he had it, he slid down on to his tummy and began crunching happily away.

'He's so gentle!' I thought back to the snappy chihuahua and a Labrador that had lived next door to us growing up. She'd been lovely but could get a little over-excited about food, and occasionally forgot her manners. Hector, apparently, had perfect table manners.

'He's cute, right?'

I laughed. 'He is.'

The thoughts from earlier still tossed about in my brain but for the moment I chose to ignore them and took comfort from the simple joy of the dog and the gratitude of seeing Jed's relief that his four-legged friend seemed far more settled now he was in a home and not a kennel.

35

The next few weeks passed quickly as spring began to strengthen and melt into summer. Jed and I spent time together walking the dog and just chatting or watching TV or reading in the evenings. In a way it felt very familiar but it also felt very strange.

After too much wine one night, I blurted out a question as to why Christine never visited his apartment.

I saw the subtlest tense of his previously relaxed shoulders. Hector, lying across Jed's stomach like a large, furry hot water bottle looked round and gave a small whine. He'd sensed it too. When Jed didn't answer, I persisted.

'It's just that, for a couple, you don't seem all that... coupley.'

'We're fine.'

'So how come you don't spend much time together?'

'We spend enough.'

'She never comes here.'

'Her apartment is closer to the areas she likes to frequent.'

'So, you stay there?'

'Is this twenty questions? I think you're getting to your limit.'

I shrugged. 'Just asking.'

'Why?'

'What?'

'Why are you asking?'

Why was I asking?

'Just nosy, I guess.'

'Occupational hazard?'

'Something like that.'

'What are you writing?' He nodded at the laptop closed on the coffee table in front of me. 'I've seen you bashing those keys.'

'Oh... just bits and bobs. A couple of letters to

papers, opinion pieces, you know. Just trying to keep my hand in for when I get a job. Which could do with being sooner rather than later, to be honest.'

'I'm not rushing you out.'

'I know you're not, but you have a life to live and you've been more than generous already. I need to start earning some money and trying to get myself back on my feet. The doctors are happy with how I'm doing.' I peered at my wine glass. They probably wouldn't be as happy as I was about that third glass of wine, but on the whole they were pleased.

'I'm serious about not rushing. It's kinda nice to have the company.'

'Company is not something a billionaire is short of, I'm sure. Especially one that looks like you.' Jed looked away, a slight colouring to the light tan of his cheeks. 'And doesn't that just bring us back round to the same conversation. If my staying here has messed up your relationship with Christine—'

'It hasn't.'

'But you've just said you like the company, so you could have... better company.'

'What makes you think there's anything wrong with your company?'

I gave him a look. 'My company has no benefits.'

'It has plenty of benefits.' His expression was serious and I realised he'd missed the point.

'Not the sort of benefits I was referring to...'

The penny dropped and he gave a short nod. I waited for something more but it turned out that was his sole reply.

'I'm going to take Hector out for his ablutions. You look beat.'

'Beaten by wine. I seem to have lost my capacity for alcohol along with my job and all my contacts.'

'I'm sure all of those will return when it's time.'

I hauled myself from the slouching position I'd slithered to and rested my elbows on my knees, my chin on my hands, and looked up.

'When fate decides?' I raised a disbelieving eyebrow.

He put a hand down to haul me up. 'You know I don't believe in all that.'

'What do you believe in?' I asked, closer now than I'd planned to be to this man I'd once loved with everything I had. A man I was scared I might be able to fall right back in love with if I wasn't careful.

'Lots of things. I believe that we sometimes meet people for a reason. That they're in our lives to help us learn a lesson or help us move in the right direction.'

'Bet you didn't think you'd be meeting me again if you could help it!' A small giggle escaped, aided by the wine, punctuated by a hiccup. 'Oops. Apols.'

'It wasn't a plan, no.' He looked down at me. There was nothing harsh in his eyes and, for once, I couldn't read him.

'I messed up the plan.'

'Maybe you're not in charge of the plan.' He pushed my hair back off my face, where it had now fully covered one eye. His eyes lingered on me, one hand still holding mine from where he'd helped me up. I felt his chest expand and somewhere deep inside, I felt something flame.

'You should get some rest,' he said softly, brushing the recalcitrant hair back again. With that, he bent, kissed me tenderly on the cheek and turned away, calling the dog. When they left the apartment, I headed back to my room, telling myself it hadn't meant anything. But as I looked in the mirror, I could feel the touch of him, the solidness of his body against mine, and wished it hadn't felt so good.

36

A few weeks later, my hand drifted up to push the same bit of hair back from my face. I hadn't been to a hairdresser in months, hiding the fuzzy parts, which were growing still far too slowly for me, under caps and hats. However, the rest, once so neatly (and expensively!) kept in style, had been left to grow out. I really ought to try to do something about it but I was worried about spending the money. I'd been doing my best to make my savings go as far as possible.

Thankfully, with the help of Jed's books, the internet and a fully paid-up annual Oyster card I'd bought (thank you, past me) after an article I'd sold got syndicated to several other places, Hector and I had been out exploring all over London. We'd discovered parks and oddities and peaceful spots. We'd even had a little tramp along the side of the Thames, descending some stairs I hadn't even known existed and taken in a view of London from the shore I'd never seen before.

Let's face it, I hadn't noticed much from above this level either. I'd passed hundreds of people a day at times, walked by beautiful architecture, magnificent history and all of it had just passed me by entirely because I never took the opportunity to look up. A helicopter flew overhead and Hector and I both raised our eyes to the sky. I recognised it at as an air ambulance. Watching its path, I sent up a silent wish that whoever it was heading to or already ferrying to hospital would be OK. Yes, my life definitely wasn't where it was supposed to be, where I'd thought it would be, but the one thing I knew was that I'd been lucky that day. I just hoped the person that emergency crew were helping would be as lucky.

I tucked my arm around Hector now he'd finished inspecting the area, full of exciting new smells, and had come and sat next to me. I loved the way he'd sit as close as possible to me his body against mine firm and fuzzy and warm. He'd put the weight he'd lost back on now and the vet had passed him as fully fit and healthy. We were still waiting on news from the family with regards to Bert's wishes for Hector's care. They didn't seem that interested and Jed had asked his solicitors to redouble their efforts to find out who Bert had used to make those wishes legal. Apparently the lawyer, failing to grasp just how important this was to Jed, had told him that short of phoning every solicitor in London, they may not find out until something turned up in the house clearance. Jed, unusually sharp, had told them that they'd better start making those damn calls then. An apologetic voice on the other end had immediately acquiesced, clearly unwilling to risk losing an account that was likely worth a hell of a lot more to the firm than that particular lawyer, should he mess up.

Cuddling the dog to me, loving the weight of his head on my shoulder, I sent up another wish that he was able to stay with Jed. Somehow. Whatever it said in Bert's will, I couldn't imagine how Hector could be any happier or more relaxed than he was in the home that Jed had made for him already.

A plop of rain hit my cheek, then another and another as the sky darkened and the downfall began to gain some momentum. Quickly, Hector and I got to our feet and scooted back towards the steps, me holding his lead with one hand and the rail carefully with the other. A side effect or possibly a benefit, depending on which way you looked at it, of the accident was that I took more care now. I looked before I leapt, which probably wasn't a bad thing.

'Good job we visited your friends at the home this morning, boy, isn't it?' I said to him as we hurried along to the nearest Tube. Carol had rung a few days after Bert's funeral and asked if there was any way Hector would be able to visit. The old folks were missing their weekly visit. Jed had looked pained. The start-up had an important meeting which he'd said he'd attend with them upon being asked, and also had several important meetings of his own to deal with.

'I could go with him,' I found myself saying as I listened to Jed's apologies for not being able to make it this week, seeing how upset that made him. I knew, because I knew Jed, that if he could have shuffled things to make it work he would have, so they must have been absolutely non-negotiable meetings.

Jed turned to me.

'I mean, if that's OK with Carol? I'm going to be hanging out with him anyway so it's no trouble to take a trip to the home if you can give me some directions?'

Jed muted the call momentarily. 'You sure you don't mind?'

'Not at all.' I gave a shrug. 'Might be nice.'

It *had* been nice, as it turned out. It had, in fact, been lovely. It was great to see Carol again, in happier circumstances, and to see Charlie, Gerry and all the others that Jed had introduced me to at the funeral and wake. I'd only intended to stay about half an hour but over two hours later, I was still sitting there nattering, as Hector moved from person to person to say hi and snuggle for a bit. It became the first of several visits.

'Oh, it's so wonderful that you're bringing him to see us,' a lady called Doris beamed as she stroked Hector's champagne fur and he tenderly rested his head on her lap, covered with a pale pink crocheted blanket. 'We did miss him. And Bert, of course. I was telling your chap, Jed, once about how we had one of these,' she nodded at the dog and ran her hands down one silky ear, 'when I was a little girl. He was a big one, just like Hector, and gentle too. He'd lie by the door when my sister and I went to bed at night, like a big guardian teddy bear. Oh, I loved that dog. I really did. I was inconsolable for weeks when he passed away.'

I rested my hand on top of the one not stroking the dog. 'I can imagine. What was his name?'

She curled her fingers around mine for a moment. 'Murphy,' she replied, smiling, her thoughts clearly swirling back to a time long ago. 'He'd come from a litter of puppies an Irish chap had brought into the pub. That sort of thing happened back then.' She shrugged. 'My father had no intention of us getting a dog. He had enough mouths to feed, he said. It was always said as a tease, although it was true. We didn't have much money to spare most weeks. But Dad was a curious sort, so he went over with his mates to have a look at these little bundles of fur. Tiny, they were. Probably should have been with their mum still, really, I shouldn't wonder, but us lay folk didn't know things like that back then. Anyway, this particular puppy toddles over and sits right on his foot. All these blokes around him and he sits there. Right on the top of Dad's boots.'

She chuckled and I passed her a drink as it began to turn into a cough. 'Thanks, love,' she said, passing it back. 'He was a big chap, was Dad, but a right softie really. So, he reaches down and lifts this little scrap of fur up. Of course, that was it. Once he'd looked into his eyes, he was done for. It was funny, though. The way he wandered over and sat with Dad, out of everyone. It was like he chose us. Loyal as they came. They do say they choose you sometimes, don't they?'

'I suppose. I have to say, I don't really know too much about dogs. We didn't have one growing up and I was always too busy to have one in my previous job.'

She gave my hand another pat. 'Well, you're a natural now, by the looks of it.'

'Hector makes it pretty easy.'

'Yes, he's a good boy, that's for sure. So, you and Jed are keeping him?'

'Oh. No, there's no me and Jed. I'm just a friend. But I know he'd like to keep Hector if he could.'

Doris was looking at me. 'I've been around a while, lovey, and I think our Jed would like to keep more than the dog.'

I shook my head. 'It's complicated.'

'Only ever as complicated as you make it.'

I wasn't about to get into my disastrous love life with Doris, especially as they clearly all adored Jed. I'd had plenty of 'are you crazy' looks when I'd broken up with him before – some of them from my own mirror. I didn't need a repeat of that.

'Jed's happily seeing someone else, but,' switching the subject, 'as for Hector, Jed's still trying to find out what Bert's wishes were, but he doesn't know which solicitor he used to make the provisions for his dog's welfare after he'd gone.'

'Oh, that would have been Carltons and something. He's used them for years. I think he said his original will was done by someone else, nearer where he used to live with his wife, before she passed away. But anything in the last ten years or so would be them.'

'Doris! This is great. I don't suppose you know where they are? Or their full name?'

She paused, thinking. 'I don't know exactly where they are but their name is Carlton, Swindlers and Gentry. I remember because Bert said the name made him laugh and that was a good enough reason to use them.'

Pulling my phone from my bag, I did a quick search. She was right! There was a firm of solicitors by that name about twenty minutes away.

'Oh, Doris! You're a star!' I'd given her a big kiss on her cheek and we'd set off for another hour or two exploring before rain had stopped play. Jed had mentioned he was going to be pretty busy today but to ring if there was an emergency. I knew he'd be eager to have the information but didn't think it classed as an emergency. So, instead of calling him, I messaged him to explain what Doris had said and sent a link to the solicitors. Now it was up to him. I crossed my fingers for luck and sent it on its way.

Shaking off the rain back home, Hector sent a bit more my way. I grabbed a towel from the coat rack as we stepped inside and gave him a quick dry off before letting him free to do his customary scoot around the apartment to make sure everything was just as it should be.

His toenails skidded to a halt on the floor as one sky-high heel stepped out from the kitchen, shortly followed by the designer-clad body of Christine Goldberg, sparkling socialite and heiress to an absolute fortune. I say designer-clad. Perhaps partially designer-clad would have been a better term. And the designer shirt she was wearing was Jed's.

'Oh.' She looked down an autocratic nose at me. Hector got a similar look. He went to give her a sniff and a friendly hello but she stepped back with disinterest. His head tilted and I came to stand beside him, reaching down and ruffling the fur on his head, hurt on his behalf at the rejection. She turned her head to the kitchen. 'I thought you said your lodger was out?'

Lodger? Also, RIGHT HERE!

Jed came into view. Thankfully he was more dressed, but still on the rumpled side. Great. This wasn't awkward at all.

'Hey,' he said, looking almost as uncomfortable as I felt. 'I didn't think you were back until later?'

'No. I... umm, didn't intend to be. It started raining so we headed back a bit early.' I eyed the bottle of champagne, open, on the counter. 'Sorry,' I added. 'I can go out again.'

'No, don't be silly.' Jed's smile felt warm even as I felt a thousand icicles piercing me from his girl-friend's direction.

'You've rather ruined the mood now.' Christine let out a sigh and turned back, strutting into the kitchen on the thin spiked, red-soled heels, and poured herself another glass of champagne.

'Sorry. I thought when you said you were busy, you meant with work, it didn't occur to me you might have meant... something else.'

'It was work,' he said, almost too quickly.

I raised a brow and smiled. 'It's fine, Jed. I'm not the fun police.'

'That's a matter of opinion.' The WASPy accent drifted out. Christine had made a pretence of saying it under her breath but I was clearly meant to hear.

I flushed and began to apologise again but before I could open my mouth, Jed had turned his head slightly and I could see the tension in his jaw. 'Knock it off, Christine. She lives here too and she can come and go as she pleases.'

My stomach was churning. The atmosphere was uncomfortable and, for the first time, I didn't feel welcome.

'I'll go out. I can go and stay with Henry and Ava for the night.'

'Don't they have a permanent spare room?' the voice came again.

'Christine!'

'What?' she snapped, coming to stand beside him, still full of confidence despite being half dressed. I guess that's what money and no one ever saying no could do for you. 'Why do you even need a lodger? It's not like you need the money!'

'She's not a lodger!'

'I'm going to go,' I said, feeling almost sick with discomfort and a hint of something else I wasn't sure of and certainly wasn't about to admit to. Life was complicated enough.

'No!' Jed held out a hand.

'Great idea!' Christine's dark eyes flashed at me, answering at the same time.

'Hector?' The dog was by my side in moments looking as unhappy as I was at the tension now filling his normally calm home. 'Come on, boy.' I grabbed his lead again and quickly exited the apartment. I hadn't even taken my coat off.

'Off out again?' the concierge asked cheerily as she saw us heading out, only minutes after we'd returned.

I waved and smiled and hoped that would be enough of an answer. My mind was busy thinking about what my next step was. Christine was clearly unhappy about me staying and I wasn't about to get in the middle of something. I knew now I'd never totally lose the feelings I'd had for Jed but that didn't mean I wanted things flung in my face. And it also didn't mean that I wanted to be an obstacle to him being happy with someone else. He deserved to have that. From what I knew in the media, gossip I'd heard in my old life, and my recent encounter, I was pretty sure Christine Goldberg didn't deserve Jed, but that was his decision, and his alone.

37

I pushed open the shop door and felt the familiar peace envelop me.

'Hi!' Ravi's smiling face greeted me and his sister, Sunni, soon popped her head out from behind another stack of books. 'How's you?'

'Oh... OK.'

'That doesn't sound very OK. I'll make tea.' Sunni zoomed off before I could stop her. They didn't really serve tea but a few favourite customers got treats. I, and now Hector, had become some of those elite.

'Here.' She placed the tea on a low table and gestured for me to sit next to her on a worn leather couch while Hector munched his way through a couple of dog biscuits. 'Now, what's up?'

'What makes you think something's up?'

'One, your face, and two, we saw you pass the window in the opposite direction not ten minutes ago.'

'Maybe I just decided I needed to come to my favourite bookshop after all.'

Sunni fixed me with a look. 'I refer you back to my first point.'

'Which was?'

'Your face.'

'What's wrong with it?'

'It's saying something's upset you.'

'It's not supposed to be saying anything.'

She gave a shrug. 'Is it Jed?'

'Not really.' I sipped the milky chai. 'Well, sort of. More just an awkward situation.'

'Oooh, sounds intriguing.'

I gave her friendly bat on the arm and she giggled, high and melodic, which at least made me smile. 'It isn't intriguing. It's awkward and... yucky.'

Yucky. This was the best I could do? I had a

feeling I wasn't going to be seeing that Pulitzer prize any time soon.

'So, tell me.'

'Do you mind if I don't? Not right now?'

Sunni watched me for a moment then reached out, pressed my hands for a moment and shook her head. 'Not at all. Stay there as long as you like. And drink your tea.' She gave Hector, who by this point was now curled up in front of the sofa, his back pressing against it, a quick fuss and then bustled off back toward the stack of books she'd been working on when I'd entered. I looked down at the dog. He twitched a furry eyebrow at me.

'Either Sunni was just being extremely diplomatic and not prying, or she decided that no gossip was worth suffering that pong you just released.' He watched me. 'Couldn't you have saved that little gem for her highness back in the apartment?' Hector didn't answer, and instead decided it was time for a nap. I gave his side a pat. 'Maybe next time, eh boy?' I said quietly before glancing over at my friend. 'So long as Sunni didn't think it was me!' Hector gave a small snore and let off another.

* * *

I checked my watch and knew we'd have to leave soon. Ravi would be closing up and, although I'd contemplated asking if I could stay on their couch, and knowing they'd probably even agree, I had to get Hector back for his dinner at some point. I'd decided I'd just drop him off and leave again. Both Henry's and Ava's phones had gone to voicemail but I was pretty sure they'd call back before it got too late and I'd be able to arrange something for the night. They might even be able to help me come up with a plan for the future as it was clear I'd outstayed my welcome at Jed's, at least in Christine's eyes.

As I gathered my things, having paid for the book I'd started and was now halfway through, the bell above the door jangled loudly as someone rushed in from the rain that was now descending in torrents.

'Sorry, we're just closi— oh, hi, mate!' Ravi's voice called.

'Hey, buddy.'

I recognised the voice. The couch, me and

Hector were all hidden from the door behind a large bookcase and momentarily, stupidly, I wished it could stay that way. The tension from earlier zipped back into my body and I felt that wave of awkwardness wash back over me.

'Have you seen Milly today?'

'Yep, they're over there.' I could see the cash desk and Ravi standing at it, pointing in my direction.

'Great, thanks, pal.'

Seconds later, Jed was standing by the couch and an over-excited dog was winding himself round his legs and pushing into them as though he hadn't seen him for years. Jed crouched and gave the dog all the fussing he was after, or at least a good dose of it, before he looked at me. Playing for time, I thought. And I couldn't blame him. The easiness had gone. Popped like a balloon with one spiky red-soled heel.

'I've been looking for you. You didn't answer your phone.'

'Oh. Sorry. I had it on silent.'

That wasn't a lie. I had. It had vibrated so I had seen him call several times and chosen not to answer, not because I was trying to be difficult but because I was still stung from Christine's words and I just wasn't ready to talk. But now he was right in front of me and I had no choice.

'I was just getting ready to come and drop him off.'

Jed frowned.

'What do you mean?'

'I'm staying with Henry and Ava tonight.'

I hope.

'And I'm not sure I can take Hector. I haven't had a chance to talk to them but...' I drifted off as Jed's forehead creased more.

'What are you saying?'

'I'm saying I'm staying at my brother's. It's not difficult.' I suddenly felt tired and sore and snappy and I didn't need Jed pretending to ignore the massive elephant in the room. OK, so she wasn't massive. She was a size eight, and five foot nine, but it made me feel momentarily better to refer to her as an elephant. Metaphorically only, of course. I actually really like elephants.

'Why?'

'Oh, come on, Jed, you know why!' I snapped,

gathering my things. 'We need to leave. Ravi needs to close up.' I walked away from him, waving to Sunni and Ravi as I headed towards the door, Hector trotting by my side on the lead. Jed followed me out and we stood for a moment, watching the rain. Small rivers ran down the road as the drains struggled to cope with the sudden influx of water. I turned toward Jed and handed the lead over. 'Here, you take him back. I'm going to head straight to the Tube.'

'You don't need to do that.'

'I do and I am.'

'Have you actually spoken to Henry?' he asked, moving slightly to block my path. It wasn't intimidating and I knew he'd move if I said something.

'I don't need to.'

'They're in Paris.'

My head snapped up. 'What?'

'Remember, he said last week? Ava's parents are going to have the kids for the week while Henry and Ava go to Paris for a break.'

'Oh.' That explained things a little more. Henry and Ava had always been much better than me at unplugging. I had the number of their hotel, as would all the parents, which meant they had the freedom to turn their phones off for a few hours and just relax and enjoy each other's company in the city, childfree, for a while.

'Milly, come back to the apartment. Please.'

I shook my head.

'Christine's gone.'

I raised my eyes slowly.

'I'm sorry about what she said. Tact isn't her strong suit. Things just come out of her mouth a little uncensored. She doesn't mean it.'

Seriously?

'I appreciate what you're trying to do and understand that you'd want people to see your girlfriend in her best light, but I was there, Jed, and I both saw her face and heard her words. Please give me the credit to recognise the difference between a person being tactless and a person who knows exactly what she's saying.'

He remained silent and I knew I'd hit the bullseye.

'Come back. Where else are you going to go right now?' Concern threaded his voice.

'That's not your problem, Jed. It hasn't been

your problem for a long time! This was all a huge
mistake from the start.' I pushed him aside and
stalked off down the street. I had no idea where I
was going. Anywhere but that apartment. I'd dis-
tanced myself from being made to feel like nothing.
Like I was a nobody. Oddly enough I'd sort of got
used to it in my job when I'd told myself exactly
what Jed had just said – that these people were just
tactless. That they didn't mean what they said. But
they did. They'd meant it just as much as Christine
had. I might have barely anything to my name, but I
knew I was worth more than that.

The sound of a horn blasting coincided with my
body being yanked forcibly backwards. Shaken
from my turbulent thoughts, I looked up. A bus
passed by, soaking me with its wake, the driver's
eyes momentarily leaving the road in order for him
to turn and shake his head angrily at me.

'Milly?' Jed's concerned voice drifted into my
conscious. 'Milly?'

I realised his free arm was wrapped around me,
soaked from the rain while Hector looked between
the two of us, clearly sensing all was not well as he
pressed up against me. His fur was all tight curls

and he'd almost shrunk in size as it lay flat against his body.

'I'd have looked,' I said, trying to calm the shake I felt throughout my body. The bus, the horn, the people, the noise. 'I would. I wouldn't have...'

'OK.' Jed nodded. 'I know. Just me overreacting, I'm sure.'

'Thanks, though.' The words sounded stiff and unnatural. Suddenly all I wanted was to go home. But I wasn't really sure where that was. Or if I even had one.

Still shaken, and unsure and unable to think what to do, I gave in and we walked the short distance back to the apartment saying little. Hector looked between us from time to time, as though sensing the ripples in his previously calm pond. Jed leant over and gave him a couple of reassuring pats on the side as we waited for the lifts.

'You OK?'

I nodded but inside my brain was roaring. The noise from outside was still overwhelming me in the quiet of the foyer. The sound of the horn was still ringing in my ears despite the heavy glass doors insulating us from it all. I'd lost my focus and

I'd been taken right back to the accident. I'd told Jed I would have looked before I stepped off the kerb and he'd gone along with that. But I didn't remember if I'd already begun stepping out... Would the bus driver have sounded his horn if I was still on the pavement? Was he just making sure? Had Jed really overreacted or had he possibly just saved my life?

38

'Did I step off the pavement?'

'Huh?' Jed looked down at me as the lift doors closed with a whisper.

'Just now. Did I actually step off the pavement?'

He hesitated and I felt a rush of anger flow in from nowhere. 'It's not a difficult question, Jed! Did I actually step into the road just now, yet again, or were you actually overreacting?'

The doors opened at the penthouse but I stayed in the lift.

'Aren't you coming in?' he asked, one hand holding the doors open. My eyes drifted to the front door of the apartment. Jed's gaze followed momentarily before he focused back on me. 'You didn't step off but I wasn't sure if you were going to. I panicked and I grabbed you. I'm sorry if it freaked you out.'

'But the bus driver?'

He shrugged. 'Maybe someone's stepped out in front of him before. Or someone in the previous street just did and he had to brake suddenly. Maybe he's friends with the guy who was driving the one who hit you before? Maybe he's just super cautious and observant and was being better safe than sorry. There are lots of explanations.'

'I can't even be trusted to cross a road. I've got no job, no home, no friends and my niece has more road sense than I do!' Tears filled my eyes and my nose had begun to run, adding to the massive headache thumping in my temples.

'Come here, honey.' Jed reached for my hand, despite the fact he'd just seen me wipe my nose on the back of it. With the gentlest of tugs, he pulled me from the lift and wrapped me in his arms. 'You're doing just fine. I'm sorry if I made things worse. I saw you by the edge of the sidewalk and my mind spun out of control. I panicked.'

'Wouldn't want to lose your lodging income. Not that I pay you.'

'You take care of Hector much of the time. That's worth a lot.' He stood me back a little so that he could look down into my face, searching my gaze. 'But you need to forget what Christine said. That's not true and you know it.'

'Do I?'

'Yes. At least, you should. Come on, let's get you inside and warm and dry.' My coat, previously pristine thanks to Jed's dry cleaner, was still dripping, making a small puddle on the floor just outside the apartment.

'Sorry if you got extra wet, doing your heroic bit.'

He glanced down at himself as he unlocked the door. 'Don't worry about it. I wasn't all that heroic. I pretty much used you as a shield from the spray. You caught most of it.'

I gave a weak smile. 'Guess that makes us even then.'

'I'd say so,' he replied, indicating for me to go first.

The place was as warm and welcoming as before, but I couldn't shake the image of earlier. Christine posing there in heels and one of Jed's crisp designer shirts. Her remarks. Her look of disdain.

'Do you want to have a bath or shower or something to warm up while I sort dinner?'

'That'd be nice, thanks. Is there anything I can do?'

'Nope. What would you like to eat?'

'I don't mind. Whatever you choose will be fine.'

Jed gave me a long look.

'What?'

He smiled and waved it away. 'Nothing. I'll call you when it's ready.'

* * *

A couple of weeks later, I was still a little jittery but I'd done my best to quell the unhelpful thoughts, and a visit with Henry and Ava and the kids to the zoo had helped. I did have my phone out but only to take some pictures with the children, wanting the memories to look back on. But for much of the time, it stayed firmly in my bag and I noticed the world, and the people around me. I also noticed all those who weren't doing that. Noticed that they were surrounded by all this incredible natural history, and it was completely passing them by, just as it had passed me by for so many years. But I wasn't that woman any more, and I never would be again.

Henry had asked if Jed wanted to come but he'd had plans that day. The slight twitch on his face suggested to me they were with Christine and he did seem genuinely upset that the arrangements had clashed. I believed him. I'd seen him with my family. Jed wasn't the type to fake emotion. His connections were deep. I guess that was part of what I struggled to understand about his and Christine's relationship. It just seemed so... casual. And casual was not Jed's style. He was all or nothing. I'd loved that about him. I'd never had to second guess how he felt about me. He made sure I knew. But things changed. I changed. And maybe he had too. Maybe I'd been instrumental in that. Whatever it was they had, I guess it worked enough for the man he was now. And it sure as hell seemed to be working for her.

*　*　*

'A party?'

'Yeah, I'm sorry it's so late notice. I didn't even know it had been planned until a friend messaged me checking the time.'

Jed had just informed me that there was to be a party tomorrow night at the apartment. He didn't exactly look thrilled at the prospect.

'You don't look too happy about it.'

'I'd have liked to have been consulted about a party being thrown in my own apartment, I admit.'

'So, cancel it.'

'I can't. It's for my birthday.' He made a gesture, raising his palms.

'Couldn't she have held it at one of her many homes?' I sniped, probably not very attractively.

'It seems not.'

I gave a snort.

'What?'

'I'm just amazed at the way you let her walk all over you.'

'I don't let her walk all over me.' Jed's accent

grew a little thicker, although his voice remained calm.

'You do! She's used to everyone saying yes to her, and you're exactly the same. Whatever she does, she gets away with. However rude she is, she gets away with it. Just because she has money. But I guess she has other attractions that work on you as money isn't an issue. Unlike your lodger.'

'Oh, man! Are you still going on about that? I apologised already!'

'I haven't mentioned it since that day and the whole point is you shouldn't be the one apologising!'

'She's sorry.'

'Oh, no she's bloody not. Even you must be able to see through that, Jed. If you can't, then you're not the man I knew.'

'Maybe we're both different people now.'

'I think we are. I, however, feel like I'm an improved version.'

'And I'm not? Is that what you're saying?' The Louisiana drawl was thick now.

'No. I'm just saying some of the company you keep is questionable.'

'Well, as you chose not to be that company four years ago, I guess that's not really your concern now, is it?'

'Nope. I don't actually give a shit. Have fun at the party.'

'Where are you going?'

'I don't know.'

Jed took a deep breath, the broad chest expanding momentarily before he blew it out slowly.

'Look, I'm sorry. I don't want to fight. You're invited to the party.'

'Oh, really? Christine invited me?'

'I invited you. I want you to be there.'

'They're not my sort of people.'

'You don't know them.'

'If they're like her, then I do. I've met enough of her type, and I don't want to be here. I'm sorry.'

'Just for a little while, then? I don't want you to feel you're not part of things. You live here too. Some are my own friends and they're all decent people. I promise. Ravi and Sunni are coming with their partners, too. If you don't feel up to it after a while, then feel free to go and lock your door. I just... it might be nice for you to meet some more people. Make some friends.'

I doubted that anyone in Jed's circle would be interested in being friends with someone way down the ladder like me, but it would be nice to socialise with Ravi and Sunni. I'd had to stop going into their shop quite so much as the stock presented too much temptation and, although I'd managed to sell a few of the pieces I'd begun writing, I was a long way from having income I could really class as disposable. I tried to pay my way as much as possible with Jed, getting groceries, and paying for takeaway if I ordered. He'd objected to start with, but soon realised that I needed to do this. He still flatly refused to take any money for the rental of the room, though, saying that my dog-sitting duties more than covered that. I knew the price to rent a slightly tacky room so, although I guessed dog-sitting fees in London were probably pretty high too, I was fairly sure I was coming out of that particular deal better off.

* * *

The party wasn't as bad as I'd feared. I'd given Jed his present in the morning. A copy of the latest Lee Child that he'd mentioned he hadn't got around to buying yet. He'd always been a huge fan of the author and when I saw his shelf was missing the latest, I did some vague enquiring as to whether he was still into him, wrapping it up in a general conversation about books and authors. I next spoke to Ravi, who managed to track down a signed copy from one of his contacts, making it that extra bit special.

'This is brilliant, Mils. Thank you.' Jed's smile widened as he saw the signatures of the joint writers, Lee Child being in the process of handing the reins of Jack Reacher to his younger brother. Both had signed it. Jed gave me a kiss on the cheek and wrapped me within a huge hug. 'I kind of wish this thing wasn't happening tonight so I could start it!'

I grinned. 'You'll get to it soon enough.'

* * *

Looking around the room, that certainly didn't look like it would be anytime tonight. This lot looked set to be partying for many hours to come. I'd spent some time with Ravi and Sunni and their partners before they'd all headed back to collect their respective children from the grandparents. It was fairly easy to tell who were Christine's friends and who were Jed's. As he'd promised, the ones he introduced me to were pleasant and chatty and I'd had a good natter about books with someone who owned a publishing house. But we hadn't talked work. Instead we'd talked about books we loved solidly for forty-five minutes and it had been great. Until the accident, and finding Ravi's shop and the local library, I'd forgotten how much books had been a part of my life. I'd escaped into them for fun as a child and now I was using them as an escape from the uncertainty of my future. The man saw someone else he knew, excused himself and melded into the party. I moved to the window and looked down on the city below.

'Did you tell him about the book you're writing?' a deep, soft drawl whispered closely. I felt the tips of my ears, thankfully hidden by my hair, go pink.

'What book?' I asked, not turning.

Jed moved in front of me, lifting a fresh glass of champagne from a passing server, handing it to me.

'Thank you.'

'So? Did you?'

'I don't know what you're talking about,' I said, burying my nose in the coupe glass. When I looked up, Jed was grinning at me.

'Yeah, you do.'

'Have you been spying?'

His head tilted a little to the left and one brow rose.

'No, sorry. I don't know why I said that. How did you know?'

'Just an educated guess. You've been sending pieces off, I know. But when you're working, at times you have a different look on your face. Like you're somewhere else. And you're super secretive about that notebook. You always close it when I might be coming near the table. Subtly, of course. Except it got so often, it made me begin to wonder what you were up to. And then I remembered you used to say you'd love to try fiction one day.'

'You remembered that? That was years ago.'

'It was. But I hadn't forgotten. I'm glad you're doing it.'

'Thanks.'

'How's it going?'

I gave a shrug. 'It's still a bit of a mess. I'm sort of just telling myself the story at the moment. Hopefully I might get something half-decent out of it one day. Depending on circumstances.'

'If you're enjoying it, you need to make time to do it, whatever happens.'

'Easier said than done.'

He pulled a face.

'So, what's it about?'

'I'm not telling you.'

He wiggled his brows. 'Oooh, is it naughty?'

I let out a laugh with a burst, trying to keep the bubbles from the champagne I'd just sipped from going up (or coming down) my nose. 'No, it's not naughty!'

'Damn. So why won't—'

'Hello.' Christine appeared and slid her arm possessively around Jed's waist as she kissed his cheek, lingering a little too long and then making a big deal about the lipstick she'd left on there. There wasn't any but I got the point. 'You two look like you're having fun. Can anyone join in?'

If he told her I was writing a book, I would kill him on the spot, birthday or not.

'Just something Hector did earlier,' he said, easily, exchanging a brief, private look with me.

'Oh.' She frowned. At least, I guess she did. Her brow didn't move but her lips pouted. Then her eyes fell on the book I'd bought Jed, lying on a small side table nearby. 'Huh, you have it already.'

Jed opened his mouth to speak but she was there first. 'Oh, well. I was going to wait but I can't. There's two parts to your birthday present. I'm pretty sure you're going to like the first and I know you're going to love the second.' She dropped her voice on the word love and I found an especially interesting part of the ceiling to study.

'So, you've ruined it a bit already having this,' she pointed at the book, 'but never mind. It doesn't matter too much as I have something much better.' Christine stood her champagne glass on the dust jacket of the book, the condensation leaving a ring on the paper. Quickly, Jed picked it up and wiped it dry on his shirt. She rolled her eyes.

'So, Daddy has a friend of a friend, oh, it doesn't matter,' she flapped her perfectly manicured hand. 'So, next week you and I are having dinner with Lee Child and his wife!'

'What?' Jed's mouth dropped open a little.

'I told you it was much better than just a silly old book.'

'Wow!' Jed looked at me, still holding the book in his hand. I gave him an encouraging smile and really hoped that Jed actually got a chance to talk to the man he'd always admired.

'Where's that dog of yours?' Hanif, one of Jed's friends I'd met earlier, asked Jed, accidentally stomping on Christine's triumph. She flashed him a dirty look. He shrugged it off and I tried not to smile.

Jed looked around. 'I don't know. He should be here somewhere.'

'I shut him in one of the bedrooms. He was on the couch. I didn't want dog hair all over our guests' clothes.' Christine brushed a non-existent piece of lint from Jed's shoulder. 'I know you're more re-laxed about these things but some of the clothes in here are worth a fortune.' She gave me a glance then looked away. My top was Gucci, but it was two years old. It may as well have been off a market stall in Christine's eyes. 'We don't want anyone getting dog hair all over them, do we?'

Jed had moved a step apart. 'You shut him in a room?'

Hanif gave me a quick glance, pulled a face and made a fast exit the way he'd come. Smart man.

'It's not a big deal, Jed,' Christine said, glancing around, her smile fixed at the other guests around them. I hovered, unsure how to make a subtle exit and wishing I'd tagged along with Hanif.

'It *is* a big deal. My dog is allowed anywhere he damn well pleases and I don't give a shit if *your* friends get hair on them. If they're that bothered, they shouldn't wear the precious clothes outside. Hector's not a shedder, anyway.' His voice was quiet but serious. 'Where is he?' He began to walk away.

'I'll go,' I said, seeing an opportunity for escape. 'I'll take him out for a walk.'

'Thanks, Milly,' Jed smiled, touching my arm briefly.

Christine remained silent, her nose tilted in the air.

I headed back towards the kitchen and grabbed a couple of dog treats and an extra poo bag, just in case. Finding Hector curled up on my bed, looking very forlorn, a few choice words flew about my head. He had no bed in there. The fact he was on mine was very unusual and he shot off, his button eyes then raised to me, worrying he was in trouble. There were no toys in there either. She'd just shoved him in and shut the door. At least she was equal opportunities – animal or human, Christine Goldberg could be thoughtless to all.

I took him out to the hall and attached the lead to his collar. As I slipped my arms into my coat, I heard low voices close to the doorway of the next room.

'I don't know what you're so upset about! It's just a dog. I put him out of the way, that's all.'

'He wasn't in the way! And he's my dog, and it's my apartment. You should have said something.'

'I'm not used to having to ask permission for things.'

'It's not asking permission. It's called discussion. It's what people do.'

'Fine. I'm sorry.' Her voice was placating now.

'Can we go back to the party now? We're supposed to be having fun for your birthday. I don't want to fight.'

I headed out and closed the door behind me. The evening was mild and Hector and I took a good long walk around the area, nodding at a few other fellow dog walkers out for their evening perambulations. It was a relief to get out of the apartment for a while. I knew I needed to get back to finding a way to fund somewhere else to live. Jed was with Christine and she was clearly unhappy at the arrangement. Tomorrow I'd redouble my efforts to find some more work opportunities and start replenishing my living fund a little quicker.

39

Having stayed out as long as possible, I could see even Hector was ready to head back. We entered the apartment quietly and I took him in on the lead to get a drink, quickly mopping his chin before it could drip anywhere.

'You OK?'

I turned. Jed was behind me. 'Yeah, we're fine.'

'Was he all right?'

'He looked a bit fed up when I went into my bedroom but he's fine now.'

'Thanks.'

'No problem. I'm sure she didn't mean to upset you. Maybe she just doesn't really do dogs much.'

'You'd never had one either.'

'I learned.'

'You're a natural.' He smiled and gave Hector the fuss he was pushing against his leg for.

Suddenly the chatter fell to silence as the high-pitched ting of a fork against crystal rang out. Both of us turned to where Christine was standing in the middle of the living room. Centre stage. Her natural place.

'Could I have your attention, please?' She smiled widely and posed happily as she made the announcement. 'Where's the birthday boy?' Seeing him next to me, she called him over, her gaze cooling a little as it fell on me. For a moment I told myself I was being paranoid, but a couple of exchanged glances near me told me I hadn't imagined it at all. As the first bars of 'Happy Birthday' rang out, I took Hector into my room, along with his bed and all his favourite toys and settled him in. He placed his favourite soft toy between his jaws and began mouthing, his eyes soon closing with the soothing motion, his paws wrapped around it.

A few moments later, we both jumped as an almighty cheer erupted from the other room. I guess Christine's second present really was a good one. I gave Hector a few strokes until he settled again, put my noise-cancelling headphones on and got ready for bed.

* * *

The next morning, Hector and I were out early. I had no desire to bump into a victorious Christine parading around the apartment in even less than I'd bumped into her in before. And it had been Jed's birthday. Frankly, if I'd had anywhere else I could have gone or been able to afford, even the tiniest hotel room in London, I'd have been there now. As it was, my headphones had worked at shutting out the party and I was now sitting with the dog in the quiet of the early morning at a cute little coffee shop a certain distance from the apartment. I'd stay there for a while, making some notes on some articles I'd been thinking about, send out some enquiries on spec and maybe do a bit more on my novel. Then Hector and I could have another walk before making our way to see our friends at the care home. That should pretty much fill the day and keep us both out of the way.

I'd bought a paper on the way and began to flick through it, sipping my hot chocolate, when someone spoke my name. I looked up into the early sunshine. The man was vaguely familiar but I couldn't place him and I'd obviously lost my knack of hiding that because he laughed, even white teeth showing as he did so.

'You don't remember me, do you?'

I shook my head. 'Should I?'

He put a hand on his heart. 'I always hope that beautiful women remember me but I suppose that is more to do with my ego.' He held out his hand. 'Dmitri Vasilov. We met at Jed's party last night.' His accent was Eton and Oxford overlaid with a thin veneer of Russian.

'Oh.' I took his hand. 'I'm sorry. Of course.' I tried to play it down as though as I did remember him after all. He was quicker than that.

'You still don't remember, do you?' He laughed again and waved a hand. 'Would you mind if I joined you both?'

Why not?

'Please. And I am sorry I didn't remember you.'

He signalled to the waiter and placed an order, checking if I wanted anything else.

'It's fine. It was a busy party,' he said, once the waiter had gone.

'Yes. It was a bit.'

'We didn't really get to talk so it's totally understandable.'

'But you remembered me.' I pulled a face.

'I never forget a beautiful woman.'

I smirked and wiped some whipped cream from my upper lip. 'That's such a line.'

He studied me a moment. 'Perhaps. But true. And usually one that works.'

'I doubt that.'

'You'd be surprised.'

'I would.'

'Perhaps because most women I meet already know who I am.'

'And who are you?'

'I already told you.'

Should I know him? Was he in the movies? He looked good enough to be. And clearly he had money. The way he dressed, even casually, exuded a confidence and the distinct whiff of wealth.

'Vasilov?'

He nodded, now sipping at the espresso the waiter had brought.

I should know this. It felt like a test, and one I was failing. Once I'd have known and retained all this sort of information in case it came in useful. But the accident seemed to have knocked things other than the stuffing out of me. The doctors had said my memory function might be damaged. It was hard to tell. Only time would do that. I hadn't noticed anything to start with but in instances like this, things I knew I'd have remembered before now just floated in the ether, refusing to come to me. Henry had said maybe it was that I didn't need any of that crap in my head any more, and my brain was just being more efficient.

Then something began to trickle in. Vasilov. Russian. Oligarch. Two sons. Eldest Dmitri.

'Ohhhh.'

'There you go. Although actually it was quite refreshing for someone not to assume things before even meeting me.'

'But you want people to know who you are,' I teased him. 'You wanted me to know who you are.'

'I was trying to impress you. I've found it helps.'

I let out an amused huff of air. 'Not with everyone. Money isn't everything.'

'It's quite a lot. Especially when you have quite a lot.'

'But it doesn't always make you happy.'

'It makes me pretty happy.'

I couldn't help but laugh. Yes, he was slightly arrogant but he was also poking a bit of fun at himself.

'I can see that.'

'Do you have plans today?'

'I'm looking for jobs this morning and then Hector and I are going to visit a care home. His visits cheer them up.'

Dmitri leant down and gave the dog a pat. 'I can see how that would be nice for them.'

'Why do you ask?'

'I'd like to spend the day with you.'

I swallowed the mouthful of frothy chocolate I'd just taken. 'You're not backwards in coming forwards, are you?'

He frowned, his mouth smiling. 'I don't know that phrase.'

'It means you're not shy.'

He laughed again. 'No, shyness is not one of my traits. So, are you turning me down? Wait, I think I might need another coffee to help my ego to revive.'

I grinned. 'Somehow I think your ego is pretty resilient.'

'You didn't answer my question.'

'I need to find some more work and take Hector out.'

'It's a weekend. Work can wait.'

'Easy for you to say.'

He let out a sigh. 'What do you do?'

'I'm a writer.'

'Oh? Of what?'

'I used to be a fashion journalist but I... sort of stopped.'

'You had an accident.'

'How did you know?'

'Jed mentioned it last night.'

'Oh. Right.' My hand went to my hair, ensuring the slides were still in place, holding longer strands of hair over the parts that were now growing out around where the stiches had been. I'd have scars but once the hair was long enough I'd find a hairdresser who could help me find a style that hid them a bit more if I found they bothered me.

'So, what you do write now?'

'Various bits.'

'*Male* have been asking me for an exclusive interview for months.'

'That's nice for you.' I wasn't quite sure what the correct response was to this.

'What if I say they can have it but only if you do it?'

'What?'

'I'll give them the interview but I won't do it with anyone but you.'

I knew that *Male* used freelancers. I'd even done a couple of pieces in the past for them, but I wasn't sure they'd want anyone but one of their senior people on something like this if they'd been asking him for months.

'Why would you do that?' I asked, genuinely intrigued.

'Because I admire your work ethic.'

'I've not had much of one for the last few months.'

'I think that's forgivable considering you'd been in a coma.'

I fixed him with a look. 'You've been asking about me.'

'I have.' He was unapologetic. 'So? Do we have a deal?'

'What's the deal?'

'You interview me for the piece.'

'What do you want in return?' This was the bit that had me worried.

'You spend the day with me.'

'You are persistent.'

'I am. When it's something worth being persistent about.'

I shook my head and Dmitri ordered us another drink each, plus a selection of pastries.

Moving the paper to the side to make space as the waiter returned, I knocked it too far and it fell on the ground. Hector gave it a sniff, found it of little interest and went back to people watching. As I picked it up, a page fell open. I stared at it as I returned to my vertical position.

'Milly?'

I heard Dmitri's voice as though through a thick fog. He called me again but all I could focus on were the words in front of me.

THIS TIME IT'S FOR REAL

Below it was a half-page picture of Christine kissing Jed on the lips, clearly taken at the party last night. Her hands were either side of his face and, this shot, taken from the left-hand side, clearly showed the huge ring on her third finger. My eyes drifted back to the headline.

Dmitri touched my hand and I jumped.

'Sorry,' he apologised. 'Are you OK?' His gaze fell to the paper then lifted back to me. 'You didn't know.' He wasn't asking. It was a statement.

I shook my head, but it made sense now. The cheer from last night. The promise that he'd like her second present. That second present was a proposal. And clearly Jed had liked it very much.

40

'Are you still in love with him?' Once again, Dmitri was direct. 'You were together before, I understand.'

'No,' I said. 'I'm not.' I'd told myself this several times since that night he'd looked at me so tenderly. But I wasn't. I couldn't be. I wouldn't allow myself to be. 'I just...' Jed would be out of my life now. I had a feeling he would be out of Henry's and the children's too and that made me even more sad. I understood the control some people needed over their partner. What I didn't understand was how the Jed I'd known, the one I thought I still knew, could let that happen, but Christine was used to getting her way. I looked down at the dog. We were still waiting to hear back from the solicitors. Apparently Bert's paperwork had been misfiled. I only hoped Hector had a happy place to go to because it was clear that he wouldn't be welcome when Christine moved in. Once I'd thought Jed wouldn't have stood for that but he'd accepted a proposal barely hours after discovering she'd shut the dog away with no consideration. She certainly hadn't checked if he'd needed to visit outside. It occurred to me briefly that that was probably why she'd shoved him in my room. If he peed or did something more on the bed, it was only mine. And as I was only the lodger...

'Were you serious about your offer?'

'Yes.'

'Then let's do it,' I said, forcing strength and defiance into my voice.

'Great. I'll call now.'

'It's Saturday. The office is closed.'

'I have the editor's direct number.' He leaned forward conspiratorially. 'Like I said, I'm quite in demand.'

I rolled my eyes at him, determined to keep a lid on the emotions that were churning inside. 'My first question is going to be: how do you manage to keep so modest?'

Dmitri threw his head back and laughed as he dialled. After a short conversation, he passed the phone over to me. After another short conversation, I had a commission that paid more than I'd made in over six months slogging my guts out before the accident, and an offer of potentially more work for them, depending on how this went. I handed the phone back.

'I just need to call the care home and rearrange the visit.' I'd be sorry to miss seeing my friends and them seeing Hector, but they could be a little relentless in their teasing about Jed and I wasn't sure I could deal with that today.

Dmitri nodded, relaxed and in no rush. A few minutes later, I'd called Carol and apologised and said I'd get something else sorted. Perhaps it was Jed's turn to take the dog to see them, anyway.

'I just need to go and take Hector back to the flat first.' Suddenly saying 'home' didn't seem right. 'Do I need to change while I'm there?'

'You look perfect just as you are.'

I gave him a smile and a teasing eye roll but it

was actually nice to be flattered, even though I was pretty sure it was just another of Dmitri's lines.

'Would you like me to walk with you, or wait here? Or I can have the car collect you when you're ready.'

'If you don't mind the walk, the company would be nice.'

Dmitri seemed pleased by the answer, and he called the server over and paid the bill, refusing any contribution from me before we headed back to the flat. Nerves danced in my stomach as we rode the lift up to the penthouse. Stepping out, we walked straight into Christine, who'd obviously just left the apartment.

'Dmitri,' she said, with a cooing voice. 'What are you two doing together?' She looked at me as if this truly baffled her.

'I'm taking Milly out for the day,' he said.

'Oh, that's kind of you.'

I bit my tongue. Her tone was grating, insinuating that I was, once again, being looked upon as a pity case.

'Congratulations, again,' he said. 'You've made

the papers already. I guess someone last night was pretty quick at selling their photo.'

She hesitated, then flashed a smile. 'Thanks,' she replied before turning her snooty gaze to me. 'Do you know how long you're planning on staying here?'

'I...'

'It's just that, well, Jed's too sweet to say it but it wasn't supposed to be a long-term arrangement. He thought you'd be here a few weeks at the most, rather than months. And it has been a little... inconvenient for our relationship.'

I felt the flush creep up my chest and flare across my face.

'Jed's never mentioned anything.'

'Well, no, he wouldn't. You know what he's like. Always very generous to any charity case.'

'I'm not a charity case!' I shot back.

'It's nothing to be ashamed of, darling.' Her use of the word contrasted sharply with the icy tone in which it was said.

'I'm not ashamed. Jed was helping me out as a friend.'

'Oh, for goodness sake! You're not friends. He's

friends with your brother and has some gallant streak about helping out. Why would he want to be friends with a woman who discarded him like you did? And just because you've decided you want him back now doesn't change any of that. Luckily, he has someone now who knows his true value.'

My mind was spinning but my jaw was set. As I opened my mouth to reply, the door to the apartment opened and Jed stood there. He was dressed in his old jeans, one of his favourite checked shirts and his feet were bare. There were dark circles under his eyes as though he'd been up all night.

'What's going on?'

'Nothing,' I answered before anyone else could.

Christine flashed me a look, turned and gave Jed a wave, then gave Dmitri another kiss on each cheek before stepping into the lift. Jed's eyes shifted between me and his friend.

'You were out early.'

'Yes. And I'm going back out.' I unclipped the lead from Hector who trotted off into the kitchen and could soon be heard lapping from his water bowl.

'Oh yeah? Anywhere nice?' He was guarded, reserved. Not like the Jed I knew, but maybe I didn't really know him any more. If what Christine had said was true, as far as he was concerned, I was cluttering up his apartment, and what had meant to be a short stay had turned into a longer one. It wasn't like I hadn't been keeping an eye out, but prices in London were so crazy, nothing was even remotely in my budget.

But I was pretty much recuperated now. I still got tired more easily than I used to, but I wasn't due to see my doctor again for several months now and I could get there on the train. As I wasn't hounding the fashion set any more, I didn't have to be city-based anyway. I'd go back to the original plan I'd had of finding a cheaper area to live. The piece I was about to do for *Male* would certainly boost my coffers and I hoped that once the editor saw that one, I could convince him to give me more. The magazine had liked my work before and I'd make damn sure they liked me enough to continue using me. I had to.

'I don't know. I ran into Dmitri at the coffee shop and he's taking me out for the day. I've rung Carol and said I couldn't make the visit today but

perhaps you might be able to if you're free. Or another day if you're able to spare the time. As I won't
be around, it will be more difficult for me to continue with them, anyway.'

I kept my voice steady but inside I felt sick at
the thought of not seeing Hector's funny, fuzzy face
every day. I loved him so much, it hurt. I knew I
might as well admit now that I'd been trying to hide
from the fact that I still loved Jed too. I always had.
Even when we'd been yelling at each other, and
walking away, I'd still loved him. I thought I'd
packed it all away in a box marked 'never to be
opened', but somehow the tape had come off and
those feelings had drifted out and back into my
heart. But I didn't want them. I wanted to toss that
box and all it contained as far away as I could. Jed
had clearly managed to do that and all I was to him
now was a charity case. Yes, he'd been worried
when I got knocked down but, as he'd said, we had
history and it wasn't easy to turn that off. But the
rest of it, it was obvious now. He was famous for his
philanthropic nature and gestures. And I was, as his
fiancée had just so kindly pointed out, just another
of those. It was time to go.

'What do you mean, you won't be around?' Jed asked, catching my hand as I turned to go.

'I'm moving out.'

His eyes shifted back to Dmitri. 'Do you mind if we have a private chat?'

'I do,' I said, before Dmitri could answer.

Jed looked at me, frustration on his face. 'Can we talk about this?'

'There's nothing to talk about,' I said, lightly. 'You've been very kind letting me stay but it's time for me to get out of your way and move on.'

'You're not in my way.'

I'm sure as hell in your fiancée's way!

'Look, Jed. I have to go. I've kept Dmitri waiting long enough already.' Jed threw him a dark look.

'Do you know when you'll be back? I think we need to talk.' He shoved a hand through his hair.

'No idea. But there's really nothing to talk about. I got a job this morning so I can finally afford to move out and let you have your home back.'

Jed began to speak but then stopped again, his eyes shifting to Dmitri, who was doing his best to keep out of the way of the conversation and was now standing looking out of the window in the small foyer, his back towards us.

'I don't want you to get hurt.' Jed stepped close, his body almost touching mine, his mouth close to my ear as he whispered the words.

Bit late for that, I thought.

'He's a playboy. You don't know him like I do.'

'And I won't get to know him standing here, will I?' I turned away.

'Milly, please. I need to talk to you.'

I slid my hand from where Jed had caught the fingertips and turned to press the lift call button. 'I think it's probably your mother you need to talk to first. Your engagement photos are all over the papers already.'

Jed closed his eyes. 'Shit.'

The lift arrived and Dmitri indicated for me to go in first. 'Congratulations, by the way,' I said as the doors closed.

41

I'd seen this glittering life from the sidelines, but now I was a part of it, and I wasn't sure how much I liked it. Clearly it suited some people, like Dmitri and Christine who'd known little else, but it felt odd to me and out of kilter. Even though I'd been staying in the most beautiful apartment until very recently and knew that Jed was part of this elite, he'd never acted like it. He'd just seemed like the same old Jed I'd known before the meteoric rise to fame and fortune.

After I moved out, I'd found a tiny studio flat an hour and half's train ride from London that was available almost immediately. Dmitri had been kind enough to offer me a room at one of his family's hotels for the night but in the end, having popped into the bookshop to say goodbye, I'd ended up staying with Sunni and her family, relishing the fun and laughter and wonderful Indian food for the night before I could collect my keys.

Henry had called a couple of times when I messaged them my new address. I'd included a line saying that I didn't want to talk about Jed, pre-empting any conversations of that type. I thought I'd got over him before, but obviously something had lingered. This time I was going to do it properly and the best way to start on that path was to not fill my head with talk, pictures or thoughts of him. I'd kept away from the papers, kept off social media, and discussions with my family and new friends were limited to any other topic but him. It still hurt like hell and I'd had no idea just how much I'd miss Hector too. It was like I'd had part of my family ripped away from me and the pain was raw and intense.

'You're miles away,' Dmitri said quietly, in accordance with the hushed atmosphere of the restaurant. I'd seen him quite a few times now and

although I liked him, I knew it wasn't going anywhere. I had a feeling he did too. Luckily, neither of
us seemed to mind and were happy to continue to
see each other as friends.

'Not really,' I smiled and sipped at my wine.
'Just thinking about the interview. I'm so glad the
editor liked it.'

'Of course he did. I had no doubts. And two
more commissions.'

'I know! I can hardly believe they're sending me
to New York to interview Brad James. Thanks so
much for your help, Dmitri.'

He shook his head. 'This is all down to you. I
merely made an introduction.' We both knew he'd
done a little more than that but I did realise that if
I'd have made a hash of it they certainly wouldn't
have offered me more work or business class tickets
to New York. I tipped my glass towards him.

'Thank you. I'm grateful for the introduction.'

'But not *that* grateful.' A blush tinted my cheeks,
already not helped by the wine. He laughed. 'I'm
sorry. I shouldn't tease you. It's just you look so cute
when you blush. It's very refreshing. I thought it
was a lost art.'

'It's not an art! I can't help it. Believe me, if I could stop it, I would. So, you shouldn't tease.'

'You're right. I shouldn't. But it's so much fun.'

I gave him a light kick under the table and he laughed. 'Again. So refreshing. I don't think I've ever had a date kick me.'

'It's not really a date.'

'I live in hope.'

'Oh, somehow I don't think you're too hard done by.'

Jed was right. Dmitri was a playboy and it was a role he clearly relished. Obviously for some women the wealth, the power, the name itself was quite an aphrodisiac. He'd already told me that a few women would be more than happy to have him place a massive old sparkler on their finger.

'I'm not interested in that yet. I will be, in time. Or with the right woman.' He gave me a look that lingered a little longer than usual. 'But I'm still having fun.'

'You think marriage means that all fun automatically stops?'

'No, not at all. I think, with the right person, it can be the most fun of all, but I want to be sure that

I'm ready for it.' His face was more serious now. 'I don't want to mess it up. If I make that commitment, I want to do it right and for the right reasons with the right person.'

I'd known him for a little while now and we'd always laugh when he tried to pull a line, already knowing it wasn't going to work on me. But this wasn't a line. This was the real Dmitri Vasilov. I'd got a hint of it in the interview, and I'd been able to tease more of his personality out than the run-of-the-mill profiles had done. He'd teased me that perhaps it had been a bad idea saying he'd only talk to me as I'd got under his skin far more than anyone had in print before. However, when I told him even more people would adore him when they saw beyond the uber-rich playboy veneer and realised there was more to him than the shallow perception mostly circulated at present, he cheered up enormously.

'And now, time for pudding!' As if by magic, a waiter appeared at our table. I'd noticed this in several of the restaurants we'd been in. I don't know how they did it but it was a neat trick. I'd also noticed the press outside some of the places we'd been out to. When Dmitri had found out I'd never been in a helicopter, he'd immediately summoned his own up, and thankfully the weather had complied with a clear blue sky. We'd toured the skyline of London, flying a route down the Thames before turning off and heading over to Oxfordshire to one of his favourite restaurants. Apparently a photo had appeared in the media the next day of Dmitri with his arm around me, by the helicopter. I was told it looked intimate, but the truth was that I'd suddenly mis-stepped, trying to avoid a pile of sheep poo, and Dmitri had steadied me, both of us laughing about it. Of course, that wasn't the headline the media had gone with and even Ava had been on the phone asking about it. Explaining that it was not a romantic tryst but a friend catching me before I ruined a pair of four hundred quid suede shoes by coating them in poo, Ava laughed, but I could hear the slight disappointment in her voice.

No, Dmitri wasn't for me romantically. As a friend, however, he was fun and generous and occasionally cheeky. He operated in an entirely different world that suited him and that I was able to enjoy in short bursts, as his friend. I'd told him that first day I wasn't still in love with Jed, but I think he'd known even before I did that wasn't true. Christine had accused me of the same. It seemed that everyone had known but me. I also appreciated that Dmitri had abided by my request not to mention Jed when we met, even though I knew they would see each other socially. He'd made a couple of attempts but I'd stopped him and each time he'd held up his hands, honouring his promise.

I hadn't seen or spoken about Jed for several months now. Avoiding the media was actually refreshing. I saw the headlines occasionally at the train station or if someone held up a Metro during their commute on the train when I'd travelled into the offices of *Male* and been offered a position of senior editor. I loved the atmosphere of the office and feel of the magazine and the editor was warm and open and down to earth. Best of all, I was able to work from home for a good proportion of the time. There were still pressures but nothing like the crazy routine I'd been used to or that I would have had if I'd got the position at *Vogue* I'd been so desperate for I'd stepped in front of a bus for it.

I'd also finally finished my novel. It had proved

a perfect distraction when everything had come crashing in and once I'd done my work for *Male* and a few other freelance jobs, I took time to step away from fact and escaped into fiction – into my Victorian mystery, inspired all those months ago by the trip I had taken to Old St Pancras. It was another world, and one I could write a guaranteed happy ending into, even if I couldn't ensure my own turned out that way. The novel gave me a focus and an escape. And it gave me hope. It also gave me a contract for another two books and an advance. And I knew none of it would have come about without the accident.

I was healthier, had more energy rather than running on pure adrenaline, and could wear what I liked without worrying about how much I would be judged by those I was working for. I was also happier. I knew my heart wasn't healed yet and, in all likelihood, wouldn't be for a while. All that time I'd thought I was getting over Jed Matthews, I'd just been supressing feelings and that never ends well. Things have a tendency to spring back up, usually when you're least expecting them. I'd finally admitted that I'd hated leaving that day years ago but

I was too proud to talk about it. Instead I'd focused everything I had on work, with no space for anyone else and now, having spoken to my parents and Henry about my new position, realised just how extreme I'd become about it. They'd all been worried about me. Seriously worried. But all I'd seen, all I'd taken from it, was that they didn't care. That they weren't supportive of my chosen path, when actually the opposite was true. They'd cared very much. I just hadn't taken the time to look up and really see that. Now I did.

* * *

'Hi,' I answered the phone to my editor a few days later.

'Milly, got an assignment for you.'

'Fab, fire away.'

'The interviews on Vasilov and James have been some of our most read pieces. Circulation is up and bloody loads of hits online.'

'That's great.'

'So, got another one for you. Can you get up to London tomorrow?'

'Sure.'

'Great. Appointment's at ten o'clock. Claridge's. Reception will let you know which room.'

'Got it. Are you going to tell me who it's with or is it a surprise?' I laughed.

'Oh, sorry, I am a daft sod. Thought I'd told you. It's with Jed Matthews. Tech billionaire chap. Been trying to get one with him for ages.'

The laughter died in my throat.

'Thanks, Mils. Look forward to seeing the piece. Toodle pip.' And he was gone before any of the versions of 'No, I can't' could make it out of my mouth.

I sat staring at the phone. I'd done everything I could to avoid any talk or news of the man for the past several months and now my boss wanted me to sit face to face and do an in-depth interview with him. I couldn't. What if Christine was there? Gloating. Preening. Sneering.

So what if she is? I snapped at myself. You've dealt with plenty like her and worse over the years. And you can deal with her now if you have to. Just like you can deal with this job. That's all it is. Another assignment. Get the interview and get out.

Maybe it will be just what you need. Finally put a lid on the whole thing, once and for all.

Pep talk done, I went online and booked my train ticket for tomorrow. At this point, I'd have normally boned up on my subject matter. Found out some key achievements, his background, what he liked to do in his spare time and written notes to help me get below the surface. But this was Jed Matthews. I already knew him – far better than I wished I did.

42

I knocked on the door precisely at ten and heard the softly drawled, 'Come in.' Taking a deep breath, I entered. Two seconds later I was practically on the floor, having been excitedly charged at by Hector, who was almost folding himself in half with his madly wagging tail, his face pushing against mine as I knelt down to him.

'Hello, boy!' I whispered, trying to hold it together and hearing the crack in my voice. God, how I had missed this bundle of fur and fun and utter love. I hadn't expected him to be here. To be honest, I thought the poor pooch would have been sent packing pretty quickly after I was if Christine had anything to say about it. And she tended to have something to say about most things, it seemed. Plus, there were Bert's last wishes for him. I made to push myself up and a large, tanned hand reached out towards me. Ignoring it would seem petty. Plus, my thigh had gone to sleep where Hector had been standing on a muscle.

'Thanks.'

I brushed my dress down and made sure I had my 'professional' expression fixed on before I finally lifted my face to meet Jed's. The smile I'd loved wasn't there and there was a wariness in his eyes I'd rarely seen.

'Don't look so worried. It won't be painful.' I tried to lighten the moment but judging by the look on his face, it was going to take a truckload of helium to even get near doing that.

'Apparently not for you.' The words were soft and his accent was a little stronger. His face was more tanned than it had been the last time I saw him, too.

'Been on holiday?' I asked, trying again to disperse the distinct cloud hovering above us. 'You look tanned.'

'I went home for a while. Back to New Orleans, I mean.'

Privately I wondered how the introduction of his fiancée to his mum had gone. Bea hadn't seemed thrilled about Christine before, but then Bea was an open-hearted woman and if she saw that the woman made her son happy, I knew she'd have been her generous, welcoming self.

'I hope your mum's well.'

'She's good, thanks. Carol was kind enough to take care of Hector while I was gone.'

'He lives with you now?'

That devastating smile broke through as Jed's eyes turned to the dog, who now had his nose in my bag, seeing if there might be anything interesting in there for him. I felt bad that there wasn't.

'He does. The solicitors eventually unearthed Bert's paperwork and turns out that special provision he said he'd made for Hector turned out to be me.' As Jed bent and gave Hector's coat a ruffle, it was obvious that Bert couldn't have made a better provision for his pet – or his friend.

'That's really wonderful, Jed. I'm so pleased for both of you.'

The bright, intense gaze lingered on me for a moment before he replied. 'Thanks.'

'So,' I said, trying to shift my focus back to a more professional view, 'where would you like to do this?'

He shrugged. 'I don't know. Where do you normally do these things?'

'It's usually up to the interviewee.'

'Interviewee...'

'Yep,' I smiled, pointing my pencil at him. 'Are you happy for me to record this?'

'Is that what you normally do?'

'Generally. It helps me make sure I've got everything and that it's all in context. But if you're not comfortable with that...'

'I don't mind.'

Bloody hell, this was going to be harder work than I thought.

'How do you usually prefer to be interviewed?' I tried another tack.

'I don't.'

'Oh. But you have something to say? I know *Male* have been trying to get an interview for years but it's pretty well known you don't like to give them.'

'I don't,' he repeated.

OK, this was getting ridiculous. I let out a sigh. 'So, if you don't mind me asking, why did you agree now? Why am I here?'

'Because I needed to see you and you wouldn't return my calls. And from what I understand, you don't even want my name mentioned in your presence.' The flash of hurt that scanned his face squeezed my heart.

'Why do you need to see me?'

'Because you didn't even say goodbye. We never got to talk.'

'Jed, there was nothing to talk about,' I said, giving up all pretence of professionalism. 'There wasn't then and there isn't now.'

'Because of Dmitri?'

'What?'

'You and Dmitri. We all saw the pictures.'

'Oh, for goodness sake. You of all people know what the papers are like. We're friends and that's it.'

'Dmitri doesn't just make friends with someone like you.'

'Like me?' I bristled, 'What's that supposed to mean? Someone from one of the lower classes, you mean? It just goes to show what you know!'

Jed was holding up his hands. 'That's not what I meant. It came out wrong. He was asking about you at the party the moment he saw you. And usually what Dmitri wants, Dmitri gets. Especially when it comes to women.'

'Well,' I snapped, 'he didn't "get" me, not that it's any of your business.'

He shook his head. 'No, I'm sorry. You're right. It's not. I just didn't want you to get hurt by him.'

'Dmitri is nothing but kind to me. And clearly he does make friends with women,' I said, settling myself into a chair, as it seemed I'd be waiting for-ever for Jed to make a decision as to where this in-terview was going to take place. 'Or perhaps I'm just special,' I smiled. 'Shall we begin?'

Hector came and sat in front of me, settling himself down and resting his head on my foot.

'You *are* special,' Jed said, the words were soft and gentle and not helpful at all.

I did my best to keep my face neutral. My feel-ings were another matter but this was my job. A job

I liked and I was not going to let Jed Matthews screw it up for me.

'We really ought to get started. I'm sure you have plenty of other demands on your time today and I'd hate to end up rushing.'

Jed didn't move for a moment, then took the armchair opposite me.

'So, you're happy for me to record this?' I asked again, just as I had done with Dmitri and the other interviewees I'd now seen for *Male*.

He shrugged an OK.

'Great.' I set the recording going and put it on the small table between us, then began my questions. Jed was initially stiff and uncomfortable, but as the conversation continued and I steered it into areas I knew he was passionate about, he relaxed and the zeal I recognised shone through. Unfortunately, I knew I'd have to ask about something else he was passionate about and I wasn't exactly looking forward to it, but I was a professional. I could do this. I'd turn in another great piece, keeping my editor happy, which was my main goal.

'Do you feel—'

'Ravi told me you sold your novel.'

I looked up, thrown for a moment. I'd kept in touch with my friends at the bookshop, and they'd already told me they wanted to hold a launch party there when it came out.

'Oh, er, yes. I did.'

'That's great, Milly. I'm really happy for you.'

'Thanks. So,' I began again. 'Do you feel that...' I stopped as Jed got up. Hector pushed himself up off my feet and plodded over to him.

'Is something the matter?'

'Yes. This. I can't do it.'

Shit! He had to do it! I couldn't go back to my editor and say he'd walked out.

'We're nearly done, I promise,' I said, in my most soothing and persuasive voice. 'Just a couple more questions and I'll be out of your way.'

He turned back to face me, shoving his hand roughly back through his hair, worn a little longer than usual, as he did so.

'Don't you get it, Milly? I don't want you out of my way. I want you in my way all the time!' He spread his hands. 'I always have.'

43

I stared up at him.

'Please say something,' he said after a few moments.

My mind felt full and blank all at the same time. I looked down at my questions. They swam in front of me and I placed a hand on them as if to hold the words in place. I didn't know why he was saying this. It wasn't fair. I didn't want to be here in the first place but he'd got me here in a way he knew I couldn't refuse, just to say something like that. It wasn't fair.

'Do you feel that your relationship—'

'Milly!'

'Jed! Please don't. I need to get this interview done for my editor. You, of all people, know that now I've managed to get my career back on track, and in a healthier way, I don't want anything to mess it up.'

He came towards me, crouched down by the chair and I looked into those eyes that had so capti-vated me that first time. 'You know I would never try and ruin anything for you. I know what this means for you. And I was relieved to hear you seem to be in a much better, happier place now with work. Maybe with everything.'

'Ravi and Sunni talk too much,' I smiled and pulled my gaze away from his. This was easier when I wasn't looking straight at him.

'I'm afraid I have to admit I badgered Henry and Ava for some information too.'

I thought back to the instructions I'd given to my family and friends. They weren't to tell or ask me anything about Jed, but I hadn't stipulated the restriction worked the other way. It hadn't occurred to me that he'd even ask, and Christine certainly wouldn't have encouraged any thought or enquiry on that front.

'Oh. Right. Well, yes. Which is why I'd really like to just get this finished, if you don't mind.' I rushed on. It certainly wasn't the usual form to have the interviewee quite so close. He'd now perched on the small table that had separated us, and I could smell his aftershave. The one he'd worn years ago. I'd always loved it on him but when I met him again, he often wore a different one. A more spicy, sharper scent than this woody, earthy one that, to me, had suited his whole being better. But what did I know about that? What I did know was I had to get this finished and then never see Jed Matthews again.

'Do you feel that your upcoming marriage to heiress, Christine Goldberg, will give you even more exposure to enable you to get your voice heard about things you find important?' I lifted my eyes briefly and his brow was furrowed, as though he didn't understand the question. I rephrased it. 'You're well known for trying to avoid the limelight, whereas your fiancée appears to be happy to embrace it. Do you feel this could actually be an advantage in—'

'No.'

'Oh.'

Silence.

'Are you able to elaborate at all on that?'

He smiled for the first time. 'Yes. Quite a bit.'

'Great,' I replied and made a gesture indicating he should.

'I'm not getting married. I don't have a fiancée. Is that enough elaboration for you?' The words were spoken softly and felt like they were enveloped with a sense of relief.

I opened my mouth to say something but couldn't pick just one from the many questions whizzing around my brain, so I closed it again. Jed waited.

'Since when?' I eventually asked.

'Since the night of my birthday. We were never engaged.'

'But the cheer and the ring and... and when Dmitri and I ran into Christine at the lift, she told me that now she'd be moving in, she wanted me gone quickly.' I remembered the conversation and its sting. 'That you both wanted me gone. That you'd only meant a couple of weeks when you offered me the room and I'd already long overstayed my welcome.'

Thunder rolled across the blue gaze. 'Is that what she said?'

'Yes.'

'None of that was true.' He gave a small laugh that momentarily cleared the storm from his eyes. 'Quite the opposite, actually. Which probably explains why she was so intent on making you believe something else.'

'I don't understand. It was in the paper. That it was for real this time. And nobody's said that it wasn't.' I reached forward and paused my recording.

'Do you have to be somewhere after this?'

I shook my head. 'No, but I do need the interview.'

'Which I promise I'll finish. But if I didn't say something I was going to explode. Come on, let's sit somewhere more comfortable.' He put out a hand and I took it, letting him help me gently from the armchair and towards a cosy looking couch in another part of the suite. 'Do you want a drink or anything?'

'I'm beginning to think I need one,' I half laughed. 'But tea would be lovely.'

He grinned. 'I should have known that, really. I've lived here long enough. Tea is always the right choice, whatever the occasion.' He made a call on the hotel phone, placed an order and then came towards the sofa. 'May I?'

'Of course. It's your room.'

'It's your space.'

'Just sit down and tell me what the hell is going on!'

'Well, the party, as you know, wasn't my idea, but by the time I found out, it was a bit late to cancel on everyone. Some people were coming from pretty far afield. Of course, I had no idea what Christine had in store. It was, as a lot of things were with her, a bit of a PR stunt. She'd begun to see that she was getting less coverage in the media. People have short attention spans these days so she needed something to grab some more headlines.'

'And that was?'

'A proposal. But, of course, it couldn't be somewhere quiet. It had to be another show. She was the one who sent the photos to the papers. She had someone take photos on her own phone and she sent them off straight after.'

'So, you were engaged?' I said, confusion creasing my face.

He shook his head. 'I never said yes, Mils.'

'So, her second present to you was... herself?'

'Yep. But I didn't want to marry her. I've told her that from the beginning. I wasn't looking for anything serious. And neither was she. Yes, she liked me but she liked that I fit the status and could get the attention she appreciated even more.'

'Maybe she changed her mind. Was actually thinking of settling down after all?'

Jed pulled an amused face. 'Christine will never settle for one thing. And certainly not one person, at least not for very long. It's just not the way she's made. She's seen other men when we've been going out. Exclusive relationships are not her style.'

'She didn't seem to feel that extended to you – at least not where I was concerned. And I was only the lodger.'

He took my hand, almost unsure for a moment, enquiring, but as I let him, he relaxed and wrapped it within one of his own large ones.

'You were always a hell of a lot more than the lodger to me. I thought you knew that.'

I shook my head. 'I always just assumed it was you being you, and kind and doing Henry a favour and... stuff.'

'I thought the fact that every time you mentioned moving out I changed the subject or found reasons why you needed to stay just that bit longer might have given me away. I was under no illusions that you'd ever be interested in restarting our original relationship but, God, I'd missed your company. The easiness of being around you. Even down to ordering takeaway without a shopping list of instructions. I love it all and I'd missed it all. Your humour, your laugh, your face. Everything about you. And when Hector took to you straight away, I knew I'd been right. And I knew, underneath it all, I was still in love with you. We'd got lost along the way and maybe we should have fought harder, I don't know.'

'I lost sight back then of what was important.'

'I think we both did.'

'But you never said anything.'

'I nearly did so many times. But then I thought

if you really didn't feel the same, and I wasn't convinced you did, then you'd feel really awkward and move straight out, so I kept quiet and pretended I could still be happy with just friends.'

'And Christine?'

He blew out a sigh. 'I kept telling her we were done. That it wasn't working, but she wouldn't have it. It was crazy. I guess when you're used to everyone agreeing to your every whim it can be a bit of a shock when someone suddenly doesn't. She just wouldn't hear me. That time you came back early?'

'The kitchen interruptus?' I raised a brow.

'Yep. She turned up dressed like that, under her coat, obviously. I'd told her the night before that it was over. Again. And then she turns up like that and I opened the door and she's grabbing at my shirt.'

'OK, enough details, thanks.'

He squeezed the hand he still held.

'When she arranged that party, we'd split up. For good, I thought. And I thought she'd got the message, finally. She seemed OK about it and that she understood but asked that we could be friends. She explained that she wanted to have the party for me anyway, as she'd already arranged it all. I guessed she'd soon move on to the next guy anyway, so I'd shrugged and said whatever, just relieved that she'd finally accepted no as an answer.'

'It didn't seem like you were split up at the party.'

'I know. That was when I realised it had all been an act and she was about to play the finale.'

'The proposal?'

'Yep.'

'But she clearly thought you'd accept. I mean, not many people ask and actually expect a no, really, do they? Especially an heiress.'

'She knew I wasn't going to ask her but she also knows how much I value marriage and family. I'm not getting any younger and I guess she thought I might just go for it. Get caught up in the moment. So you're right, I don't think it occurred to her I'd ever say no. That anyone would say no. That's not something that happens in her world.'

'But the cheer? It didn't sound like you said no.'

'I didn't say anything! She asked me to marry her, shoved her hand out with the ring already on it and kissed me, then it all kind of snowballed and suddenly everyone was congratulating us. I was mad as hell but I couldn't stand there in front of all her friends and make a scene. Even she didn't deserve that. It would have been too humiliating.'

I wasn't sure I agreed with him – she was pretty free to try and humiliate others when it suited her. But it didn't surprise me that Jed chose not to make a scene.

'So, what happened?'

'I'm surprised you didn't hear once everyone left.'

'I have excellent noise-cancelling headphones. And Valium.'

'Fair enough. Suffice to say there was a lot of screaming. I need to replenish my stock of drinking glasses and I'm also a serving bowl down.' He peered at me. 'How many of those pills did you take?'

'Enough, apparently.'

'Christine passed out eventually and I put her in the spare room. When she woke up the next day, shortly before you came back, she started again. And then she asked if there was someone else. Specifically, you.'

'Oh.'

'And so I told her. That yes, I was still in love with you. I knew it the moment I saw you rushed in from that ambulance, but I also knew you'd moved on. But having you in my life again had made me realise that you were all the things I wanted, and Christine was none of those things. Initially I'd thought she was fun and carefree but it was soon apparent that she had fun at others' expense, and she was too carefree with her words and didn't mind if she hurt people with them. People can be quite different sometimes once you get to know them.'

'They can.'

'Like Dmitri.'

'Meaning?'

'He's a good guy. Yes, he's a playboy. I was right about that, but he's got a good heart.'

I rested my head against the back of the sofa. 'This interview was his idea, wasn't it?'

Jed pulled a face that dropped his friend right in it.

'I need to have words with Dmitri. Has he been feeding you information, too?'

'No.' He shook his head. 'He's too loyal to you to do that. Although he did tell me he's tried to tell you a couple of times that the engagement wasn't really an engagement.'

I thought back to the times Dmitri had started to mention Jed's name and I'd stopped him. 'Oh!' I shook my head. 'If he even began to say something about you, I stopped him. I didn't want to hear it. I needed to get over you and I thought the more I kept you out of my head, avoiding hearing about you, or seeing you in the press, the quicker it would happen.'

'Get over me?' Jed asked, sitting up a little more.

'I thought I'd done it. It had been so long since we split up, and we'd had so many rows towards the end anyway. I thought anything I'd felt would just shrivel once I left our little flat, like a plant starved of water.'

'And did it?'

'No. I shut it away in a box and thought that was enough. But then I got hit by a bloody bus and you walked into my hospital room and back into my life, and no matter how much I sat on that box, determined to keep it shut, eventually it just sprang open and all the contents spilled out everywhere as bright and vivid as the day I first met you. But you were with someone else, and I thought I'd messed it up so badly and treated everyone as if they weren't important, that even entertaining the thought of you still feeling anything for me seemed ridiculous. Then Christine told me I was just another charity case, I knew you had a good heart, and you'd even said at the beginning, you would have done it for anyone.'

'Blame that on self-preservation.'

'I didn't know, and her words made sense. I felt so awkward and humiliated, I just had to leave.'

'I was going to tell you how I felt the moment you got back, but then I saw you with Dmitri and you were so determined not to speak to me.'

'I was hurting and trying to process the engagement thing and the fact I'd been imposing on you the whole time and that you'd just been too polite to say anything. It was mortifying. I was angry with myself for still loving you, and knew I had to leave and never see you again. Do it properly this time. Really move on.'

'And have you?'

'In some ways. I have a better life-work balance. I feel more appreciated, and I have a small group of friends I love and value. I'm not missing out on family moments any more, and I'm present in the world now, appreciating it rather than letting it just pass me by.'

'That all sounds great, Mils. It really does. Henry did say you seem happier, and you look great.'

'Thanks.'

'I'm sorry about getting you here under false pretences. I guess that was kind of a sneaky trick. But the magazine have been asking, and I've read the interviews you've done for them. They're great. I decided that maybe it was time to let the world in a little, if it meant I could talk about the things that are important to me and spread the word further. Dmitri said his charity causes got a real boost following the publication of his profile.'

'Yes, he mentioned that. That's great. And, so long as you let me finish the interview, it's not entirely false pretences.'

'I know I'm not the one supposed to be asking the questions, but do I get just one?'

'I guess I could allow one.'

'Have I missed my chance with you?'

I was about to answer when a knock at the door announced room service. Jed dropped his head onto my shoulder and let out a sigh. 'Perfect timing.' He briefly squeezed my hand, then let go and headed to the door, followed by Hector who obviously needed to inspect anything new happening. The trolley was rolled in and, despite it being late morning, a delicious afternoon tea sat upon it, with fine china plates, cups and saucers. A large silver teapot sat on one side and a matching coffee pot on the other.

'Would you like me to serve, sir?' the waiter asked.

'No, that's fine. I got it. Thanks,' Jed said, signing for the order and slipping a note into the man's hand as he handed the small wallet back. He closed the door behind him and then returned to the sofa.

'I was only expecting a cup of tea,' I laughed.

'I was only expecting a run-of-the-mill meeting that day several months ago until I got that call from the hospital. I guess sometimes we get more than we bargain for.'

'I guess we do,' I said, looking up.

His eyes were on me and he was closer now. 'You didn't answer the question.'

'You noticed that, huh?' I said, softly, unconsciously leaning a little more towards him.

'I notice everything when it comes to you.' His voice was low and close to my ear, the warm breath sending ripples of delight and something much more basic to places that hadn't rippled in a long time.

'Is that so?'

'Yes, so answer the damn question.' His lips brushed my neck and I lost my focus.

'I heard a quote once.'

'Uh huh,' he replied, coming back up. His face was now inches from mine, eyes sparkling but earnest.

'That sometimes you need a second chance because you weren't quite ready for the first one. Maybe we weren't ready for our first chance. But I know I'm ready now.'

His kiss was gentle but quickly became something more powerful, more raw, and I returned it with the same desperation. We'd tossed one chance away but both of us had learned from it, me more than anyone. I'd learned so much in the last several months and one of those things was that I loved this man. I always had. And I always would. I had nearly lost my life and thought I'd lost everything, but that wasn't true. I'd found what was important. Who was important. My family. My friends. My Jed. I'd found life. Things were definitely looking up...

Find out what happens one year later in this exclusive Epilogue from Maxine Morrey

http://bit.ly/ThingsAreLookingUpEpilogue

ACKNOWLEDGMENTS

As always, to James – thank you for everything.

An absolutely huge thank you to the amazing team at Boldwood Books, especially the brilliant Amanda and Nia. You have created such a special place with Boldwood that is so much more than just a publishing house, and I am so honoured to be a part of it. Thank you for all your help, belief, enthusiasm and support. I can't tell you how much it all means.

More thanks go to the wonderful Sarah Ritherdon, my editor, for her support and love of this book, despite having to also deal with home schooling. Writing yet another book during Tier systems and Lockdowns meant that confidence wasn't always abounding but her response to the first reading of this made me cry with happiness and relief.

Thanks also to the brilliant copy editor and proof reader who both did excellent jobs as usual tidying up the whoops moments.

I don't think any of us expected the pandemic to have gone on for so long and I didn't expect to be writing a second book amongst it all. It's not been easy for anyone and I'm sending out love to anyone who's struggling. Thank you to my writer pals for being there during all this – Rachel Burton, Victoria Cooke, Rachel Dove and Rachel Stewart especially – one day we'll get those hugs and cocktails!

Big hug and thanks to Jo P for all her support, WhatsApp chats and our currently virtual Afternoon Teas. Can't wait until we can do real ones again – assuming we can work the tea strainer!

I'd also like to say thank you to Mick Hill for allowing me to dedicate this book to his wonderful wife, Shirley, who we sadly lost suddenly last year. She was the loveliest, sweetest lady and supported my books from the very beginning, always asking when the next would be out. It filled my heart. So, thank you to you both for that and for the wonderful friendship you have always shown to my parents. They don't make many like you two.

As usual, I'd also like to send a big thank you to the bloggers who help spread the word about my books. Your time, reviews and support are very much appreciated.

And last, but not least, thank you to my wonderful readers. I wouldn't be able to do this if you didn't choose to read my books and I am still stunned and thrilled that you do. I don't think that feeling will ever change. I am so grateful for your lovely comments, and hearing that my books have brought a smile, especially throughout these difficult times has meant so very much. Thank you.

MORE FROM MAXINE MORREY

We hope you enjoyed reading *Things are Looking Up*. If you did, please leave a review.

If you'd like to gift a copy, this book is also available as an ebook, digital audio download and audiobook CD.

Sign up to Maxine Morrey's mailing list for news, competitions and updates on future books.

http://bit.ly/MaxineMorreyNewsletter

Explore more uplifting reads from Maxine Morrey.

 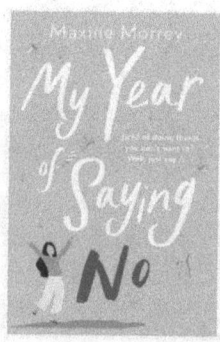 

ABOUT THE AUTHOR

Maxine has wanted to be a writer for as long as she can remember and wrote her first (very short) book for school when she was ten.

As time went by, she continued to write, but 'normal' work often got in the way. She has written articles on a variety of subjects, as well as a local history book on Brighton. However, novels are her first love.

In August 2015, she won Harper Collins/Carina UK's 'Write Christmas' competition with her first romantic comedy, 'Winter's Fairytale'.

Maxine lives on the south coast of England, and when not wrangling with words loves to read, sew and listen to podcasts and audio books. Being a fan of tea and cake, she can (should!) also be found out on a walk (although preferably one without too many hills).

Instagram: @scribbler_maxi (This is where she is to be found most)

Twitter: @Scribbler_Maxi

Facebook: www. Facebook.com/MaxineMorreyAuthor

Pinterest: ScribblerMaxi

Website: www.scribblermaxi.co.uk

Email: scribblermaxi@outlook.com

ABOUT BOLDWOOD BOOKS

Boldwood Books is a fiction publishing company seeking out the best stories from around the world.

Find out more at www.boldwoodbooks.com

Sign up to the Book and Tonic newsletter for news, offers and competitions from Boldwood Books!

http://www.bit.ly/bookandtonic

We'd love to hear from you, follow us on social media:

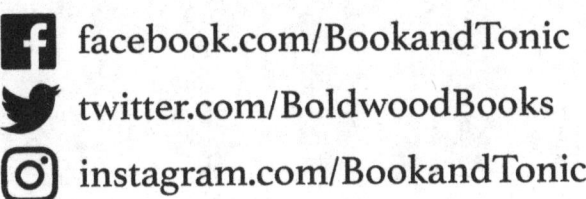

facebook.com/BookandTonic

twitter.com/BoldwoodBooks

instagram.com/BookandTonic

* 9 7 8 1 8 0 1 6 2 8 1 7 4 *